LONESTAR SECRETS

OTHER NOVELS BY COLLEEN COBLE INCLUDE

Cry in the Night

Lonestar Sanctuary

Anathema

Abomination

Midnight Sea

Fire Dancer

Alaska Twilight

The Rock Harbor series

Without a Trace

Beyond a Doubt

Into the Deep

The Aloha Reef series

Distant Echoes

Black Sands

Dangerous Depths

LONESTAR SECRETS

COLLEEN
COBLE

THOMAS NELSON
Since 1798

NASHVILLE DALLAS MEXICO CITY RIO DE JANEIRO BEIJING

Published in Nashville, Tennessee. Thomas Nelson is a registered trademark of Thomas Nelson, Inc.

Thomas Nelson, Inc., books may be purchased in bulk for educational, business, fund-raising, or sales promotional use. For information, please e-mail SpecialMarkets@ThomasNelson.com.

Publisher's Note: This novel is a work of fiction. Names, characters, places, and incidents are either products of the author's imagination or used fictitiously. All characters are fictional, and any similarity to people living or dead is purely coincidental.

Library of Congress Cataloging-in-Publication Data

Coble, Colleen.
Lonestar secrets / Colleen Coble.
p. cm.
ISBN 978-1-59554-487-2
1. Texas—Fiction. I. Title.
PS3553.O2285L665 2008
813'.54—dc22

2008017106

Printed in the United States of America

09 10 11 12 13 RRD 6 5

For my brother David Rhoads,

who should have been a cowboy

1

MILES OF EMPTY ROAD STRETCHED AHEAD OF HER. SHANNON ASTOR HAD babied the old Jeep along I-10 west from San Antonio until the traffic ran out. She watched a million stars in the sky through the windshield as the hill country gave way to desert and the sun began to peek above the dark horizon in her rearview mirror. The Big Bend area was only an hour away now. She smelled smoke from the wildfires in southwest Texas and hoped the flames didn't get any closer.

Shannon glanced in the rearview mirror, and her heart melted with tenderness. Her daughter Kylie slept peacefully in her booster seat, her head resting against the back of the seat. The glimmers of sunrise gilded her pale blonde hair. Shannon would do anything for her, even go back to the place she'd sworn never to set foot in again.

She was doing the right thing. She could never get ahead with the cost of living in San Antonio, and facing her demons back in Bluebird Crossing was worth getting her daughter out of the slum apartment. This job was her lifeline to something better for Kylie.

Her cell phone rang, and she grabbed it off the seat beside her before the chimes to "The Last Unicorn" could awaken Kylie. Who would be calling at six in the morning? Her friend Mary Beth's name flashed across the screen. Shannon flipped her phone open. "Mary Beth, what are you doing up?" Only silence greeted her at first. "Mary Beth?"

"I . . . I shouldn't have called," Mary Beth gasped out. Music blared out of a radio in the background.

"What's wrong?" Shannon struggled to make sense of the sounds flooding into her ear: road noises, music, labored breathing.

"Listen, I don't have much time. I . . . I'm going to be away for a while." Mary Beth ended the statement with a sob.

Shannon pulled to the side of the interstate and stopped the Jeep. "Mary Beth, have you been drinking?" Her friend had been known to tie one on every now and then.

The short bark of laughter on the other end of the line sounded all too sober. "I wish it were that simple."

Shannon heard the sound of screeching tires and the road noises. Mary Beth's gasps were louder. "Mary Beth? What's happening?"

"I was trying to help you. I had no idea it would come to this."

"Help me? What are you talking about?"

The phone went dead in Shannon's ear. Was Mary Beth in trouble? Or was Shannon reading too much into the strange call? She tried to call Mary Beth back but was dumped into her voice mail. Shannon punched in Horton's home number. He'd be up having his morning tea by now.

His proper British voice answered on the second ring. "Horton here. Shannon, have you broken down already?"

Hearing his voice made her long for the safety of her little apartment in San Antonio, even if it was a hole-in-the-wall. "Horton, have you heard from Mary Beth? I think she might be in some kind of trouble."

"What's happened?"

Shannon told him about Mary Beth's call. "Do you think something's wrong?"

He cleared his throat. "Maybe she had an argument with a boyfriend. Who is she dating right now?"

Shannon rubbed her arm. "I don't know. I think probably a married man. That seems to be her normal mode."

"What can I do to help?"

She glanced at her sleeping daughter. It would do no good to overreact. "Nothing. I'm sure I'll hear from her soon. If she calls you, let me know."

"Will do, my dear. Are you sure you don't want to come back? Your position hasn't been filled."

"I can't let this opportunity slip through my fingers. The clinic will be my own, the pay is good, and Kylie will get a chance to grow up in wide-open spaces."

"Be careful, my dear. I'll let you know if I hear anything about Mary Beth."

"I'm sure everything will be fine," Shannon said, more to reassure herself. She was beginning to regret she'd called Horton over something so silly. Driving through the night must have set her nerves on edge. "I'll call when I get to town and see if you've heard anything more." She disconnected the call and drove on into the dawn.

TALL AND IMPOSING, THE OLD HOUSE DOMINATED THE TEXAS LANDSCAPE and loomed over the weathered barn and outbuildings. Chickens still scratched in the thin dirt, and the buildings were even more ramshackled than she remembered. The Chihuahuan Desert wind moaned through the eaves of the old house, and the familiar sound made Shannon realize she was really home. Even though it wasn't much, it was theirs.

Her work here was cut out for her. At least it was better than the trailer she'd lived in for so many years, and she'd hoped to show the town right off that she was a landowner now, not the quiet kid they'd been only too happy to ridicule. There was nothing to be gained by sitting here looking at it. She dropped her Jeep back into drive and accelerated toward the ranch.

"This isn't it, is it, Mommy?" Kylie looked up from her coloring book and peered over the edge of the door out the window. A dilapidated windmill creaked painfully around its axis. "It's scary."

With her uncle gone, it wouldn't echo with his disapproval any longer. "It just needs some work, sweetie. Uncle Earl lived here fifty years, and I don't think he painted a board. We'll get it shipshape in no time." Well, it would maybe take awhile. It would be several weeks before she had any money coming in.

She pointed to the side yard. "Look, we have a barn. We'll get a pony, and you can have a dog. In fact, Moses might still be here." She whistled for the old stock dog. "Here, Moses. Here, boy." Only the wind answered her. If Moses was still around, maybe he was roaming the desert.

Every bone in her body ached from driving all night, and her nerves were shot after Mary Beth's mysterious call. She parked the vehicle in front of the hitching post by the porch, then sat listening to the groaning windmill. The sounds had echoed her own pain when her parents died.

"Are we going to get out?" Kylie asked, fidgeting.

"Sure, baby." Shannon opened her door and moved around to unbuckle her daughter's car seat.

Kylie hopped out and took her hand. "Do we have to go in? Maybe there's ghosts."

"No ghosts. It's just a little dirty and run-down, but I'll give it a good cleaning," Shannon promised. "Our old apartment was way worse. Here you'll have your own room and a playroom too." She took Kylie's hand and they stepped past straggly creosote bushes that scented the air. The porch steps sagged as though to swallow them whole. She and her daughter mounted the porch and approached the door. The key in her hand needed to be jiggled in the lock before the door would open.

Stale air that stank of mouse droppings rushed to meet them. Kylie wrinkled her nose and pulled back on her mother's hand. "I don't want to go in. It smells nasty."

"I'll soon have it smelling like Pine-Sol and lemon," Shannon promised. But after letting her gaze sweep the foyer lit with dim morning light, her courage faltered. She was too exhausted to face the monumental task. They should have stopped for the night so it didn't seem so overwhelming.

Kylie tugged on Shannon's hand. "Can I sit out here until it's better?"

Shannon hesitated. Her gaze swept the barren landscape. There was nothing to see but the unbroken panorama of yucca and prickly pear cactus, and the crags and peaks of the hills until the desert met the Chisos Mountains in the distance. She'd once loved this devil's playground even when it was as hot as his home, but today it felt lonely and dangerous.

She rested her hand on the top of her daughter's hair, and the contact filled her with determination. "I need your help, honey." She took her daughter's hand again and led her into the foyer.

The flowered wallpaper was peeling and faded. A layer of grime dimmed the olive green paint on the woodwork. Shannon sneezed at the odor of decay. She could see their footprints in the dust on the scarred wooden floors. It seemed the moment her uncle died three months ago, the desert stepped through the doors and windows to reclaim the house.

She heard a squeak when they entered the kitchen, and a mouse ran for cover along the counter before disappearing from view.

"Ew, a mouse," Kylie said. "We're not staying here, are we, Mommy?"

Shannon grabbed a broom from the corner and shook the cobwebs from it, but the rodent didn't reappear. "You'll love it after I get it fixed up. I've got some mousetraps in the car." She stepped to the utility room on the other side of the kitchen and lit the propane gas water heater. It began to rumble and chatter. "We'll leave our stuff in the car until we get it clean."

The last thing she wanted to do was clean, but she had to have this place in better shape before she'd allow Kylie to sleep here. Nightfall wouldn't make its appearance for another twelve hours. Plenty of time to at least get the main rooms clean and the beds ready. Everything would have to be washed, every stitch of bedding, every towel, every kitchen utensil.

A monumental task when she was tired to the bone. But it was nothing new. Many nights she'd had to rush to the vet hospital and work all the next day on little or no sleep.

She looked under the sink and found cleaning supplies. She wiped off the table and the counter, then dived back under the sink for cleansing powder. While she was on her hands and knees, she thought she heard tires crunching on gravel outside. She sprang to her feet to peer out the window. Nothing there. She sure was skittish.

"Are there any horses in the barn?" Kylie asked. "I can go pet them with my sister."

Kylie's invisible playmate. Shannon never had the heart to tell Kylie of the real sister who died at birth, but somehow the little girl had never let go of her unknown sibling. "I don't think so." But now that she thought about it, Shannon realized Felipe Mendoza, her uncle's old ranch hand, hadn't come to greet them. He was always around the house. And where was Moses, the ranch dog?

"Tell you what, Kylie, you can play on the porch for a little while with your toys. I've got to get some things out of the car." And make a quick stop in the barn. Shannon took her daughter's hand and led her to the porch. After digging out a tub of toys and depositing them on the porch with Kylie, she made the little girl promise not to leave the porch.

Shannon went to the side yard where the big old barn stood. She glanced behind her to make sure she could see Kylie, then walked toward the building. The door yawned open, an unusual state. The hair on the back of her neck stirred. She told herself it was her exhaustion, but her senses tried to sample everything around her as she walked across the flat sand toward the outbuildings.

The barn needed a coat of paint and boards replaced. The desert claimed everything left uninhabited. She hurried to the barn and peered inside. "Hello? Felipe?"

She heard a dog whine, then begin to bark, an agitated sound that made alarm bells go off in Shannon's head. Her cell phone was inside the house in her purse. She could call the sheriff, but it would take him awhile to get here. What if Felipe had fallen and was lying injured? Moses would never leave him.

She ducked into the barn. The aroma of dust, hay, and manure struck her. Funny how after five years in the city, the normal smells of a ranch overpowered her when she didn't used to even notice them. She glanced through the open tack room door. Only bridles and saddles there.

Dust motes danced in the air, and she sneezed. "Felipe?" she called again.

Moses broke into another frenzied round of barks, and she followed the sound. She passed several stalls, unused now. No livestock lowed or rustled in its hay. "Moses, where are you, boy?"

The dog whined and barked again. Shannon climbed over a gate when she couldn't open it and then over the railing at the back of the stall. There she saw Moses, a border collie, standing over what she took to be a pile of clothing. A second later she registered that it was Felipe lying in a mound of hay.

"Felipe!" She dropped to his side and rolled him over. He was quite dead. She scrabbled back on her haunches and fought the shriek building in her throat. Kylie would be frightened if she heard her mother scream.

"Stay calm, stay calm," she muttered. She called the dog to her, and Moses came reluctantly with his tail between his legs. "Good dog," she crooned, burying her face in his fur. The dog's musky scent and rough coat soothed her nerves. He whined and licked her face.

She had to get hold of herself. Her legs trembled when she released the dog and stood. Moses made a move as if to go back to his watch at Felipe's side, but she grabbed his collar and dragged him from the barn with her. The barn door screeched when she shut it.

Even though Felipe had likely died of natural causes, the fact there was a dead man in her barn made her race to the house to get to her daughter. Kylie was still on the porch with her stuffed unicorn, and the tightness in Shannon's chest eased.

Her daughter saw her and jumped up with her gaze on Moses. "We have a dog?"

"His name is Moses. We'll take him inside with us to the living room, and you can pet him."

Moses looked up at the sound of his name, and Shannon called him to her. She ran her hands over him. No broken bones or abrasions, though his coat was rough and dull. She made a mental note to get him on better food.

A vehicle rumbled up the drive, and she squinted at the vaguely familiar male figure in a shiny black pickup. Rick Bailey, from the adjacent Bluebird Ranch, climbed out of the truck. A pretty woman with black curls was with him, and a little girl hopped out of the backseat. A border collie leaped from the truck bed. Shannon struggled to remember the dog's name—Jem.

She broke into a run. Rick would know what to do.

TWO CUPS OF TEA LATER, SHANNON STILL HADN'T STOPPED SHAKING. THE sheriff and his deputies were still in the barn investigating, but the sheriff said the cause of death was likely a heart attack. Felipe had suffered one three months ago.

Rick's wife, Allie, though hugely pregnant, had washed some utensils, then made Shannon sit down and drink some tea. The girls squealed and giggled in the living room, unaware of the drama playing out in the barn. Betsy was about Kylie's age, and the two had hit it off immediately.

"You should come home with us," Allie said. About thirty, she was short with dark curls and a ready smile. "This place isn't going to be ready to live in for a while."

Shannon glanced around the kitchen. "I know it looks bad, but cleaning will make it livable." Grit irritated her eyes, and she rubbed at them. It was only ten in the morning, but she longed to crawl into a bed with clean sheets and sleep for a week. Or at least two hours.

Allie watched her. "I've got cleaning stuff in the Jeep and came prepared with rubber gloves. What do you think, Rick?"

"I'd feel better if you both came home with us," he said. "There might be scorpions and spiders."

Shannon shuddered, then shook her head. "I want to get settled in before my job starts. I'll be too busy once things start happening there. I can't wait to get started. Me—a vet. It's about time."

The Bureau of Land Management and a West Texas mustang rescue organization were sponsoring the Mustang Makeover, a demonstration to the public of what great horses were up for adoption through the agency. She'd been hired to replace Big Bend's departing vet, Grady O'Sullivan, and her first task would be to make sure the mustangs stayed in good shape through the makeover training. The BLM tried to preserve as many wild mustangs roaming the western ranges as possible, and the herds needed thinning—by being either adopted or, in the case of the older horses, put down. Shannon meant to save as many of the mustangs as she could.

"The Mustang Makeover starts this afternoon at one. You're the vet in charge, right?"

"Sure am." Her smile widened at the thought. "I thought I wasn't supposed to be there until tomorrow."

"You're not. But if you want to take a look at what's waiting for you, we'll be glad to run you over."

"Have you seen Jewel around?" Shannon asked in a too-casual voice. Her pulse sped up as she waited for his answer.

Rick's smile extended to his kind blue eyes. "Not in about a week. He's still roaming the hills though."

"Who's Jewel?" Allie asked.

"He's a horse my dad bought before he died. I named him and pretended he was a unicorn in disguise." Shannon never forgot her first glimpse of the stallion. As he stood silhouetted against the sunrise, she was sure she'd seen a horn on his head. For as long as she lived here, she'd tried to surprise the horse to see the horn again. Even now, as an adult, she wasn't sure it had been an illusion.

"I'll look for him tomorrow." The stallion's black coat had received many of her tears over the years. He was probably about eighteen years old now. She longed to see him.

"Let's get to work," Allie said.

"How about you sit at the table and talk to me while I work?" Shannon said, her gaze going to the woman's stomach.

"Girl, I'm pregnant, not dying. And cleaning is my thing."

"If you're only eight months, you're having one half grown."

Allie laughed. "It's a big boy. He'll probably come out twirling a rope."

"Or looking for a bull to ride." Shannon laughed, remembering the delicious sensation of awaiting the arrival of new life, of watching the babies move under her skin. "I'm not going to be responsible for the kid wanting to clean sinks instead of helping his dad muck out the stable. I'll work and you direct."

"Give it up, Shannon," Rick said. "My wife is a little powerhouse of energy. But we'll give her something easy to do."

Allie stuck her tongue out at him, picked up her pail of cleaning supplies, then went toward the screen door. "Let's get to work."

Shannon stood and threw open the cabinet doors. Having people here chased away the ghosts she'd glimpsed waiting for her.

THE SCENT OF HORSES, HAY, AND MANURE FILLED JACK MACGOWAN'S NOSTRILS. Some might have found it distasteful, but it meant money and excitement to him. He carried his saddle across the open field while his daughter, Faith, ran ahead of him with the mustang's halter. The desert had been roped off into makeshift corrals, and the place was as busy as a small town. Other horse trainers and numerous spectators thronged the dusty lot. News reporters with cameras and microphones roamed the open field as well. The mustangs that had been transported here snorted and neighed in the paddock.

"Stay back from the fence, Faith," he called. "The mustangs are dangerous." His practiced eye took in the horses racing around the corral. Nostrils flaring and eyes wild, most of them had never been this close to people before. He spotted a particularly handsome specimen. The stallion's coal black coat gleamed with sweat. Good lines, muscular.

Faith stopped two feet shy of the fence, but her face reflected her longing to climb it and see the mustangs up close and personal. Jack reached her and dropped the saddle.

"See the filly, Daddy?" she said, pointing to a small sorrel. "Can I have her?"

"You already have a pony." His gaze went over the sorrel's lines. She'd always be small, but she had a nice form and bright eyes. "Looks like she's limping, sweet pea. We want to take a good one home."

"Maybe she really needs a home," Faith said, her gaze tracking the horse. "Maybe she doesn't have a mommy either."

Jack winced. She'd been making statements like that more and more lately. He chose not to answer. He noticed Buzz Bollinger directing trucks of supplies from within a cloud of dust. The old mining camp with shacks that had housed a generation of workers would be the training ground for the bronc busters. Now weathered to gray, the old wooden buildings were hardly the lap of luxury.

Luckily for Jack, he lived close enough to stay home and drive here every day.

He waved to Buzz. "Let's go check in, Faith," he said. He picked up the saddle again and walked toward Buzz.

The big guy was going bald. He had to be nearly fifty by now, but he was still as skinny as a rattler. He looked up and saw Jack. "Howdy, pardner," he said in a terrible John Wayne imitation.

Jack grinned. Everyone who knew he collected John Wayne memorabilia tried that on him. "The Duke would roll over in his grave. You sound like Clint Eastwood."

Buzz slapped him on the back. "Jack MacGowan, you old bronc buster, I haven't seen you since you got thrown by that big bull in Cheyenne. How's the leg doing?"

Jack put down the saddle and shook Buzz's hand. "Pains me some during monsoon season. It's a good reminder of why I gave up the rodeo. You remember Faith?"

"Who could forget that cotton-candy hair?" Buzz ruffled her soft blonde tresses. "I thought I saw her on the other side of the camp a few minutes ago."

"We just got here. All the trainers arrive?"

"Yeah, they're all checking into their digs." Buzz made a face. "We'll be roughing it for a few weeks. You're lucky your ranch is just over the hill."

"How'd you decide to come here for the training?"

"It's out of the limelight. I thought you all could do your work in peace, at least away from casual gawkers. The media is here, but they won't bother us much until we're ready to show our stuff."

"How's my competition look?" Jack hadn't seen any of the other trainers yet, just stock handlers. At least none he'd recognized.

"Stiff. Tucker Larue is here. Breathing fire and brimstone and claiming he's going to toss your rear into the nearest cactus." Buzz shook his head and grinned. "Think you can handle him?"

"No problem." Jack had hoped not to run into his old nemesis for a while. Larue didn't know the meaning of "friendly competition." He was always out for blood. Some men hated to lose, and Larue was one of them.

Jack exhaled. "We got a vet here to check out the horses?"

"Yep. She'll be here tomorrow."

Faith tugged on his hand. "Daddy, butterflies!"

Jack glanced at the sprawling butterfly bush by the bunkhouse. Dozens of butterflies covered the shrub. "You can go look at them," he told her.

She ran to the bush and knelt to study the insects. Jack turned his attention back to Buzz. "What's the vet say about the mustangs? They all in good shape?"

Buzz shrugged. "She hasn't seen them yet, but the boys will be taking more than a gander or two at her. She's a looker." His attention caught on something over Jack's shoulder. "Hey, she's here today."

Jack turned to follow Buzz's gaze. A slim woman with nearly white blonde hair stood talking to Rick and Allie Bailey. Something about her rattled a memory, but he couldn't catch hold of it. "Did she go to school here?"

Buzz chewed on his unlit cigar. "Yep, she's from here. Old Man Astor's niece, Shannon."

Shannon Astor. Jack's face burned and it wasn't from the sun. He doubted he'd ever get over the guilt. He managed to smile and act natural. "She was the brain in school. Even though she was two years younger, lots of us in biology class went to her for tutoring. Man, that was eons ago. Another world. She's been gone awhile. What's she doing back here?"

"Old Earl left her the ranch, what's left of it. It's only pert near a hundred acres, not worth enough jingle for a good steak dinner. But she told me she wanted to raise her daughter where the air wasn't filled with car exhaust."

Jack frowned. He'd graduated with Earl's son, Curt. "I bet that went over well with his son. Losing the ranch, I mean."

Buzz shrugged. "Curt's a horse lawyer in Austin. He'd never live in the desert again. That land's small potatoes to him. I'd heard he suggested his dad give it to Shannon."

Jack was only listening with half an ear. He needed to get Faith and go back to the corral. He turned to find her and realized there were three little girls entranced by the butterflies.

Watching them lean in with intent faces made him smile. Until he realized that two of those little girls had identical blonde hair and dark blue eyes. He blinked to clear his double vision, but nothing changed. Two little girls so alike it was hard to take in. Not quite identical, but almost. He stared at one, then the other, as he felt the world he knew shift under his feet.

2

SHANNON'S GAZE TOOK IN THE MELEE OF DUST, HORSES, AND MEN. HER adrenaline surged at the thought of the coming days. She had been discussing the merits of the various horses with Rick, and she was so engrossed she'd barely heard Allie say she was taking the girls to look at the butterflies.

She understood horses better than people.

"You're having to hit the ground running," Rick said. "You sure you're up to it?"

"I'm thrilled at the opportunity. It was good of Grady to suggest me for the job."

"We're gonna miss him as our vet."

"But now you'll have more of his time as your pastor, right?"

Rick nodded and grinned. “It’s been a long time coming for him and Dolly.”

Shannon smiled up at him. “You sure got a darling in Allie. I love her already.”

His grin widened. “Me too. I never dreamed I’d be so lucky. God dropped her right into my lap, and neither of us had a choice about it.”

She couldn’t spot her daughter or Allie in the throng of blue jeans, boots, and cowboy hats. “Where’d she go with the girls?”

“Over by the bunkhouse. There’s a mass of butterflies on the bush, and Kylie was begging to go see.”

“Kylie is nuts about butterflies.” She fell into step beside Rick to skirt the line of cowboys checking into their bunkhouses.

Kylie’s blonde head caught her attention and she smiled at the rapt expression on her daughter’s face. Wait a minute—where had Kylie gotten that pink shirt? She’d worn a blue shirt that matched her eyes when they’d left the house. Shannon had never seen this one before with its ruffled neck and sleeves.

Shannon and a man called out names at the same time.

“Kylie!”

“Faith!”

The child in pink turned toward the man who’d called her Faith. Shannon stopped and stared. The little girl who looked so much like her daughter ran to the man, who lifted her in his arms. Her fists clenched at the familiar embrace from a stranger. She’d taught Kylie better.

She started toward him to yank her daughter away. With his back to her, she didn’t recognize him. Then she saw past him to Betsy, hand in hand with —Kylie? Shannon blinked hard, and her gaze went back to the other child, whom she now realized had hair a shade darker than Kylie’s.

Kylie spotted Shannon. "Mommy, I found my sister!" She tugged her hand out of Betsy's and ran to her mother.

The man turned around with his daughter in his arms. She recognized him immediately. The green of his eyes had always made her think of the desert in springtime. Jack MacGowan. She'd sworn his actions had killed her latent crush, but her stomach still churned at the sight of him, and her nails bit into her palms. She'd hoped he'd moved on. Last she heard, he was following the rodeo circuit, much to his father's dismay.

The years had been kind to him. At thirty-four, he still had thick and curly hair. His muscular frame didn't carry an ounce of extra weight. Only the lines around his eyes betrayed the passing of time since he'd been a star quarterback and she'd been the studious sophomore with the handmade clothes. She struggled past her anger to remember the name of his wife. Blair Stickman, captain of the cheerleading squad. They'd dated all through high school.

He came toward her. "Shannon, good to see you after all these years." He glanced down at Kylie, who was clinging to Shannon's hand. "Our girls look so much alike, it's bizarre."

Shannon couldn't take her eyes off Faith long enough for it to sink in that he was acting as though he hadn't destroyed her life. "I thought she was Kylie at first."

He put Faith down. The girls linked hands and began to chatter as if they'd been friends forever. "I don't get this," he said in a soft voice.

A thought too horrible to contemplate began to form in Shannon's mind. She couldn't put her mind around the girls' astounding similarities. It wasn't possible. That kind of thing didn't happen except in the papers.

"When was Faith born?" she asked. The girls couldn't be more than a few months apart in age.

"She's five. She'll be six on April 14."

"That's Kylie's birthday," she said. Before her mind could replay that day five years ago, she made herself focus on Jack. "Faith was born in the local birthing clinic? I kind of remember that now that you mention it. Your wife is Blair, a redhead?"

He lifted a brow. "Yeah. Was. She died."

"I'm sorry," she said mechanically. She hadn't heard about Blair's death and wasn't about to dwell on it now. The ramifications of her memories caused Shannon's gut to plunge. Jack had nearly black hair. Blair's was red. Where had Faith's pale blonde hair come from? It couldn't be, could it? And the way he studied her—the concentrated frown, the suspicious glint in his eye—made her mind go too dull to think this out.

"I've got to go." She scooped up Kylie and rushed away. Jack called after her, but she hurried on. Her blood pounded in her ears, and her breath came in gasps.

But she couldn't outrun the implications of the girls' resemblance. *No, no, it couldn't be.* She wouldn't let herself even consider the possibility. Kylie struggled in her arms, crying out, and Shannon slowed to a stop and kissed her daughter's soft cheek. The little-girl scent calmed her enough to help her think.

There had to be some other explanation. Something that didn't require a huge effort to get right. She didn't have the time, money, or energy to climb the mountain looming ahead.

"Mommy, I want down. I want to talk to my sister," Kylie said, still struggling.

Shannon realized Rick was calling her too. And how did she even answer Kylie? Out of breath, she turned to see Rick running after her. Allie waddled behind with Betsy. She waited to let them catch up.

Rick reached her. "What's going on? You ran off like a cougar was chasing you."

"I've got things to do before nightfall. This can all wait until tomorrow when I'm supposed to be here."

"Did Jack say something to upset you?"

"No, no, nothing like that." Shannon wished she could confide in someone, but this was too personal. Too hurtful.

Allie reached them. Her face red and her breath hitching in her chest, she paused and put her hand on her belly. "Where's the fire?"

Shannon hated making a fool of herself. Her face burned. "Can we go back to the house? I've got so much to do." Her vision doubled and blurred, and she blinked hard but it didn't clear. Stress did that to her.

"Sure," Rick said. He helped his wife to the truck.

Shannon got in the back of the big crew cab with the girls and buckled them in their car seats. Her thoughts whirled all the way back to the ranch. Her suspicions were crazy. But the thoughts nagged and dug further into her swelling incredulity.

"You want to stop at your office and check it out?" Rick asked.

"I'll do that tomorrow." Right now, she wanted to be alone and think this through. She fell silent as Rick drove to the old ranch house.

Rick parked in front of the house. "You need anything else from us?"

"No, I'm fine."

Allie glanced at her husband. "Honey, take Betsy home for her nap and come get me in a couple of hours. Okay?"

He nodded. "How about I take Kylie too? She's already asleep back there. She and Betsy can play when they wake."

Shannon glanced at her sleeping daughter. Though she hated to be away from Kylie, she needed some space to think. "You sure? They might be a handful when they're fresh."

"I can handle them," Rick said.

"You're the husband of the year." Allie blew him a kiss, then got out of the truck and lumbered to the porch.

Shannon brushed a kiss across her sleeping child's forehead, then followed. She longed to share her fears with Allie but wasn't sure anyone would understand. Her suspicions were too outrageous.

A faint fragrance hung in the air when she entered the house. Shannon sniffed. "Do you smell that?"

"What?"

"A man's cologne." Could Rick's have lasted this long? Maybe it was her imagination.

"I don't smell anything," Allie said.

Shannon went to the coffeepot and dumped out the cold, stale coffee. "I'll make some fresh coffee."

"No caffeine while I'm pregnant. But I've got decaf tea in my purse if you want to start some water."

Tea might calm her. Shannon set down the carafe and put on the teakettle. It was the same stained white one she'd used all her years here, but she hadn't noticed this morning when Allie cleaned it up and made tea. Was it only this morning she'd arrived? Fatigue blurred her vision around the edges again. The familiar motion of clutching the kettle's chipped handle comforted her.

Once the women cupped steaming mugs of tea in their palms, she and Allie settled on the lumpy sofa in the living room. Shannon wrapped her hands around the warm cup even though heat shimmered in the room. Her uncle had always hated air-conditioning.

"Your expression could scare small children," Allie said. "You ready to talk about it?"

Shannon bit her lip. "You didn't think it odd that Kylie and Faith looked so much alike?"

"I was surprised," Allie said. "But I've heard of those kinds of things happening. Don't they say everyone has a look-alike somewhere? Are you thinking she's adopted or something? By someone in your family?"

"Not exactly." If only that were a possibility. She took a sip of her peppermint tea. The herb's bite cleared her head. Was there anyone left in her family who might have a child so amazingly similar? There was only Curt, and he was dark-haired like his dad. Shannon took after her mother. No other cousins. And Faith had been born *the same day.* In the same tiny birthing clinic.

Her teacup rattled in her hand, and she set it down before her shaking hands spilled it. "Kylie had a twin," she said.

Allie choked on her sip of tea. "You gave her up for adoption?" she guessed.

"Never!" Shannon said. "She died. At least that's what they told me. Jack said Faith was born on April 14 in the clinic. Kylie was born the same day in the same place. What does that tell you, Allie? I just keep going over and over it in my mind. What if my other daughter and Jack's were switched? What if Jack's baby died and he took one of my girls?"

Her past with Jack didn't inspire much trust, and she wouldn't put anything past him.

Allie held up her hand. "Okay, I'm lame, but I'm not getting it. Start at the beginning."

Shannon sighed. She was going to have to go through the whole thing. "I got pregnant my final year in college up at Sul Ross State in Alpine. Kylie's father, well, let's say he was less than thrilled. He lit out for Dallas and left me on my own. I came home that summer to stay with my uncle one last time so I could have my babies here. I found out four months before I delivered that I was having twins—both girls."

She fell silent, remembering the shock. The thought of raising one child had been daunting. Realizing there were two had been overwhelming. "When my water broke, I went to the clinic. The delivery seemed uneventful, fairly quick and easy. Rylie—my first baby—was perfect in the delivery room. I kissed her warm cheek and touched her pink skin. She wasn't a bit blue. Then Kylie came, another perfect baby girl."

Not wanting to relive the shock of that day, she stared out the window at the mountains in the distance. Allie touched her hand, and she refocused on her new friend's face. "Then they told me Rylie had died. I don't know what happened." She set her tea on the table and gripped Allie's hand. "But what if she didn't die? What if Jack and his wife took her?"

"You mean on purpose?" Allie shook her head. "I don't really know Jack well, but Rick thinks the world of Jack. And if that's what happened, where's his other child, the one his wife delivered?"

"They showed me a dead baby." Shannon rubbed her head. "Ridiculous, huh?" She still couldn't get the possibility out of her mind. Jack's family had money. And connections. Could the babies have been switched deliberately? It wouldn't be the first time he'd tried to take something that belonged to her family.

"A DNA test would tell you the truth," Allie said.

Shannon pressed her fingers on the bridge of her nose. "You sound like you believe it's possible."

"Anyone who looks at those two girls has to consider it. Go back over the birth. Tell me what you remember."

Shannon nodded and stepped back five years.

THE PAIN HAD EASED WITH THE EPIDURAL. THE SMELL OF ANTISEPTIC AND the cold embrace of the delivery table made her shudder. If only she weren't going through this alone.

"Here comes baby number one," the doctor called out. "I see the head."

"Bear down hard," the nurse said. Her badge read Verna. She was in her late fifties with dull auburn hair.

Shannon's life had narrowed to this small, sterile room. After today, she wouldn't be alone anymore. She'd have her babies. Shannon bore down with all her might, her moans locked behind her teeth. If there was one thing her uncle had taught her, it was that an Astor didn't cry. It took everything she had not to allow even a gasp past her lips.

"Good job," the nurse said. "It's a girl!"

Moments later the doctor deposited a small body on Shannon's stomach. Shannon ran her hand over the tiny head, still white and sticky with vernix. "You're Rylie," she whispered.

"One more time," the doctor said. "Give me all you've got, Shannon."

Shannon closed her eyes and concentrated on the task. She'd have years with her tiny daughters once they were safely here. A few minutes later another baby girl joined her sister. "Hello, Kylie," she said to her new daughter. The little one mewled.

She was a mother now. The strength of her maternal instincts surprised her. She nuzzled the babies, kissing their soft cheeks and inhaling the aroma of their newness.

"Let me check them out." The nurse slid her palms under Rylie.

Shannon hated to let the nurse take them to the warmers, and she ran her palm over Rylie's head one last time, then did the same to Kylie.

"They look good," the nurse said. "Good Apgar scores. No problems here."

"Thank God," Shannon whispered. Weak tears leaked from her eyes. If only there were someone to share the joy with. Shannon's uncle had declared he was too ashamed to come for the births, and who knew where the babies' father was by now. She had to face this like she'd faced every other trial in her life—with no help.

Verna smiled at Shannon. "I'm going to take your girls to the nursery and get their tests. You'll have them back by the time we get you to your room."

"Could you take a picture first?" Shannon pointed to the camera on the stainless-steel tray. Verna smiled and took two pictures before whisking away the babies.

Dr. Madison joked as he stitched her up, but Shannon barely heard. She was eager to touch her daughters again. When she finally got to her room, there was only one baby there. "Where's my other daughter?" she asked the nurse who wheeled her in.

"Let me check." The nurse bustled away.

Shannon checked the tag on the baby's wrist. It read "Astor Baby 2." She touched the fuzz on Kylie's head and brushed her lips over the baby's soft skin. She'd do anything for her babies. Somehow she'd give them a good life.

Glancing at the clock, she realized the nurse had been gone fifteen minutes. A vague alarm began to tickle Shannon's spine. That alarm changed to panic when half an hour passed. All of it a premonition of the nurse's return and the announcement that Rylie had died.

SHANNON BLINKED AND SHE WAS BACK IN THE DINGY LIVING ROOM WITH Allie's compassionate gaze on her. Shannon swallowed hard. "I asked to see my daughter, to hold her one last time, and they brought her."

"Were you sure then it was the same baby?"

Shannon struggled to remember the tiny blue face. "I wasn't suspicious, if that's what you mean. I'd gotten such a brief glimpse of her in the delivery room."

"What reason did they give for her death?"

"The doctor said her lungs weren't developed properly," she told Allie. Even now, her throat closed and her eyes burned. She often thought about being reunited with her daughter in heaven.

A frown creased Allie's brow. "Wouldn't that have shown up in the delivery room? You'd think she would have been struggling to breathe from the moment she was born."

The thought had crossed Shannon's mind more than once. "I couldn't let myself think about it too much. I still had Kylie. She's been the joy of my life."

"Do you still have that picture?"

"Yes, just a minute." Shannon stood and went to the stack of boxes against the wall. She found the right one and pulled the tape from the top, then rummaged through Kylie's collection of unicorns until she found the photo album. "Here it is." Returning to the sofa, she flipped it open and showed Allie.

Allie ran her finger down the page. "Wow, the girls look identical."

Shannon's thoughts lingered on the little girl she'd seen today. Faith. The last thing she needed was one more problem to deal with, but she couldn't walk away from this. "I have to find out for sure if Faith is my daughter."

"You'd need some kind of reason to request a blood test. Or you could exhume the body of the little one who died and see if she's yours."

"How did Blair die?"

"Freak accident, really. A little over a year ago, she went up in a hot-air balloon that crashed. She'd been doing all kinds of crazy things—driving a race car, going bungee jumping. Rumor has it that she was diagnosed with breast cancer and wanted to try everything before she got too sick. Shannon, you okay? You went white."

"Fine, I'm fine." Shannon ignored the sick churning in her stomach as the full ramifications of what faced her began to sink in. "Let's see if we can find the nurse first and talk to her. Her name was Verna Jeffers."

"I've heard the name. Can't think in what context though," Allie said.

The women hashed through the situation for another hour and a half until the rumble of a vehicle floated through the open window.

"I think Rick and the girls are here," Shannon said. Car doors slammed, and she stood at the sound of small feet.

The girls burst into the room. Kylie spoke first. "Mommy, I'm hot. I think my sister is sick."

Shannon suppressed a smile. Kylie often claimed things about her imaginary sister. Her smile faded when she took in her daughter's flushed face and recalled the events of the day. Shannon had often heard of the connections twins experienced. She touched Kylie's head. No fever. But she *looked* like she might be feverish. Spots of red stained her cheeks, and her eyes were glazed.

Call Jack.

She resisted the impulse. Even if Faith had a fever, Jack wasn't likely to welcome advice from a stranger. Besides, the last thing she wanted to do was talk to him. She pulled Kylie onto her lap. "You're okay, peanut. You and Betsy want some apple slices? Maybe that will make you feel better."

"My sister is sick," Kylie said, her voice insistent. "You should help her, Mommy. You always make me feel better."

Shannon bit her lip. What if Faith really was sick? She didn't have

Jack's number, but she was tempted to find it. Her glance went to Allie, who interpreted it.

"I know his number," Allie said.

Cornered. With Allie and the girls staring at her, Shannon dug out her cell phone. "What is it?" He could only hang up. A little humiliation was a small price to pay for peace of mind.

She punched in the number as Allie quoted it. The phone rang on the other end. A woman's voice, heavily accented, answered. "Mr. Jack's house."

Shannon's words dried up on her tongue. She could handle Jack, but a stranger on the phone would think she was nuts. She wet her lips. "Um, could I speak to Mr. MacGowan?"

"He no in."

Maybe this woman was Faith's nanny. At least she might know if the child was all right. "I was wondering if Faith is all right?"

"This is nurse? You no come now. Miss Faith has fever and cough, but I fix her. She will be okay."

Standing too far to hear the words on the other end of the phone, Kylie put her hand to her mouth and coughed. "I'm sorry, I'm not a nurse. I just wondered if she was okay." She closed her phone before the woman could answer.

"Your friend has a little cough and fever," she said to Kylie. "But she'll be fine."

"She's not my friend. She's my sister." Kylie took Betsy's hand and the two little girls went back to the living room.

"I think Faith is my daughter," Shannon whispered.

Obtaining the proof, then getting her back might prove to be the most formidable task she'd ever faced, and she wasn't sure she was up to it. Was it even the right thing to do?

3

DOSED WITH VICKS AND ENRICA'S HOMEOPATHIC CONCOCTIONS, FAITH would be fine by morning, Jack thought. He tore through the books on the shelf in his office. Blair had kept meticulous records of Faith's early years. He hadn't been good at keeping up with pictures and memorabilia since Blair's death. When he found the baby book, he dropped into the leather chair at his desk and flipped it open.

"Mr. Jack, what you doing?" Enrica Torres—his housekeeper, Faith's nanny, and an indispensable member of the family—stood by his framed movie poster of John Wayne in *North to Alaska*. Five feet two and nearly as round as she was tall, she ruled the household with an iron hand muffled by velvet. "Something is wrong, *sí*? Did you check Faith?"

He took off his cowboy hat and ran his hand through his hair. "I checked on Faith a few minutes ago. You've got her on the mend, Enrica. She'll be all right after she rests. Has Wyatt come home yet?" His golden retriever had gone missing this morning. Jack had fired a ranch hand the night before, and he feared the guy had taken Wyatt as revenge.

Enrica shook her head. Jack studied her a moment. She had been Blair's childhood nanny and never left the family. "Do you remember the night Faith was born?"

"*Sí,* I remember. The nurse think our Faith will die—I see it on her face. But we pray and show them all a miracle." Her brow furrowed. "Something is wrong?"

"Maybe. Do you remember anyone else in the clinic having a baby?"

She nodded. "A young woman in the next room. She have twins. But one baby die. I hear her sobbing all night long and pray for her."

Jack's gut gave a hot squeeze. Twins. He stared at the entries in the baby book on the desk.

Faith Ann MacGowan. Seven pounds, seven ounces. It had been touch and go from the moment she arrived. Her Apgar scores weren't good. She was flaccid and blue. He barely saw her before Blair's aunt Verna rushed her to the nursery. He and Blair held hands and prayed for her recovery, and God delivered a miracle to their arms a few hours later. When they next saw their baby girl, she was pink and beautiful.

But what if it was the wrong baby? Faith didn't resemble either of them.

There was no denying his daughter looked amazingly like Shannon's little girl. And like Shannon. Blonde hair so pale it was almost white. And those striking azure eyes. A boulder formed in his throat. It wasn't just the coloring. The heart-shaped face, the set of the eyes.

"Mr. Jack, you scaring me." Enrica put her hands on her nonexistent waist and glared at him.

"Enrica, I saw the woman who was in the other delivery room today. She has a little girl who looks exactly like Faith. Nearly an exact copy. I couldn't tell them apart when I saw them standing together."

Enrica's brow furrowed. "A woman call just now. She ask if Faith is sick. How she know this?"

Shannon had called? Did she know something already? "She asked if Faith was sick?"

Enrica nodded. "Like she already know."

Maybe her daughter was sick too. He wanted to bury the questions, ignore the possibilities. But he knew Shannon wouldn't let it lie. He'd seen the fear and speculation in her eyes. She would poke around until she found out the truth. But this was his fear talking. It had to be. Faith was his daughter. *His.*

COYOTES YIPPED LONG INTO THE NIGHT, A SOUND SHANNON HAD GROWN unaccustomed to in the city. She punched her pillow and stared at the shadows on the walls. The pillows, even with clean cases, smelled dusty and old. She'd buy some new ones as soon as her first check came in. But it wasn't the smell of the bedding that kept her awake. She rolled over and glanced at the clock. Two in the morning. Her arm around her stuffed unicorn, Kylie slept soundly in a cot against the wall until her room was ready.

Where was Mary Beth? Shannon glanced at her cell phone. She sat up and reached for it, then dialed Mary Beth's number. It just rang until she got her friend's voice mail. She closed the phone and tried to lie back down.

A creak echoed from somewhere in the house. An old house always made strange noises. It was nothing. Then the noise came again, and she sat back up. She slid out of bed, then lifted the mattress. Her fingers groped along the box springs until she found the butt of the pistol she'd put there before going to bed. Moving quietly so she didn't awaken Kylie, she crept to the dark closet and reached up onto the highest shelf where she'd put a box of bullets. She loaded the pistol, then her feet moved to the door.

She twisted the doorknob and the door creaked open, the sound like a crack of thunder to her ears. Her pulse galloped so loudly in her ears she couldn't hear anything. Moonlight dappled the carpet from a window at the other end of the long, narrow hallway. She tiptoed along the worn rug to the top of the stairs. By sheer effort of will, she stilled her pulse and her breathing and listened to the quiet house. She'd thought the noise was from downstairs.

If she'd been thinking, she would have had Moses sleep inside by her bed tonight. She gripped the handrail with one hand and held the gun steady with the other as she descended the staircase. The coyotes howled again, and the sound raised gooseflesh on her arms. Had she been dreaming?

The house was perfectly quiet now. Not a creak, not a whisper. When she reached the bottom of the stairs, she saw a trail of light cutting through the floor and leading to the front door.

Moonlight. The door stood wide open.

SHANNON SAT ON THE SAGGING PORCH SWING AND WATCHED THE SUN IGNITE the shrubs and bushes across the ranch. The thick scent of creosote and sage intensified with the warmth. She was still a little unnerved by finding the door open, but she couldn't remember if she'd shut it securely or not. The stress of the last two days had taken a toll on her memory of the events of the past few hours.

Once everything was up and running this morning, she'd get the locks changed. She buried her fingers in the dog's fur, taking comfort from his warmth. Shannon should have called Horton yesterday when she arrived, but things had spiraled around her so fast she hadn't had time, though worry for Mary Beth hovered in the back of her mind. It would be the first call she made this morning.

Her thoughts went to the child she'd seen yesterday. "Faith." Saying the name made it all the more real. Her daughter Faith. Shannon was sure of it.

Allie had volunteered to watch Kylie this morning while Shannon went to the medical clinic and looked at the records of the birth of her girls. Then she'd try to find Verna Jeffers. The nurse was likely in her sixties by now, but she might still be working.

Shannon rose and stretched, then went inside to get ready. She wanted to be at the old mining camp by ten, so she'd better get a move on. After showering and dressing, she sat at the old black phone in her uncle's office. The sheriff had made a call and activated the service immediately. She dialed Horton's house.

"Horton Chrisman," he said. He'd never lost the last trace of his English accent.

"It's Shannon. How is everything?"

"Not the same without you, my dear. When I got to the clinic yesterday morning, there had been a break-in. All my files were strewn about the floor."

She tensed. "Are you okay?"

"I'm fine. It was probably a burglar."

"And you haven't seen Mary Beth?"

"No, I'm sorry. Not a word. I tried to call her but got only her voice mail."

"Same here." She told Horton she'd check in a few days later and gave him her number at the ranch.

By seven thirty she was standing outside the birth center in Bluebird Crossing. The small building was only one story. It had five delivery rooms and a few exam rooms. Two doctors in the area had started the clinic to make sure women didn't have to drive two hours to give birth. The sight of the terra-cotta and white facade took her back five years to the mixture of grief and elation she'd felt when she'd driven away from the building with an empty car seat. And one cradling a tiny baby girl.

Had she left one behind?

Shannon studied the clinic, her gaze slipping past two women who stood smoking by the road. She hadn't been here since her girls were born. The memory of that night was branded so deeply in her psyche that even now her muscles tightened and her teeth wanted to chatter. She'd never felt so alone, then or now. It was the night she finally realized that if she was going to make anything of herself, it was up to her. The night she faced the fact that she'd be raising Kylie on her own. The night she vowed she'd prove one mistake didn't have to ruin her life.

Now here she was, back in the town she'd promised to leave in her dust. God sure had a sense of humor. She pushed through the glass door of the clinic and stepped to the check-in counter. The gum-popping twentysomething girl with pink streaks in her hair handed over copies of the records once Shannon signed the release form.

"Does Verna Jeffers still work here?" Shannon asked as she thrust the papers into her purse.

The girl fingered one of the four studs in her ear. "Miss Verna?

Nope, she retired last year. She's in the phone book if you want to give her a call. She help deliver your baby?"

"Yes. Thanks for the information."

"No problem. Hey, you hear about the wildfires up north? They might move this way."

"I haven't had the news on. Are they bad?"

"The news said they're the worst outbreak since the winter of '05 and '06."

In Texas, talk of fire was as common as conjecture about rain. Shannon thanked the girl again and hurried back out to her Jeep. She glanced at her watch. She had an hour and forty-five minutes before she had to be at the mining camp. Shannon drove to a gas station, where she looked up Verna's address and phone number, then headed along the road to the small house.

The potholes along the dirt road were big enough to swallow her Jeep, and a wash ran across the road in front of Verna's house. The road likely hadn't been graded since the last time Shannon was in town. During monsoon season, Verna was probably stuck here.

Shannon eased the Jeep through the sandy bottom of the wash and into the driveway. The place was a double-wide that had to have been put here back in the seventies. Dents left by hail dotted the siding, but the neatly landscaped yard stole the attention from the house. Bird of paradise, ocotillo, and oleanders lit the yard with a blaze of color.

Shannon walked along a brick pathway to the house, waving away bees and inhaling the fragrance of the blossoms that filled the air. Verna had made a desert museum of her yard with the native plants and habitat for lizards.

A woman in overalls and a wide straw hat was coming down the steps from the house with a spade in hand. She pushed the hat off her forehead and smiled at Shannon. "Can I help you?" In her sixties with blue eyes in a tanned face, she was as slim as a girl.

Before Shannon could answer, tires spit gravel behind her, and she turned to see Jack MacGowan in a big blue truck. He barely waited for the truck to stop before leaping out of the vehicle and striding into the yard. His gaze flickered from Shannon to Verna. "What did she tell you?" he asked Shannon.

Shannon thought about playing coy and acting as though she had no idea what he was talking about, but the suffering in Jack's expression was enough to silence her. "Nothing. I just got here. How's Faith?"

"She's fine. The fever broke about midnight. It's just a cold. How did you know she was sick?"

"Kylie told me," Shannon said, waiting to see if his reaction was anything like hers had been.

Jack's head rocked back as though he'd been slapped. "Kylie? How did she know?"

"She has sometimes told me things about her—her twin." Shannon forced herself to watch him, to notice the agitation in his hands, the fear in his eyes. She needed every bit of ammunition she could find to fight him.

"Jack? What's going on?" Verna's voice was tremulous.

"We need to talk to you, Aunt Verna." Jack took her arm and guided her to a garden bench.

Verna's gaze lingered on Shannon's face. "I know you," she said. "Shannon Astor, isn't it?" The spade fell from her fingers onto the ground. Her hand shook when she lifted it to tuck a stray lock of gray hair behind her ear.

"Yes. You remember me?"

"You told me you were leaving this wide spot in the road and never coming back."

"I changed my mind," Shannon said evenly. "I need to know what you did that night. How you switched the babies. Don't try to lie. I know it's true. I've seen Faith. She's my daughter."

"You don't know that," Jack said. "She's mine."

Verna held her hands up in front of her face. "I want you to go now."

Shannon folded her arms over her chest. "I'm not leaving. Tell me what you did." She glared at Jack. He had to want the truth.

Jack's hand was shaking when he wiped his forehead. "We need the truth, Aunt Verna. Did you switch the babies?"

Shannon glanced at his stony face and hoped she'd never see him stare at her like that. Surely the woman would crumble and tell the truth.

Verna shook her head. "How could you think such a thing?" Her voice trembled.

"The girls look alike. Totally alike," Jack said.

"That happens sometimes." Verna grabbed her spade and turned toward the house. "I have to go now."

Jack moved after her, but she disappeared inside the house, and the lock clicked. Jack shook the doorknob. "Aunt Verna, you have to talk to us." He rattled the door again, but the woman didn't reappear. He rejoined Shannon in the yard.

"Faith is Kylie's twin," she told him. "You know it's true or you wouldn't be here either."

"Not necessarily." But his voice held no conviction.

Shannon sank onto the bench. "We have to know the truth. I can have Faith's DNA checked if Verna refuses to talk."

"I don't want to put her through that."

"I'd just need some strands of hair or a swab from her mouth. She doesn't have to know yet what it's all about." Shannon didn't hold out much hope that he'd cooperate. She wouldn't if she were in his shoes.

He focused that glacier stare on her. "I'm not giving up my daughter." He couldn't hold her stare and glanced away. "I already know the truth. It's just a coincidence."

Shannon found room in her heart for pity, even for a man like Jack. "Can't you hear the desperation in your own voice? I think we know this can't be a coincidence."

He balled his fists and strode back to the front door. "Aunt Verna, we're not leaving here until you tell us what happened that day."

Shannon joined him and called out through the door. "If I have to get the sheriff involved, I will. We need to know the truth."

The door slowly opened, and Verna peered out. Her face was white, and the hand on the door frame shook.

Shannon tried to find an ounce of pity for the woman who was trembling in front of her, but a hard ball of rage settled in her belly. She knew what she was going to hear. It was as clear as the blue sky and the hot sun pressing down on her head. Verna had given her daughter to this man and passed his dead child off as Shannon's.

4

JACK PRIDED HIMSELF ON HIS COURAGE. HE'D VAULTED ATOP THOUSAND-pound bulls, ridden broncs guaranteed to break bones, faced a charging bull. But bracing himself now for what he feared was coming turned his muscles to mush. "Aunt Verna, what happened?"

Blair's aunt stepped away from the door. "Come in. I need to sit down." She showed every one of her years as she staggered down the hall to the living room and dropped onto a green chenille sofa. Pictures of Blair and Faith covered nearly every surface of the table stands and the coffee table.

Shannon followed them. She grabbed the back of a chair and leaned on it. "You played God with our lives, didn't you?" A sob punctuated her question. She swiped a strand of blonde hair behind her ear.

Verna began to weep. She fished a hankie out of her sleeve and dabbed her cheeks. When she nodded, Jack's stomach plunged into his boots. If only he could awaken from this nightmare. Things had been bleak when Blair died, but at least he'd had his daughter. He couldn't lose Faith—he just couldn't.

Verna clenched the hankie in her lap. "The secret is killing me. I had to believe I did the right thing. I wanted to help everyone. It seemed the best. Haven't you ever stayed quiet so people you love could be happy?" She stared up at Shannon with a plea in her eyes.

Shannon nodded. "Some secrets aren't made to be kept forever, and this is one of them," she said. "I realize you thought you were helping, but tell us the truth."

"Truth is always better," Jack said. "There's never a good reason to keep a secret from people you love. It always comes out and hurts in the end. What did you do?" The word *secret* left a bad taste in his mouth. His father was secretive in ways that always left Jack out of everything.

"What I thought was best. I heard Blair's panic when the baby wasn't breathing, and I knew she couldn't go through that. Not when I could fix it and help you too." She kept her gaze on Shannon. "I didn't want to hurt anyone. But you would each have a baby then. It seemed fair."

The strength ran out of Jack's legs and it was all he could do to continue to stand and stare down at Blair's aunt. He shuddered and thrust his hands into his pockets so the women didn't see them shaking. "Our baby died, and you gave us her baby?"

"Of course she did." Shannon's voice trembled. "She thought you were entitled to a live child because you're the great Jack MacGowan. Upstanding citizen, son of the senator. Who better to gain a beautiful, *live* baby girl? And who better to be rid of the burden than a down-and-out unwed mother?"

He winced at her assessment. And at the rage in her voice. It sounded like she hated him. And no wonder, after what he'd done to her. He had hated himself enough over the years for it too. "What were you told?" he asked.

She continued to stare at Verna. "That my daughter, who was perfect in the delivery room, had died. Underdeveloped lungs was the reason given." The fire was gone from her voice, and tears pooled in her eyes. She sagged against a wall. "I can't believe it."

"I thought you'd understand," Verna said in a piteous voice. "Would you have made it through college and vet school with two children?"

"That's hardly the point!" Shannon said.

His daughter hadn't been perfect in the delivery room. She hadn't been breathing. He drew in a deep breath. "How did you manage this?" he asked Verna.

Verna rocked back and forth with her arms clasped around her. She didn't look at either of them. "I was the nurse on duty. Your baby had just died. I couldn't tell you or Blair. When we took Shannon to delivery, those babies were so beautiful, so perfect. I was alone in the nursery with them. It was an easy matter to switch the wrist tags and tell the doctor one of the twins had died."

"Didn't he think it a little suspicious that a perfectly healthy baby died and one at death's door lived?" Jack demanded.

"It was old Doc Crasley," she said as if that explained everything.

It did. The old doctor had been white-haired when Jack was a kid. By the time Faith was born, the physician had been ancient.

"Don't you think I should have been the one to make the decision about what was best for me and *my* daughters?" Shannon demanded. She swiped at an errant tear that trickled down her cheek.

"I was just trying to help," Verna whispered.

"What was so important about making sure Blair and Jack had a baby?" Shannon asked, her voice trembling. "What gave you the right to play God?"

"Blair had tried for four years to have a baby," Jack said. "It was a miracle she carried Faith. Er, our baby. She suffered five miscarriages in those four years, and the doctor didn't think she could carry a child." He winced, remembering the trauma of that time. The tears, the sullen anger and despair he'd tried to coax Blair through.

"I'm sorry," Shannon said. "For Blair, for all of us." She sounded as though she really meant it.

"I meant no harm," Verna whispered.

"How are we going to sort this mess out?" Shannon muttered, more to herself than to Jack.

Jack glanced at her. "You want to go somewhere and talk?" he asked.

Her head came up and she stared at him. "What will talk accomplish? You don't want to give up Faith, and I'm not giving her up either." She blinked at the moisture in her eyes. "I was cheated of her first five years. From the time Kylie could talk, she's spoken of an imaginary friend—her sister. She hurts when Faith has hurt. The girls have been cheated of their time too. Last night was just one time of many that Kylie has told me something about her sister being sick or hurt."

He'd heard of the twin connection. Faith had an imaginary friend, too, and he had indulged her fantasy, never suspecting it was real. He sighed and took off his cowboy hat, then ran his hand through his hair and put it back on. What could they do? He saw no way out of this.

"We have to fix this," Shannon said. "But I don't know how."

Fix it? Jack didn't like the sound of those words. "Do you want to put the girls through a custody battle? Let's talk about it."

"We both know what kind of man you are, Jack MacGowan."

He winced. "I was a kid, Shannon."

"You were eighteen. Hardly a kid anymore."

"Look, I've apologized. You want me to do it again?" But they both knew a simple apology would never wipe away his guilt.

Her fingers curled around the strap on her purse. "Where do you want to go talk?"

"How about the drugstore café in town? I'll buy you breakfast."

She glanced at her watch. "We both have to be out at the mustang training in forty-five minutes."

"The camp is only a five-minute drive from town. We'd have a spell to talk." He needed time to think this out, figure out a solution that let him keep his daughter. "Wait, I've got a better idea. You think about your solution, and I'll do the same. We'll meet at the café for dinner."

"I have a daughter to get home to," she pointed out.

So do I hovered on his tongue, but they both knew his claim to his daughter was as flimsy as butterfly wings. "I don't like to train longer than a couple of hours at a time. How about we take a break for lunch?"

"I packed my lunch."

"Enrica packed me one too. We could find a place to eat where we won't be disturbed."

"Fine." She rushed for the door.

Jack wanted to feel sorry for her, but she stood poised to strip him of his daughter, and he couldn't find the grace not to blame her. He peered out the window and heard the door to her Jeep slam. Couldn't she just be happy Faith was being raised by a doting father? She had another daughter. The tires spit dirt when she took off.

"Am I in trouble?" Verna asked in a weak voice.

He saw no sign of remorse in her. She'd said she was sorry, but he knew she was only sorry to be caught. "If lawyers get involved, there may be a lawsuit."

"Will I go to jail?"

"It's possible. It was a criminal thing to do." Pain began to pulse behind his eyes, and he pressed the bridge of his nose.

She twisted her hands in her lap. "It seemed right at the time."

There was no right here. Fixing this seemed impossible. "Are you crazy?" He shouted the words, not caring that she cringed from him. "Don't you care that my daughter is about to be ripped from me? How is she going to feel when the only home she's ever known is torn apart?"

Verna held up trembling hands as if to ward him off. "After all I've done for you, this is the thanks I get. If not for me, you wouldn't have a daughter at all."

Jack squeezed his eyes shut. He was about to lose everything that made life worth living, and Verna thought she deserved a medal.

JUST WHEN SHANNON THOUGHT THE TREMBLING HAD STOPPED, IT WOULD start up again. She longed to see the little girl she'd only glimpsed yesterday. Would she be just like Kylie with her ability to sing perfectly on key? Did she talk in her sleep? Did she love stuffed animals and unicorns?

Shannon's eyes kept blurring with tears. She hated to cry. Her nose ran, and her throat hurt from holding in the pain. Did Faith talk about her twin the way Kylie did? The minute Kylie had seen Faith, she'd claimed the girl as her sister. It had been hard to get her to sleep last night with all her chatter about finding Faith. Had Jack dealt with any of that?

She glanced at her watch. Allie would offer a good shoulder to cry on. Shannon whipped into the Bluebird Youth Ranch's driveway and drove back the long, winding lane to the ranch house. She sat for a moment watching the girls trying to rope calves with Rick. She finally got out and walked to the porch, where Allie sat snapping beans.

"I didn't expect to see you until this afternoon," Allie said. Her smile faded when Shannon neared. "What's happened?"

Shannon dropped abruptly onto the top step of the porch. "I saw Verna Jeffers. She admitted to switching my daughter with Jack's dead daughter."

Allie's hands stilled their task. The color leeched from her cheeks. "I can't believe it. Why would she do something like that?"

"She said she knew it would be hard for me to raise two children, but I'm sure it was for Jack and Blair. She's Blair's aunt. What am I going to do to get Faith back, Allie? Jack has money, power, and prestige here in the area."

"Get a lawyer?" Allie began to snap the beans again.

"No judge is going to rip Faith from her home and give her to an unwed mom who's a hundred thousand dollars in debt with school loans. It will be several years before I make any kind of decent money." Her head began to pound from thinking about it.

And what judge would grant Shannon custody if her medical records came to light?

Allie tossed some broken beans into the pan. "You should at least talk to someone. Wouldn't the law be clear about it?"

"Maybe. I don't know, but I'm scared. Look at the house. It's falling down around our ears. A home study will show the sharp contrast in living conditions."

"Rick can help you hire a good attorney."

"With what? He'll want a retainer." She held up her hand when Allie started to speak. "And don't offer to loan me money. I wasn't fishing."

"We could help you out, Shannon."

Her eyes burned at her new friend's generosity. "I appreciate it, but I'd rather figure this out on my own. I needed someone to talk to, so thanks for listening." She rose. "I'd better get out to the mustang training. Jack wants to talk over lunch about our 'options' and I have no idea what to suggest."

"A custody split maybe?" Allie said.

"I can't see Jack as the kind who will want to share. I predict he'll try to buy me off. Want to lay bets?" Shannon grinned, her mood lightening as she thought about how she'd answer him if he dared try it.

"You seem to have a chip on your shoulder about Jack. What's happened between you two?"

"It's complicated."

"I've got time."

Shannon sat back down. She didn't want to remember that past pain, but maybe it would help to talk about it. "I loved my parents. They were like shooting stars, exciting and vibrant to be around. But not stable. I always knew they loved each other more than me. They were always looking for a new way to make a million overnight. No crazy scheme was too extreme to try. So that meant we often didn't have enough money for clothes, though I never went hungry. After one of my dad's 'opportunities' went south, we moved in with my uncle. He was a sour man and never spoke to me unless it was to tell me to do something."

"Your parents let him?"

Shannon shrugged. "What choice did they have? He was putting a roof over their heads while they were out looking for Spanish treasure."

"I've heard the legends around here."

"My father believed they were more than legends. Anyhow, that's how I happened to move here. I tutored Jack and his sister in biology.

I thought we were friends. You know about Jewel?" She waited until Allie nodded. "I told Jack I thought Jewel might be a unicorn, that one night I thought I'd seen a horn on his head." She nearly winced waiting for Allie's reaction. This wasn't something she talked about.

Allie didn't laugh. "Rick says there's something different about that horse."

"Do you think I'm crazy?"

Allie shook her head. "I've seen strange things in this land. So what happened? Did Jack make fun of you?"

"Not then. He promised not to tell anyone. Two days later, a bunch of boys saw me. They circled around like a pack of wolves and wanted to know if it was true that I had a unicorn. I had to admit it."

"So Jack *told* them?"

Shannon nodded then held up her hand. "Wait, there's more. The whole school thought I was a little crazy after that. In the halls, people gave me a wide berth. Even my so-called friends. They cut me loose. No one sat next to me in class. My reputation grew in the years after my parents died. I got quiet after their death. First with grief, then with fatigue. My uncle expected me to do everything around the ranch, the housework, the barn work, everything. My silence just added to my schoolmates' perception that I wasn't right in the head. It didn't help that I was thought of as poor white trash."

Allie winced. "I'm so sorry, Shannon. But you're strong and smart. Couldn't they see that?"

Shannon shrugged. "They believed the great Jack MacGowan, star football player, son of the senator. But Jack isn't trustworthy. If he says he'll do something, I'll never be able to believe him. And he has my daughter."

"No wonder you don't know what to do. Rick thinks the world of

Jack. Maybe he's changed. Did you ever confront him about how he broke your confidence?"

Shannon nodded. "He said he was sorry, that it just slipped out when he was talking with his buddies. But it was too little too late. He gave me my first lesson on not trusting people."

"It sounds like it was that way with your parents too. They weren't there for you much."

Shannon never liked to face that fact, but she gave a reluctant nod. "I suppose. But it made me strong. And I want my daughter—daughters to be strong too. Life is hard enough without expecting too much from other people. And I can't assume Jack will do right by Faith now that he knows the truth."

Allie grabbed the cordless phone on the swing beside her. She handed it to Shannon. "Call an attorney."

Shannon's fingers closed around the phone. Maybe it wouldn't hurt to at least contact a lawyer. She knew no one though. Wait, wasn't Horton's brother an attorney? "My old boss has a brother who might know what to do. I've still got the contact information in my phone. Horton had me put it in as his next-of-kin." She scrolled through her address book and found the number.

Did she even want to know? She bit her lip as she punched in the number. When the man answered on the other end, she explained who she was.

"Horton has often spoken of you," Duncan Chrisman said. "Is my brother well?"

"He's fine," Shannon said hastily. "Um, this is a legal matter, and I didn't know who else to call."

"What can I do for you? No charge for any advice. You've been good to Horton."

"It . . . it's a custody issue." Shannon told him the situation. She wasn't sure she liked the sound of his repeated "uh-huh" and "I see."

When she finally fell silent, he cleared his throat. "The law is not clear, I'm sorry to say. In previous cases similar to this, the decisions have been split. You'd think it would be pretty open-and-shut. The child was stolen from you, deliberately switched by a member of the family. But the fact Mr. MacGowan was unaware of the deception muddies the water. And the court will look at what is in the best interests of the child. I would suggest you come to an equitable arrangement out of court. If you go before a judge, there's no telling what ruling you might get."

"What judge would want to separate twins and the connection they feel? Doesn't the fact that they're twins make my case stronger?"

"Perhaps." Duncan's tone was slow and measured. "But the judge also might feel that because you have another child, you were less harmed. The other child is in a good home, I assume?"

"The father is a widower, so she has no mother."

"And you are unmarried, right?"

Shannon didn't want to admit it. "Yes."

"So neither situation would be as ideal as a married couple. What is the man's financial situation?"

"He's Senator MacGowan's son, if that tells you anything."

"Oh dear. Any judge in the state will look at that and the senator's long reach. Again, my advice for you is to settle this amicably."

Shannon gave a heavy sigh. "I'm not quite sure how to do that."

"The two of you could always marry," Duncan said with a chuckle.

Shannon caught back a gasp. *What a stupid idea.* But she kept the words to herself.

"But on a more serious note, surely the man will be reasonable and allow you visitation."

"I don't want visitation. I want my child back."

"I doubt you'll accomplish that without a court battle. I could check for someone in your area."

"There's only one attorney here and he's in Jack's pocket." Shannon rubbed her eyes. "I'll think about what you've said. Thanks for your time."

"I'm glad to help. Call if you need anything else." The phone clicked off.

Shannon handed the phone back to Allie, who had sat quietly listening. "He says to settle out of court. It's just as I suspected. Jack is holding most of the cards."

"Then maybe you should talk to Jack."

"I will, but I have no idea what to tell him. He's not going to give up custody."

"Would you? Besides, Faith loves Jack. Would you want to tear him out of her life?"

"No," Shannon admitted. She'd seen how close father and daughter were. She'd be a monster to want to rip that apart. But she wanted the daughter who had been robbed from her, the sister denied to her daughter.

With Jack, Faith had a good name, prominence in the community, security. She wished Kylie had that kind of life.

SWEAT LATHERED BOTH JACK AND THE HORSE. HE TOOK OFF HIS HAT AND wiped the perspiration from his forehead. The stallion wasn't going to be easy to train. He was aggressive and muscular, so Jack had to be on his toes with this one.

"Having trouble, MacGowan? Want me to teach you how it's done?"

Jack didn't have to turn around to recognize the taunting voice. "Larue, don't you have better things to do than to watch me? It didn't look like you were having much luck with that mare of yours earlier."

A bullwhip cracked, and Jack whirled to see the tip coming his way. He ducked, but the whirling leather took the hat from his head and tossed it into the water trough. Tucker Larue's laughter floated on the wind as he walked away.

Jack glared after him but held his tongue. Any reaction would play into Larue's game. He lifted his soggy hat from the water and hung it over a fence post. His head would be exposed to the late morning's brutal sun, but maybe the hat would be dry by the time he had lunch with Shannon.

What was he going to say to Shannon?

"MacGowan, I thought sure you'd tear that boy a new rear end," Buzz Bollinger drawled. "You mellowing in your old age?"

Jack glanced at the organization's supervisor. Buzz had hired Shannon to work this event. Maybe he could offer some insight that might give Jack an angle to solve this problem. "What's the deal with the new vet?" he asked, his voice casual. "She's not the friendliest one."

Bollinger propped a muddy boot onto a rock. "Thought you knew her from school."

"She was much younger."

"Rough life, I guess. Way I heard it, she came here when she was thirteen, looking like an angel but all starch. Her daddy was one of those men who would take supper money to gamble on some new get-rich-quick scheme. Her mama was a looker like her though. They were chasing one of the desert's legends. A rockfall buried them. Their bodies were never recovered."

"I remember hearing that," Jack said. "They were on some

harebrained scheme to find a Spaniard's burial site. There was some big hoopla about digging out their bodies, but no one was sure about the location, and the daughter wanted to let them be."

"You know more than I do then," Bollinger said.

Only because Buzz's words had opened a floodgate of memories. Ones he'd like to forget. Like the betrayal in her eyes at school in the lunchroom when his friends mocked her and twirled their fingers around their ears to imply she was crazy.

"I moseyed around town asking questions about her before I hired her," Buzz said. "Grady said she was the best helper he ever had. When she left here, she put herself through college and veterinary school. One thing that bothered me a bit was someone at the café said she was just a little off, if you know what I mean."

"That's not true," Jack said quickly.

"You sound like Grady. He said the rumors were just cruel lies."

"She's got a daughter," Jack said. "Is the dad around?" Shannon would be a formidable enough adversary by herself.

"I don't know anything about that. I was only interested in what kind of person I'd be hiring."

Jack had already figured that out. Shannon was as tenacious as a Gila monster. "I'm surprised she came back here. The pay can't be very good."

"I wondered about that too. She told me her school bills were crippling, but she's got a free place to live here."

Bills. Maybe if he was lucky, Shannon could be bought off.

SHANNON WRAPPED THE HORSE'S SWOLLEN LEG AND RAN GENTLE HANDS over the mare's fetlock. "You'll be all right, girl," she whispered. The horse nuzzled Shannon's hair as if to say thank you.

Shannon packed up her supplies and headed toward the far training paddock. At least she had something to keep her mind off the amazing turn of events that had disrupted her life. She longed to know Faith better, to see her girls laugh and play together. She didn't have the faintest idea how to accomplish that. She skirted a cactus and stood on a rock for a better view. The trainer hadn't seen her yet, that's the way she liked it.

She hadn't seen the man's face, but something about him seemed familiar. About five-eight, he was thin with lots of nervous energy that he focused on the mustang. The young mare strained against the long lead as she galloped along the sand in a circle around him. Shannon was about to turn and walk away when she heard a distinctive crack behind her. She spun back and saw a bullwhip flip through the air and land on the rump of the mare. The animal screamed and danced away from the whip.

No! Her fists clenched, Shannon leaped from the rock and bolted for the paddock. The guy's back was to her, and he was swearing so loudly he couldn't hear her approach. He raised his whip again, but before he brought the rawhide down on the mare, Shannon reached up and snatched it from his hand.

"What the—" The man whirled to face her. Red suffused his swarthy face, which was twisted into an angry grimace.

Shannon retreated in shock. She'd had no idea he was here.

With his gaze locked on hers, the anger faded from Tucker Larue's eyes. "It's you," he said. "I wondered when you'd come to see me."

"Tucker?" she said, struggling to keep her tone even. No, not now, not here. This was the last complication she needed. She hadn't seen him in over five years, and she'd hoped never to lay eyes on him again.

"At least you remember my name." His smile widened, but it still didn't reach his eyes. "I'll take my whip back now."

"You will not. You're getting a citation for using it on this horse. One more and you're done here." She turned to stalk away, but Tucker's arm snaked out and seized her around the waist. He hauled her back against his chest. Struggling with him was like trying to escape the grip of a boa constrictor. "Let go of me," she said. "Or you'll have citation number two."

He released her. "I didn't hurt that animal. She doesn't like the sound of the whip. Go ahead. Take a look at her. There's not a scratch on her."

Shannon gave him an angry glare, then walked over to where the mare stood trembling. The mustang danced away at Shannon's approach. "It's okay, girl. You're okay," she said soothingly. The horse snorted, then calmed when Shannon ran her hands over her withers. She found no cuts or abrasions on the mare.

"See?" Tucker was standing close behind her. His hand grabbed the heft of her hair. "You've still got that beautiful hair."

Shannon tugged her hair from his grasp. "Step away from me," she said. "You're in my personal space." A sheen of perspiration broke out on her forehead. She had to keep him away from her girls.

"I'd like to get closer," he whispered in her ear, but he moved away. "Shannon, did you keep the baby?"

Shannon swallowed hard and avoided his smiling gaze. "It's none of your business. And I don't care to discuss my personal life with you."

"I think I have a right to know. It was my kid too."

She thanked God he'd lit out the second he heard she was pregnant. He had no idea there were two. She struggled to keep her composure. "Oh? You want to support a baby?"

"That's not the point. A father has a right to know the truth."

"Not a father like you." Shannon ignored his question and glanced at the mare again. "Since she's not hurt, I won't write you up this time, but if I see you using the whip even to scare her, I will. There are better ways to train a horse."

"Fear puts a little respect in a horse's eyes. And a woman's," he called, his smile broadening.

Shannon wanted to slap his smirking face, but she let her withering glare wipe the grin from his face before she turned and stomped back to headquarters. She didn't remember him being so obnoxious. Evidently, time hadn't improved his character.

5

SHANNON HAD WALKED WHAT SEEMED LIKE MILES AND CHECKED COUNTLESS mustangs for abrasions, lacerations, and other injuries. The horses were all in decent shape except for a few contusions from the transportation here.

She cringed at the thought of telling Jack about Tucker. There were enough wrinkles in this problem without the man adding another one.

Her cell phone rang in the clip at her waist. Her fingers fumbled with the clip and she stared at the display. Mary Beth's name flashed across the tiny screen. Finally.

She flipped it open. "Mary Beth, where have you been? You've scared me to death."

Mary Beth's laugh came, but it was forced. "Sorry, I . . . I had no idea you'd be worried."

Was she *whispering*? Shannon straightened and gripped the phone tighter. "Are you okay?"

"I . . . I think so. I will be. He just has to understand."

"Understand what?"

"I can't go into all of that now. I just called to make sure you got to Bluebird okay. How's Kylie?"

"Fine. We're both fine. The job is interesting. Are you sure you're okay?"

"Ask me next week." Mary Beth's voice sounded full of tears.

"Is it that guy you're seeing?" Shannon asked, lowering her voice and hoping her friend would open up.

"Sort of. Listen, he's coming. I have to go. Don't call me. I'll call you when I can."

The phone clicked off before Shannon could answer. Her legs were wobbly, and her vision doubled for the second time in two days. She wished she'd brought her cane. Stress worsened her condition, and she'd hoped to keep it hidden for a while. She glanced at her watch and managed to make out the time. Jack would be waiting for her. Inhaling a few deep breaths, she prayed for a calm spirit.

Buzz fell into step beside her. "You okay, Shannon?"

Great. The big boss himself would find out all too soon that she had feet of clay. "A little tired. Um, where's the mess hall? I'm supposed to meet Jack."

"I'll show you. A little worn out?"

She seized the excuse he offered. "Exhausted. I didn't get much sleep last night even though I'd been up over twenty-four hours. I never asked you how you happened to pick me for the assignment," she said. "I'm grateful for the opportunity."

He smiled. "You came highly recommended. Grady sang your praises. He told me he'd never seen anyone with your natural instinct with animals and that he could always count on you to show up at his office after school. A couple of other people recommended you too. Jack's dad for one."

"The senator? I'm surprised he even remembered me."

"He said you used to take care of his collies when he brought them in to the vet's office."

"His border collies. Great animals." She struggled to remember their names, but the memory eluded her. "I didn't even know he knew my name."

"The senator doesn't miss a trick."

"Have you known Jack a long time?"

"A fair spell. He was a teenage rodeo star when I was running a rodeo in Phoenix. He's a good trainer. I can't say the same about some of our other contestants."

Shannon grimaced. "Why'd you let Tucker Larue enter?"

Buzz shrugged. "He met the requirements. I can't pick and choose favorites and have a fair contest."

Maybe she could get some information out of Buzz. He didn't seem to be holding anything back. "Tucker doesn't seem to like Jack. I saw them snarling at one another in the west paddock yesterday."

Buzz raised his brows. "You've noticed, eh? The two have clashed at more rodeos than I can count. Larue has a competitive streak too. If he loses, he makes sure the winner suffers in some way."

It was so clear now, six years after she'd first met him, that she'd been dazzled by Tucker's shiny belt buckles, snakeskin boots, and

Stetson hat. She'd been fair game for a slick operator. She only prayed her girls didn't have to suffer for her stupidity.

"Here we are," Buzz said. "I see Jack is already at the far left corner. Looks like he wants some privacy." Amusement lingered in his voice.

"We, ah, have business to discuss."

"Sure, sure." He patted her hand. "If you need anything, you let me know, Shannon."

"Thanks, Buzz." She headed for the back table. Buzz was a great guy. She'd thought she didn't have a shot at this job, but he'd given her a chance. She was as weak as cactus tea by the time she got to where Jack waited. With her legs about to give out, she sank onto the bench. "Sorry I'm late. Have you been waiting long?"

He stretched out his long, jean-clad legs. "About five minutes. I wasn't sure you'd show."

She blinked her blurry eyes a few times. Thankfully, her vision was beginning to come back to normal. "I said I would."

Jack's gaze stayed on her. "I thought maybe you'd decided to see a lawyer first."

She met his gaze with her chin up. "It may be too complicated to do anything but consult an attorney," she said.

He frowned. "Are you okay? You look pale and upset."

"I didn't sleep last night." If she told him about her open door at midnight and finding Felipe when she arrived, he would use it against her and say the ranch wasn't safe for Faith.

She dug her sandwich out of her bag to gain some time to think. There was no easy way out of this situation. She knew he would have a suggestion though. Men like Jack always did. Men who took control of a situation, who cut the Gordian knot with one thrust of the sword. Men who thought they knew the best answer to any question. She could sense his eyes on her, looking for any sign of weakness. She forced her gaze up to lock with his.

His color was a little pale. "Have you come up with a solution?"

She laid her turkey sandwich on the table and unzipped the plastic bag. He was asking *her*? She took out her bottle of hot sauce and poured it on her sandwich. The only solution that would be good for the girls terrified her, but she had to remember her twins were the important ones in this problem. Not her and not Jack.

"I'll be honest, Shannon. I'm scared spitless." He leaned forward and stared at her. "Faith is the best thing in my life. She's all I've got, just like Kylie is all you've got. She's my family. I can't lose her." His voice broke.

If he was trying to play to her emotions, he was doing a good job. A lump formed in her throat. Faith probably adored her daddy. A little girl should have a daddy. Kylie should have one too. She asked about her father off and on, and Shannon never knew what to tell her. Tucker had never so much as called to see if the girls had been born or if Shannon was all right.

Except he was here now. And she couldn't tell Jack.

SHANNON UNCAPPED HER BOTTLE OF WATER AND TOOK A SIP, THEN STARED at Jack. He couldn't read her expression. "I have a suggestion," he said. "Look, don't take this wrong, okay? I've got plenty of money. I know things are rough for you, trying to raise your daughter by yourself. I'll pay off your school loans, give you a fresh start. Just sign over Faith to me."

She choked on her water. "*Sell* you my daughter? What kind of monster do you think I am? This has nothing to do with money. I've cared for Kylie and myself from the beginning. I'm not some helpless damsel waiting to be rescued from a life of poverty."

He'd worried she'd take it wrong. He held up his hand. "I didn't mean it like that. I wanted to help you and Kylie. A court battle will hurt us all."

She glared at him. "I want to know my daughter," she said. "She's my flesh and blood. I've never washed her hair, bought her a shirt, or kissed her cheek." Her voice broke and she blinked damp eyes. "I've never heard her say 'Mommy' or listened to her sing. I've never read a bedtime story to her or tucked her into bed at night after listening to her prayers. That's what's been stolen from me, Jack."

He pressed his lips together. "That's not my fault, Shannon." Not hers either, but he didn't say it.

Shannon's mouth trembled, and she looked down at her hands. Some emotion he couldn't read passed over her face. Could it be fear?

"Has Faith ever said strange things about having a sister?" she asked. "She has, hasn't she? Kylie has talked about it almost from the time she could first put sentences together. The second she saw Faith, she *knew*. How can we deprive them of the closeness twins can share?"

He clasped his hands together. "How can we give them that and keep their worlds from coming apart? Especially Faith's? If you take her away from me, she'll hate you. And a court battle might not even get you custody. I don't doubt you could give it a good shot, but the judge looks at what's in the best interest of the child. It's possible all you'll accomplish is alienating Faith when she finds out what you're trying to do. She loves me, you know."

"I'm sure she does." She pressed her fingers to her eyes as though her head hurt.

"You've got an idea. I can see the wheels turning," he said. He flattened his palms against the top of the table and leaned forward. "What is it?"

"Do you have a girlfriend, Jack?" she asked, her tone careful.

He frowned. He didn't want to tell her he'd only begun to think about dating again. "What's that got to do with anything?"

"Just answer me. Maybe nothing. Maybe everything." She didn't meet his gaze.

"No. I haven't seen anyone since Blair died. Raising Faith is the most important thing in my life. Are you ready to marry or something? You think having two parents is the most important thing in a kid's life? I'd normally agree, but not if you rip a daughter from her father's arms."

Shannon finally stared up into his eyes. He thought he saw pain or fear there. Maybe both. "Spill it," he said. "I have no idea where you're going."

She wet her lips. "I do think having two parents is important. You're going to think this is a crazy idea, and maybe it is, but hear me out."

His heart softened toward her when he saw the way she trembled. He kept forgetting this was hard on her too. "You can trust me, Shannon. I want what's best for all of us."

Her face was expressionless. "That's all I want too—to see the girls happy and whole." She clasped her hands together. "I have to worry about the future, about Kylie's future. She has no one who cares about her but me."

"I'm sorry," he said softly. "That has to be scary for you. But you're young. You've got many years ahead of you."

"That's what Blair thought," she said, not seeming to notice his wince.

Was she asking for a trust fund for Kylie? He could do that without another thought. Hope leaped to life.

Her gaze searched his. "This isn't about what we want. This is about the girls. Faith needs a mother and Kylie needs a father, someone who would love her even if I'm not there. Could you love her, Jack?"

"Of course I could. She's part of Faith." Did she want him to promise to take Kylie too? "What's this all about, Shannon? I don't know where you're going with this. Are you asking me to take Kylie if something happens to you?"

"I'm asking for more than that. I want stability for both girls. I think we should marry." Her voice quavered, and she stared down at her hands. "Believe me, it's the last thing I would want for myself. But I'm not the important one here—it's my girls who matter. And a stable home would be best for them."

Marry. The word made the blood drop from his head to his boots. He gripped the edge of the table. What a stupid idea. She must be crazy after all. He sank against his seat back. "Marry you? You mean, like a wedding license? Legally?" Jack stood on the edge of a precipice and couldn't see what lay below.

"That's usually what *marry* means." She batted moist eyes.

Jack realized a fly was heading straight for his mouth. He clamped his lips shut and stared at Shannon. Maybe she hadn't said what he thought he heard. But no, he could see by the wariness in her eyes that she'd just suggested they get married. It was the craziest idea he'd ever heard, but if he gave her his gut reaction, it might close all dialogue between them on how to sort out this mess.

"Tha-that's an interesting idea," he said slowly. "I'm not sure I'm tracking what you have in mind though." He studied her. She was a beautiful woman. Her straight blonde hair touched her shoulders, amazing blue eyes just like his daughter's. Slim but shapely in all the right places.

But he didn't love her. Heck, he didn't even *know* her. She was tenacious and strong, a woman who had put herself through school and was raising her daughter alone, both admirable traits. But for all he knew, she ate bats for breakfast. Her pretty face could hide anything. Like every other man he knew, he'd seen *Fatal Attraction* and shuddered.

She pushed her hair out of her face. "I know it's a shock. I'm not proposing a real marriage, of course." Her words came out in a rush, and she wouldn't meet his gaze. "I'm sure your ranch house has tons of space, and we could each have our own wing or something. It would be a marriage in name only, just to provide for our girls."

"At least you're saying 'our' girls." He couldn't believe he was actually thinking about this. "We wouldn't be putting them through a very public court battle," he said slowly, allowing the idea to sink in. He wouldn't run the risk of losing his daughter.

Of course there would be trade-offs. He'd have a woman in his house to consider every time he did something. He'd have two children, not just one. He wouldn't be able to look at another woman. Not that he'd dated anyone since Blair died, but the idea had begun to stir in his heart, even though he'd pushed it away. A marriage would effectively put an end to that idea.

He studied her downcast face. "In fact, the girls wouldn't have to know anything other than that we're getting married."

She frowned and raised her gaze. Her guarded expression had vanished, replaced with longing. "I want Faith to know I'm her real mother."

Blair's face flashed across his mind. Her laughing face framed with red curls, her chocolate eyes dancing with the zest of life. He shook his head. "Blair was Faith's mommy in every sense of the word. They were very close. Faith cherishes the memory of her. I don't want to ruin that."

Shannon winced, but she nodded. "Fair enough, but you have to be willing to let her know the truth at some point. I want the girls to know they're sisters, twins. That's an important thing for wholeness for them."

She had a point, though he didn't want to admit it. Still, he wasn't ready to just jump on this idea. There had to be another way around the problem.

"Don't answer now," she said as if she saw the indecision on his face. "Think about it. Pray about it. Nothing has to be decided yet." Her blue eyes darkened to midnight. "I know I'm hardly the wife material you might have had in mind. And frankly, I don't really trust you, Jack. You broke your word to me once."

His gut tightened. "I've apologized more than once, Shannon. I was a stupid kid, and it just slipped out. You have to admit it was crazy to think that horse was a unicorn."

"I never said he was!" Now she was finally looking at him. "I said in the moonlight it looked like he had a horn. I just asked if you believed unicorns could be real. You made me sound like some kind of nutcase."

"Look, let's just start over. That's all in the past. We were kids, and I was stupid. I admit that. Can't you just let it go?"

The high color on her face began to ebb, and she finally nodded. He saw Larue approaching. At least he wouldn't have to pursue this until he'd had time to examine the idea.

Larue's black eyes roamed over Shannon, and his crooked smile held a predatory gleam. He stopped by Shannon's chair, his hip close enough to graze her shoulder.

She tipped her head up to see who had joined them. "Tucker, were you looking for me?"

"I've never stopped looking for you," he said in a sultry voice. His hand brushed across her blond locks.

Shannon's smile faded, and she scooted away a few inches. "Any problems with your horses?"

"Couldn't be better. I'm going to win this competition and the money." He flashed a grin Jack's way.

"If you don't need Dr. Astor for anything, then vamoose," Jack said. "This is a private discussion."

"You trying to hog the pretty lady all to yourself?" Larue's hand brushed her hair again.

Shannon jerked away, leaping to her feet. "I'll thank you to keep your hands to yourself. I'm an official of this competition and I expect to be treated with respect. I'm not some bimbo out for a good time."

Larue stepped back and held up his hands. "Whoa, sweet! I like to see passion like that in my women."

Jack stood with his fists clenched, but he never got the chance to defend her. She jabbed her finger in Larue's chest. "I'm not one of your women and never will be." She grabbed her lunch from the table and stalked off. She didn't look back.

Jack was grinning when Larue glanced at him. The man strode off with a scowl. Jack's admiration of the little veterinarian rose a couple of notches. She was no man's fool.

6

She should have her head examined. Shannon groaned at her own stupidity as she continued her rounds to check on the mustangs. Jack must have wondered at her sanity. She couldn't believe the words had come out of her mouth either. Was she trying for a repeat of the way he'd hurt her in the past?

She needed to quit worrying. God had seen her through this far. She had to trust he would continue to lead her. The anxiety about her future ebbed. When the day's training was over, she drove to town. She hadn't seen her office yet or set up her answering machine. Probably everyone in town knew she was here by now. She scanned the buildings, looking for a brown stucco building on the next corner. She spotted it. A rail fence framed the edge of the property. The landscaping could use some work—weeds poked through the gravel mulch in the yard.

She parked in the dirt lot and grabbed her bag. As she approached the front door, she noticed it looked a bit grimy. Grady O'Sullivan had probably only stopped by if he forgot something, because his friends all knew to call him at the church office if they had an animal in trouble.

She unlocked the door and pushed it open. A man standing at the filing cabinet turned when the door hinges creaked. She nearly screamed, but then she recognized Grady's red hair.

She put her hand to her throat. "Grady, you nearly gave me a heart attack."

"A bit jumpy?" He smiled and approached her with his hand extended. "Welcome back to town, Shannon. I always knew you'd make it."

Over the summers during high school and college, she'd worked for Grady. She'd taken care of the animals he kept overnight, checking in on them until bedtime and again first thing in the morning. She'd done his filing and answered the phones and learned so much. He was one of the few people who didn't listen to gossip about her.

She ignored his outstretched hand and hugged him instead. His shirt smelled of lemon wax. "You been waxing the church piano again?" she teased.

He returned her hug. "Guilty as charged."

As pastor of the tiny church in town, Grady was the jack-of-all-trades. During her teen years, Shannon had seen him cleaning fans, unclogging the septic, and doing everything in between.

"I hope to see you at church on Sunday."

"You will." She stepped away and glanced around.

The small office didn't hold much other than utilitarian black furniture coated with ten years' worth of pet hair. A battered desk and new file cabinets blocked off the actual office area. From memory she knew the hall led to three examining rooms. A door at the end of the hall opened into a large garage-like space where animal crates lined the walls. The room was where overnight patients were kept.

Her domain now. The surreal thought made her stop. Who would have dreamed she'd come back to town and take over the business?

She followed him back to the filing cabinets. "Grady, I wish you'd let me pay you for the business."

"The business was here when I came, Shannon. When old Majors died, I stepped into his shoes. I'm just happy to have someone relieve me of the responsibility. Getting calls at night for animal illnesses and from people with problems got to be more than I could handle. And I trust you." He turned a smile on her.

"It doesn't feel right," she muttered.

His grin widened. "You hate feeling obligated. So don't. I'm the grateful one. And Dolly is even more grateful. At least I'm not having to slip out of bed two or three nights a week to go work on a foundered horse."

"Is it that bad?" She frowned, wondering how she was going to handle that with no one to look after Kylie at such hours.

He grinned. "Okay, maybe I'm exaggerating. But it happens several times a month, at least. How are you going to handle those calls with Kylie? Have you thought it through?"

"I thought I might hire a housekeeper once I have some money coming in. I've lived on a shoestring budget long enough to be able to make it while paying a salary out, I think." She gestured to the door to the animal area. "We have any patients in the back? And who checks on them at night?"

"Two cats with urinary tract infections and a dog that got hit by a pickup. I just checked on them, but I know you'll want to as well. They're doing fine and will be released tomorrow. I rented out that little apartment garage in back to a woman who checks on the animals through the night until Cassie comes in for the day."

"Thanks for keeping things rolling until I can take over the office. Once the Mustang Makeover is over, you can forget all about this place."

"You'll see me around from time to time. Caring for animals is in the blood." He studied her face. "You were born to be a vet, Shannon. You've got a gentle touch that creatures sense."

"You always know where you stand with animals," she said. "If they wag their tail or lick your hand, you're in."

Grady laughed. "I know you. You'll work yourself to death for them. But don't forget to have a life too."

"I won't." She went toward the hall door. "I'll check on the patients." She left Grady in the office and stepped into the big room in the back. Both cats began meowing and rubbing up against the cages. She opened the first cage and ran her hand over the black cat's fur. It began to purr. "You're not sick, are you?"

She lifted the kitty and put her face against its fur. The tension she'd been under began to ease. Grady said she had a way with animals, but in truth, animals had a way with her. Their unconditional love made her believe there was goodness in the world. She never felt inept when caring for someone's pet.

After checking the others, she put a message on the answering machine directing people to call her cell phone, then hugged Grady good-bye and drove to the Bluebird Ranch. The aroma of green beans cooking wafted out on the breeze through the open window. Allie was probably canning the beans she'd snapped this morning. Or else she was cooking them for supper.

Allie saw her through the window and waved Shannon inside. When Shannon stepped into the kitchen, she saw rows of canned beans cooling on every available surface. Allie's face was red, and her forehead was damp as she bustled from stove to counter with a hot can in some tongs.

"Should you be working this hard?" Shannon asked.

"Did you change your name to Rick?" Allie sent her an impish grin, then set down the jar and wiped her forehead with her apron. "This is the last batch. Hey, the girls have been begging for Kylie to spend the night. Is it okay with you?"

The thought of going to that empty house alone set Shannon's nerves on edge, but she nodded and went to pour a cup of coffee from the carafe. She spooned in sugar and cream and took it to the table. It was only five, so by the time she got home she might get some cleaning done.

"How did it go with Jack today? Did you talk about the girls?"

"We did." Shannon managed a weak smile.

Allie brought a cup of tea to the table and sat beside Shannon. "What was his suggestion on how to work this out?" she asked.

"For me to just sign Faith over to him and he'd pay off my school loans. You owe me, girl. I won that bet." It gave her no pleasure to be right.

"What did you say?"

Shannon looked away. "I don't want to tell you. It was the stupidest idea of the century. I still can't believe I said it." If she could roll back time, she'd take it back.

"What on earth? What happened?"

Shannon sipped her coffee and wished she'd never brought it up. The taste of the drink purged the bile on her tongue. Hot and strong, the way she liked it. She set her cup on the table. "I told him I wanted us to marry."

Allie's jaw dropped, and her eyes widened. "Wait, I'm not following you here. Say it again, only slower."

"You heard me. M-a-r-r-y. Marry as in a wedding. I told him we should get married and provide both parents for the girls." She rubbed her forehead. "It seemed the only answer. He has to think I'm a total idiot."

Allie still hadn't said anything. Shannon dared a peek at her friend and found her staring back with a thoughtful expression. "What?" she asked.

"What *were* you thinking? I want to know how you came up with this idea." She wagged her eyebrows. "He's a hottie. One look and you were smitten, right? Oh wait, I know. His housekeeper slipped you a little love potion when you weren't looking."

Heaven forbid. Shannon studied her hands: the unpolished nails, the nick on her forefinger. The truth was going to come out anyway. "I have MS, Allie." When Allie gasped and Shannon saw tears pooling in her friend's eyes, she smiled. "Hey, it's not a death sentence or anything. But my vision comes and goes, and I have trouble walking sometimes. I just want Kylie cared for if I become unable to work."

Allie reached across the table and gripped Shannon's hand. "We'll help if you need us."

Shannon returned the pressure of Allie's grip. "Thanks. I want Kylie to have two parents. I think Jack would love her because he already loves Faith. They're two peas in a pod. Neither of us could tell them apart. It made some kind of sense at the time I suggested it. Now I'm not so sure."

"What did Jack say?"

A giggle forced its way up Shannon's throat. "To say he was appalled would be an understatement. I could have plucked out his eyes and used them as marbles."

Allie laughed. "So he refused right off?"

"No. I told him to think about it. He was happy to grab an excuse not to answer." She laughed again. "He probably won't go for it."

"If he doesn't, what are you going to do?"

Shannon sobered, realizing again there were no easy answers. "I don't know. I want to know Faith. I suppose we'd have to share custody in some way. I'm not just turning her over to Jack."

"Those poor girls. This will be hard to explain."

"Maybe not so hard for Kylie. She's asked about her twin sister for years."

Allie's flush was beginning to fade. "Kylie talked about Faith all day today too."

Shannon rubbed at a stain on her jeans. "Jack must have loved his wife very much. He didn't want me to tell Faith that I'm her mother." Maybe he'd loved her so much he'd have trouble letting Shannon into Faith's life.

"Faith has to suspect something." Allie's voice was thoughtful. "She would have noticed how much she and Kylie look alike. Kylie told me she'd told Faith they were sisters. It's so strange how certain your daughter is even without confirmation from you."

"That twin connection is very strange and a little intimidating. I don't know what I'm going to do if Jack says no. Fight it out in court, I guess."

"I think you'll have to. It's a weird tangle."

Shannon rose. "I'd better get home." She longed to take Kylie with her, but she didn't want to disrupt the fun she was having with Betsy.

Allie walked her to the door. "I wish you'd spend the night. I hate to think about you out there all alone."

"I don't mind. I want to get things squared away for Kylie and me to make a home there." Even though every bone in her body ached, she had more filthy rooms to address. She and Allie had only cleaned the kitchen, the bedrooms, and the bathrooms. She told Allie goodbye, hugged her daughter, then went out to her Jeep.

Her cell phone lay on the seat. There were two missed calls. She scrolled through them and saw that both numbers were from Mary Beth's cell phone. She didn't dare call back—her friend had told her not to. She studied the keypad. What could it hurt to send a text message though? She keyed in a quick question. *R U good?* It was a joke between them. Mary Beth often said she'd rather be right than good.

Rick was walking toward the house and detoured to the car. "Hey, Shannon. You keeping those cowboys whipped into shape?"

She wondered if he knew about her and Tucker. Probably not. She was too wary of everyone, even Rick. "I'm working on it." She eyed him. He'd listen if she told him about the trouble, maybe even offer advice. She launched into the story about Mary Beth's call, her unease about the way her friend was acting, and her fear there was trouble brewing.

Rick's smile had long since dimmed as the story unfolded. He tipped his hat back from his forehead. "How did you meet her?"

"We were roommates at college. She went into nursing while I went into veterinary medicine. On the one hand, she's this dedicated nurse who cares about her patients, but in her private life she's always a little on the wild side. Some weeks she blows her whole paycheck on lottery tickets. Once she bought some land in Mexico that was supposed to be developed for a big resort complex. She thought she'd make four hundred thousand dollars overnight. It's still sitting there."

"Out for fast money?"

Shannon thought the label too restrictive, but she wasn't sure how to explain her friend. "Not for herself. She always sees ways she could help other people if she just had the money to do it."

He frowned. "A cop-out to justify her greed maybe."

"I don't think so. She really cares about people. She's always taking care of me. Before I left, she insisted on giving me a free tetanus shot just because she was afraid I wouldn't keep it current out here. She does the best she can."

"Who does she hang around with?"

"She works a lot of hours. In her spare time she sometimes works at the Republican Party headquarters in town. She visits the children's hospital and plays games with the kids. She goes scuba diving when she can."

"A Jill-of-all-trades," he said dryly, his nostrils flaring.

"She's not what you think," Shannon said. "Yes, she gets into scrapes occasionally, but there's no malice."

"Anything you want me to do about it?"

Shannon shook her head. "I just needed to talk to someone about my worry, and I didn't want to burden Allie with it."

"I've got a buddy in Special Ops. I'll ask him to run a check on her, see if there's anything hinky going on."

"Thanks, Rick, you're the best." At least there were a few people in town she could trust.

7

SHANNON CHECKED HER CELL PHONE AFTER SHE LEFT THE BAILEYS' RANCH. Nothing back from Mary Beth. A ramshackle house stood empty about a mile from her ranch. Tied up in an estate dispute, it had been deserted for as long as she could remember. As she passed the shack, she thought she heard something through her open window. She slowed and listened. There it came again. It sounded like a dog howling.

She whipped the vehicle to the side of the road and parked. When she hopped out, she heard the sound again. It *was* a dog. She jogged toward the shack. "Hey, boy," she called. "Where are you?" The dog howled, and the despair in the pitch prickled the back of her neck.

She bounded up the rickety steps to the rotted porch. Pushing open the unlatched door, she stepped into a room thick with tumbleweeds, dust, and spiderwebs. Grimacing, she started to back out, but the dog's wail came again. Some of the webs held fat black widows and she shuddered. But she couldn't leave the dog in distress here either. Maybe there was another way through to the back room where the dog's cries were coming from.

She retraced her steps to the porch and went around the back. Peering in the broken window, she saw the room was the kitchen. And on the floor, tied to the leg of a broken-down table, was a forlorn golden retriever. She rushed to the door and tried to open it, but it was locked and too solid to break through. She could leave the dog here and go to the ranch after an axe, but the dog's whine came again, and she knew she couldn't desert it.

She ran back to her vehicle and rummaged in the back for a weapon against the spiders, even though the thought of going through them made bile rise to the back of her throat. The broom was tucked along the side where she'd packed it to use at the office.

She grabbed it up, and wielding it like a sword, she charged the shack. She chopped her away through the room and swept away the webs. Keeping her gaze averted from the black bodies that scurried away from her sneakers, she ran to the kitchen. It wasn't much better in here. The broom banished the closest webs and their inhabitants, then she untied the dog and unlocked the back door. Stepping into the night with her prize was like winning a race.

She knelt and took the dog's muzzle in her hands. "Who put you in there, sweetie?" The dog licked her chin. Shannon examined the golden and found no abrasions, nothing worse than dehydration and hunger. Someone had put this fine boy in the shack to let him die, and if she ever found out who had done it, she'd . . . she'd . . . well, she didn't know what she'd do, but it wouldn't be pretty.

Her hand touched his collar and tag. It read "Wyatt" and had a phone number. She recognized that number. It was Jack's. One thing she knew—he'd never hurt his dog even if he'd hurt her.

There were bottles of water, something everyone in the desert kept handy, in the back of her Jeep. She uncapped a bottle and poured some into her palm and let the dog lick it up, then repeated the process until Wyatt had lapped up enough. Next the dog scarfed down several handfuls of the cat food she carried in her bag for strays. Once she loaded the dog into the backseat of the Jeep, she headed toward Jack's.

She passed the turnoff to the Bluebird Youth Ranch, then drove another five miles to Jack's ranch. She'd been by here many times, but never through the gate. The palatial house and extensive barns and white paddocks were as nice as something from a magazine. Beautiful racehorses grazed in the irrigated fields. Shannon stopped just inside the gate and got out. She had to touch one of those sleek coats.

"Here, girl," she crooned, climbing the white rail fence. She extended her hand to a sleek black horse that stood at least sixteen hands. "You're gorgeous." The mare was also very pregnant and acted agitated.

"Isn't she?"

She whirled at the sound of Jack's voice. "Did you raise her?"

He jumped the fence and joined her. "Yeah. She was born to Fancy Stockings. She's one of our best mares. You've got a good eye."

She'd heard of the famous racehorse. God said not to covet, but it was a hard commandment to obey when she let her gaze linger on the horses. Good lines, bright eyes, high energy. Horses were her weakness. If it were up to her, she'd have dozens. "She's about to foal."

"I've been watching her," he said.

Shannon stooped and ran her hand over the mare's teats. They were waxed and about to burst with milk. The tail and rump muscles were soft and relaxed. It would be soon. Within a day.

"You here to see Faith?" Jack's voice interrupted her thoughts.

She turned her attention on him. "Actually no. Are you missing a dog?"

His smile froze. "Did you find Wyatt?" The color left his face. "Is he all right?"

She gestured to the Jeep. "See for yourself."

He leaped the fence and bolted for the SUV. When he yanked open the back door, the dog leaped on top of him. The excited barking made Shannon smile. It was days like this that made her glad she'd been able to follow her dream.

Jack was on the ground with the dog licking his face. He turned his laughing face to Shannon. "Where'd you find him?"

"You're not going to like it." She told him about finding the dog tied in the abandoned house. "He was hungry and thirsty, but he's okay," she added as he sprang to his feet with his brows drawn together. "Do you have any idea who would do something like this?"

"Harry Slocum," he said through gritted teeth. "I fired him the night before Wyatt went missing. He told me I'd be sorry."

"All's well that ends well," she said. "Wyatt will be fine." The dog came to her and licked her hand.

"How much do I owe you?"

The warmth she'd developed toward him evaporated. "Don't be an idiot." To her surprise, he just nodded and thanked her. She'd expected him to press the issue.

Her gaze went back to the mare. "She needs to be inside. That foal is coming any minute."

"Come along. I'll show you the setup in the barn." He vaulted the fence and grabbed the mare's mane.

She followed her master toward the barn, so Shannon did the same. The barns were white monoliths, freshly painted and in top condition. Jack led them to a stall that had been prepared for foaling. She was glad to see he had fresh straw ready.

The mare lay down in the stall as soon as she entered. Shannon could see the sac protruding, and moments later the mare's water broke, staining the straw. "You should have been more prepared for this, Jack," she said. "Her tail isn't even wrapped."

Jack wore a worried frown. "I'm a bit behind since Harry left."

Shannon didn't interfere. She would likely not have to. Most horses foaled in about an hour with no problems. The mare vocalized occasionally with groans. Standing shoulder to shoulder with Jack, Shannon watched a process she never tired of. The foal's front feet slid into view, soles down and close together. Next came the fetlocks, then the foal's head appeared. Minutes later a foal slid onto the straw.

Shannon's smile beamed out until she realized the foal was very small and wasn't moving. Her throat closed. No! Nothing could happen to this little one. She sprang into the stall and wiped at the little colt's nostrils and blew gently. Nothing. *Breathe, breathe.* She fought tears and panic as she kneeled, rubbing the colt's tiny chest. Blowing into his nostrils again, she prayed for a miracle. Perspiration popped out on her forehead as she fought the inevitable for what seemed an eternity.

A hand fell on her shoulder. "Shannon, it's over," Jack said.

She shook off the press of his fingers. "No, I can save him." She bent to her task again, but Jack knelt beside her and pulled her gently away from the unmoving colt. Tears sprang to her eyes. "I'm sorry," she whispered.

Shannon bolted from the stall with tears streaming from her eyes. Sobs tore from her throat. She'd lost him. Her first foaling as a vet, and she'd failed. She was vaguely aware of Jack following her with drooping shoulders.

He put his hand on her shoulder. "This wasn't your fault."

She shook off his hand and tore for her Jeep. She would never get used to a dead baby. Never.

WALLY TATUM'S OFFICE WAS LIKE A WILD WEST MUSEUM. WANTED POSTERS of long ago plastered the walls. A set of bighorns dominated one wall, and a pair of spurs reputed to have been worn by Jesse James resided in a display case. The leather sofa creaked under Jack as he waited to be called back to see the attorney.

He knew Wally was here. Jack had seen his old Cadillac parked under the streetlight. That big car was a fixture around town. Wally washed it every day, and even the interior was in pristine condition.

The lacquered door at the end of the hall opened, and Wally stepped out. He could have been a dead ringer for the famous outlaw with his waxed mustache, ruffled shirt, and pressed jeans.

The attorney motioned for Jack to join him, and Jack sprang to his feet. "Thanks for coming to meet me," Jack said. "I know it's late."

Wally's spurs jingled as he walked down the hall to his office. He sniffed. "Smells like the fires are getting closer."

"The news said the wind had shifted this way." Jack had been keeping a worried eye on the situation.

Wally closed the door behind them and motioned for Jack to have a seat. "You said it was urgent."

"It is." The black leather chair swallowed Jack's bulk, and he struggled to sit more upright.

Wally put his boots on his desk. "So shoot. What's got you showing your fangs?"

Jack told him about the baby switch. The more he explained what his aunt had done, the longer Wally's face grew. "So what are my chances of keeping my daughter?" Jack asked with a trace of desperation.

Wally's long fingers twirled his mustache. Jack could almost imagine him as a gunslinger from the 1800s planning his next gunfight. Wally would never be a decent poker player, and Jack knew before Wally spoke that the news wouldn't be good.

Wally put his feet back on the floor and leaned forward. "This is deep water, my friend. We might have had a better chance if the nurse had been a stranger and was acting out of the goodness of her heart. But she's Blair's aunt. She had a personal interest in it. It would appear that you might have even had a hand in it as well."

"I didn't. I had no clue!" Even though Jack had been expecting this news, his gorge rose. He couldn't lose his daughter.

Two days ago his life had been good. Faith was happy and healthy, and although Jack missed Blair, he'd been content to watch their baby girl grow. His horse ranch business was good, and he had a place of respect in the community, a church home, friends around for support. He could sense a major shift happening in his life, feel the shimmy beginning like the tremors before a major earthquake.

He curled his fingers into his palms. "What can I do?"

"Get her to settle this out of court if you want to continue to see your daughter. Maybe some kind of joint custody would appease the woman. Is she a good mother?"

Jack thought of the way her face lit up when she talked about

Kylie. Of the sacrifice she was willing to make for her daughter. Of the pain in her face when the foal had been stillborn earlier. "I think so. She's put herself through school and still managed to provide for her daughter, who seems happy and well adjusted."

Wally nodded. "Good. If she loves her kids, she'll want what's best for Faith. That's the best shot you've got."

Jack rose and shook the attorney's hand. "Thanks, Wally. I'll see what I can do." He went back down the carpeted hallway and outside under the stars. His legs barely supported him, but he made it to his truck. He slammed the door behind him and leaned his forehead against the steering wheel. His stomach heaved.

Sharing custody wasn't an option. He looked forward to seeing Faith every day, to tucking her into bed at night after a story. He loved taking her riding out over the desert and teaching her survival lessons. She brought purpose and joy to his life, and he knew she would be devastated at being wrenched from his arms. He often saw the problems divorced friends endured and how their children suffered from the conflict. He couldn't put Faith through that.

Which meant he had to put his head on the chopping block.

SHANNON HAD NEVER BEEN SO GLAD TO GET HOME. IT WAS ONLY NINE thirty, but it felt like midnight at least. She warmed up a bowl of soup, then tore into the house. By the time she cleaned what would be her office, her initial burst of energy was gone and it was eleven. She went to get a coke from the fridge and glanced out the window. There he was. Jewel stood as if waiting for her by the barn. Just the medicine she needed after such a stressful day. Shannon's smile was so wide it almost hurt as she ran to the horse. "Jewel," she called.

The black coat glistened. Jewel snorted and tossed his head, then stepped out to meet her. Power radiated from the massive stallion. The muscles along his withers rippled. Age hadn't stolen his strength or the clear light in his eyes.

Shannon stepped closer, a bit unsure of herself when so close to those massive hooves and hard teeth. What if he had forgotten her? But no, he dropped his head and stepped closer. She threw her arms around his neck and breathed in the good scent of horse. His soft lips nuzzled her hair and neck, and he snuffled loudly in her ear.

She ran her fingers over the white hair of his freeze brand. "I'd forgotten how beautiful you are," she whispered. "And how big."

The sun was down, but the stars made a carpet of light in the sky. The thought of racing over the desert on Jewel's back tempted her beyond resistance. She wrapped her hand in his mane and vaulted onto the horse's back. He bucked a little and she held on tightly. Maybe she'd have to get off. He hadn't been ridden since she left here. But he settled down and turned to trot into the desert. The blackness of the night made her heart tattoo against her ribs. She'd gotten used to city lights and sounds, and the velvet night made her wonder what hid in the hills watching them.

Jewel took off as if she'd told him where to go. She couldn't see the canyon in the dark, but Shannon knew it loomed nearer with every fall of Jewel's hooves. "Whoa, boy," she said, her voice as loud as the coyote yipping for attention over the next hill. She shouldn't have come out at night. Even Jewel might not be that surefooted with her on his back.

Jewel stopped, and Shannon sat on his back gazing up at the rock formation ahead. Her parents were buried up there, along with more Spanish treasure than she could fathom. And a fabulous sword inlaid with emeralds that hadn't seen the light of day in over four hundred years. She made a mental note to come back in the daylight, make sure the site hadn't been disturbed. No one knew where it was but her, and she planned to keep her parents' secret.

A red glare lit the night to their north. The wildfires were still burning out of control, and the horse shifted uneasily. Shannon studied the glow. Wasn't that awfully close to the Millers' ranch? She decided to ride closer and see if she could gauge the blaze's distance.

Jewel snorted and pranced in his tracks when she turned his face toward the fire, but he finally acquiesced to obeying her. "Good boy," she murmured, patting his neck. She clung to his back as he picked his way through the rocks and shrubs, eventually reaching a narrow path covered with a thin layer of dirt.

As she neared, she saw tongues of flame leaping from bush to bush. The roar of the fire made Jewel snort and rear. The wind brought the thick smoke swirling around Shannon's head. The fire had nearly reached the Millers' barn. Men shouted and ran in the surreal glow of the flames and the drifting ash.

Something in the sky caught her attention. Smokejumpers? She stared, transfixed at the sight. Parachutes billowed out and drifted down toward the ranch. The hum of a plane overhead caught her attention, and she saw more jumpers leap into the night air.

Shannon had to help. She dismounted. "Go, boy," she said, slapping the horse on the rump. Jewel leaped away, and she saw him disappear over the rocky hillside. She ran toward the ranch.

ASH AND SOOT COATED JACK'S THROAT AND TONGUE. WHEN THE CALL HAD come in, he left Faith with Enrica and drove here like a madman, then immediately began to kick dirt onto the flames. The heat baked his face and cracked his lips.

The smokejumpers were directing the volunteers from the surrounding ranches in how to fight the fire. A low-flying plane buzzed overhead, dropping water on the inferno racing toward them.

"Here." A tall smokejumper with dark eyes peering out from under his helmet handed Jack a shovel. He turned and pointed behind them. "We're putting out our line of defense there. Dig up the vegetation. If the fire has no food, it'll die out."

Jack nodded and jogged back to where other men and women were tearing at the shrubs and digging up the weeds. It was going to be a long night. He tore into the sod, but it was hard going. The desert sun had baked the soil into something that resembled fired brick. They needed more help.

From the corner of his eye, he saw a figure rushing toward him. Shannon—here? Her wind-tossed hair caught the glow from the fire. She was dressed in jeans, boots, and a yellow shirt that was open at the neck.

"What are you doing here?" he asked when she reached him.

"I was out riding and saw the flames. What can I do?"

He wanted to tell her to get to safety but knew she wouldn't go. He thrust his shovel into her hands. "Dig. I'll get another shovel."

She nodded and began to work at the soil. He snagged another shovel and came back to find the smokejumper he'd met working alongside her. They worked in silence for about ten minutes until the firefighter stopped, took off his helmet, and wiped his forehead.

The man looked like he had Native American blood. Straight dark hair, square face, high cheekbones. And eyes that spoke of suffering. When he turned, Jack saw the right side of his face was horribly scarred by fire. He caught Jack staring and turned as though to make sure Jack got a good look at his disfigurement. Jack averted his stare.

Shannon paused and put her hand on the small of her back. "Do you do this every day?" she asked the smokejumper.

The smile he threw her twisted the scars on his cheek. "During fire season. It's early this year. When so much rain comes in the springtime, the desert heat turns the vegetation that grows tinder dry. I'm busy for months after a wet spring." The firefighter bent to his task again.

"Why aren't you at home?" Jack asked Shannon. "Where's Kylie?" He knew his voice held censure when Shannon squared her shoulders and glared at him.

"She's perfectly fine. Allie wanted to keep her overnight until I get the house ready. Besides, she and Betsy were having fun." She narrowed her eyes. "I hardly think that's any of your business."

He started to speak, then shut his mouth. She was right. He hadn't married her—hadn't even *agreed* to marry her. He turned back to his work. The fire was moving closer. They'd managed to clear a path about four feet wide.

"It's not going to be wide enough to stop it," the firefighter said. "Tell the owners to evacuate."

Jack nodded and grabbed Shannon's hand. "Come with me. I'll need help persuading Harriet to leave."

Shannon fell into step beside him. "Why won't she go?"

"She was born here. Her great-grandfather built this place. She's eighty-five and as strong-willed as a bull. She won't believe even a fire could take her home from her."

"You think it's not going to be stopped?"

He gestured toward the flames flaring from bush to shrub. "Do you?" Her gaze swept the scene, and his did the same. The blaze was burning hotter than ever. It had just crossed the line of bare dirt they'd worked so hard to make.

"I guess not," she said.

THE TWO OF THEM MANAGED TO CONVINCE HARRIET TO LEAVE. OR RATHER, Shannon managed it somehow. Her crisp professional manner disarmed the older woman, who reluctantly agreed to go to the daughter's, just for tonight. When Jack loaded the last of Harriet's valuables into the back of her old pickup, he turned to thank Shannon and found her gone.

The scarred firefighter, his shoulders slumped, was walking this way with the rest of his crew, having been momentarily relieved by a shift in the wind. Jack blocked his path. "Any of you and your crew are welcome to spend the night at my house."

The man swiped a grimy hand against his sooty cheek. "The Bluebird Ranch is putting us up, but thanks for the offer."

"You see where the blonde lady went who was helping me?" Jack asked.

"She whistled for her horse and rode off that way." The firefighter pointed away from the fire toward Shannon's old ranch.

"Thanks. What's your name?"

"Buck. Buck Carter."

Jack put out his hand. "Jack MacGowan." The man had a strong grip, something Jack liked. He dropped his hand to his side. "Thanks again for the job you did here tonight."

"It's what I do. Most of the time."

"What do you do when you're not fighting fires?"

Buck shrugged. "I'm an outfitter in Arizona. Mogollon Rim country. Firefighters have been called from all over to fight the fires here, so I came to join the fun."

Jack hardly called it fun. "Like I said, my home is open if you ever need it." He clapped the man on the back and went to his truck. He should go home, but he was still high on adrenaline. He turned the truck toward Shannon's ranch. The decision couldn't be put off any longer.

In the desert with no streetlights and only his headlamps illuminating the landscape, the stars were brighter. Jack's eyes burned from fatigue and smoke, but his lips were tight with determination. He would do whatever was necessary to keep his daughter.

He turned into the unkempt lane that led to the old Astor homestead. Only one light shone out of a window. The porch light wasn't on, and not even a security light highlighted the barn and the yard. This wasn't a safe environment for Kylie and Shannon. He parked and strode to the door. The porch boards were spongy and weak under his boots. This place was going to take a lot of work to make it livable.

His fist fell on the rickety screen door. A dog began to bark from inside the house. At least she had some kind of protection. He banged the door again.

"Who's there?" Shannon's voice was sharp, but fear hovered under the confident tone.

He should have identified himself right away. She was bound to be afraid out here all alone. "Shannon, it's Jack."

"Jack." Her voice rose with relief.

He heard her fumble with the lock, then the door opened and she peeked out. Her long blonde hair lay loose. She was dressed in pink pajamas with a dog pattern. Her feet were bare.

"It's awfully late," she said.

"I know. Can I come in a minute?"

With obvious reluctance, she shoved open the screen door and stepped back. She held on to the dog's collar. The border collie was snarling and growling like he wanted to eat Jack alive. "Quiet, Moses," she commanded. "He's a friend. I think."

Jack held out his hand for the dog to sniff, then Moses licked his fingers. "Good dog," he said. He followed Shannon to the kitchen, an ancient room with old-fashioned linoleum, metal cabinets, and a chipped porcelain sink. She had guts to move into a house in this kind of shape.

"I just fixed some hot chocolate. You want some?"

"No thanks." He stood with his hands in his pockets. She smelled good even from here. She must have raced home and gotten a shower the minute she stepped in the house.

"Coke?"

"I'll take that," he said, knowing she meant any soft drink she happened to have in the fridge. He accepted the cold Mountain Dew she got out of the rusting refrigerator for him. "This place is going to take a lot of work and money."

"You should have seen it the day we moved in," she said, a slight smile tilting her lips. "Have a seat."

He pulled out a shaky chair and sat down gingerly. To delay the inevitable, he popped the top and took a sip of his drink. The cold rush of liquid wet his burned throat. He set the drink on the table and watched Shannon as she sipped her cocoa and avoided his gaze. She knew why he was here, and she was as nervous as he. Neither of them wanted to broach the subject, but he'd have to do it. He cleared his throat.

She finally lifted her gaze to meet his. "I assume you've thought about my suggestion?" The muscles in her long smooth neck convulsed, and she glanced away.

"Yeah. I decided you're right. Marriage is the best solution."

Her startled gaze flew up to meet his again. "I . . . it is? I mean, great."

"You laid it out pretty clearly. A stable home with both parents, the bonding that is best for the girls, no court battle that will hurt Faith. Or Kylie."

He realized Shannon was no more pleased at the thought of marrying him than he was of marrying her. "When do you want to do this?" he asked.

She circled her cup with her hands. "Are you sure? I mean, this is a big step."

"Yeah, it is. But let's not have any false expectations going into this. I'm doing it only because it's best for my daughter."

"And for Kylie," she said. Her color began to come back to her cheeks and she straightened. "I expect you to treat Kylie with the same love and devotion you give to Faith. She needs a father and Faith needs a mother."

"Agreed," he said through clenched teeth. "But you've got to let me pick the time to tell Faith. I have to prepare her. Her memories of Blair are precious to us both, and I talk about her mother to her all the time. It will be hard for her if I just announce it with no preparation." A sense of loss descended on him. This vivid personality here in the kitchen with him would soon overshadow any memories Faith had of her mother.

Her tired gaze held a challenge. "As long as it doesn't drag on too long. Kids are smarter than you realize, Jack. Kylie knew the minute she saw Faith that they're twins. Faith suspects something, I'm sure.

For someone who hates secrets, you're suddenly willing to hang on to this one."

That stung, but he didn't bother defending himself. He was only looking out for his daughter. Faith had talked about Kylie, but she was only five. He doubted she would put together something like that. "There's no waiting period for marriage in Texas. We can get this done as soon as you like."

She glanced away, but not before he saw the glimmer of pain in her eyes. "Have you ever been married?" he asked. She shook her head, and he felt as low as a sidewinder. She'd probably dreamed of what her wedding would someday look like. Blair had planned every detail of their wedding for six months.

But he was no Prince Charming—especially when he was being forced into it. "Do you need time to get a dress?"

She tilted her chin up and met his gaze. "This is hardly a love match, Jack. I thought we'd just go see the justice of the peace and have it cut-and-dried."

"I'd rather get married in church," he said.

Her pale brows arched, and she blinked. "Ch-church?"

He nodded. "This marriage might be for our children, but I mean to honor the vows and I hope you do too. This won't be an open marriage where you get to sleep around."

"Of course not!" Color flooded her face and she stood. "Just because I made one mistake doesn't mean my morals are questionable. Do you make a practice of insulting your wife? If so, I might reconsider this idea."

He stood, towering over her and hating himself for the tactic. "You've agreed and we're both stuck with this deal. You've got me lassoed and on the ground." Was he trying to get her to back out by being deliberately unpleasant?

He took off his cowboy hat and ran his hand through his hair. "Look, I'm sorry. I'm not normally such a jerk. We're both under a lot of stress. Can we start over? When would you like to get married? I'd like you to have a pretty dress, and I'm happy to pay for it."

"I'll buy my own dress," she said. Her voice went husky. "Let's plan for next Saturday, ten days away. I'll need to go to Alpine to look for something."

"How about we have Faith and Kylie be flower girls?" he said.

Her gaze searched his. "Are you sure you want to tell Faith right away that you're remarrying?"

He saw the gratitude in her eyes. "It's not like you can just move into the house with no explanation. I think the girls will squeal at the thought."

"I know they will as long as you're sure. I'll need to get them dresses."

"I'll have Enrica get them."

"Enrica?"

"My housekeeper, nanny, whatever you want to call her. She was Blair's nanny, too, and she adores Faith."

"I'd rather get the dresses. I'll want them to go with mine."

"Fine." He dug out his wallet and slapped five hundred dollars on the table. "Get whatever you need for them."

"I can pay for the dresses."

She tried to give the money back, but he stepped away. "It's my contribution to the wedding. You shouldn't have to foot the whole bill. I'll check in with you tomorrow." He fled the house so he didn't have to look at her forlorn face.

8

THE CREAKING OF THE OLD WINDMILL KEPT SHANNON AWAKE FAR INTO THE night. At least she told herself that was why she tossed and turned on the old mattress. What kind of future was she setting herself up for, marrying a man she didn't love? Or know? Some kind of insanity must have swept over her for her to suggest such an idea.

She rolled over, plunging her face into the sheets scented with sage from the outdoors. It was so hot the heat shimmered in the air. She would have to get up in three hours, and she hadn't slept more than fifteen minutes. Her eyes drifted shut until something creaked overhead. Clutching the thin sheet to her chest, she bolted upright in the bed and listened to the house, which had fallen silent again. Barely daring to breathe, she strained to hear past the blood pounding in her ears. There, the noise came again, right over her head.

On the rug beside the bed, Moses growled. He stood, and the moonlight through the window illuminated the bristling fur on his neck. The sight caused the hair on the back of Shannon's neck to do the same.

The creak came again, and she looked up at the ceiling. Was someone in the attic?

There was no one to send to check it out—it was her house, her job now. But she wasn't going up there. The best defense was retreat. With a gun. But it was all she could do to reach over and retrieve the revolver from the bedside stand. Her bare feet hit the cool floor, but she didn't take time to find her slippers. Moses moved to her side, and she curled her fingers around his collar. The sensation of his warm fur strengthened her resolve. Her feet knew where to avoid the creaks in her bedroom floor, and she moved across the dark room to the door.

It opened with a whisper. She sidled into the hallway with the gun trembling in her hand. She faced the direction of the attic door at the end of the narrow hall. Even from here, a draft swirled around her bare ankles. Squinting, she could make out the stairway.

The door to the attic stood wide open.

A chill raced down her spine. She had to get out of here. With her hand still clutching the dog's collar, she raced for the steps down to the first floor. Growling and lunging, Moses tried to tug away from her toward the attic stairs, but she hung on to him. With him beside her, the fear wasn't overpowering.

Her bare feet pounded down the steps. By now, the terror had climbed on top of her back and was digging in its claws. She released Moses long enough to struggle with the lock on the front door. The dog didn't try to go back upstairs, but he kept turning his head to stare up at the landing.

And he kept growling.

Panting, she fumbled with the dead bolt, but her hands were stiff and it wouldn't unlock. She dared a glance over her back at the stairs but saw nothing. Yet. She renewed her efforts at the door until her thumb found the right way to flip the lever. The old door creaked open, and she shoved the screen door so hard it banged back against the siding. She winced and glanced behind her again, but no dark form raced toward her from the stairs. The cool rush of air cleared her head when she stepped out onto the porch.

She'd left her cell phone on the nightstand, but she wasn't going back after it. The cool dirt on her bare feet made her realize she was hardly in a position to summon help. No shoes, no phone. Her gaze touched her Jeep. No keys. She'd left them on the kitchen counter.

Had she overreacted? Moses was still growling, so she didn't think so. Still, it could have been an animal in the attic.

An animal didn't enter by the stairs or open doors.

Shannon gulped. Someone was inside the house. She took a tighter grip on the pistol. "Come with me, Moses," she said. Her voice shook. She and the dog mounted the steps again. She put her hand on the screen door handle but couldn't bring herself to pull it open. What if the guy was right inside the door waiting for her?

She had the gun. That should scare him off. With sudden decision, she jerked the door open and stepped into the entry. The darkness closed around her. She raced to the kitchen and reached the counter. Her outflung hand touched the bowl that had held her soup last night. Her fingers moved on until she touched the keys. Snatched them from the counter. Turned to run back outside.

And ran up against an immovable object. A giant of a man.

His hands came down on her arms, pinning her hands to her sides. He gave a soft chuckle. Shannon writhed away from his grip, but she couldn't shake his hands from her arms enough to bring up the gun. The near silent struggle in the dark kitchen, punctuated only by gasps, was the stuff of nightmares.

Moses barked and lunged at the man, who kicked him away, but the dog kept coming. Shannon heard fabric tear and realized Moses had taken a bite out of the guy's trousers, but the big man had been unperturbed.

"Where's my money?" he whispered in her ear.

"I don't know what you're talking about!" She wrenched her arm away, but his fingers didn't give.

His hand came up and wrapped around her hair, loose on her shoulders. "Pretty hair," he said. "It might not look so good torn out by the roots."

She winced when his grip tightened painfully. "I don't have any money." Her mind raced. Couldn't he tell by looking at this place that there was nothing of value here?

His voice could cut a diamond. "Don't play games with me. It's not . . . healthy. We both know you have the money and we want it back. You've got a day to turn it over or someone you love will bear the consequences."

The pain in her head made her faint. "Don't hurt my daughter! I don't know what money you're talking about. I'd give it to you if I had it." What did she have? An old ranch house that was falling down around her ears. Nothing a man like this could want.

"I don't like games," he said in a cold voice. "I wouldn't hurt your daughter—what kind of a man do you think I am? But your friend Mary Beth, well, that's another story. You've got twenty-four hours to hand it over."

"Mary Beth?" She should have pressed her friend for details.

Shannon's gut had told her something was wrong. "What kind of trouble is she in?"

He grinned, but the grimace held no mirth. "Her worst nightmare. Me. Yours, too, if you don't listen." His grip tightened on her hair. "I thought I'd stop by and give you motivation to listen to me."

If she could bring the pistol up and point it at him, she'd have a chance, but her hands had no room to maneuver. A flash of inspiration struck and she quit struggling. Standing passively with the man's hands gripping her, she waited.

Her acquiescence slackened his grasp. "You're going to cooperate, huh?" He sounded disappointed.

"Just tell me what you want," she said, keeping her voice resigned. "What money? How much?"

"I thought you were through playing games. The boss won't be happy." He leaned down and his breath touched her face. It smelled of cloves.

She turned her head and his lips grazed her cheek instead of her lips. His grip loosened even more, and she managed to bring up the gun and jab it into his ribs. "Let go of me," she snarled.

"Wha—" He took a step back.

The added room gave her courage to point the gun higher, right at his heart. "I don't have any money. I don't know anything." She leaned over to flip on the light.

Her movement allowed him to whip around and dash for the door. As the bright light spilled into the room, Shannon caught only a glimpse of a broad back and dark hair above a denim jacket. She reflexively fired the gun. The bullet dug into the wall at his side, spewing plaster.

The screen door banged, and she heard the sound of feet running across the gravel. The wall propped her up or she would have fallen. Moses licked at her hand. "Thanks for helping me, boy." She sank to her knees and buried her face in his fur. His scent and warmth strengthened her. She stood again, holding tight to the gun, then hurried out to the porch with the keys. She should go upstairs and get dressed, but she had to get out of here before the guy came back.

She had no doubt he *would* be back. With a grudge.

WHEN THE SUN THREW A GOLDEN BLANKET OVER THE BLUE HILLS AROUND the ranch, Jack hadn't slept a wink. He'd been all too happy to climb out of bed at six and tend to the livestock. It gave him something to do to forget his circumstances.

By the time Enrica called him in for breakfast, he had come full circle back to the realization that there was no other way to ensure Faith stayed with him. He'd just agreed to marry a woman he didn't know. And while that was a scary thought, another frightening situation loomed.

He had to tell his parents. Today. This morning. Even now he could hear the rumble of his father's big Caddy.

He gulped down a last swig of strong coffee to fortify himself, then went out to the big porch to greet his parents. At least he wouldn't have to listen to his mother's cries for long. He had to get out to the training corral in another hour.

The hot breeze blew down from the hills, carrying with it the scent of mesquite. He loved this ranch, the pillars of black igneous rock that stood like ancient guardians along the hills, the desolate majesty, even the jackrabbits scrabbling over the hardpan desert. When he was a kid, his mother's housekeeper used to scare him with stories of the unforgiving land. The devil, she said, was sealed up in a cave on the south bank of the Río Bravo del Norte. As a boy, Jack often watched the nearby mountains to make sure the devil didn't escape on a swing hung between them.

This country's other name was El Despoblado, the land of no people. More creatures than human inhabitants lived here, and Jack never wanted it to change. Development of the land was a topic of contention between him and his father. Now, watching his dad stride up the driveway with Jack's mother, Jack could see from the great Senator MacGowan's confident smile that he was here for a reason Jack wasn't going to like.

Jack stepped down to the brick walkway to embrace his mother, who hurried ahead of the senator. Her light flowery scent reached him before she did. When he hugged her, he could feel her ribs, but he knew better than to ask her if she was dieting. She was always dieting, and no amount of chiding on his part lessened her determination to fit into a size four.

He brushed his lips across her cheek. "Good to see you, Mom."

"Jacky, you're not dressed. Did you forget?" His mother's voice was softly reproachful.

"Forget?" Then it hit him. Several months ago his parents had coerced him into a trip to Austin to meet the daughter of another senator. "I'm not going to be able to make it, Mom." He turned from the hurt in her eyes to shake his dad's hand.

"What's this?" his father demanded while gripping Jack's hand. "Not going? You have to go. I paid two hundred dollars for your ticket."

"I'll pay you back, Dad." Jack gestured to the porch. "Coffee? Enrica made some killer coffee cake this morning to go with it."

"Don't change the subject," his father said, his scowl growing as dark as the hills. "Carleen is expecting you. Why, she even told her mama she'd bought a new dress. I won't be humiliated like this. Get your suit and get in the car. We don't have a lot of time to waste."

Jack didn't let his smile slip. His father would take advantage of any weakness. "I'm training horses, and there's an even more important reason I can't go. Sit down on the porch and let me explain." At least out here there was no chance of Faith overhearing.

His mother clung to his arm. "You should have called us," she whispered as he led her up the steps to the seating area at the end of the porch. "You know how your father hates to be caught off guard."

His father liked to know everything and reveal nothing. Jack shrugged. "I forgot." Like that excuse would satisfy either of them. He'd been so upside down with worry over losing Faith, he couldn't remember the last time he'd even looked at his calendar.

His mother settled onto the plush cushion and smoothed her skirt. The senator dropped into the seat beside her, and his brows came together. Jack didn't want to sit, but he forced himself to perch on a chair and appear nonchalant.

"What's this about, Jack?" his father demanded.

"It wouldn't be right to go out with another woman when I'm engaged." Nothing like dropping the bomb all at once. He waited for his mother's gasp and his father's brows to rise before plunging on. "In fact, I'm getting married a week from Saturday. I hope your schedules will allow you to come."

"Ma-married?" His mother put her hand to her throat. "You're teasing us, Son."

"I'm spot-on serious, Mom. Her name is Shannon Astor."

"Astor? As in old Earl Astor?" the senator put in. "His niece is the new vet in town."

"That's Shannon. My fiancée."

"I remember her," his mother said, tipping her head to one side. "She helped you and your sister with biology one year. Studious little thing, but no presence. She barely looked up from her books. And wasn't there some talk about her being not quite emotionally stable? Are you sure about this, Jacky?"

"I'm very sure. In spite of losing her parents, she went on to make something of herself. She's a good person. And one of the strongest women I know." To his surprise, he found he meant the words. Shannon was someone to be admired. She'd be a wonderful role model for the girls. He wanted Faith to grow up to be able to stand on her own. Shannon had done just that.

His father still had said nothing. He glanced at his watch. "We'd better go, poppet, or we'll be late." He rose and held out his hand.

His mother fluttered to her feet. "Senator, we need to talk about this." She put her hand on Jack's arm. "Don't rush into anything, Son."

"I'm not, Mom. Will you both come to the wedding? I know Leah can't." His sister was abroad.

His father put his hand on her shoulder and ushered her toward the steps before she answered. His glare pierced Jack.

Jack followed them. "Look, Dad, I'm not some puppet to be used to help you climb the political ladder." His dad turned with hooded eyes and tight lips. Jack knew he should have kept his mouth shut.

"Just what I would have expected you to say, Jack," the senior Jack MacGowan said. "You have never supported my dreams. All you want is wrapped up here in this ranch." He waved his hand toward the barns and outbuildings. "You could make something of yourself if you'd try. Yes, you're the rooster in this tiny yard, but you have it in you to be more than that—to really *be* someone of substance."

"We don't all have to be in the limelight to be reaching our potential," Jack said, keeping his voice even. "There's something to be said for raising a family and being part of my community." He watched his mother flinch, then hurriedly get into the blue Cadillac and shut the door.

His dad snorted. "I suppose that's a slap at the way I was gone some when you were growing up. Sometimes sacrifices have to be made." He turned back to the car and got under the wheel.

"I don't want to sacrifice my daughter on the horns of my ambition," Jack said to the dust billowing from the back of his father's car. He stood and watched the wind catch the particles of sand and swirl them away. Just like his words.

9

AFTER FLEEING THE RANCH, SHANNON SPENT THE REST OF THE NIGHT AT THE Bluebird and decided, at Rick and Allie's urging, that was where she and Kylie would stay until the wedding.

All day, she barely went through the motions at the mustang camp. She was supposed to turn over the money—whatever it was—in a few hours to the big guy. But she was no closer to figuring out what they wanted. Would he really kill Mary Beth?

Rick's buddy had discovered nothing out of the ordinary in his check on Mary Beth. Grabbing a bottle of water from the big iced bucket by the mess hall, Shannon sat on the ground and pulled out her cell phone. No answering text message from Mary Beth, but then, Shannon hadn't expected one. Still, she'd hoped. Mary Beth's sister might know something, but Shannon didn't have a phone number. The guy wanted money. Could Mary Beth have put money in Shannon's account? It wouldn't be the first time. Mary Beth was always trying to help out without Shannon's knowing, though usually she could only spare small amounts like a hundred dollars. Still, it wouldn't hurt to check.

She dialed the bank's automated number and followed the prompts to get to her balance. Three hundred twenty-six dollars and two cents. Hardly worth terrorizing her and Mary Beth for. And exactly what her bank register said. She closed her phone and sighed.

"Everything okay?" Jack's voice spoke above her head. "You were scowling."

She scrambled to her feet and dusted her jeans. "You would, too, if you had a bank balance like mine," she said before she could stop the words.

"Listen, we're practically married. If you need money, I'd be glad to help."

"I don't need anything, but thanks."

They stood staring at one another. Shannon wished she could tell him about the problem, but the last time she'd shared anything with him, he'd ruined her life. She couldn't risk it again.

SHANNON'S DEADLINE TO DELIVER THE MONEY HAD COME AND GONE WITHout a hint that the intruder's threat was real. But Mary Beth's failure to call Shannon kept her mind focused on the worst. There'd been no text message answer from her, no phone call. Only silence.

Could her own ignorance make her responsible for the death of her friend?

Saturday morning, Shannon and Allie decided to go shopping for dresses. Kylie had taken the news that she was marrying Faith's daddy with her usual enthusiasm. It was all she talked about.

"There's nowhere to buy a nice dress around here," Allie said, tying a bow at the end of Betsy's braid. "I think we should go to San Antonio."

"That's over six hours away!" Shannon wanted to look nice, but she didn't plan to spend the entire weekend on a shopping trip for a sham marriage.

Allie cast a sly glance at Rick. "Not when your husband has a plane."

By plane, San Antonio would be a short hop. Many large ranchers had small planes, but she hadn't suspected Rick did. A plan began to form in Shannon's head. She glanced at Rick. "Would you have time to take us?"

Rick's gaze settled on his wife's swollen belly. "I can make arrangements. At least then I'll make sure Allie isn't overdoing it. I got her an oxygen setup when I found out she was pregnant so she can fly with no problems."

Allie brushed a kiss across his lips. "I thought you'd see it that way."

He draped his arm over her shoulders. "When do you girls want to leave?"

"As soon as you can get the plane ready. I need to call Jack and see if I can take Faith."

"It's ready. I was planning on offering my services." He grinned when Allie gently punched his stomach. He stooped to scoop up Betsy. "Let's get out of here."

Shannon smiled, but a hollow sensation settled between her shoulder blades. She'd never seen a more tender look than Rick bestowed on Allie. She would never experience loving banter or have a man want to protect her. Her marriage wouldn't change a thing. Only her last name and her place of residence.

One other important thing would change, she thought, glancing at Kylie. Her daughter would have a father. And that was worth everything.

She picked up the cordless phone. "Give me a minute to call Jack." She punched in the number, surprised to find she knew it by heart already.

Jack's deep voice answered. "MacGowan."

"Jack, good morning. I'm, um, I'm going to go buy the dresses for next Saturday." She couldn't bring herself to say the word *wedding*. "I wondered if Faith would like to go? I don't have to take her since she and Kylie are the same size, but I thought she might enjoy the outing." A long pause followed, and she was beginning to wonder if they'd lost the connection before he finally answered.

"She's not here. Enrica took her over to play with her granddaughter. I don't think I can contact them. Enrica refuses to have a cell phone. She thinks they're dangerous." He cleared his throat. "Nice of you to think of her."

"She's my *daughter.* Of course I think of her." He seemed to forget that fact so easily. Shannon longed to do so many things with Faith.

"And mine," he said with an edge to his voice. "You should have called earlier to make plans. Besides, I haven't told her about the wedding yet."

"Why not?" Shannon failed to keep the disappointment from her voice. Moses nudged her hand, and she rubbed his ears.

"I was waiting for the right time. I'll tell her when she gets home."

Did he think Faith would be upset? Faith seemed to like Shannon, so surely she'd be happy. And the girl already loved Kylie. "Can I bring the dress over for her to see tonight?"

"My parents are coming for dinner, and I don't want to subject you to them yet. How about Sunday? You can come over for dinner after church."

So he was ashamed of her. Her eyes stung. "Fine. I've got to go."

"Wait, Shannon. Maybe I can track down Enrica. Give me an hour."

"Everyone is ready to go. Rick is flying us to San Antonio, so we can't really wait. I wish we could. I'd love to have had her with us." And it was her fault. She should have called last night, but she'd put it off.

For just a moment, she thought about asking him to come with her. She wanted to tell him about the guy who wanted something from her. But would he even believe her? Maybe he'd think she was making it up to get his sympathy. Besides, if he still thought her imagination had the better of her, he might back out. In the end, she said nothing until he finally spoke.

"Okay, sorry," he said, really sounding as though he meant it. "I'll see you later."

Shannon put the phone down. She could have kicked herself. It wasn't like her to let fear rule her, but she'd let it make her put off the call. "Let's go," she told the Bailey family. "Time's a-wasting." She followed Rick and his family out to a small hangar behind the barn. The plane was already outside on the sand. "No runway?"

Rick opened the plane door and deposited Betsy inside. "The desert makes a fine one." He helped Allie into the plane and held out his hand to Shannon.

"I have something else I need to do," she said in a voice too soft for Allie to hear. "I'd like to go by my old apartment." She had told him about what the guy said when he broke in.

"You forget something?"

She shook her head. "I want to see if Mary Beth is there. If she's not, maybe I can find clues to what's going on. Maybe there's something in her room."

Rick frowned, then gave a reluctant nod. "You should ask your fiancé to go with us."

"I haven't told him," she said, pressing her lips together. Shannon saw the condemnation in his eyes and sighed. Her guilt about not telling Jack was bad enough without Rick adding to it. "I don't trust him, Rick."

"You're marrying him," he pointed out.

"Only because it's the most logical way to make sure both girls are taken care of. Allie told you, didn't she? About my MS? I can't risk him using all these problems against me in a custody battle."

"She told me. But Jack isn't that kind of guy, Shannon. You've got him pegged wrong. I know he did something stupid in school, but didn't we all?"

Shannon shrugged, then turned to climb into the plane. She spoke over her shoulder. "I can't risk it. Not yet." She settled into the back with the girls while Rick took another walk around the plane.

Allie turned around in the front passenger seat and lifted the oxygen mask from her face for a moment. "What were you and Rick talking about? You both looked tense."

Shannon glanced at the girls, but they were busy talking. She leaned forward and spoke in Allie's ear. "He wanted me to tell Jack about the break-in and the demand for money."

Allie gave a mock shudder. "A fate worse than death." Her smile dropped off. "You *are* marrying the man. Don't you think he should know about this? What if the guy follows you there?"

"And face Jack's arsenal? Not likely. He'd have to get in the gates, get past all of Jack's employees, then get into that mammoth house that's probably locked up tighter than Fort Knox. I just have to stay safe until after the wedding. Just a week. I can do that. He hasn't tried anything while I've been at your house."

"It's only been one night," Allie said dryly.

Shannon sat back and didn't answer when Rick climbed into the plane. Allie put her mask back on, and he started the engine. They were soon flying over the peaks and valleys of the desert. From the air, it appeared even more desolate. The girls peered in rapt attention out the windows.

Were the Baileys right? If Shannon thought either of her daughters was in danger, she'd tell anyone who would listen, even Jack. But Mary Beth was the one in danger. Still, just because Jack had been disloyal, did that mean she had to be as well? She chewed on her lip and wished she knew the answer.

Kylie climbed into her lap. Shannon pointed out the window. "Look, there are the sky mountains," she said, gesturing to the Chisos and Sierra del Carmen Mountains.

"Why do they call them that, Mommy?" Kylie asked. It was her first time in an airplane.

"I know," said Betsy. "They're supposed to be holding up the sky, but it's not true. The mountains don't do that—God does."

Shannon smiled at her. "Exactly right, but it's fun to know the myths and legends around the place where you live. And there are lots around here."

"Tell me a story, Mommy," Kylie demanded. "About the gold in the hills."

"How do you know about the gold?"

"Mr. Larue asked me if you'd ever taken me to see it. Have you seen it, Mommy?"

Tucker had talked to Kylie. Everything in Shannon tensed. "When did he ask you about it?" she demanded.

Kylie squirmed. "Don't squeeze me so tight," she whimpered.

Shannon loosened her grip on her daughter's arm. "Sorry, sweetie. When did Mr. Larue ask you about it?"

"When I was outside looking for the unicorn. Yesterday." Kylie slid off Shannon's lap and scooted over to sit by Betsy.

The unicorn? Had Kylie seen Jewel? Shannon huddled into the corner and tried to think above the roar of the plane. How did Tucker talk to Kylie without anyone seeing? Kylie's trusting nature scared Shannon. "You're not supposed to talk to strangers," she told Kylie. "How many times have I told you that?"

"He said he was your friend."

Shannon's fingers gripped Kylie's chin and she forced her daughter to look her in the eye. "If someone is my friend, I'll introduce you. Understand?" Kylie nodded and puckered. Shannon hugged her tight.

How did Tucker know about the gold? Or that Shannon might know where it was? He might use Kylie as leverage to get her to talk. She rubbed her forehead and wished she'd never seen that cave.

Kylie tugged on her arm. "Do you need to rest, Mommy?"

Shannon smiled at her daughter. Kylie was intuitive and noticed when her MS was kicking up. "I'm okay, sweetheart. I'll just close my eyes for a minute."

Kylie put her finger to her lips and turned back to whisper with Betsy. Shannon smiled and rested her head against the window. Today would be a long day. Shopping was not her favorite thing in the world.

Rick landed at the small field airport. Within half an hour, they were in a rented car and heading to a bridal shop. The little girls were in heaven looking at the frilly white dresses.

"What colors do you want?" Allie asked, flipping through the racks.

Shannon gazed around the packed store. She'd only been out of the city a few days and already it felt like another planet. "I . . . I have no idea. Let's do bright periwinkle if we can find it. The girls would look darling in that."

"Not pink?"

"Too vapid for them. And for you." Shannon reached for a splash of bright fabric. "Here, this would look great on the girls."

Allie held the dress under Kylie's chin. "Darling. It makes her eyes look brighter. I'll have her try it on while you look for yourself."

Shannon drifted toward the women's dresses. A smiling woman came toward her and directed her to the informal styles, then promised to be back to help her. Shannon touched the chiffon of a beautiful creamy gown. It fell from a high empire waist in soft folds.

This wasn't the way she'd thought she might be picking out a wedding dress someday. In her dreams, she'd thought maybe her fiancé's mother or sister would go with her since she had no family of her own. Allie was a good friend to have made this trip with her, but Shannon still had no love waiting for her at the end of the aisle. There was no excitement propelling her through these tasks, no gigging late-night chats with a gaggle of attendants, no parties given by friends and family.

Allie and the girls rejoined her. Shannon smiled at Kylie. "You look so pretty, sweetie. Do you like it?" Her daughter nodded and kept craning her neck to stare at herself in the banks of mirrors around the store.

Allie caressed the chiffon dress. "Let's try this on. It's so you." She and the girls followed Shannon to the huge dressing room.

Shannon shucked her jeans and T-shirt, then slipped the dress over her head. She turned for Allie to zip her up and found herself staring at her image in the mirror. A stranger stared back. One with a soft, tremulous mouth as though she really were a bride whose groom waited with open arms.

She averted her gaze from her face and stared objectively at her silhouette. When had she last worn a dress? Maybe to her graduation from veterinary school. No, that had been a pantsuit. She'd wanted to look professional. Turning this way and that in front of the mirror, she admired the drape of the gown and the way her neck appeared longer.

"It's perfect! You have to have it," Allie said.

"If you say so. Now let's find you a dress."

Anything so she didn't have to dwell on the reality facing her. Seven days of freedom left. Shannon made sure her hands didn't tremble.

THE WOMAN WAS ENOUGH TO DRIVE HIM TO DRINK. JACK WOVE THROUGH the San Antonio traffic toward the bridal shop. He'd called Rick to find out where they were heading, then called in a favor from a friend with an airplane. Faith was in her booster in the backseat. He could see her face in his rearview mirror, but he still didn't know how he was going to tell her he was getting remarried.

And telling his daughter that Shannon was her real mother would have to wait until later. Much later.

He found the bridal shop with no problem. After he parked, he got into the backseat of the rental car with his daughter. Faith had already unfastened her seat belt and was ready to get out.

She stared up at him with a question in her eyes. "Aren't we going shopping for a dress, Daddy?"

"Yes, we are, baby girl. In just a minute. I wanted to talk to you about something first." With her big blue eyes fastened on him, he wasn't sure how he'd find the words to tell her their lives were about to change. "It's a special dress we're buying. Miss Shannon and Kylie are inside too."

Faith slipped out of her seat and started to climb over him. "I want to see Kylie! She's my bestest friend."

She's so much more than that. Jack gulped and grabbed his daughter so she couldn't escape the vehicle. "In a minute. That's not all I have to tell you. We're going to buy you and Kylie dresses so you can be in a wedding."

Her smile widened. "Like flower girls? Me and Kylie both?"

He nodded. "Just like that."

"Who is the bride?"

"Miss Shannon."

Faith wrinkled her nose. "She doesn't have an engagement ring. Maybe her bridegroom is poor. Schmendrick was poor. I'm going to marry someone rich like Prince Lir."

"This isn't a movie like *The Last Unicorn*. And she's not marrying someone poor. I just didn't get her an engagement ring. There wasn't time." Too late he realized he'd blurted it out. "I mean, Miss Shannon is going to marry me."

"And move into our house?"

He nodded. "But you don't have to share your room with Kylie. We'll redo the bedroom right next to yours."

"She can share my room. We'll be just like sisters!" Faith wiggled to get down. "I want to go see her! I like Miss Shannon. She's nice. But she's not my mommy."

Jack found himself wanting to agree with her, but he said nothing. Now wasn't the time to go into that. His daughter would need to hear the truth in small sips, not in one gulp. "Let's go find Kylie," he said. Taking his daughter's hand, he wound through the parking lot to the store.

He'd never entered a place like this. Faith paused to stare at the mannequins in the store window, and he cringed at the sight of the white dresses. A peek beyond the display didn't reassure him. A store packed with women browsing rows and rows of dresses.

Hardly a place for a cowboy.

Even the quick gulp of air didn't help, tinged with exhaust as it was. He opened the door and led his daughter inside. And ran right into Shannon. Literally. His hands came up to steady her when she rocked back on her heels and clutched at the bagged dress she carried. "Sorry."

She pulled away. "What are you doing here?"

"I tracked down Enrica, and Faith has never been known to turn down a chance to go shopping. She's like her mother that way." Too late he realized he'd blown it again. He rushed on and averted his gaze from Shannon's face. And her cheeks that had reddened as though he'd slapped her.

The girls rushed into one another's arms. "We're going to be real sisters," Kylie said.

The girls' giggling and squealing were attracting attention. Jack would rather be mucking out stalls than encountering the curious female faces. "So are you already done here?"

"We are. Rick is bringing the car around." Shannon went past him to the door.

Allie smiled at him as she went past, and Jack saw the sympathy in her eyes. At least someone knew how hard this was. He grabbed the girls' hands and followed the women. The relief of being outside again was enough to let loose with a yell, but he didn't.

He saw Shannon with Allie by a white Taurus. He waited for traffic, then crossed to the parking lot to join them.

Rick leaned against the front fender and waved when he saw Jack. "Glad you could make it," he said when Jack reached the car.

"Not in time. Where we headed to now?" He intercepted a glance between Rick and Shannon. She'd narrowed her eyes in a warning glare at Rick. What was going on?

"Actually, you're here just in time," Rick said. "I'm going to take Allie and the girls out for lunch, and Shannon needs to run an errand. I'm sure you won't mind taking her."

"Rick!" Shannon protested.

Rick spread his hands out. "It's the best way," he said, glancing at the girls. He turned his gaze back to Jack. "I'll let her explain it. You have a booster seat for Faith?"

Jack glanced at Shannon's red face. What was going on?

"I'll get it." Whatever Shannon's errand was, she didn't want him to know about it.

10

THE BAILEY FAMILY AND THE TWINS LEFT WITH A WAVE. SHANNON COULD strangle Rick. She'd have to handle this very carefully so she didn't have to explain to Jack what was going on. "I need to run by my old apartment," she said.

Jack folded his arms across his chest. "That's all? I expected to find Rick's throat slashed after that glare you shot him. Or is it you just don't want to be in my company?"

"It's complicated," she muttered, glancing around. "Where's your car?"

"Over there." He pointed and she headed toward it. He unlocked it before she got there. "Where are we going?" he asked once they were buckled in.

"My apartment isn't far. Turn left out of the mall." Her mind raced through how she might handle this. Maybe she could get him to wait in the car. That would work. She told him where to turn, and fifteen minutes later, he parked on the street outside her old apartment in the projects.

One big problem. She didn't have a key any longer.

When she made no move to open her door, Jack glanced at her with a question in his eyes. "You're not going in?"

"Sure, just thinking. You can wait here. I won't be long."

"Fine." He tugged his cowboy hat forward, leaned his head back, and closed his eyes.

Whew, she'd dodged that bullet. She hurried toward the building, an aging structure missing chunks of brick. The old tile floors were chipped and loose inside the main door. Her apartment was on the second floor, and there was no elevator. She stared up the dirt-caked flight of stairs. All the way up the steps, she prayed to find Mary Beth inside the apartment.

By the time she reached the second floor, she was panting and her leg was hurting. The apartment was at the end of the long, poorly lit hallway. There were few long-term renters in the building, and none on this floor, so there was no one she could ask for help.

Her old life suddenly didn't seem so far away. The sound of a child crying was followed by a slap and even louder wailing. Paint flakes crunched under her feet. The odor of marijuana wafted around a teenager with sullen eyes who brushed past her.

Anything Shannon must do to make sure Kylie never came back to a place like this would be worth it. Seeing her old home with new eyes, she hated that her daughter had ever endured this.

A man exited the door at the end of the hall. On the left. Her door.

Shannon took a quick turn into a stairwell before he could see her. She'd seen that tall figure before, and the glimpse of his curly hair made it hard to breathe. Pressing back against the brick wall in a dark corner, she watched his shadow pass her hidey-hole. She waited until his footsteps faded.

Shaking, she wobbled along the hallway to the apartment door until she stood in front of apartment 222. The doorknob appeared too grimy to touch, even though she'd washed it often when she lived here. The door too. The dirt must have crawled right up the minute she was gone.

She shook her head at her fanciful notions and reached out to touch the knob. It turned under her fingers, and she heard the latch click. He'd left it unlocked. She pushed open the door. "Mary Beth?" she called, flinching at the stale odor that rushed out. The blinds were shut, and the room was dark. She flipped on the light switch and closed the door behind her. She tried to lock it, but he'd broken the knob getting in.

No one answered her, and the apartment felt empty. Her slim hope of finding Mary Beth here evaporated. The sooner she looked around and got out of here, the happier she'd be. She doubted the man would come back, but the hair still stood up on the back of her neck. Her gaze swept the room and the meager furnishings—a sofa and two wooden chairs. Clean though. She'd made sure of that. Two of Kylie's crayon drawings still decorated the refrigerator.

She headed for Mary Beth's bedroom, passing the one she'd shared with Kylie on the way. The two twin beds were still in the tiny room, though someone had removed the mattresses and leaned them on the far wall. No dust bunnies huddled under the rusting springs yet. In this room she'd studied and mothered between her working hours. Looking back, it seemed impossible she'd managed to graduate from vet school.

She averted her gaze and hurried on to Mary Beth's room. The door was closed. She pushed it open and stared at the mess. Even on her worst days, Mary Beth was never this messy. Contents from the painted dresser lay scattered on the floor. The bedclothes were rolled up and in a corner. The mattress was off the bed too.

He'd searched the apartment of course. It had been a waste of time to come here after she'd seen him.

She slumped against the doorjamb. If what he sought was here, he would have taken it with him. She turned to go when she remembered the hiding place she and Mary Beth had sometimes used for their meager amounts of savings. Mary Beth put other things in it as well. Retracing her steps to the living area, she went to the tiny kitchen. She climbed onto the counter, just a piece of plywood covered with linoleum, and ran her hand along the grimy cabinet top. The wall was ancient brick. She found the loose one and pulled it out. It was too dark to see the makeshift cubby, so she stood on her tiptoes and ran her hand inside.

"What are you doing?" Jack asked behind her.

She nearly fell off the counter. Grabbing the top of the cabinet for support, she glared down at him. "You scared the life out of me!"

"You were gone so long, I thought I'd better check."

She wiped her dusty hands on her jeans. "How'd you know which apartment?"

"I called Rick to have him ask Kylie."

Smart man. And maybe useful. Her fingers had barely brushed something in the cavity, but she couldn't reach the back of the hiding place. "Could you climb up here and get something for me? I can't quite reach it."

"Sure." His big hands circled her waist, and he lifted her down from the counter.

She fell against his chest, and for a moment, it was as if they were embracing. His breath stirred her hair. "It must have been sweltering in the car," she said, pushing away.

He dropped his hands and stepped back as if she were the one who was hot. "It was." He climbed onto the counter and stood. "Here?"

She watched him stick his hand in the cavity. "Yes."

"What am I supposed to be looking for?"

"Whatever's in there," she said. His lips compressed, and she knew he thought she didn't want to tell him. This current situation was something that she wanted to put behind her and never look at again. There was no need to drag him into it. If she could just find whatever money Mary Beth had taken and give it back, this nightmare would be over. Especially for Mary Beth.

He extracted a paper bag wrapped around a booklike shape. "Here you go." He tossed it down to her. "Why didn't you just admit it was your diary?" Grinning, he jumped down from the counter. He thrust the package into her hands.

"Thanks," she said.

"We ready to go? Rick said they were done with lunch. We can grab some fast food and meet them at the airport."

She was dying to see what was in the sack. "Let me run to the ladies' room a minute." She started to tell him to go on down to the car, then thought better of it. Having Jack here made her feel safer. "I'll just be a minute."

She hurried to the bathroom and shut the door behind her before unwrapping the bundle. A book fell out. Leather-bound and expensive with a design embossed on the front. Nicer than she'd ever seen in her friend's possession. She flipped it open. The paper was thick and costly too. There was no name in the front, and the first few pages held rows of figures.

She glanced at her watch. Jack would be getting impatient. This would take some deciphering. After putting the book back into the bag, she flushed the toilet so he wasn't suspicious, then washed the apartment's dirt from her hands.

If only she could wash the problems away as easily.

TUESDAY MORNING, AFTER SHANNON DISCOVERED HER JEEP HAD A FLAT, Rick offered to drive her to work. On the way, the text message jingle sounded on Shannon's cell phone. She inhaled quickly, then called up the message. It wasn't from Mary Beth.

Time's up. Way up. Look under your seat.

Her mouth went dry. She reached under the seat. Her fingers encountered a box. Shoe-box size. She pulled it out and lifted it to her lap. It was lightweight as though it contained nothing, but something told her she wouldn't like the contents. For a moment she wanted to toss it into the back and ignore it. But she couldn't do that. Mary Beth's life was at stake. She stared at the top of the shoe box—"Nike," the box read.

"What's that?" Rick asked.

"I just got a message telling me to look there," she said. Holding her breath, she lifted the lid and stared down at a mass of brown. What on earth? Then it hit her. Mary Beth's hair. All of it, by the looks of the amount in the box. Shannon slammed shut the lid and took several deep breaths.

Another text message signal sounded. *Next time I'll send her head.*

She texted back. *I don't have what you want.* Panic beat against her chest. Was Mary Beth all right? *Don't hurt her.*

Rick veered across the road then centered his truck and pulled it to the side of the road. "What is it?"

"It's Mary Beth's hair! The guy just texted me. He said the next time he'll send her head." She grabbed her phone and dialed the Midland station of the Texas Rangers. The officer she spoke to promised to send out someone to pick up the hair. Not that having it in their custody would find Mary Beth.

If she was even still alive.

"He let more than twenty-four hours go by," Rick said. "Any idea why?"

"When he didn't contact me, I'd hoped he found what he was looking for in our old apartment. Or else he'd figured out I didn't know anything. But I should have known better. Mary Beth would have called me if she was okay. I went through that journal I found, but I couldn't make it out. It's just a financial ledger of some kind. In the back was a love letter from Mary Beth to some guy, but there's no name."

"Maybe it's the guy's ledger."

Shannon shuddered. "To be betrayed by the man you love would be the worst thing I can imagine." Which was why Jack's betrayal in school had hurt.

Rick let her out and she went to work. By afternoon the weather had turned even hotter. The wind blew stinging dust against Shannon's cheeks. She glanced at the yellow sky, dark and threatening, as she ran her hands over a mare's legs. A true dust storm was headed this way. Likely the trainers were packing up their gear and getting things stowed away before it hit.

"I think she'll be okay," she told the trainer, a cowboy who proudly wore his rodeo buckles, a different one every day. "It's just a sprain."

He thanked her and she hurried toward the parking lot. Rick could read the sky as easily as she did, and he'd be ready to get home and make sure everything was battened down and ready.

Another four days and she'd be a married woman. The scariest part of that equation was that she knew little about Jack and how he might expect her to behave. Facing him across the dinner table every night was just the beginning. He ran in different circles than she did. She was a cowgirl at heart, one who was happier around horses than around people, especially people with money. Maybe she was judgmental. She might find Jack's circle down-to-earth and interesting. It was bound to be different though.

Seemingly out of nowhere, a rope whooshed over her head and settled around her waist. The loop tightened with a jerk, and she stumbled. The next thing she knew, she was facedown in the dirt with the wind swirling grit in her eyes. Hands seized her feet and wrapped rope around her ankles.

She rolled onto her side so she could peer up. Tucker was grinning down at her. "Untie me," she said through gritted teeth. "What in Sam Hill do you think you're doing?"

"Fifteen seconds to bring the calf to ground," he crowed. "Just practicing, darlin'."

"Practice on a post. Untie me. Now." And when she got loose, she was going to sock him.

"Ask me nicely," he said, his grin widening.

"Tucker. Get these ropes off me." Vainly she struggled against the rough hemp.

"You never could take a joke." He knelt and unwound the rope from her ankles.

She got to her feet and pushed his hands away from her waist. "I can take it from here." She widened the loop and stepped free of it. The words she wanted to lash him with stayed locked behind her teeth, and she had to keep them there. Giving in to her anger would be playing into his hands. He lived to get someone's goat.

As she turned to leave him, his hand snaked out and grabbed her wrist. "Not so fast. I want to talk to you."

"A storm is coming, in case you haven't noticed. Keep it quick."

The crooked smile that used to thrill her was in perfect form, but today it only raised her level of alarm. What did he want? She prayed it wouldn't involve Kylie.

"I talked to Kylie the other day. Cute kid," he said. "She looks just like you." He swiped at her hair, but she danced away, and his eyes hardened. "I started thinking about something you said when we were together. You mentioned some Spanish artifacts your parents had been looking for. But here's the interesting thing—I've been doing some research on those artifacts, and none of the books mentions a sword inlaid with emeralds." He leaned closer. "Way I figure it, your parents found that treasure. And you saw it."

The cold hand of fear gripped her spine, but she managed to look him in the eye and keep her voice even. "You can dream up anything you like, Tucker. Just leave me out of your delusions."

She wheeled and walked toward the parking lot at a pace that wouldn't seem as though she was running. Her heart beat against her ribs, and she prayed he didn't follow.

She thought the story of that treasure had died long ago. But when cowboys got together, they resurrected tales, so she should have expected this.

Rick was waiting at the truck when she arrived at the lot, and he frowned when he saw her face. "What's wrong?"

"Nothing. Just Tucker being himself."

"You sound like you know him well."

"Too well." Changing the subject might help. "You had a fresh batch of kids due this afternoon, didn't you?" The Bluebird Ranch was a camp that helped abused kids by connecting them with abused horses.

He nodded. "They're here. Seven of them. They took to the horses right off. Allie has them mucking out the stalls right now."

"Fun. They'll want to head back to the city, especially when they go through this sandstorm."

"They always want to run scared, but it won't take long for them to settle in. Allie is great with them."

"You two make a perfect team."

He beamed. "We're grateful God opened the door for us to make a difference with these throwaway kids."

"And the throwaway horses."

"Those too," he agreed. He glanced at the sky. "We'd better move on home. That storm will be here in an hour."

She nodded and climbed into the truck. Rick accelerated down the road toward home. The roar of another truck passing them caused Shannon to glance up. Tucker waved and grinned as he barreled past, and Shannon leaned her head against the window and wondered what she was going to do about him. So far he hadn't made any demand to see Kylie, but Shannon feared it was coming. He was all about power, and forcing her to admit him into Kylie's life would be the ultimate power trip.

They reached the Bluebird Ranch, and Buck, the fireman Shannon had met a few days ago, came rushing down the steps. The fire in their area had been put out, but Rick had invited him to stay to discuss coming to work at Bluebird. Rick had been thinking about adding overnight mountain campouts to the program.

Rick and Shannon jumped out of the truck as he reached them. "What's wrong?" Shannon asked, her first thought rushing to her daughter's safety.

"The wind has already torn off one of the barn doors. Bluebird got out."

The mare was Betsy's favorite. No one could ride her except the little girl. She'd be devastated if they didn't recover the horse.

"You batten down the hatches and I'll go look for Bluebird," Shannon said. "Make sure you call Moses in." She headed toward the barn. If only she had Jewel. The horse had an uncanny ability to know what she needed to do. Even whistling for the stallion would be useless in this wind. She'd have to do the best she could with Cupcake.

Glancing at the sky, she knew she didn't have much time before the sandstorm hit. It could be deadly for her or the horses to be caught out in this.

11

WITH THE SHUTTERS CLOSED AND THE BARNS LOCKED UP TIGHT, JACK settled into his favorite chair by the massive stone fireplace in his office. He had his favorite dog-eared copy of *Riders of the Purple Sage* in his hand, and he looked forward to a comfortable evening reading with his dog at his feet while the wind howled outside.

The phone rang, but he let Enrica answer it in the kitchen. She knew not to disturb him when his office door was shut unless it was an emergency.

A few moments later, a tap sounded on his door, and he sprang to his feet. "Come in."

Enrica poked her head in. "Mr. Jack, Mr. Rick on the phone. He say he need help. Miss Allie having pain, and he must take her to clinic.

Miss Shannon out looking for lost horse. No one there for the *niñas*. He ask can he bring them here."

Jack tossed his book down and glanced out the window. Dust swirled outside, turning daylight to dusk. The wind was already making fine drifts of sand along the fence. The thought of Shannon outside in this brought him bolting out of his chair.

He grabbed the phone from the desk. "Rick? Drop the girls off here. Enrica will keep them while I go look for Shannon. How long has she been out there?" He glanced out the window at the swirling sand again. It wasn't nearly as bad as it was going to get, according to the news.

Rick's voice vibrated with worry. "Only about half an hour. I told her not to stay out long. I'm sure she'll be back soon. I thought you'd keep the girls, so we're already on our way."

Shannon would do just about anything for an endangered horse, and Jack didn't trust her to turn back if she didn't find it. "I'll go out looking for her. What direction did she head?"

"West from my ranch on horseback. We're outside now."

"I'll come out to get the girls." Jack punched off the phone and beckoned to Enrica as he left the office. "The girls need to stay here," he called over his shoulder as she hurried after him. "And I need to go look for Miss Shannon."

By the time he reached the porch, Rick had brought Betsy and Kylie to the steps. The sky was an angry brown and it was hard to see past the swirling sand. The girls ran up the steps to him, and he was struck again by how much the girls looked alike. A wave of love washed over him, surprising him with its strength. He'd been worried about being able to care for her as much as he did Faith. But clearly he had plenty of love to give.

To their mother too? He was less certain of that.

He squatted by the girls. "Faith is in the kitchen. Enrica is getting ready to bake cookies with you all," he told them. He didn't mention the cookies would be wheat-free and made with pure maple syrup instead of sugar. Somehow Enrica made them tasty that way.

The girls squealed and ran past him into the house. "Get going," he told Rick. "Let me know how it goes."

Rick nodded and ran toward the truck. He called back to Jack, "It's about two weeks early though. Allie thinks it's false labor, but I want her checked."

Jack watched him jump back into the truck and accelerate away. He pulled the collar of his denim shirt up around his neck and settled his cowboy hat a little more snugly onto his head, then headed to his truck. The sand stung every exposed patch of skin, and the grit in his eyes made it hard to see. He reached the vehicle and had second thoughts. Shannon was most likely headed this way on horseback. He'd be better off to try to meet her across the desert. He'd take his four-wheeler. He should find her before the storm got bad enough to foul his engine. If she was hurt, he could get her back faster too.

Just to make sure she hadn't come back, he detoured into the house to call the Bluebird. The phone would ring into the barn and the bunkhouse if no one in the house picked up. When he finally reached the youth worker in the bunkhouse and found out Shannon still hadn't returned, he jogged to the barn and fired up his four-wheeler, then rolled out across the yard to the desert.

Away from the buildings, the sandstorm was much worse. He could barely see, then remembered a helmet with a shield in the compartment behind him. He stopped and dug out the helmet. The shield helped, and he was able to point the four-wheeler in the right direction. The storm began to intensify, but he managed to keep going.

The brown cloud transformed familiar terrain into a moonscape of strange shapes and impressions, but he'd been out in many a sandstorm over the years. Shannon likely had, too, but not for quite a few years. She might have forgotten any survival skills she once knew, and he pressed his foot down harder on the accelerator.

The sandstorm made him hit several big rocks in the dirt he would have otherwise missed, sending the vehicle airborne twice. He reached the shelter of a big rock that blunted the fury of the wind and sand. Fishing out his cell phone, he saw he had one bar and a text message. It was from Rick. All was well with Allie and he was going to get the girls. No word from Shannon.

Jack texted back that he hadn't found Shannon, but that Rick shouldn't worry if they were caught out in it. He would find shelter somewhere for them both. Brave words, but his arms were sore from hanging on to the grips on the four-wheeler. He didn't want to entertain the thought that he might not find her.

A sip from his canteen washed the grit from his throat. He started the bike again and headed out into the storm. Bluebird Ranch property was just ahead. He slowed the vehicle and peered through the intensifying dust. The four-wheeler slowed more than he intended, and he realized he had the four-wheeler gunned as much as he could. The sand must be fouling the engine. He had barely reached Bluebird Ranch property when the engine began to cough and sputter.

It died before Jack could form a backup plan. He sat on the vehicle seat and thought about his options. Giving up was not one of them. His skin burned from the assault of the storm. The thought of Shannon out in these conditions increased his sense of urgency, but he had no idea where to look. Cell phones wouldn't work in this morass of sand. He and Shannon were isolated.

He tried to think of any shelter she might find out here. There was an old shack by the abandoned copper mine north of his location. It would be a long, painful walk though. He glanced at his vehicle and knew trying to restart it would be a waste of time. There was no help for it but to start hiking. He pulled out a handkerchief and tied it around his nose and mouth. He couldn't make out the outcroppings that signaled the location of the shack, but he knew this area well and recognized other rocks as he jogged past them. The ground sloped upward, and he saw a clear landmark: the large grouping of prickly pear cactus close to the shack.

Picking up his step, he glimpsed the outline of the building. The weathered wood wouldn't keep out all the sand, but it would help. As he neared, a short burst of barks was quickly hushed by a woman's voice. He stepped onto the rickety stoop. The door was off its hinges, and the front windows were cracked with missing panes.

"Shannon?" he called.

Her blonde head bobbed up in the window. "Jack," she said, her voice wobbling with relief. "How did you find me?"

He stepped through the doorway into a space where the dust still swirled in the air, but the volume was much reduced.

Moses came to greet him and pressed his cold nose against Jack's hand. Jack rubbed his ears. "You okay?"

Her appearance answered his question. Her hair was a golden tangle from the wind, and the stinging sand had left her skin reddened. It might be mistaken for a sunburn. Her shirt and jeans held a brownish tinge from the sand embedded in the cloth. In the back corner of the building he saw two horses.

She nodded toward the horses. "I'm fine, but Bluebird has an injured fetlock. I knew we'd never make it home, so I brought the horses here. I tried to call Rick, but the storm was too bad to get through."

He glanced around the one-room shack. It held a couple of broken-down stools, some trash, and a small iron kettle upside-down in the corner. Several inches of sand covered the scarred wooden floorboards. Drifts of sand piled against the walls and in the corners.

His gaze reverted to Shannon, and he tugged his kerchief from his face. "You realize this storm won't blow itself out until morning. We'll be stuck here all night."

"I know. You didn't have to come looking for me. I know how to take care of myself."

Even though her chin was tipped up, he had clearly read the relief in her face when she saw him. "Rick was worried, and he had to take Allie to the clinic. She was having contractions."

She began to pace. "The baby isn't due yet!"

So like her to be worried about other people. A wave of some kind of emotion rose in a mist as thick as the sand, but Jack refused to examine it. "Allie thought it was false labor, but Rick wanted to make sure. Allie's fine and they're back home now."

"Where are the girls?"

"They were at my house with Enrica. Rick and Allie have them by now again."

She smiled then. "Thank you."

Did nothing ever frighten her? Blair had been strong, too, but Shannon's was a different kind of strength, one of quiet determination. He was beginning to realize he liked a strong woman.

He walked farther into the room. "Seeing Kylie again, I was blown away at how much alike she and Faith are. It's amazing." He shoved his hands in his pockets and glanced around the dirty cabin. "It's going to be pretty uncomfortable here tonight."

She gestured to the animals. "I was about to unsaddle the horses. We can use their blankets and the saddles will make a pillow."

She really did have it together. This woman didn't need rescuing. The deflation that rippled through him caught him off guard. He liked to be needed, and Shannon was an island unto herself. The future with her was as murky as the sand-filled air.

THE WIND HOWLED THROUGH THE HOLES IN THE SHACK AND ROARED through the broken window panes. Night began to fall, and Shannon set to work making the space as comfortable as she could.

When she started to unsaddle the horses, Jack sprang forward to help her. He pulled a saddle from Bluebird and carried it to the corner with the fewest number of holes in the wall, then went back for Cupcake's saddle.

The sand coated Shannon's throat and she longed to escape its choking influence. "I wish we had some way to fill the holes in the walls and the windows."

"I've got an idea," he said. He grabbed the horse blanket and took it to the corner. He dragged the broken chairs over next, then draped them over the chair backs, forming a small shelter. "Bring me the other blanket," he called above the howl of the wind.

Shannon pulled the blanket from the horse's back and hurried to the corner with it. "What are you doing?"

"You'll see." Jack took it and draped it over one side of his little tent. "Now only one side is open. It won't keep out all the dust, but we'll be safe from most of it. Climb in."

Shannon ducked under the rough wool throw. In the dim shelter, there was hardly any sand in the air, and if Jack weren't here, she might have taken a moment to spit out the gritty taste in her mouth.

She felt rather than saw him slide into the shelter with her. If she hadn't been so desperate to get out of the sand, she might have stopped to think what it would be like to be trapped in a small space with him. His male scent filled her nostrils instead of the earthy smell of sand. A pleasant change if she hadn't been so fearful of her own reaction to him.

She huddled against the wall so she didn't brush him inadvertently.

"It's better in here," he said.

She managed enough moisture to wet her cracked lips. "Smart of you to think of it. I wish we had water. I hurried off too fast to think of it. A fatal error in this land."

"Hang on." His bulk moved away and the sound of him shuffling through something was muffled by the blankets. His presence filled the tiny space again. "Here you go."

A cool canteen touched her hand. Shannon unscrewed the lid and took a sip of the sweetest water she'd ever swallowed. She would have taken another sip, but they might need to conserve it. She pressed it back into his hand. "You'd better have some too." She heard him unscrew the cap and take a swig.

He shuffled around next to her, and his voice was closer to the floor when it came. "We might as well try to get some sleep."

Cautiously Shannon stretched out and laid her head on the saddle. The good aroma of horse swept away the dusty odor in her nose. Jack's breathing was slow and even. Could he be asleep already? Shannon could imagine Rick and Allie's distress if they knew she wasn't home. Luckily, the girls probably didn't know anything was amiss. Being together would be enough of a treat. Kylie wouldn't be worrying about her mother. She became aware she was humming "It Is Well with My Soul" under her breath.

Jack's voice interrupted the howling of the wind. "We could talk for a while if you can't sleep."

"How did you know I wasn't asleep?"

"The little sounds you were making. And you were humming under your breath. Do you do that often?"

"Whenever I'm nervous. Sorry if I disturbed you."

"I wasn't asleep."

"What do you want to talk about?" Shannon found herself wanting to keep the conversation going. Somehow it was easier to talk in the dark. She didn't have to try to judge his expressions. It might be her imagination, but she thought his tone was softer. The intimacy of their situation stripped away the guardedness they usually held between them.

When he spoke, his voice was soft. "We're going to be married in four days, and I don't know much about you. What are your dreams, Shannon? What do you want to accomplish with your life?"

What did she want? Once upon a time, she'd wanted to become an expert whom the news media consulted about animals. She wanted a name that would make people back here whisper with astonishment. All that had been stripped away the moment she learned she had MS, and all that remained was the desire to be well enough to raise her daughter, to get through each day and make a home Kylie would remember with fondness. But she couldn't tell him all that. Not yet.

"Could I have another sip of water?" she asked while she tried to think how to answer his question.

He handed over the canteen, and she took a tiny sip. The cool liquid was like heaven.

"I take it you don't want to answer me?" His voice was gently teasing.

"I was just trying to think about what I want. You have to admit our lives took a surprising detour in the past week or so. You'd say an unwelcome one, but it was an exciting one for me to find out my daughter is still alive. So I want the girls to have a stable, loving home. To grow up well adjusted and happy."

"I'm getting used to the idea that I'll have two little Faiths around."

"And a wife. I'm sure that idea isn't growing on you."

"I've worried about Faith, growing up without a mother. She needs you."

And you don't, she thought. Tears sprang to her eyes, but she told herself it was a reaction against the grit in them. Her throat thickened, but she swallowed and forced a light tone to her voice. "How about you? What do you want? Politics like your dad?"

"The good Lord preserve me from such a fate," he said. "I love this land, the stark beauty of it. The Rio Grande in full flood, the hawk on the wing. The yip of the coyotes at night. I want to live a life of integrity and to teach my daughter—daughters—to do the same. To be a good steward of the land God's given me. To raise great horses that enrich other people's lives as well as my own. I don't know, maybe I sound a little pompous. I don't voice this stuff much. I just want my life to count for something good."

Shannon couldn't answer him. He'd changed from the self-absorbed young man she remembered from school. It would be way too easy to fall in love with him, and she didn't trust him. Not yet. Besides, he'd been crazy about Blair, and with good reason. She'd always treated Shannon decently even when others hadn't. Shannon could never hold a candle to someone like Blair.

His breathing slowed, and she knew he was asleep. Tomorrow

they'd ride out of here and she'd be able to keep him at a safe distance again.

When the sunlight filtered through their "tent," it didn't seem she'd slept a wink, but she must have, because she lay curled against Jack with her head on his shoulder. And she never would have gone there in her right mind. She rolled away, and he murmured something in his sleep. She didn't want to know what it was, and luckily, she heard Rick's shout outside the shack door followed by Moses' excited bark.

"Here, we're here!" She scrambled over Jack's inert frame and burst out of the door and into the sunshine—where the cold light of day assured her Jack could never come to care for her.

12

WEDNESDAY EVENING, SHANNON STARED AT THE CELL PHONE IN HER HAND. Not knowing what had happened to Mary Beth was weighing on her, and she couldn't get the image of that mass of her friend's hair out of her mind.

Did she dare call and demand to speak to Mary Beth?

What did she have to lose? Right now she had no idea if her friend was dead or alive. Shannon feared the answer wasn't one she wanted to hear, but she had to know. She called up Mary Beth's cell phone number and listened to it ring. Steeling herself for that man's voice, she waited.

Shannon's heart leaped at the sound of Mary Beth's voice, then she realized she'd been dumped into voice mail. She nearly hung up but didn't. "This is Shannon Astor. I need to know that Mary Beth is okay before I do anything else." She shut the phone and put it away.

Before I do anything else. Like she were able to do anything other than this walk in the dark. If only she had some idea of what money was in question. The man would have checked out Mary Beth's bank account, and Shannon couldn't do it anyway, because she didn't have the account number. All she could do was wait.

Her cell phone played its tune, and she froze. She grabbed it and glanced at the display, then saw Mary Beth's number. That was fast. For a moment she wanted to ignore the urgent ring. Praying for courage and the right words, she flipped it open. "Mary Beth?"

"Wrong, little lady. You should know what happened to your friend when you wouldn't play ball. Bye-bye, Mary Beth."

"I don't think so," she said, wondering at her boldness. "If she's dead, your hopes of finding the money are gone."

"We still have you."

"I want to talk to Mary Beth," Shannon said, hanging on to the phone with a death grip. "If I don't talk to her, you don't get anything." What was that noise in the background? It grew louder and she realized it was a train.

His voice came in a low growl above the train's rumble. "Give me the money, and you can talk to her then."

"We're at a standstill, then. I'm not making a move until I know she's okay." She waited for his response, but all she got was a click. He'd hung up on her. What did that say about Mary Beth's situation? Shannon prayed it didn't mean her friend was dead.

She called the Rangers again, but that was a waste of time when she had nothing to give them but the sound of a train. They made note of the call and she put her phone away. They hadn't found any trace of

Mary Beth. If this man didn't get what he wanted by using Mary Beth, would he move on to Shannon's daughters? The man had said he wouldn't touch the children, but she sensed desperation in his voice, and she had no idea what he would do next.

And the man's frustration was likely growing at his inability to get her to talk. She pressed her fingers to her eyes. If only she knew where to look for that money.

THE SMALL CHURCH HELD A HANDFUL OF PEOPLE. PASTOR GRADY O'Sullivan and his wife, Dolly. A few folks from the adult Sunday-school class Jack taught. The Baileys. Jack's parents were here, but he hadn't invited Aunt Verna.

He glanced down at his daughter clinging to his hand. The two girls wore identical dresses in a weird bluish shade. They were made of that filmy stuff that made them look like princesses. In cream leather flats, with bows in their curled blonde hair, they could have stepped from the pages of a fairy-tale book.

Shannon had done a good job, but he was ready to bolt for the door, especially after the other night in the sandstorm. He was way too attracted to her. He cracked his knuckles and made himself stand where he was.

"You nervous?" Rick asked. Dressed in a suit, he could almost be going to his own wedding.

"A little." Jack eyed Rick. Shannon had moved in with the Baileys last week, and she'd been tight-lipped about the reason why. Maybe it was the state of the house her uncle had left her. Or maybe she just needed Allie's comfort as they planned the wedding.

Jack cracked his knuckles again, then stuck his hands in his pockets.

His dark blue suit was new, and he'd had his hair trimmed yesterday. All to marry some woman he didn't know. No, strike that. He squeezed Faith's fingers gently. To keep his daughter. That's what it was all about. He had to keep his priorities in mind.

His daughter pulled her hand free and ran across the church to join her sister. They still had to tell the girls the whole truth, but Jack intended to put it off as long as possible.

Rick waited until she was out of hearing range. "Shannon has been a wild woman for three days. Pacing the floor at night, crying for no reason, eating every bit of homemade bread in the house." He grinned. "Between her and my pregnant wife, I haven't gotten a lick of work done."

A short bark of laughter burst out of Jack's mouth, and the release kept him grinning. "Enrica doesn't allow wheat in our house. Shannon's going to have a hard time of it if she gets nervous at our place." He stared hard at Rick. "You're happy, right? Married, I mean."

Rick nodded, his eyes twinkling. He leaned closer. "I didn't know Allie when I married her either."

Jack had heard rumors, but he hadn't known what to believe. "Some people said you knew her from a long time ago."

"Nope. I hadn't laid eyes on her until I found her and Betsy stranded at the side of the road. We married for Betsy's sake, and it's worked out. More than worked out. We've got a great marriage." Rick slapped Jack on the shoulder. "Give yourself a chance to discover she's a terrific gal."

Jack grunted. "You couldn't prove it by me. She could have just done the right thing. All she had to do was sign Faith over to me."

"Would you have done that? If the situation were reversed and that child was yours?"

Jack didn't want to answer. He wanted to hang on to his anger against Shannon, to hug his feelings of outrage. "Maybe not."

"You wouldn't. You'd want to know your daughter too. Anyone would. You can't blame her."

Jack shrugged. "I've been railroaded." He knew he sounded sulky. No, he *was* sulky.

Rick's grin faded. "Like I said, don't shut the door on a real marriage. It can happen."

"Yeah, right." Jack took his hands from his pocket and cracked his knuckles again. His stomach plunged when Grady stepped out the side door by the pulpit and motioned to him. This dog and pony show was about to begin.

All he wanted to do was run for the nearest exit, but he'd have to grab the pommel of this saddle and hang on for dear life.

Rick grabbed his elbow when he took a step back. "You can do it. Let's go."

Jack forced his feet to move forward, shuffling closer to the front of the church. He barely noticed the flowers hanging on the ends of the pews or the candelabra at the front of the church. All touches someone had cared about to make the day nice for them.

The next thing he knew, he and Rick were standing in front of the few guests. Grady's wife, Dolly, put her hands on the organ, and the sound filled the small church. The girls came down the aisle together, one scattering petals and the other holding the ring bearer's pillow with the fake rings.

"You've got the ring, right?" Jack whispered to Rick.

"Got it."

Allie came down the aisle in a blue dress that was shiny. She looked nice, and the love in her eyes when she saw Rick made Jack's throat thicken. Blair used to look at him like that. Now here he was, settling for a loveless marriage.

The organ pounded out the first notes of the "Bridal Chorus." He caught his first glimpse of his new bride. She wore a cream dress that left her shoulders bare and draped over her down to a jagged kind of hem. At least it wasn't a normal bride's dress. It didn't even have a train.

His gaze found her face. She looked pale, and her eyes stared straight ahead. She didn't turn to smile at any of the guests. Her mouth pressed into a straight line, she walked with a halting step. Was she trying to match the music or was she about to turn tail and run? His muscles tensed to grab her if she started to bolt. She'd gotten them both into this, and she'd see it through.

One foot in front of the other, she advanced until she stood at his side. No one gave her away. Pale as a yucca blossom, she stood swaying beside him. As Grady had them repeat their vows, Jack could barely hear her answers, though he replied to Grady's prompts in a strong voice.

"I now pronounce you man and wife."

The ominous words struck Jack in the gut. Man and wife. When he'd first heard those words, he'd thought his marriage would be forever. At that time it had been a happy thought. Today, *forever* was more of a threat.

"You may kiss your bride," Grady said softly.

Jack glanced at Shannon. Her smile seemed more like a grimace. People were watching and he didn't want to embarrass her, so he bent and brushed his lips across hers. The softness of her mouth startled him. It had been so long since he'd kissed a woman—a year in fact. He didn't want to think about her in the same category as Blair. He stepped away.

It was all he could do to offer a tight-lipped smile and his arm to his new bride. She clung to his arm as he led her back down the aisle. He knew she'd seen Verna seated in the back by the way she gripped his arm.

"Did you invite her?" she whispered.

"No," he said softly.

Verna's eyes pleaded with them as they passed out the doors of the sanctuary to form a reception line in the foyer. She was the first one out of the sanctuary door and came toward them with her arms outstretched. "I'm sorry, so sorry," she sniffled, pulling a hankie from her purse. "But it's all turned out for the best, hasn't it?"

Jack didn't know how to answer that. He maintained a tight smile for the sake of the guests coming up behind her. Shannon's arm trembled against his.

"What do you call 'the best'?" Shannon asked softly. "A loveless marriage?"

Verna dropped her gaze, then lifted it again with a touch of defiance in her eyes. "You've got a good man to take care of you. The girls are together. Blair died happy. What part isn't good?"

"How about the fact I've never tucked Faith into bed at night? I've never read her a story or nursed her. All the years I've missed."

Verna's gaze softened, and her eyes filled. "I can't give that back to you, but what you lost, Blair gained. That should bring some comfort."

To Jack's surprise, Shannon slowly nodded. He eyed her pensive face and wondered what she was thinking.

"Maybe you're right, Verna," she said. "One person's loss is another's gain. I'll try to remember that good can come from bad."

Her lips were tight, and he knew she was trying not to spoil their day. He took her hand, and her fingers curled around his as they turned to greet the rest of the guests streaming out of the sanctuary.

When family and friends finally finished hugging them, they escaped to the reception tent. One more duty with the punch and cake and they could leave. His mother had insisted on filling the tent with flowers. So far he'd managed to keep her away from Shannon, but his luck was about to end. His mother bore down on them with his father in tow. Her set face wore a smile, but the determination in her eyes told him he'd have to be on his toes to keep the truth from her and Dad.

"Shannon, you look lovely," his mother said, her teeth nearly bared. "I'm so eager to get to know you better. How amazing that the girls look so much alike."

No pussyfooting around with his mother. She went straight for the jugular. Jack brushed his lips against his mother's cool powdered cheek. Once upon a time, he'd thought the scent of face powder was a necessary requirement for a woman. The thought sent his gaze skipping to Shannon.

He pulled her forward to meet his parents. "Shannon, this is my mom and dad, Alexis and Senator Jack. You probably figured it out." He knew his smile was weak. How on earth was he going to steer this conversation away from the girls?

"I'm so happy to meet you." Shannon embraced both parents, then stepped back and tucked her hand into Jack's elbow again.

"She doesn't know you think the sun comes up just to hear you crow." Jack's dad punched him on the arm. "Wait until she lives with you a spell."

Jack forced himself not to fire back. Just because he didn't jump when his dad snapped his fingers didn't mean he was self-centered. "We'll have plenty of time for her to find out my faults."

"Well, what was the rush, Jack?" His mother tossed back a strand of hair that dared to stray onto her forehead.

Her gaze stayed focused on her new daughter-in-law, and a puzzled frown marred the smoothness of her brow. Her Botox must be wearing off. Jack tanked the stray thought and managed a smile. "I didn't want her to get away."

Shannon's fingers tightened on his arm. "We wanted the girls to get to know one another as quickly as possible."

His mother's eyes narrowed. "Why do they look so much alike? Is your child Jack's love child? The girls looked enough alike to be sisters, and they're the spitting image of you."

Jack nearly rocked on his heels. Is that what everyone thought? That he'd had an affair while he was married to Blair? "No, Mother. Look, the guests are hungry and this isn't the time to discuss the situation. I'll explain it to you later."

His mother opened her mouth, her protest in the vertical lines between her eyes. He ignored the way her hand came up. "We'd better mingle." He led Shannon to the serving line to speak with the few guests who had come.

He'd have to tell his parents the truth, and the confrontation wouldn't be easy.

SHE MANAGED TO ENDURE THE WEDDING AND RECEPTION. SHANNON KEPT remembering the way Jack's mother had stared at her—like she was an unknown species of tarantula that inspired horror, fear, and curiosity. Jack had taken his dark good looks from both parents, and their reaction to the situation had been a mirror of Jack's horror when pushed into marriage.

Facing the townspeople wasn't easy either. Several of the people who'd avoided her and mocked her in school were there, though with kinder attitudes. Amazing what Jack's mantle of approval could do. Or maybe it was the fact she was grown up now, with a vet's license. That would bestow some credibility upon her too. She wasn't any longer the poor white trash they could torment.

Large stone pillars flanked the paved drive back to the two-story home. Driving the Jeep packed with her few belongings up to the house, she trembled inside. She had to keep reminding herself she had chosen this life for her daughters, or she would have turned the SUV around and jammed the pedal to the floor.

Her face wreathed with smiles, Kylie chattered in the back from her booster seat with her arm around Moses. "I'm going to share a room with my sister. And we're going to build a playhouse with blankets."

Faith probably had a real playhouse, but Shannon didn't destroy her daughter's dream. Kylie would discover what a privileged life was like soon enough. No more buying clothes at Goodwill or taking hand-me-downs from friends at church. No more saving quarters to buy shoes or get those blonde locks trimmed.

Maybe a comfortable life would be enough compensation for a loveless marriage. Especially if the worst happened, and Shannon ended up unable to work. Her symptoms had gotten worse with all the stress of everything.

Shannon wanted to tell Jack about all of it, to share the burden. The words stuck in her throat every time she thought about it. How did she explain Mary Beth? Better to keep quiet and hope the storm passed. He already wondered about Shannon's morals. If he knew about the fix Mary Beth had pulled her into, Jack would question her judgment too.

Jack motioned her to stop by the huge front porch supported by massive white pillars. She'd barely popped the lift gate when four ranch hands began pulling out her boxes. They disappeared through the open double doors with her things. Jack lifted Kylie out of the backseat, then set her down to grab Faith's hand. Moses went to sniff noses with Jack's dog.

Shannon gathered her courage to face her future. Holding her cream skirt down in the wind, she followed him up the wide steps to the porch. Every gray board was spotless. The red doors opened into a wide foyer painted in pale green. Shannon hurried inside before he could make a move to carry her over the threshold. She could only go so far with this marriage thing, and he'd already forced himself to kiss her after the ceremony.

The color soothed her the minute she stepped onto the plush oriental runner protecting the gleaming oak floors. Some kind of spicy candle perfumed the air.

"Wow, Mommy," Kylie said, her voice awed. Her hand crept into Shannon's. "Can I sleep with you?"

Shannon was overwhelmed too. The ceilings rose twelve feet, and a curving staircase swept up to the second floor.

Jack lifted Kylie to his shoulders. "Your room is right across from your mommy's."

"And my room has a door to your room," Faith put in. Her hand crept into Shannon's.

Shannon glanced down at her unknown daughter and squeezed her fingers. It would be worth everything she had to go through to keep the girls together and to get to know this little girl who'd been stolen from her.

"I wanted to share a room with my sister," Kylie said, her lower lip trembling.

"You're tired." Shannon knelt and pulled Kylie into an embrace. "You'll see plenty of Faith. You might even get tired of each other."

"I'll never get tired of my sister." Kylie turned out of Shannon's arms to reach for Faith's hand. Both girls smiled at one another.

Jack put his hand on Kylie's head. She gazed up at him as if he were Barney and Clifford the Big Red Dog all rolled into one. "I had double beds put in both rooms. You can share a room whenever you want to. And then you can go back to your own rooms whenever you want."

Jack's gaze met hers, and she saw a surprising softness in his eyes that warmed her. At least he was showing affection to Kylie, who was lapping it up like a kitten.

"Your rooms are this way." Carrying Kylie on his shoulders, he led them up the gleaming oak staircase to a wide hallway that stretched in both directions from the stairs. He turned right and strode along the thick carpet to a set of doors at each side of the hall. Setting Kylie down, he opened the door on his left. "This is your room, Shannon. The girls have the connecting rooms across the hall. You can hear them from here very well."

Shannon peeked into the room. "It looks new. The furniture, I mean." The air held the faint odor of paint. The walls were pale pink and so was the carpet. White country-french furniture brightened the room even more. A pink-and-yellow quilt covered the pillow-top mattress, and silk pillows in both colors nearly overflowed the bed. She fell in love with her bedroom the minute she saw it.

"Daddy used to sleep in there," Faith said, still clinging to Shannon's hand. "It was all dark, but he said you'd like it prettier. Besides, he said girls need their own bathrooms for their smelly stuff. It's painted pink too. Daddy let me pick the color."

"It's lovely," she said, smiling her thanks. He'd done all this for her? She had trouble taking it all in.

He shrugged and turned to the rooms across the hall. "I let Faith pick out the color of their new stuff too. She wanted the white furniture you had."

Both rooms had double canopy beds, pink and white. Definitely girlish and sweet. A picture caught her attention. "Unicorns?"

He shrugged. "Faith loves them."

"So does Kylie." They shared glances, then she turned back to examine the room again. He'd dropped quite a bit of money redoing all three rooms. Her smile faded. Not that money made up for the distance between them. But this circumstance wasn't for her. She had to remember that. It touched her even more that he would do this for Kylie.

Jack left her to unpack. Shannon laid out Kylie's clothes first, then while the girls played, she went to her room and shut the door. Opening her suitcase, she put her clothes away, then got out her cell phone. Nothing. No word about Mary Beth since Wednesday night. It was like the lull before the storm though. Shannon was sure the man wasn't through with her yet, and the waiting was taking a toll on her health. If only she knew what to do.

13

THE DINING ROOM TABLE GROANED UNDER THE WEIGHT OF THE SUNDAY evening dinner Enrica had prepared. Jack sat at the head of the table. He could hardly bear to see Shannon in Blair's place, and it was easier to avert his eyes and not deal with it.

Faith chattered to her grandmother, but his mom's gaze kept flitting from her to Kylie. His mother's eyes glazed over at the steady stream of little-girl talk. Horses, new beds, a new sister. Faith's life was exciting, at least to hear her tell it.

The turkey tasted like sand in his mouth, and Enrica's famous dressing didn't lift him out of his dread. He ate a piece of pie, but it was like eating dust.

At seven, his mother pushed away from the table. "Enrica, you put the children to bed. I'd like to talk to the newlyweds."

Jack and Shannon exchanged resigned glances and rose to join the elder MacGowans in the living room. Shannon had so far only ventured from her room to the dining room since church, and he watched her take in the thick carpet, the ornate ceiling, the massive stone fireplace, and the leather seating clustered around it.

"It's a lovely room," she whispered to him.

Her awe touched him. Maybe he'd be able to give her and Kylie things they would never experience otherwise. But a man wanted to be respected and loved for more than his possessions. He had no idea what Shannon thought of him as a person other than her contempt for what he'd done in high school.

He dropped onto the sofa so she could sit beside him. A unified front might put his parents off a bit. His mother took the seat to the right of the fireplace, and his father sat down in the opposite chair.

His mother folded her hands in her lap. "Now children, tell us what's going on. The resemblance between the girls is—quite remarkable."

"That's because they're twins," Shannon said. Her hands lay on her thighs, and her voice didn't reveal any stress.

Nothing like jumping right into open war. Jack nodded. "That's right. They're twins."

Alexis gasped and put her hand to her throat. "Twins? I don't understand." She glanced across the rug to her husband. "Senator, do you know what they're talking about?"

His mother had called his father Senator from the moment he won his first race twenty years ago. Jack used to think it an affectation that proclaimed her own status, but he'd come to realize his mother really was proud of Dad. The endearment was more for his father's ego than for hers.

His father cleared his throat. "I think the young'uns are about to tell us, poppet. Settle down and let 'em talk."

Jack took Shannon's hand. "Both girls are Shannon's." He waited for the gasps to end. "Blair's dear aunt switched our dead baby with one of Shannon's girls."

His mother's head swung from side to side as though to clear it. "Verna did this? I don't believe it." But the color drained from her face.

"She did." Jack wasn't sure how much more to say. His mother was sure to want to know why Verna would do such a thing, and the minute she found out Shannon had delivered the girls out of wedlock, Alexis's attitude would take a major shift. At least his dad's attitude had softened. He was in his "win the vote" mode.

"What was she thinking?" Alexis murmured. She twisted her huge rings on her fingers.

"She wasn't thinking at all or she wouldn't have done it," Jack said.

Shannon inhaled, a gentle sigh, and her glance at him held gratitude. She straightened from her slouch against the sofa. "She thought she was doing me a favor. I had no husband. I was going off to college. She thought it would be impossible for me to support two children by myself."

Jack shook his head. "That was how she rationalized it. The reality is, she did it for Blair. Blair's life was wrapped up in the baby. It was a miracle she carried the baby to term in the first place. The doctor didn't think she'd get pregnant again. Verna saw her chance to make Blair happy and took it."

"Land sakes," Alexis said, her voice nearly inaudible. "How was this discovered?"

"We ran into one another and saw the girls together. Neither of us knew which was our own daughter." The memory of that horror still dogged his dreams. "They're too much alike to miss the resemblance. And they look just like Shannon."

The senator crossed one leg over the other. "So you married to take care of both girls. You did good, Son."

His wife stared at him as though he'd just sprouted cactus from his forehead. She looked back to Jack. "But you don't love one another."

"We'll learn to," Jack said. He'd mouthed the words, but did he really intend to learn to love her? He wasn't ready to let anyone take Blair's place. Shannon's hand twitched in his, but he kept hold of it. This whole thing might be harder than he'd imagined.

His father managed a smile. "Welcome to the family, Shannon. It's easy to see where the girls got their looks." He stretched out his legs. "Interesting legends in that old canyon your uncle owned. You ever go looking for Spanish artifacts with your daddy?"

Her hand clutched his tighter. "The desire to find the treasure killed my parents. I believe in letting the dead rest in peace."

"Of course. I'm sorry about your parents. You look very much like your mother."

"I get that a lot."

Jack glanced down at her. The tension in her voice made him wonder. His dad was just making idle conversation, but her cheeks had lost color and she had his hand in a death grip. "It's just legend," he said.

The senator cleared his throat. "You know the stories, Jack. Spaniards, gold coins, gold mines. The rumors picked up again in 1980 when a hiker was backpacking on a trail in the Big Bend. He stumbled on a jeweled gold cross, washed down from someplace on the hill. I always reckoned that cross was part of a treasure hidden after Indians massacred a band of Spaniards. Folks looked for more at the time, but it was all big hat but no cattle."

Shannon's fingers dug into his hand even tighter, and Jack gave her arm an absent pat.

"I reckon she could tell you more than me." Senator Jack's smile was genial. "Her pa told me he'd found the mother lode. The whole enchilada. Maybe it's buried with him."

Shannon's lips tightened, but she still said nothing.

"Any idea how much treasure we're talking?" Jack asked, glancing at Shannon.

"My dad said it would be worth at least two million," she said with obvious reluctance.

"That was over fifteen years ago. I reckon it's closer to fifty million in today's market. Folks are hungry to get their hands on artifacts."

"Fifty million," Shannon said, her voice barely above a whisper.

"Mighty fine, isn't it? You'd be a rich woman if you could figure out where your daddy found it." The senator stood. "Ready to go home, poppet?"

While Jack hugged his parents good-bye and saw them off, his mind played with the idea. Could the treasure still be out there? He had no need of the money, but his sense of adventure kicked in. He couldn't imagine touching artifacts that had been last held by a Spaniard who walked this land in the 1500s. That was only a few years after Columbus sailed. He could imagine the thick gold, the jewels.

Shannon touched his elbow. "You're thinking about the treasure, aren't you?"

"The thought has its hooks in me," he admitted.

"I hoped you'd be above that kind of greed." Her voice was low and sad, not angry.

"It's not greed."

"You don't need the money. You just want it."

"You're not intrigued at the thought of seeing something so ancient?"

Her head whipped from side to side. "I don't want to see it again." She rushed up the stairs.

It was only after he'd heard the door to her bedroom slam that he realized she'd said "again."

THE ROOM SMELLED NEW. NEW CARPET, NEW PAINT, NEW FURNISHINGS. New marriage.

Shannon lay snuggled in the big bed. She fingered the wedding band on her hand. She'd never been much for jewelry, and the ring was almost a brand of ownership. After meeting Jack's family, she realized she had a reputation to uphold. She hadn't considered how her life might change so drastically as a MacGowan.

Jack had surprised her tonight. He'd told his parents the truth about Verna instead of letting Shannon take the blame. It was a tiny piece of the puzzle that was her husband. It would take many months before she was able to make out the picture. It held a smudge because of his obsession with the treasure, though. She'd thought better of him.

The pillows under her head were the finest down. The thread count on the sheets and quilt had to be at least a thousand. They were soft as satin, and Enrica had washed them enough to get the starch out. Comfort cocooned her, and she stretched out, letting every inch of her body luxuriate in it.

She should be happy. Kylie was going to be cared for, but the uncomfortable sensation under her breastbone made her squirm in the lap of luxury. Guilt, pure and simple.

A whisper of movement caught her attention, then two small bodies leaped onto the bed. Giggling, the girls pounced on her. Shannon threw back the covers. "You want to sleep with me?"

Kylie squealed, "Yes!" Both girls snuggled under the quilt against her. The early fall night sent a chill through her open window, and the warm little bodies comforted Shannon.

With a child on each side, she closed her eyes and tried to sleep, but she realized the girls had left the bedroom door open. She should get up and shut it. Before she could summon the determination to let loose her hold on her daughters, another hint of movement caught her attention. The moonlight touched the face of the man who stood framed in the doorway with Wyatt at his side.

"Jack." Instinctively, Shannon pulled the quilt to her chin. "What are you doing?"

"Sorry to disturb you. I was just making sure of the girls' whereabouts. Looks like they're with you."

"They just got here a few minutes ago. I think Kylie was keeping Faith awake."

"Most likely it was Faith. She doesn't sleep well."

"Neither does Kylie."

He took a step into the room. "Is there anything you need?"

"No, we're fine." Before he could turn to go, she burst out, "What made you say yes, Jack? You could have fought for Faith." Her hand tightened on the shoulder of the twin on her left. *But I never would have given her up. The girls need each other.*

"I didn't want to put her through something like that. Or Kylie either."

He might have won. With his father's influence and his wealth, what jury would have awarded her Faith? "I'll try not to embarrass you. I'll learn everything I should know about being the wife you need at functions and dinners. I know how people here used to think about me, but I'll never give them cause to mock me again. You won't have to be ashamed of me."

His teeth gleamed in the moonlight, and his soft laugh made her insides flutter. She'd never heard him laugh, and the sound was as enjoyable as the song of the bluebirds she'd heard in the meadow the other day. It made her want to move closer and see the amusement in his eyes, to let his breath touch her face, to sense his indulgence of her.

She mentally shook herself. There was no future to *that* kind of relationship.

"I don't get out all that often, Shannon. My life isn't like my parents'. I like to eat at home. I look forward to having a second daughter. I don't expect you to be anyone but who you are."

"Thank you for standing up to your parents for me tonight," she said, the impulsive words blurting from her mouth when he turned to leave. Was she trying to get him to stay? How pathetic. "I mean, you could have let me take the blame, but you didn't."

"None of this is your fault."

"It's not yours either."

He shook his head. "We were both caught up in something we never reckoned could happen. I think we're dealing with it pretty well."

"Me too. Good night."

"Good night." His teeth gleamed again. Then he stepped out of the doorway.

The flutter of breeze from the evening air turned colder. Shannon told herself it had nothing to do with his absence.

JACK CHECKED THE HORSES BEFORE HE WENT TO BED. EVERYTHING WAS quiet. On his way to his room, he heard a cell phone ring from inside Shannon's room. He heard the soft murmur of her voice, then the sound of the closet door sliding open. He leaned against the wall until she appeared, fully dressed.

She paused when she saw him standing there. "Did I wake you?" she asked.

"No, I was up. A problem?"

She nodded. "A dog hit by a car. Grady is with a foaling mare and called to ask me if I could go."

He winced. "Want me to come? Enrica is here with the girls."

She hesitated, and he interpreted her expression. "Let me tell Enrica. I'll meet you at the truck."

"Thanks," she mumbled.

He rapped on Enrica's door and told her the situation, then rushed down the steps to the truck outside. Shannon was already inside with her knapsack. "How bad?" he asked, dropping the truck lever into drive.

"Bad. I'm probably going to have to put him down." Her voice trembled.

He shot a quick glance her way. "Your first?"

She shook her head. "But it's never easy."

"Whose is it?"

"Judge Julia Thompson's."

He winced. "Porter? He's a great dog."

"I remember him, I think. A collie mix, right?"

"Yeah. He's probably ten or twelve years old now." They rode in silence the rest of the way to town. Bluebird Crossing slumbered under the stars. The only lighted area they passed was the parking lot at the grocery store. At the judge's two-story stucco place, lights blazed from the upstairs and the kitchen windows. He saw movement by the street and saw Julia crouching on the tree lawn with Porter's head in her lap.

Shannon was out of the truck before he managed to throw the lever into park. He followed her to the dog and its mistress.

Julia's face was wet with tears. "Kids racing. They didn't even stop. I let him out to do his business and had his leash in my hand. He heard the kids laughing and jerked the end of it out of my hand. He was in the street before I could react."

Shannon knelt beside the injured dog and touched his head. He was panting. Jack watched her run her hands over his spine and twisted legs. His heart sank when she shook her head.

"I'm sorry, Judge," she said. "He's all busted up inside. His spine is broken. There's nothing I can do for him except put him out of pain."

"Do it then," Julia said fiercely. She pulled the dog closer and spoke to Porter in a soothing voice. "Such a good dog you've been, my friend. Go wait for me in heaven at the Rainbow Bridge. I'll be along soon. Chase some rabbits until I get there."

Shannon was weeping as she filled the syringe. It was all Jack could do to hold back his own emotion as he watched her kneel and administer the shot. Seconds later Porter relaxed in Julia's arms. The judge broke into loud sobbing and hugged her dog one last time.

"You want me to take him?" Shannon asked, her voice choppy.

"I'd like to have him cremated," Julia said. "If you could arrange that, I'd be grateful."

"I'll take care of it," Shannon promised. "Jack, would you open the back of your truck?"

"I can take Porter. He's heavy."

"I'd like to do it," Shannon said. She lifted the big dog's body in her arms and carried him to the truck, where she laid him on an old blanket. She walked back to where Julia stood on the tree lawn. "Is there anything I can do for you?" she asked.

Julia shook her head. "Thank you. For caring, for giving him peace."

Shannon wiped her cheeks. "I'm so sorry, Judge. I'll see you get his ashes back in a week or so." She patted Julia's arm, then walked back to the truck and got in.

Jack shut the tailgate, hugged Julia and waited until she was inside, then went to the truck as well. When he got inside the cab, he found Shannon with her face in her hands and her shoulders heaving. He put his arm around her. "It's okay," he whispered in her hair.

"Sometimes I wonder why I wanted to be a vet," she muttered.

He smoothed her hair, relishing its softness. Fairy hair, Kylie called it. "It's good you care. The animals can sense that."

She raised her head. "Thanks for coming with me, Jack. I . . . I needed you."

The raw words struck his heart. She wasn't as strong as she seemed, this new wife of his. He needed to remember to be gentler. He brushed his lips across her soft cheek, then moved back under the steering wheel and drove toward home.

14

THE NEXT WEEK FELL INTO AN EVEN TENOR. SHANNON RODE TO THE Mustang Makeover with Jack. After the bonding the night of Porter's death, the silences between them began to thaw to a guarded camaraderie, and she looked forward to the few words they exchanged along the way. She'd tried to call Mary Beth several more times, but the only answer was the voice mail. The man who wanted money didn't contact her again. She called the Texas Rangers daily and received the expected answer: they had no new leads. Shannon didn't know what to think, what to do. She'd never been so helpless.

In spite of the uncertainty over Mary Beth, her health was better now, and she was more clearheaded. Enrica claimed it was the food she served. The housekeeper thought gluten was the root of all evil and eliminating it would fix anything, but Shannon thought resolving her daughters' futures might play a part.

Wednesday evening of the following week, she walked out of the Mustang Makeover camp toward Jack's truck. The training was going well, and the mustangs were animals they could all be proud of. Jack wasn't at the truck yet, so she opened the door to throw in her backpack, then climbed in and pulled out her cell phone. Nothing from Mary Beth. She dialed her friend's number again, but it was with no real sense of hope.

"Shannon?" Mary Beth's whisper came over the soft buzz of the phone. "Are you okay?"

Relief made Shannon lightheaded. The sound of her friend's voice was welcome music. "Are *you* okay? I've been worried sick! Some big guy is wanting money. What's going on?"

"I never meant for it to turn out this way," Mary Beth said, her voice catching on a sob. "I wanted to help you. But I don't want to hurt him either. I love him, but what he did to you was wrong. He has to make restitution whether he wants to or not."

"What who did?" Shannon had no idea what Mary Beth was babbling about. "I'm fine, Mary Beth. You don't have to worry about me. I got a box of your hair. Are you all right?"

"That was just to scare you. He . . . he wouldn't hurt me. Not really." But she didn't sound convinced. "I've got to go. I'll try to call later." The phone clicked off.

Shannon threw the phone onto the seat and fought tears. She knew no more now than she had five minutes ago. At least Mary Beth was alive. But the fear in her voice contradicted her words. She was in trouble.

She turned her head toward the window and saw her cousin Curt outside her door with his hands in his jeans pockets. Throwing open her door, she jumped out. "Curt, what are you doing here?"

The hot wind blew his blond hair back from his face, and he was smiling. "Hey, Shannon, I thought I'd find you here. Sorry I missed the wedding."

When was the last time she'd seen him—five years ago maybe? They exchanged a brief, awkward hug. "I'd thought I could count on one person to be at my side at the wedding," she said, smiling to show him she was teasing. "But it's not like we gave you much notice. What are you doing in town?"

He smiled. "I wondered if I might get the key to the old place and get some mementos. Do you mind?"

"Not at all. Anything in particular you're looking for? Though I guess you'd know where stuff is more than I would. You've been back more often."

"Pop had a box of old papers and mementos of my mom's. It's about so big." His hands measured out about ten inches. "The top has an eagle carved into it."

"I don't think I've ever seen it." She dug out a key. "Feel free to look around though. You can leave the key on the counter. I have a duplicate."

He pocketed the key. "How's married life?"

"Fine. Have you met Jack?" She thought they'd gone to school together.

"Everyone knows the great man." His lip curled.

"You sound as though you don't like him."

Curt shrugged. "In school he had the prettiest girls, the best spot on the football team. When he ran for class president, no one ran against him. He doesn't know what hardship is."

"His wife died, Curt." And his daughter, but Curt didn't need to know that story. At least not yet.

Curt's blue eyes softened. "Sorry, I assumed he was divorced."

He put his hand on her shoulder and the warmth seeped through to her skin. "You okay, Shannon? I want you to know I'm here for you if you ever need anything. We're all the family that's left."

Her voice dried up at the affection in his voice. He'd never tried to make her feel like an outsider, so why had she always felt she stood beyond the circle formed by him and his dad, out in the dark where she was frightened all the time? Once her parents died, she'd been a phantom—nameless, voiceless, unseen. Looking back now, she wondered if some of the isolation had been of her own making. A way of dealing with her pain by keeping everyone at arm's length.

She found her voice. "I'm good. Really, Curt. Hey, whatever happened to that old motor home my parents lived in? I've been thinking about it lately. I never went through it after they died."

Curt frowned. "I'm not sure, but I think Pop had it hauled to the dump. The one on the south side of town. I'm sure Pop went through it." He glanced at his watch. "Listen, I've got to run."

Curt was probably right about the motor home being empty, but Shannon longed to take a look. Now that she was married and had the twins reunited, she had been thinking about them often. They would have loved her girls. The junkyard was on the way home. She saw Jack heading toward the truck. Maybe she could talk him into stopping a minute.

"Ready to head home?" Jack asked when he reached her.

Home. A real home with happy children. It was worth all the silences between her and Jack. "I'm ready." She climbed into the truck and faced him when he did the same. "Would you mind stopping at the old junkyard for a minute?"

He shot an amused glance her way. "You in the market for an old car?"

"Not exactly." She explained what she had in mind.

"If that thing has been there for fifteen years, it's bound to be full of nasty critters. You sure you're up to it?"

She suppressed a shudder. "Just a quick peek."

He started the engine and dropped the transmission lever into drive. "You got it."

Shannon gazed out over the dry landscape. After a lush spring, the grasses had turned to fire tinder this summer, the last bit of moisture baked out by the sun. She caught a whiff of new fires that were burning.

He turned in the drive to the junkyard. There was little rust on the decaying vehicles because of the dry climate. "You see it?"

It was hard to distinguish the jumble of twisted metal. "Not yet. There's the office. Maybe we can ask." She ran her window down and the heat blasted inside.

"I'll check." He parked and got out, then disappeared inside the office. He reappeared by her open window a minute or two later. "The guy says it's back by the fence. He knew right where to send us because someone else was asking yesterday. He didn't let them back since they had no ID. He knows I married you so he's cool with letting us go back."

Shannon stared up at him. "That's strange," she said slowly. "Did he know who it was? I can't imagine their trailer would interest anyone but me."

"He just said it was a guy. Big shoulders. Curly hair."

The guy who'd attacked her in the kitchen at her uncle's ranch? She suppressed a shudder. He was still lurking about, even though she hadn't seen him.

"What?" Jack appeared perplexed by her reaction.

She'd never told Jack about the attacks or about Mary Beth's situation. She stole a peek at his strong face. So far she'd seen only evidence of honesty and integrity. Maybe she dared trust him with this problem. "It's a long story."

He opened her door. "You can tell me while we walk back there." He grabbed a broom leaning by the main office on their way past.

Shannon launched into the story. He interrupted occasionally with a question. "So I guess the guy looking for the motor home might be that same person," she finished. Jack wasn't saying much. She peeked at him from the corner of her eye. His clenched jaw told her as much as his silence.

"Why didn't you tell me about this right away? You put our girls in danger by keeping this to yourself. I could have had my ranch hands watching out for all of us."

Her anger began to simmer. "You've not shown yourself to be the most trustworthy person in the past, Jack. I haven't seen that guy for several weeks, so I assumed he realized I didn't know anything. If I thought the girls were in any real danger, I would have asked you for help."

"You think it's only the girls I'm worried about?" He stopped and took her arm in a tight grip. "You think I wouldn't take a bullet for you too? This is a dangerous situation—for everyone. The girls could get caught in crossfire or knocked down and hurt accidentally. They don't have to be targets to be injured. Neither do you."

"Jack, I'd die for my daughters. You don't have to worry about me not protecting them." She didn't bother to temper her tone.

"I didn't say you were a bad mother," he said. "But we're a team now. I don't want any secrets in the house, especially ones as serious as this. I'm not that same kid who let you down, Shannon. I'll never do it again. You can trust me." His gaze locked with hers. "Do you think this is about the Spanish treasure? Do you know where it is?"

She tugged her arm free. "I see the motor home." Not even Jack had the right to ask her that question. Later, when she was alone, she would examine the way her blood warmed at his promise to her. Maybe she could relinquish the secrets she held close.

She stared at the vehicle's sorry state. The blue stripes on the side were sun-faded. Dents big enough to put her fist into peppered the side facing her. The window in the door had been busted out, and the motor home sat on concrete blocks instead of tires. Once upon a time, Shannon had thought it the most beautiful place in the world. Now it was nothing but a heap of metal.

She tugged on the door handle. "It's stuck."

"Let me try."

She moved out of the way and Jack's big hand closed around the handle. He twisted and tugged until the door screeched open. Stale air rushed out, and a bird squawked and flew from inside. Debris littered the floor, obliterating the vinyl. Jack took the broom and swept out the cobwebs hanging in their way.

"I don't hear any rattlers, at least not yet," he said. He mounted the bent steps and stared up at the ceiling before sweeping it clean too. He crushed several spiders that dropped down.

Shannon gasped when something dark moved. "A tarantula!" She pointed behind him.

"Step out of the way."

She moved to the front of the motor home and watched him sweep the massive spider out the door. It lay motionless for a moment, then began to crawl slowly away. Nasty things.

Jack poked his head out the door. "All clear, at least for now," he said. "You want to come in?"

She wanted to chicken out, but he'd already gone to so much trouble for her, she didn't dare. "I'll be right there." Her gaze searched the nooks and crannies she could see from the doorway before stepping up onto the floor.

"You all lived in this little place?" he asked.

"I slept in the bed over the cab, and my parents had the back bedroom," she said. "I loved it. It was like sleeping in a tree house." She started for the bedroom, but he stopped her.

"Let me check back there first." Broom in hand, he strode down the hallway. He pushed open the door, then backed away fast. "It's full of rattlers and I saw another tarantula. I don't think you want to go in there."

She didn't. Making a hasty retreat, she rushed for the steps but stopped short of them when her gaze landed on the small metal box her dad had kept his maps and notes in. She snatched it up and disturbed a scorpion that ran toward her boot. Shuddering, she squashed it before it could run up her pant leg.

"Have I mentioned I hate spiders and scorpions?" she muttered when Jack joined her.

"You braved something like this for Wyatt." His gaze held admiration, then his attention went to what she held. "What's that?"

"A box of my dad's."

"Want me to look inside and make sure there's nothing in there?"

She handed it to him. "Please."

He tried to open it. "I think it's locked. I'll get my tools at home, see if I can jimmy it."

"There might be a key at Uncle Earl's. He had a key to everything."

"We'll run over and look after supper if the Baileys don't stay too long. I'm sure you'd like me to preserve the box if I can."

Sometimes her new husband surprised her with his perception and compassion. He'd been a rock for her today. She leaned over and squeezed his hand as they walked back to the truck. His eyebrow arched, but he returned the pressure of her hand and didn't let go as they walked to the vehicle.

WHEN JACK PULLED INTO THE DRIVEWAY, HIS HAND STILL TINGLED FROM the way Shannon held it at the junkyard. "The Baileys are already here," he said, noticing Rick's truck.

"Looks like they just got here," Shannon said as the doors to the truck swung open.

They greeted their friends, then invited them inside. The aroma of pot roast filled the house, and his mouth watered. He'd have to give more of an effort during dinner tonight. The sight of Shannon in Blair's place had been painful at meals so far, he'd kept his head down and left the table as soon as he could.

"How are your mustangs coming along?" Rick asked once they went to the dining room.

"I've got two that are promising. Faith named them Gent and Dancer. The stallion, Gent, is anything but a gentleman. Dancer is beginning to show promise, but Gent's got an iron mouth and a will to match."

Rick grinned. "Sounds like my wife."

Allie balled her small fist and punched his arm. "I heard that."

Shannon smiled and left the room, returning with a bottle of hot sauce. She poured a liberal amount on her pot roast. Jack stared with open mouth. "What are you doing?"

She stopped. "I like my food hot."

He picked up the bottle. "It's pure habanero peppers."

She plucked it from his hand and dropped it back into her purse. "What else?" She forked a bite of the doctored roast into her mouth. "Yum. You man enough to try it?"

He opened his mouth to refuse, then caught the light of challenge in her eyes. The smirk on Rick's face decided him. "You bet."

He leaned over and dug his fork into her plate of food, taking a generous bite of the roast with the most sauce. The minute the sauce hit his tongue, he knew he'd made a mistake. The heat froze his vocal cords and the muscles in this throat seized. For a horrifying moment, he thought he'd choke on the lump of meat trying to make it past his esophagus.

He reached for his glass of milk, and the struggle to breathe past the pain made him so unsteady that he knocked it over. The liquid splattered onto Shannon's lap. He wanted to tell her he was sorry, but he still could make no sound.

Shannon grabbed her glass of water. "Here." She thrust it into his hand.

He downed it like a drowning man, but the heat only intensified. "Milk," he managed to croak.

Shannon shot to her feet and rushed to the kitchen. Jack looked around wildly for anyone who had milk. The girls. Lurching to his feet, he staggered around the table to Faith. Or was it Kylie? He snatched the glass she was lifting to her lips and brought it to his own. He barely heard her protest as the cold liquid quenched the fire on his tongue.

The heat had been so intense, moisture coated his eyes. He blinked until the room came into focus and managed a weak grin when Rick broke into guffaws. Shannon rushed back into the room with a glass of milk in her hand.

"Daddy, you drank my milk," Faith said, her glare accusing.

He took the glass from Shannon, who was trying not to giggle. "Here," he said.

"Big tough guy," Rick said. "Felled by a little hot sauce."

"You try it and see if you're still laughing," Jack said under his breath. He stared at his wife with new respect. "You eat that stuff all the time?"

"On everything." Her blue eyes were as bright as last night's stars. "It's an acquired taste. Try it a few more times. What, are you afraid?"

"I'm more afraid of that hot stuff than a long-tail cat in a room full of rockers."

Shannon giggled and put her hand over her mouth. "The look on your face."

Jack realized how tense things had been between them now that he'd heard her laugh. He wanted to hear more of it.

"JACK'S HUMAN AFTER ALL." SHANNON SUPPRESSED ANOTHER GIGGLE. SHE and Allie sat on the large porch while the men went to the barn to check on the horses. The night breeze carried the sound of coyotes and owls to their ears.

Allie rested her hand on her pregnant belly. "You sound surprised."

"I wasn't sure. He's bigger-than-life most times. It's the first weakness I've seen." The breeze lifted Shannon's hair and cooled the back of her neck.

Allie chuckled and pressed her fist against the small of her back. "How are things between the two of you? You seem to be getting along well. He didn't strangle you when you laughed at him."

"We're getting by. I don't know that we'll ever be more than polite roommates though."

"That's what I thought about Rick and me. Or rather, I thought we'd be enemies."

"Enemies?"

"The first time I met him, he yelled at me and implied I was a lousy mother."

Shannon winced. "And he lived to tell the tale?"

"I spared his life, but just barely. I thought we'd have a marriage of convenience only, but at the last minute Rick decided not to say the vows unless he meant to keep them. He said love was a choice and that we could choose to love one another."

"And it worked?"

Allie's white teeth flashed in the dark. "What do you think?"

"Jack said he means to honor his vows, but I'm not feeling much love come my way." Shannon laughed, but only because she didn't want to show Allie how much she was beginning to want more than courtly kindness. She wanted to surprise a fire in his eyes.

Allie studied Shannon's downcast face. "Is any love floating his way?"

"No."

"You think you could love him if you let yourself?"

Could she? Shannon remembered high school and the way she'd daydreamed about Jack. Only to be humiliated. "I don't know. I'm such a loser at love. Not that I've had much experience. The children's father was my one and only disastrous foray into romance."

"Watch Jack stare at you. And go for a trial kiss. He's a red-blooded male. He's nibbling at the bait."

Shannon rolled her eyes. "He's not sure what I'll do next."

"It's always good to keep a guy on his toes," Allie said. Her hand moved to her belly and she rubbed it.

"You having contractions?"

"A few, but they're just getting me ready. I don't think this munchkin will show up for another two weeks. I was right on my due date with Betsy."

"But you're huge. My girls were nearly a month early. You could come at any time."

Allie heaved herself to her feet. "But not tonight. Here come the guys. I'm heading for bed." She called for Betsy, and the little girl came grumbling to take her hand.

The twins followed them to the steps and each child took one of Shannon's hands. Their fingers curled trustingly around hers, and she didn't think she'd ever experienced such contentment.

Jack came toward them beside Rick, and she examined Jack's face in the moonlight. It wasn't just his good looks that drew her, but his tender way with the girls. She'd watched him with his hired hands too. He was demanding but fair. He showed his integrity every day, and that was a powerful accelerant to the attraction she'd always had to him.

When they'd waved good-bye to the Baileys, it was too late to go to her ranch for that key, so she took the girls up for their baths. Half an hour later, the girls were snuggled in the bed beside her. Their hair was still damp, and their skin still held the delicious aroma of soap and little girl. She grabbed a book from the night table and opened it. The girls loved her to read to them before bed.

She brushed her lips across the top of Faith's hair. Small differences were finally beginning to set the girls apart. Faith loved licorice, but Kylie was partial to jelly beans. Kylie had a way of tipping her head to look up while Faith took the world head-on, just like Jack. Faith's hair was slightly shorter than Kylie's. But the biggest difference was Kylie called her "Mommy" and Faith called her "Miss Shannon." She longed to change that, to see Faith's lips form the word *Mommy*.

Faith twisted a lock of Shannon's hair in her fingers. "Your hair is like mine and Kylie's. Why do you look like me?"

There was no easy answer. She'd told Jack he could decide when to tell Faith, and she'd clung to her patience. Every fiber of her being longed to tell her children the truth. They'd be so excited to know they were true sisters. Twins.

"We have fairy hair, don't we, Mommy?" Kylie said. "The fairies gave it to us."

"Well maybe not the fairies. But God did. What we look like is his decision." She smiled at the way the girls looked into one another's faces and giggled. She realized telling them the truth wasn't just about her life and what she wanted, but about the girls being better for knowing too. Their love would deepen beyond friendship.

Faith accepted her answers for now. Shannon wondered if she would remember them later when she found out the truth. She might think Shannon had lied to her.

"Read the story, Mommy," Kylie demanded. She scooted closer to her mother.

Shannon slipped open the book before Faith could ask more questions. "Are you ready to see what Alexander is up to today?" They'd been reading the Judith Viorst books, and today's was *Alexander and the Terrible, Horrible, No Good, Very Bad Day.* She plunged into the story and soon had the girls giggling about Alexander's misadventures.

A light knock came at the door. "Come in," Faith called.

The door swung open, and Jack stepped in. "Sorry to bother you, but it sounded like you all were having too much fun without me. What's going on?"

"Just a story." Shannon held up the book.

His hair stuck up on end, mussed by his hat. A few buttons had come undone on his shirt as if he'd started to get ready for bed, and maybe he had, because he was in his stocking feet.

She sensed he was lonely. "You want to read to them for a while?"

"Yes, Daddy, you read!" Faith bounced up and down in the bed. "Get in bed with us." She threw back the covers.

Shannon froze. Not a good idea. But before she could think up an excuse, Jack crossed the room in four steps and flopped onto his back next to Faith. At least he was on *top* of the covers. He playfully snatched the book from her hand, settled it on his stomach, and began to read.

The lull of his deep voice reading the book loosened the tense muscles in Shannon's back. She settled Kylie on her other arm and watched the delight on the faces of the girls. A complete family. Something she'd wanted all her life. What would it be like to belong to this family completely? To this man? Shannon couldn't wrap her mind around it. She was so used to fighting to survive, to make something of herself. She needed to learn to rest in her circumstances, but she didn't know how.

Jack nestling with them on Faith's other side was somehow right. She wondered if he was thinking of Blair, but she didn't really want to know. Not tonight. Tonight she wanted to imagine there was room for her in his heart too. Her eyelids drifted shut, influenced by the warmth of the bed and the sound of his voice.

There was an absence of sound, and her eyes flew open. How long since he'd quit reading? She glanced over and saw him staring at her.

He had his head propped on one arm, and the soft expression in his eyes made her mouth go dry.

"Sorry I fell asleep," she whispered. "You read well."

His gaze never left her face. "It didn't seem that way when you were snoring."

"I don't snore!"

He grinned. "Gotcha." His gaze drifted to the twins. "The girls are both sleeping. You want me to move them to their beds?"

She realized what she wanted more than anything was for the four of them to be together. For his warm expression to stay right there pinning her to the pillow. "Not yet," she whispered. Her gaze locked with his, and she couldn't look away.

He leaned nearer, over the top of his sleeping daughter. Close enough Shannon could feel his breath on her face. Near enough to see the flecks of gold in his eyes. She lost herself in that gaze. His head started down and she knew he was going to kiss her. Holding her breath, she waited until his warm lips brushed hers. A faint impression of skin-to-skin was all she got before he jerked back and slipped from the bed before she could say a word or even register how that kiss had felt.

"Jack?" she managed to say.

He was fleeing toward the door, but he turned at the sound of his name. "I'm sorry, Shannon, that was out of line."

"I'm your wife," she said. Where had she gotten the courage to imply she welcomed his kiss?

"Blair—" He ran his hand through his hair, disrupting it even more.

Shannon slipped out of bed, avoiding Kylie, and went on bare feet to where he stood. "I know you loved her, Jack. And she loved you.

She'd want you to be able to go on, to make a new life and be happy. Blair wouldn't expect you to mourn the rest of your life. We can make this a real marriage if we want to. If we decide to try to learn to love one another." She couldn't believe she was saying those words. He'd think she was brazen and bold, but she had to speak her piece.

Love was a choice, Allie had said. Shannon believed it too. She put her hand on his chest. His heart thumped against her palm. There was a war going on inside him, and he was the only one who could decide what their future was to be.

His hands came down on her shoulders, and he pulled her toward him. Her pulse gave a leap of joy, but it stumbled almost as quickly.

"No!" He thrust her away and fled the room.

Shannon stood in the empty hallway with the breeze from the open window blowing through her thin nightgown.

15

JACK HAD BEEN A BEAR WITH A SORE HEAD SINCE LAST NIGHT. ON THE drive to and from the mustang camp, he had barely spoken. Shannon wasn't about to ask him to go with her after work to find the key to the lockbox they'd found in the motor home. She decided to ride over to her uncle's ranch on horseback while Jack sequestered himself in his office to write out monthly bills.

She left the girls watching a video while Enrica cooked supper. It wouldn't be dark for a few hours, so she decided to take a detour through the canyon. When she stepped outside, the back of her neck prickled as though someone was watching her. She glanced carefully around the landscape but saw no one. It must have been her imagination. She hadn't seen or heard from the intruder or Mary Beth in days, though Shannon had called and texted her cell phone several times.

The trail through the canyon was a prettier ride, though a bit harder on the horse. She didn't think the mare would complain, though she wished she had Jewel to ride. With the leather reins in her hands and her knees pressing against the saddle, she was at home. The sun baked the skin on her arms, and the steady gait of the horse bounced the cares of the week off her back. Rounding the trail past the wash, she reined in the mare and glanced around. Had she heard something? Carefully staring through the piñon and mesquite trees, she watched for movement. A bird took flight, and she breathed a sigh of relief.

She urged the horse forward again just as a slither of movement came from her left. This time she wasn't going to stop. Digging her heels into the mare's flank, she took off for the house that she could see now. Almost immediately she heard the sound of hoofbeats following. She dared a glance toward the sound and saw a big man mounted on a black horse chasing her. He was too far back to tell for sure, but she was sure it was the guy who had broken into her house and attacked her in the kitchen. Had he been watching her from the hills at Jack's ranch? No wonder she'd sensed something.

She urged the mare into a full-out run. Crouching over the horse's neck, she raced for the safety of the house. She knew where a gun was stashed. If the situation hadn't been so perilous, she would have laughed at the way the man sat in the saddle. He was like a sack of potatoes, letting the horse's gait toss him around. At least it slowed him down.

She reached the house well ahead of her pursuer. Unlocking the door, she leaped inside and slammed it behind her. Throwing the dead bolt, she checked the other doors, then ran to the office and snatched up the shotgun on top of the bookcase. It wasn't loaded, so she jammed two shells into the chamber, then pumped it so it was ready to fire.

The door rattled and she ran to it. "I've got a gun!" she shouted. "I wouldn't mind taking you out."

The knob stopped its movement, then she saw the man's dark head bob past the window. He was heading to the back door. She rushed to the kitchen where she saw the keys she'd come here to find. Stuffing them in her pocket, she watched the doorknob. The weakest link was this door. Any man worth the label could kick it in. The frame around it was rotting, and the latch didn't fully connect.

But the door stayed shut. And quiet. The silence unnerved her. She could sense him waiting. She tiptoed to the sink and glanced out through the window. Her mare was still out at the hitching post. Maybe she'd try for a quick getaway. But no, that wouldn't work. He might be lurking right outside the door.

She had no choice but to call for help. Rick would be closer, but Jack would be furious if she didn't call him. She punched in the number on her cell phone.

He answered on the second ring. "Shannon, where are you?"

"At my uncle's. A guy chased me here on horseback."

"On my way."

The sound of Jack's breathing rattled through the phone. She heard his boot heels clatter over the porch, then the slam of his truck door. "I'm going to call Rick," he said. "He might get there first."

"I'm safe right now. I've got a shotgun pointed at the door." She strained to hear anything past her gasps for breath.

"I'll call you right back."

The phone went dead in her ear and she swallowed past her dry throat. Without Jack's voice, she was alone. Where was the intruder?

He wasn't likely to chase her here then leave her alone. She tipped her head to the side and listened. Was that a creak from upstairs? Stepping to the bottom of the staircase, she scanned the part of the hallway that she could see. When her phone rang, she nearly screamed.

"Rick's not home," Jack said. "I'm almost there though. Where is the guy?"

"I think he might be upstairs," she whispered. "I heard something." She glanced around for somewhere to barricade herself until Jack got there. Maybe the office. She started for the doorway off the stairway hall, but a sudden movement on the steps made her turn and swing up the gun.

The man who had attacked her weeks ago in the kitchen rushed down the steps toward her. In a split second, she registered that he was dressed in camo gear and had close-cropped dark hair and a scar on his forehead. His teeth were bared. Her gaze fastened on his handgun, and almost without thinking, she fired the shotgun. She had aimed the warning shell at his feet, and splinters flew from the steps. He recoiled when the wood exploded at his boots and nearly fell. He stood and brought his gun around as she pumped the gun again and aimed at his chest.

The breath seemed squeezed from her lungs. It was the closest she'd ever come to killing a man. "Move and your liver will be on the back wall," she said. "This is a scatter gun and there will be nothing left of you." Her voice quavered.

"If I squeeze off one round, you're dead," he said, his voice calm. "I'd say it's a standoff."

"With one difference," she panted, her fingers pressing the trigger. "You don't want to kill me because then you'll never get what you want."

He smiled and opened his mouth to speak, but the sound of Jack's truck wiped the smirk from his face.

"That's my husband," Shannon said. "You don't want to meet him."

Footsteps pounded up the porch. The door rattled, then the wood splintered as Jack kicked it in. Her attention was diverted, and in that split moment, the man bolted up the steps and disappeared around the corner.

The strength ran out of Shannon's legs, and she collapsed onto the bottom step as Jack rushed into the house brandishing some kind of automatic gun that was as big as a cannon. She smiled weakly. "You think you're taking out an army?"

His gaze swept the room. "Where is he?"

"Gone." Her hand shook as she pointed upstairs. A window shattered from somewhere on the second floor, and she heard a scrabbling sound on the pump shed roof. That must be how he'd gotten up there.

Jack started toward the door, and her teeth began to chatter. She rocked back and forth on the step until he came back inside.

"He got away," Jack said.

She was so cold. "I want to go home."

He helped her to her feet, and she burrowed against his chest instinctively. He stilled, then his arms came around her and he gripped her in a hold that was the most secure she'd ever felt.

"I've got you," he crooned in her ear.

When she was eight, she'd climbed a ladder that had been left out. Once she was on the barn roof, she couldn't get down. It was too high, too scary. Her father found her and told her he'd catch her if she jumped into his arms. And he had. He'd said those same words to her that Jack whispered against her hair. And then he'd dropped her.

There was danger in leaning too heavily on someone else. Shannon forced herself to remember Jack's reaction last night. It gave her the strength to push away. She tucked a stray lock of hair behind her ear and smiled. "Thanks."

"Why didn't you tell me you wanted to come over here? I would have brought you."

"You weren't speaking to me," she said, clamping down on her teeth so they didn't chatter. She didn't wait for his answer but shoved open the shattered door and stepped out onto the porch. The sun was beginning to go down.

"What do you think you're doing?" Jack stood with his hands on his hips and his hat pushed to the back of his head. "We need to report this to the sheriff."

"I'm fixing to head home." She grabbed the mare's reins. "I'll call the sheriff from there."

"That guy just chased you across the desert. How'd he know you were out there?"

"I think he was watching the ranch. I sort of sensed it but thought it was my imagination." She mounted and settled into the saddle. "I can't leave the mare here," she pointed out.

"I'll ride her back." He made a swipe for the reins, but the horse backed away.

"If you're worried, you can follow me in the truck. It's four-wheel drive. I can take the long way through the desert rather than through the canyon."

She wheeled and started out across the desert. She heard Jack mutter, but the wind snatched the meaning of his words. Peeking back, she saw he was following in the truck. She probably shouldn't have been so difficult. He could have ridden the mare and she could have taken the truck, but she needed the time to collect her thoughts. And her courage.

She glanced to her right and saw Jewel's outline on the craggy outcropping. Reining in her horse, she whistled softly through her teeth. The black stallion began to pick his way down the rocks toward her. He'd nearly reached her when his head came up and his ears went back. He turned to stare into the darkness behind them, then snorted and ran off.

Was that guy out there? Shannon shuddered and urged her mare into a trot.

JACK TURNED ON HIS HIGH BEAMS TO ILLUMINATE THE WAY, BUT THE MARE pulled ahead of the light and made better time than he did in his truck. There were too many holes and washes to go very fast. Just his being behind Shannon should be a deterrent to whoever was following her.

The guy could have shot her. What was the money thing all about? His response to her last night had scared the fire out of him. She burned as hot as the Triple-M brand in his mind, scorching his memories of Blair, tossing his notions of what he had planned for his life onto a bonfire.

He killed the engine and watched Shannon dismount. She dragged her left foot as she led the mare to the barn. He got out and jogged to intercept her. "You go on into the house. You're limping. Did the guy hurt you?"

"No, I'm fine."

But she didn't protest when he took the reins from her, though she followed him into the barn. "Supper is probably on the table," he said. "Enrica's gonna be meaner than a junkyard dog if her meal's ruined."

"All the more reason to wait for you." She gave a mock shudder, and they began to walk together toward the barn.

"Did you whistle for that horse? The big black stallion?"

"That's Jewel. My dad got him just before he died. My uncle let him roam the ranch."

He wouldn't mind getting a closer look at the stallion. "You want to bring him here?"

She looked at him for a moment. "I don't know that he'd come. I'd like him to get used to staying on the property though. He could roam for miles."

"Where'd your dad get him?"

She hiked the leg of her jeans and propped her booted foot on a bale of hay. "I'm not really sure. He's got a brand on him that shows he's a thoroughbred. He has this lovely fluid motion when he moves. And he can run like a devil wind."

"I'd like to get a better look at him." Something nagged at him, a memory or story his dad had mentioned. "With all the excitement, did you get the keys you went after?"

She dug in her pocket and pulled them out, jingling them in front of his face. "Yep."

He finished currying the horse, then took the keys. "Quite a fistful. What do they all go to?"

"Who knows? Uncle Earl kept everything he ever owned. This hunk of keys is an accumulation of his whole life."

"Did your cousin find what he was looking for?"

"I don't know. I haven't talked to him. I didn't see the keys I loaned him on the counter though, so I'm guessing he hasn't. I'll check in with him later."

He motioned for her to go ahead of him out of the barn, then slid the door closed. "I'll call the sheriff while you go get the box."

"Back in a minute." Her gait was awkward as she ran ahead of him and disappeared inside.

The limp he'd noticed several times before they married was back. He should probably insist she see a doctor. He called the sheriff and explained what happened, then stopped to pet the dogs. Shannon met him in the foyer when he stepped inside the door. The aroma of fried chicken greeted him. She had the metal box in her hand.

"Let's go to the office," he said. "Quick, before Enrica comes after us with a butcher knife." He liked the sound of her laughter, but she quickly muffled it and followed him down the hall to the office. He swung the door shut and she set the box on his desk.

"Enrica will be pounding at the door any minute. How'd she do fried chicken with no wheat?"

"Rice flour," he muttered, peering at the tiny lock. He sorted through the jumble of keys on the ring. Not many were small enough to fit. He tried three and none of them opened it. "There's one more." The key slid easily into the slot, and there was a click when he turned it. "Got it!"

He straightened and peeked inside, rustling through the papers. "Seems critter free. You want to go through the papers by yourself?"

She hesitated, then shook her head. "I'd like you to stay."

He could drown in the deep water of her eyes. He slid the box toward her, and the lid slammed shut again. Her hand shook when she reached toward it. "What do you think is in it?"

"I don't know, but it's a piece of my parents." Her fingers fumbled with the box, but she managed to get it open again. She touched the papers lying on top, and they crackled under her hand. "Old newspaper articles." She lifted them out one by one, opened them, and laid them on the desk. That was it. Nothing but the papers.

Jack stood by and let her have quiet for the job. He flipped on the desk light. "You could sit down," he said when he noticed she swayed where she stood. "You look exhausted."

"I am." She dragged her foot as she went around to the chair and dropped into it.

He moved the pile of papers and the box across the desk to her. She picked up the first article and began to read. "This is so strange," she said. "It's an article about a stolen racehorse." She held it up to him. "He looks like Jewel. This says his name is Five Lives."

He held the article under the lamp and scanned it. "I haven't seen the horse up close and personal, but it resembles him. I saw Five Lives race once—he was poetry in motion. Do you remember what Jewel's brand looks like? There's a picture here."

"I didn't see the picture." She held out her hand and he gave it back. Her lips pursed as she read. "That's it—that's his brand." She chewed on her lip. "He must have been stolen."

"I can try to find out more, get in touch with the owner."

She winced and lurched to her feet. "Oh, Jack—no, please! I can't lose Jewel. He was hurt when he came here. Someone beat him. I'm the only one he trusts. I can't give him back to some monster."

Jack glanced back down at the clipping. "The newspaper article says he's worth over a million dollars."

"Surely not now. His racing days are over."

"If he's really Five Lives, his owner could make a fortune on stud fees. Finding his owner is the right thing to do, Shannon."

Her eyes pled with him. "Not yet. Let's figure this out first."

He couldn't say no with her face soft with yearning. Nodding, he opened the door. "I'll poke around quietly and see if the owner is even still looking. Maybe he's dead or out of racing."

She went past him into the hall. It would kill her to turn over that horse, and Jack found himself praying fervently that she wouldn't have to. Even if he kept her at arm's length, he didn't want to see her hurt.

16

THE HOUSEHOLD SLEPT. ALL EXCEPT FOR SHANNON. COULD HER DAD HAVE stolen Jewel? Or rather Five Lives, if that was really his name. She wouldn't have thought he would do something like that, but maybe he'd thought to sell the horse and get enough money to fund his treasure hunt. How well did a kid know her parents? And was there any connection between Jewel and Mary Beth? Could the horse be the basis of the money the guy wanted? But no, Mary Beth never even knew about Jewel. Shannon hadn't mentioned him.

Maybe her dad bought the horse not knowing he was stolen. Shannon liked that possibility better. But if he didn't know, why would he have kept those clippings locked up? Unless maybe he'd found out later and hadn't been any more willing to turn the horse over to his abuser than she was. Her head hurt from thinking about it.

Maybe some hot cocoa would help her sleep. She slipped out of bed and tiptoed out the door and down the steps. Jack had night-lights along the floor for the girls, and she had no trouble seeing, even with the vision in her left eye blurry. When Enrica saw her today, she'd asked Shannon if she'd eaten any bread, and sure enough, she'd had a piece of cake at the mustang mess hall. A cowboy had brought it in to celebrate his birthday. Maybe Enrica was onto something.

She warmed milk on the stove—no microwave for Enrica—then dumped in some hot chocolate mix. A few minutes later, cupping her hands around the warm cup, she inhaled the steam and moved to the table, where she eased into a chair.

Jack was noticing her unsteadiness. He'd commented on her limp. How much longer could she keep her secret? And should she? How could she think of making this marriage real if she remained unwilling to let him know about her MS?

She sipped the drink, letting the chocolate sit on her tongue. A noise came from behind her and she saw Faith shuffle into the kitchen, rubbing her eyes. "Hey, sweetie, what are you doing up?"

"I woke up and went to your room, but you were gone," the little girl said, her eyes accusing.

"Want some milk, baby girl?" Jack asked, appearing in the doorway behind Faith. He wore a Dallas Cowboys T-shirt and dark blue pajama bottoms. He was barefoot.

Faith nodded and stepped closer to Shannon. Shannon lifted her onto her lap. Jack poured the little girl a cup of milk and handed it to her. Shannon inhaled the sweet scent of this daughter she hardly knew, relishing the warm weight of her on her thighs. Life didn't get much better than this. If she'd never come back to the ranch, she wouldn't have run into Jack. She had much to be thankful for even if she lived the next fifteen years as an unloved wife.

"Where's the hot sauce?" Jack teased, looking into Shannon's cup.

Faith wiggled off Shannon's lap. "I didn't bring it down, but I can run and get it for you."

"Sadist." He scooped up Faith and set her on the counter, then opened the refrigerator and peered inside. "How can you stand a hot drink? I'll have a coke." He extracted a Mountain Dew, popped the top, and took a swig.

"All that caffeine will make it harder to sleep."

He gave a pointed glance at her hot chocolate. "You're the pot calling the kettle black."

She grinned and took a big swig. "This little bit never bothers me. You'll be up all night."

"I couldn't close my eyes anyway. I did a little searching on the Internet after you went to bed. I found Five Lives. His owner still has a reward out for information leading to his whereabouts. It sounds like he was a doting owner. The kidnappers might have been the ones to mistreat him."

"Doting owner? Just because the owner knew his value doesn't mean he treasured Jewel. I see men like that all the time. They spend their last penny on an 'investment' but put the horse down the second they can't milk it of any more money."

"You don't want to believe it because it might mean your father was the one who hurt him."

She stood and went to the door. She blinked back the moisture in her eyes. "You didn't know my father. He never would have hurt a horse."

"Everyone has secrets. We don't know what this is all about, but sticking your head in the sand won't get us closer to the truth."

Faith yawned and rubbed her eyes.

"Ready for bed, baby girl?" he asked. She nodded and he scooped her up.

Shannon didn't have the energy to move as the sound of his steps faded. Could her father have stolen a horse? True, she didn't want to believe it. If he had, it was to save Jewel, not hurt him. She was sure of that much.

MONDAY MORNING, WITH THE WEEK'S WORK AHEAD OF HIM, JACK STOOD talking to Buzz. "When you going on your honeymoon?" Buzz asked with a wink.

Never. Jack bit back the word. It wouldn't do to air their situation to the world. "Maybe when the mustang breaking is over." Now that he'd said it, he realized a vacation might ease the tension in the house. Since Wednesday night, when Shannon suggested they work on making a real marriage, he'd been unable to think of much else. When he watched her sleep with her hair loose on her shoulders, she'd been the most tempting thing he'd seen in months. It had been all he could do to resist her.

He'd never been one to rush into anything. This hurried marriage was bad enough, but if he made a move he'd regret later, he'd think back to this time and wish he'd thought out his actions. So he was going to do that—take the time to ferret out what was best. The conflict they'd had over the fate of the horse muddied the waters even more.

Questions lurked in Buzz's eyes, but Jack didn't intend to answer them. He was fooling himself if he thought the town hadn't guessed the reason for the marriage. One look at the two girls should have laid everything open.

Tucker Larue swaggered up before Buzz said anything more. His bullwhip secured to his belt and his mustache waxed to a fine curl, Larue didn't appear to have worked up a sweat with his horses today. Jack had managed to avoid the man for a week, but his luck couldn't hold on forever.

When Larue saw Jack and Buzz, he stopped and hooked his thumbs in his belt loops. "My stallion is already ground broke, MacGowan. Looks like you're losing this round."

"Got a saddle on him yet, Larue?" Jack couldn't help the taunt. At least Dancer let him drop a saddle on her back. He hadn't managed to stay on her yet, but she was progressing.

Larue gave a slow smile. "I think your bridle slipped off your little filly. I saw her smiling and batting those baby blues at a couple of cowboys today."

Jack lifted his brows. He knew Larue was talking about Shannon. "I bet you weren't one of them." He nearly grinned when Larue's face darkened and the man stalked away.

He was going to have to make sure Shannon knew not to give the wrong impression here. Cowboys were quick to respond to a pretty face and a flirtatious smile. Or even a smile that wasn't flirty. He waved to Buzz, then went to his truck. Shannon was standing by the passenger door, waiting. Her blond hair tied back in a ponytail, she appeared younger than he knew her to be.

He slid under the wheel and waited until she'd settled on her side of the truck. "Larue seemed to think you were flirting today." He nearly winced. That hadn't come out the way he intended. Even he could hear the accusation in the words.

She glared at him, her gaze a blue laser. "I didn't say two words to Tucker," she said. "I told you I'm not interested in other men. Besides, why would you care if I was? You haven't said a thing to me for the past two days! I come home. Play with the girls. I try to help with supper, but Enrica won't let me. You stare at your plate all through the meal, then vanish to your office until time to put the girls to bed. I feel like a pariah or something. I don't have a real place in the family. I'm like a poor cousin you've taken in."

She rubbed her forehead. "I'm sorry, I sound like a fishwife," she muttered.

"I don't know what to talk about," he mumbled. He focused on the road. He couldn't begin to explain how his attraction to her the other night had put him on his guard. He couldn't let her creep into his heart unless he was sure he wanted her there.

"The kids notice the tension between us. We have to at least try to be friendly, even if we're not friends. And just for the record, I don't flirt. Not ever."

You did the other night. The thought made him grip the steering wheel and stare at the road. He didn't want to remember the way she'd looked or how long it had taken him to get to sleep in his empty bed.

She turned her head and stared out the window. He glanced over at the smooth curve of her jaw and the long line of her neck. "I didn't mean to accuse you. I was repeating what Larue said," he said.

"Larue is an annoyance, nothing more." She still wouldn't look at him.

Silence stretched out along with the road for the next five miles. He reached the driveway and turned into it. "What do you want me to do?"

She turned to catch his gaze then. Her mouth drooped. "You sound like you think I'm going to ask something hard. I'd just like a little courtesy. Normal dinner conversation. Addressing me once in a while instead of the girls when we're playing games at night. I feel a little left out. And you still haven't told Faith I'm her real mother, have you? It's been over two weeks."

He couldn't stop the frown that sprang to his face. "I'm waiting for the right time."

Shannon rubbed her head. "I love her dearly, Jack. I want her to know she has a real sister, a mother who loves her. Blair has been dead for over a year. Faith needs me in her life, all of me, her mother. And her sister, her twin."

His fingers tightened on the wheel. "Blair was her mother!"

She flinched, and there was moisture hanging on her lashes when she looked at him. "There's room for both of us, Jack. I don't want to take away her love for Blair, but it's not my fault she was stolen from me." Her voice broke. "I know it's not your fault either, but please don't shut me out of her life because of your loyalty to Blair. I think she'd want Faith to have my love too." She shook her head and broke eye contact with him. "I have five years of lost time to make up. You have to tell her, Jack. It's the right thing to do."

He parked by the garage and got out without saying another word. Stalking to the house, he wondered why he'd ever thought this would work. She had him trapped. Legally, she was his wife. A court battle would prove she was Faith's mother.

But why did it feel so wrong? Telling Faith that Shannon was her mother would be letting go of the last bit of Blair. He had nothing left of her now. Not even a child they'd made together. And to think of putting anyone in Blair's place still pained him.

He bounded up the stairs and rushed through the door to his

office. He found Enrica dusting his desk. The faint odor of lemon wax hung in the air.

Her head came up when he barged through the door. "You mad, Mr. Jack?"

He sank onto his chair. "I don't know what to do, Enrica. Shannon wants me to tell Faith she's her real mother." He snatched the picture of Blair off his desk. "I can't do it."

Enrica rubbed the gleaming surface of the desk without saying anything for a long minute. "Miss Blair. She not perfect." Enrica nodded to the picture. "She no saint. You forget the fights sometimes, Mr. Jack."

"We never fought," he protested.

Enrica smiled and picked up a vase from the bookcase behind her. "Miss Blair throw this at you. I fix. See crack here?"

Transfixed, he stared at it. He remembered that argument. She'd wanted new drapes for the living room and he hadn't wanted to spend the money or deal with the mess. With the door cracked open, he remembered other fights—about Faith's bedtime, which movie to see, where to go to dinner. Blair had liked things her own way. She liked being the big man's wife, having the best of everything, making a splash in town and getting her picture in the paper.

She wasn't a saint. And neither was he.

Maybe he'd put her on a pedestal after her death. She would be horrified if she knew it. He put his head in his hands. It was about time he faced the truth and tried to make things better for the family he had left. What Shannon wanted was her right. And Faith's.

THE GLAZED DISHES, DEEP ORANGE AND GOLD, REFLECTED HER SCOWL. Shannon placed the plates on the table and went to get the silverware.

Her hands needed to be busy so she didn't throw something. Jack was never going to tell Faith the truth.

"Miss Shannon, you should not work." Enrica snatched the silverware box from her hand. "This my job."

"I like to do it," Shannon protested. She tried to get the box back, but Enrica turned and moved to the dining room. Shannon sometimes wondered if she'd ever be more than an outsider here. She wasn't trying to take Enrica's job, but she wanted to be part of the family. Someone who did more than occupy a room upstairs.

"Will Faith be home from her grandparents' in time for supper?" she asked.

"*Sí.*" Enrica's gaze shot to Shannon. "Miss Faith's *abuela* fears you take Miss Blair's place."

Shannon gaped at the housekeeper. "I've never even met the woman."

Enrica nodded. "When she come to pick up the *niña*, she ask many questions. I see fear in her eyes."

Shannon hadn't given much thought to Blair's parents. Of course they would want to keep their daughter's memory alive. Of course they would resent the woman who took Blair's place. They hadn't come to the wedding, and neither she nor Jack had expected them to show. She needed to make more of an effort to assure them she intended to help Faith hold on to the memory of her mother.

"They are here now," Enrica said at the sound of an engine outside.

"I'll go get her," Shannon said. She stepped out onto the porch and stood by a white pillar. A woman dressed in black slacks and a black silk blouse got out of the white Lexus. She got Faith out of the backseat, and Shannon caught a glimpse of a man at the steering wheel. Faith held the woman's hand and chattered all the way up the brick walk. Her focus never left the woman's face, and as they neared, Shannon understood. If Blair had lived, she would have been a copy of this woman in her fifties.

Shannon stepped down the steps. "Hello, I'm Shannon." She held her hand out to the woman, who took it with obvious reluctance. "You must be Mrs. Stickman."

Mrs. Stickman released Shannon's fingers after the merest touch. "Yes. We've had a fine time, haven't we, Faith?"

"I want to stay with you, Grammy," Faith said, her voice full of tears. She hung on to her grandmother's hand.

"Kylie has been counting the minutes until you got back," Shannon said.

Mrs. Stickman's eyes held sorrow. "Thank you for being so good to Faith," she said. "You can't always count on that with a stepmother."

Maybe she'd never seen Kylie and had no idea of the reality of the relationship, so Shannon held her tongue. But no, surely she knew. Verna was her sister.

The door behind her flew open and Kylie burst onto the porch. "Faith, you've been gone *forever*!"

Mrs. Stickman gaped at Kylie, then stared back at her granddaughter. She blinked at the moisture in her eyes. "I didn't believe Verna when she told me," she said quietly as Faith darted up the steps to Kylie and the two went hand in hand into the house. "Have you told Faith?"

"Not yet." Shannon met her gaze. "And I'll do all I can to make sure Faith treasures her memories of Blair. Her sweet spirit is a tribute to her . . . her mother."

Mrs. Stickman dabbed at her eyes. "Thank you. I don't know what to say. I'm just thankful Blair never had to deal with this. Faith was her whole world. As she is mine. I hope you'll never prevent her from seeing us."

"Of course not! Grandparents are so important to a child's life. Kylie has none."

Mrs. Stickman's mouth sagged, but then she smiled. "Would you consider letting us have Kylie when we take Faith? There's room in our hearts for another grandchild."

Tears sprang to Shannon's eyes, and she wanted to open her arms and hug the other woman. This kind of acceptance was something she'd craved all her life. "I'd be honored," she said in a choked voice. "Kylie has always wanted a grandma and grandpa."

"Could I have them both in a couple of weeks?"

Shannon nodded, her throat too full to speak. The other woman exchanged a brief hug with her, then went toward her car with a spring in her step.

"Nice to meet you," Shannon called over her shoulder as she stepped toward the door. She couldn't wait to tell Kylie. But first Jack had to tell the girls the truth.

The aroma of beef enchiladas filled the hall. Shannon went to the kitchen and wandered to the stove. The rice and beans were bubbling away on top, and flans sat cooling on the windowsill. Enrica must have stepped out of the kitchen a minute.

Shannon's stomach rumbled at the same time that her cell phone rang. She pulled it off her belt and glanced at the number. Mary Beth's name flashed across the caller ID screen. Shannon froze. She didn't want to answer it, but she had to. She flipped the phone open and put it to her ear.

"Shannon?" Mary Beth's voice was breathless and weak. "Everything okay?"

Shannon's heart leaped. "I'm fine. There's a guy after me. What does he want?"

"Money that belongs to you!" Mary Beth's voice was fierce. "Run a scanner over your arm and keep it. Don't give it up, no matter what he tells you. He's not going to hurt me. At least I don't think so. Oh no, here he comes." Her voice cut off.

Jack's silhouette filled the doorway. "Who was that?"

She glanced at his broad shoulders. He would stand by her. Keeping him informed was the only way he could protect them. *No secrets*, she reminded herself. Other than the MS. That was one secret that would take time to gather the nerve to tell.

He stood staring at her with a frown crouching beneath his dusty cowboy hat. "Shannon? What's wrong?"

She realized she'd been staring at him for several long moments and settled onto a bar stool at the gleaming granite island before her knees gave out. "It was Mary Beth, the friend I roomed with."

"The one in trouble?"

She nodded. "She told me to run my scanner on my arm."

"What scanner?"

"I think she must mean the scanner I use to identify pets and livestock. Owners put a chip in them with their name and contact information. But I don't know how she would have put a chip in my arm." She frowned. "No, wait. She gave me a tetanus shot before coming here."

"Is the chip that small?"

She nodded. "We insert it into animals on the end of a needle."

"What would be the point of putting a chip in your arm?"

"I don't know. She was cut off before she could tell me anything more. All she said was, 'Keep the money. It belongs to you.' But I have no idea what she's talking about."

He stepped closer and ran his fingers down her bare arms. His big, warm hands sent chills down her back. She wanted to draw away, but a response like that would make more of the incident than he intended. It would make her look foolish. "It was here," she said, touching her upper left arm.

His hand probed her skin. "I don't feel anything," he said. He dropped his hands and stepped back.

"It's too small to feel. Only a scanner will pick it up."

"What would be on a chip that small that someone would want?"

"I don't know. Mary Beth didn't say what it was. I'll stop by the office in the morning and get my scanner. See what I can find." She tipped her head to look up at him. "Let's check on the girls. I want to make sure they're safe."

"No one will break in here. This place is like a citadel. I've got ten ranch hands and an arsenal no criminal would want to mess with. At least not if they're smart." His voice dropped to a threatening growl.

It helped to have someone else shoulder this with her. To feel protected. Even with her parents, she'd often been their second thought. They'd get so caught up in their search for the Spanish treasure that dinner would be cold hot dogs and beans. She'd put herself to bed many nights.

He started toward the door, then turned. "I thought about what you said."

"Which part?"

"About telling Faith. I'm going to tell her tonight. I'd like you to be there."

Her lungs squeezed. Her daughter would finally know her. Faith seemed to like her. She and Kylie were so much alike. "Tonight? What changed your mind?"

He shrugged and didn't look at her. "It's time."

There was more to it than that. "How are you going to tell her? I like to have important conversations plotted out ahead of time in my head. She might not be receptive."

"I thought that might be the case. It doesn't matter though. The time has come for the truth." He glanced up and their gazes locked. "I want her to remember and love Blair, but I don't think that's going to happen."

"Do you have a book of photos of the two of them together? That might help. I'll do what I can, Jack. I don't want to replace Blair. There's room for me too."

He nodded. "Faith has a book, but she's got it about worn-out."

She tried to keep the happiness from her voice. "If you're sure about it, we can do it tonight."

"I thought you'd be overjoyed," he said.

"I am." She managed a smile. "I want to handle it right. And Blair's mom asked to take both girls next weekend. She wants to be a grandma to Kylie too."

His smile was genuine. "That's great!"

"When do you want to do it? Tell the girls, I mean."

"When we put them to bed. Faith will be relaxed and ready to listen."

17

It was a long evening while Shannon waited and wondered how her daughters would take the news. Kylie didn't seem to be jealous of Faith, but would the truth change things?

Just to settle her mind, Shannon peeked in on the girls playing in Faith's room. They were surrounded by stuffed animals, though their unicorns held center stage. The scent of Jack's spicy cologne announced his arrival beside her.

He stood in silence watching with her before speaking. "They love those unicorns," he said with a laugh. "Do you still believe in unicorns, Shannon?"

Her gaze lingered on the unicorns. "Faith in anything is a funny thing. It veers between total acceptance and more questions than I can count. Sometimes I'm as sure there are no unicorns as I am that there is a God. But then night comes and I question everything I know to be true. There is never any certainty of the unseen. We *hope*. That's what we do as Christians, and that's what I do with unicorns. Maybe like C. S. Lewis's Jewel, that glimpse of a unicorn I sometimes see is a glimpse of Jesus."

From the corner of her eye, she saw him stare at the girls. "They trust so completely. A lot like you did when I knew you a lifetime ago, Shannon." He turned her to face him and his gaze locked with hers. "Only now do I see how I killed something in you when I broke your faith in me. I'm sorry. Truly sorry. I wish I could go back and see that trust in your eyes again."

All his other apologies had come with a curl of the lip, as though she had no reason to be upset. This was the only one accompanied by a shamefaced expression and deep sincerity in his eyes. She blinked back tears. "I forgive you. It worked out for the best, you know. Without the motivation to prove everyone wrong, I might not have gone on to school. So maybe I should thank you."

He held up his hand. "Don't, Shannon. Let me wallow in my guilt awhile. I deserve it."

She chuckled through her tears. "I'm okay, Jack. Really. You're helping restore my faith in people." She brushed her lips across his cheek and ignored his shocked intake of breath. "Let's go to supper." She called to the children. "Girls, come and eat." They trooped downstairs together.

The girls chattered through supper, each vying for Jack's attention. Faith told her father about the new colt that had been born in her grandpa's barn. Kylie told them about Enrica taking her for a walk to look at butterflies. After the meal, Shannon and Jack each read a story to the girls. Seated together on the overstuffed leather sofa in the massive family room, Shannon almost could believe they were the perfect little family.

Fantasy could be its own reward.

Jack dropped a kiss on Faith's blonde head. "Time for bed, kiddos."

"Aw, Daddy, one more story," Faith said.

Jack's gaze caught Shannon's. "Okay, but only when you're in bed. Go get your pj's on, both of you."

Faith scrambled down from his lap, and Kylie did the same. The sound of their feet rushing up the steps made Shannon chuckle. Her smile died at the somber expression on Jack's face. "Are you having second thoughts?" she whispered.

"No, just trying to figure it out. I'll make it a story."

"Do you want me to tell her?"

"No, this needs to come from me. Why would she believe you? I was there."

"So was I." Her voice went sharp. "I held her when she was still covered with goop." Her throat thickened. Rylie—Faith—had stared up at her as if memorizing her face. If only Faith could recall that memory.

He glanced away. "I'm sorry."

She stood. "We'd better go up." Her back stiff, she stalked away from him. He was doing it again, minimizing her role in the girls' lives. She marched up the steps and down to the bedroom.

The girls had taken to sleeping in the same bed. They took turns between the two bedrooms. Tonight they were both in Kylie's canopy bed. Their scrubbed faces with damp wisps of hair on their cheeks peered over the top of the pink and lavender quilt. They each had their stuffed unicorn. Identical ones, even though they'd been purchased miles apart before Faith and Kylie had ever met.

Shannon kissed each soap-scented cheek and tucked the covers around the girls. She sat on the edge of the bed and brushed Kylie's hair back from her face.

"A story, a story!" Faith began to chant. Kylie took up the singsong with her.

"Enough, both of you," Jack said. He sat on the other edge of the bed and took Faith's hand. "You ready?"

"You don't have a book, Daddy," Faith said.

"I don't need a book for this story," Jack said. "It's, er, very familiar to me." He cleared his throat. "Once upon a time, there were two beautiful baby girls. They were as alike as Daisy and Candy, our kittens."

"Like us," Kylie said. She gripped her sister's hand.

"Just like that," Jack agreed. "Their mother looked just like them. They were all blonde and beautiful. And they had the deepest blue eyes their daddy had ever seen. As deep as sapphires, as dark as the blue of the sea."

Did he think she was beautiful? The girls drank in his words. Shannon wanted to tell him to stop. Maybe this was the wrong thing for Faith. She watched her little girl's face, so sweet and innocent. Would this disrupt her life? She opened her mouth, then closed it again. The girls needed to know they were twins.

He cleared his throat. "Something happened at the hospital so that the girls got mixed up with another baby. The other baby died, and one little blonde girl went home with her mommy, and one little blonde girl went home with her new mommy and daddy."

Kylie frowned fiercely. "That's a bad story! The little girls need to be together. Like me and my sister."

Faith nodded. "Tell another story, Daddy. I don't like that one."

"There's more to it. I think you'll like the ending. The little girl was very happy with her mommy and daddy. And the other little girl also was very happy with her mommy, though she wished she had a daddy too."

"What are the little girls' names? They need names," Faith said.

"How about if we name them after you two?" Shannon asked gently.

Faith nodded. "I like that."

"The little girl who went home with her new mommy and daddy was Faith, and the other little girl was Kylie," Jack said. His voice was hoarse. "But Faith's mommy died."

"Just like my mommy," Faith said.

He nodded. "And Kylie and her mommy came to town. They went to a stockyard where they met Faith and her daddy. As soon as they saw the two little girls together, Faith's daddy and Kylie's mommy knew they were sisters. It couldn't be anything else. They looked too much alike."

The eyes of both girls were huge. They were watching Jack with rapt attention, hanging on his every word.

"Kylie's mommy went to the hospital. She found out about the mix-up with the babies. Kylie's mommy was very upset when she found out she had missed seeing her little girl grow. She went to Faith's daddy to talk about it."

Shannon's muscles clenched, and she leaned forward. Surely he wasn't going to tell the girls that she'd proposed marriage. She licked her dry lips and waited for the girls to finally understand it all.

"When the mommy and daddy talked it out, they realized they both loved the little girls so much that they wanted them to be a family. So they married each other. Now they can all be together and live happily ever after."

"And the little girls can be sisters like they were supposed to,"

Kylie whispered. Her gaze sought Shannon's, and the innocent blue eyes held a question.

"It's not a real story. Is it, Daddy?" The sweet pink had left Faith's cheeks.

"Yes, baby, it is. Miss Shannon is your mommy."

"But you're my daddy." Faith launched herself from under the covers and into Jack's arms. Sobs erupted from her throat.

"Of course I'm your daddy." He smoothed her damp curls back from her face. "But now I'm Kylie's daddy too. And you have a new mommy. We're a family."

Tears streamed down Faith's face. "I already have a mommy." She jerked from Jack's arms and slid out of bed. From under the bed she pulled a tattered photo album. She carried it to the bed and flipped it open. "See, my mommy's holding me. You're there too, Daddy. We're a family. Grammy says Mommy is watching me in heaven."

Shannon looked into Blair's proud face as she smiled down at the infant in her arms. So happy. They'd been the perfect family. "I'm sure your mommy is watching you from heaven, sweetheart. And she'll always be your mommy. I'm not going to take her place." She wanted to say more, to tell her daughter that there was room for two in her heart, but the little girl was too young to understand yet.

Jack closed the book and pulled Faith onto his lap. "Your first mommy loved you very much. But she's in heaven and can't be here to take care of you. Miss Shannon is here to love you and take care of you. She can be a mommy too. You're very lucky to have two such wonderful mommies."

Faith buried her face in Jack's shirt. "But you're *my* daddy."

"I'll always be your daddy." He hugged her tightly to his chest. "Always."

Kylie tugged on the sleeve of Faith's pajama top. "But we're real sisters, Faith. I told you so."

Faith raised her face, and her gaze found Kylie's. "Sisters," she echoed with a question in her voice.

Kylie nodded. "We're twins, aren't we, Mommy?"

Shannon's throat thickened. "Yes, you are, sweetheart. Faith is your big sister. She was born a minute before you."

Faith finally looked at Shannon. "I'm the big sister?"

Shannon nodded and leaned forward to touch Faith's blonde hair. "You are. I'm so glad we found you, baby girl. I've missed you so much."

Faith pulled away and put her head on Jack's chest again. "Only Daddy calls me 'baby girl.'"

"Then I'll come up with another name for you. I want you always to love your daddy. And your mommy."

"You're not going to take me away, are you?" Her blue eyes darkened.

"Of course not." For the first time she realized she'd done the right thing in forcing the marriage issue. If she'd tried to get Faith through the courts, the little girl would have been terribly hurt. "Neither of us will ever leave you. We are your family forever."

"Forever!" Kylie jumped up and began to bounce on the bed. "Sisters forever, Faith. Forever!" She managed to pull Faith to her feet to jump with her, but Faith's eyes held tears, and her mouth stayed sullen.

At least one of the girls was excited. Shannon's gaze locked with Jack's. That hadn't gone as well as she'd hoped.

Jack leaned down to kiss Faith, then straightened with a frown. "You've got a fever, Faith. No wonder you're grumpy."

"I'm not grumpy," she said with a sullen glare at Shannon.

Shannon touched her older daughter's forehead, but the child flinched away. "Is your throat sore?" she asked. Faith nodded and tears gathered in her eyes.

"I've got some Dimetapp," she said. "Let me get some."

"Ask Enrica first," Jack said. "She has some homeopathic concoction that works wonders."

Shannon touched Kylie's forehead. "You're hot too. Is your throat sore?"

Kylie nodded. "But I'm okay, Mommy. You should rest. I saw you limp today."

Heat flooded Shannon's cheeks, and she didn't look at Jack. "I'm fine, sweetie. Let me see what Enrica has to help you."

She hurried to the door and downstairs to find the housekeeper. Her cell phone rang when she reached the kitchen, and she saw Grady's number roll up. She flipped it open. "Hey, Grady."

"Sorry to bother you," he said in a hoarse voice. "I've got the flu, and the Mitchells' horse has foundered. Can you go?"

She hesitated. It was her job, and she had no choice, but she hated to leave when the girls were sick. "On my way," she said finally. "I know where it is." She closed her phone and slipped it back into her pocket. "Enrica, the girls are sick with sore throats and fever. Jack said you have some miracle medicine."

"I take care," Enrica said, her dark eyes concerned. "You tell Mr. Jack you go?"

"Yes, I'll do that. Thanks." She hurried up the steps to the girls' room, where she found Jack in a chair beside the bed reading a story to them. "I . . . I have to go," she said. "Foundered horse and Grady is sick too."

He frowned and stood. Taking her arm, he led her into the hall. "You'd leave the girls when they're sick?"

"What choice do I have? It's my job."

"What about your job as a mother?"

Her throat swelled with tears that wanted to move to her eyes, and she swallowed them down. "Are you saying you don't want to care for sick kids?"

"That's not it at all. But this is your chance to show Faith you care about her."

"If I don't go, the horse will likely *die*, Jack. What do you expect me to do? The girls are just getting a cold." With every fiber of her being, she longed to stay here, to cuddle her sick children, but this was what she'd trained to do. What she *had* to do. Why couldn't he see that?

He waved his hand in a dismissive move. "Go then. I'll explain it to the girls."

"I will," she said fiercely. "I love them with all my heart. But sometimes duty calls." She brushed past him and pasted a smile on her face. "Girls, I have to go tend to a sick horse. I'll be back as soon as I can. Enrica is bringing you up some medicine and when I get back, I'll make some hot chocolate."

"With marshmallows?" Kylie asked.

"Is there any other kind?" Shannon dropped a kiss on each golden head, even though Faith flinched away.

"Is the horse going to die, Mommy?" Kylie asked. "Can you save it?"

"I'll do my best," she promised. At least her younger daughter cared about something other than herself. Unlike Jack.

18

HE'D BEEN OUT OF LINE LAST NIGHT. JACK RECOGNIZED THE FACT IN THE hard light of day. He'd have done the same thing. Shannon had returned in time to brush the girls' hair and fix them hot chocolate before rushing out again to check on the horse. They were better this morning, though they hadn't said much over breakfast. Jack still wasn't sure he'd done the right thing by telling them the truth so soon. Faith clung to his pant leg like a burr as he tried to get ready for his day.

Shannon rushed into the dining room late, carrying her boots. Jeans hugged her long, slim legs, and she'd tucked her sleeveless blue shirt into the waistband. He jerked his gaze away from her curves.

She pulled out a chair and sat down to pull on her boots. "Sorry

I'm late. I didn't get to sleep until two." She straightened and swiveled to the table to dig into the bacon-and-egg casserole Enrica had made.

"You've got dark circles under your eyes," he said.

"You know just the right sweet talk, Jack," she said, her smile flashing a dimple.

He grinned to show her he was sorry about his harsh words the night before. "Was I supposed to lie?"

"A little white lie can be balm to a woman's ego." She crossed her eyes and stuck out her tongue at him.

He rolled his eyes, and she laughed. "Did you sleep well, Faith?" she asked.

Faith didn't look at her from her perch on Jack's knee. She turned and buried her face in Jack's chest. Jack's gaze locked with Shannon's, and he saw the pain in her eyes. "She'll be fine," he mouthed. Her smile fading, Shannon nodded and looked down at her plate.

"Mommy, we're going to go to the Big Bend museum today. Enrica is taking us," Kylie said.

Shannon's smile was strained, but Kylie didn't seem to notice. "That's great, sweetheart. Are you excited to go too, Faith?"

Faith pressed her head more tightly against Jack, but she gave an almost imperceptible nod. A small victory, but one that made Jack exchange a smile with Shannon. He kissed the top of his daughter's head, then lifted her away from his chest and set her in the chair though she clung to him. "I've got to go, baby. My mustangs are looking for me."

"I want to go with you today," she said.

"You'd miss the exhibit at the museum," he reminded her.

She frowned and nodded with obvious reluctance. "Okay, I'll go with Kylie." She scooted off the chair and went to sit by Kylie, who took her hand.

"Don't be sad today, Faith," Kylie said. "Enrica said we would be junior rangers. Maybe we'll see a snake!"

Shannon grimaced. "Stand very still if you do."

Jack dropped a kiss on both golden heads. "Gotta run, munchkins. You ready?" he asked Shannon.

She nodded and shoveled in one last bite of casserole. "Great breakfast," she called through the doorway to Enrica, who was in the kitchen. The housekeeper waved a hand without looking.

He held the door open for Shannon and caught a faint whiff of her shampoo as she passed. Some kind of stuff that smelled of oranges. He liked it, and it was just one of many things he liked about his new wife. Shannon was already in the truck by the time he shut the door behind them and dug his keys out of his pocket.

"I don't feel like working today," he muttered, sliding under the wheel.

"We can delay it a few minutes. I need to stop by the office and get my scanner," she reminded him when he turned the key in the ignition.

He nodded. "I remembered. I thought maybe we should check in with the sheriff about all this. You've got a description now, and he can watch for strangers."

"Aren't there always strangers passing through on their way to Big Bend?"

"Yeah, but it's mostly families, or at least couples. A strange man or two might stand out."

She shrugged. "We still don't know who it is. The sheriff already knows some big guy broke into my house. I want to find out what's going on. Let me see what the scanner shows first."

He said nothing. Glancing at her from the corner of his eye, he realized he knew very little about her. He'd told Faith the truth about her mother, but what about her father? Even Jack didn't know the truth about that. Someday Faith would ask. It was sure to happen. Maybe now was a good time to find out. It had been hard enough to let another mother into Faith's life. Allowing another father to be a part of her growing up would be even harder.

He glanced at her out of the corner of his eye. "You mind if I ask you a question?"

She narrowed her eyes. "What kind of question?"

"Who's the father?"

She didn't pretend to misunderstand. Turning her gaze away, she sighed. "Let's not go there now, Jack. Don't we have enough to deal with this morning? Save it for another time."

"What if he wants to be a part of their lives?"

She continued to stare out the window at the desert landscape. "He doesn't."

"Are you sure? Does he live nearby? What if he hears you've come back to town and comes looking for the girls?"

"He wanted nothing to do with a baby. I had to fight him about getting an abortion. No way would I do that."

"Look, just answer the question. I have to know what I'm dealing with. Does he live around here?"

She turned back toward him, her blue eyes deep pools of grief. "He was a cowboy drifter who worked at my uncle's. I met him my senior year of college and came home every weekend to be with him. I thought he cared about me, but I was wrong."

"His name," he pressed again. "I have to know, Shannon. It might be important someday for medical reasons." As well as his sanity.

"I'm not going to tell you. Not now."

"More secrets from me?"

Her lips pressed together. "If you want to call it that. I just don't see any benefit in going there, not when we have other problems to face right now. I'll tell you. Just not right now."

"Do I know him?"

Her chin jutted out, and she stared out the window. "I'm not talking about it."

Which meant he probably did. He decided to go in another direction. "What happened when your uncle found out you were pregnant?"

She blinked fast, not looking at him. "You want to see me bleed or what? You must be the kind of person who likes to pull the wings off flies."

"Sorry. I was trying to be sympathetic."

"You're about as subtle as a horse tromping on my foot. He was mad, okay? He'd have thrown me out onto the street if my cousin hadn't intervened. As it was, he wanted me gone as soon as the girls were born."

"He left you his property."

"Believe me, that was a shock." Her face puckered and her eyes clouded. "He and Curt had a huge fight just before Uncle Earl died, and Curt told him to leave it to me, that he didn't want an albatross around his neck. I think my uncle decided to do it out of spite. He wasn't a bad man. Just solitary and inept around women. He was perpetually disappointed in how his life turned out."

"How did you get through school and raise a little girl?" he asked, careful to keep his voice soft. The lady had guts. He hoped the girls had inherited Shannon's spunk and grit.

"I was lucky. I rented a room from the sweetest lady to walk the earth when I first moved to Alpine. She offered to care for Kylie for free while I finished school. In exchange, I did light housework when

I wasn't waiting tables, ran errands for her, that kind of thing. I was sorry to leave her when I went to veterinary school at A&M."

"Who took care of her when you were there? That's a lot of hours."

"She was in preschool by then, and I found a good one nearby. The owner's teenage daughter helped out after hours. She brought Kylie home and stayed with her until I made it there."

"And you waited tables too?" He waited until she nodded. "When did you sleep?"

"About four hours a night." She smiled. "It was hard, but it was worth it. How many people get to do their dream job? After college, I got a job with a vet in San Antonio, but I could only afford the worst of apartments—you saw it. I had to get Kylie out of that environment, so when I inherited the ranch, I came back here."

"To face the ridicule I'd caused," he said softly. "You're pretty amazing. I think I'm glad you're the mother of my daughters." The surprise was he actually meant it.

One shapely brow arched, and delicate pink rushed to her cheeks. "I hope Faith can accept me."

"Give her time." He'd thought Faith would cling to Shannon the minute she found out she had a new mother. Maybe she wouldn't forget Blair. His emotions were a mixed bag right now.

Her smile was shy. "Thanks for being so sweet to Kylie."

"She's easy to love. She's one of those people who give their heart first and think about it later. Faith is a little more cautious."

"Like her father."

His gaze locked with hers. "You don't give your heart easily like Kylie. Where'd she get that?"

Her lips tightened and she glanced away. "I try to think things through now."

The town limits flashed by. Bluebird Crossing, population 850. He'd lived all his life in the wide-open spaces. How had she adjusted to the confines of the city? Her love of the desert and of the horses had been evident to him the first time he'd met her. But he'd asked enough personal questions for one day.

He pulled into the parking lot of the Bluebird Veterinary Clinic. His tires crunched the gravel of the empty parking lot. "No customers."

"Nope." She thrust open her car door and began to root in her purse, then pulled out a set of keys.

Jack followed her up the walk. "Your receptionist isn't here yet."

"She doesn't come in until nine." She stopped to pet a kitten that raced to her feet from under the oleanders.

She had a way with animals. The kitten was purring at the attention. Two more crept out from behind the bushes and approached her. She dug in her purse and pulled out some bagged food, which she sprinkled on the gravel.

Jack watched her gentle touch with the kittens. "You always carry food with you?"

"I try to. You never can tell when it will come in handy. Wyatt sure was glad for it." She stood and went to the door.

Jack was close enough behind to hear her sharp inhalation. Close enough also to see that the door stood ajar about an inch and the doorplate had been busted out.

"Stay here," he said, pulling her away from the door.

THE FILE CABINET LAY ON ITS SIDE WITH ITS CONTENTS STREWN ACROSS the floor. The desk drawers had been jerked out and left upended on the carpet. Papers and pens littered the area as if an explosion had gone off in the room. A picture of her and Kylie lay upside down with shards of glass around it. The odor of a strong male cologne lingered in the air.

Shannon stood gaping at the destruction. She clutched herself, but her teeth chattered.

"I told you to stay back," Jack said. He strode from door to door checking each room.

She couldn't stand here shaking in her boots. She dropped her arms. "It's my office. I wanted to see what had happened." She gingerly plucked the picture from the debris. The broken glass had cut across her face but left her daughter's intact, and the relief flooding through her was out of proportion to the circumstances.

Her scanner. She glanced around the room, seeking the piece of equipment amid the destruction. Wading through the debris, she lifted the chair from in front of the cabinet where she had kept the scanner. There it was. She picked it up and turned it on. The light blinked and stayed steady.

"I found my scanner," she said, turning toward Jack. "It's working."

He stepped over to join her. "You think this is related to the phone call?"

"What else could it be?" Looking at the destruction, she felt as if her insides were hollowed out. It felt personal, as though someone hated her. She'd never had a personal enemy that she knew of, and now some stranger was out to terrorize her.

"Mexican vagrants maybe, looking for drugs or money."

She shook her head. "We've had illegals break into the barn or the house through the years. They're too scared to take the time to cause such destruction. This looks like someone didn't find what they were searching for, so they decided to do as much damage as possible."

He glanced at the scanner and held out his hand. "Let me run it over your skin."

She showed him how to use it and where to look for the readout. Holding out her arm, she prayed he found nothing. All she wanted to do was get on with her life.

His rough fingers steadied her arm with an impersonal touch. She stared at the nicks and cuts on his hands. Work hands that could cradle an injured horse or a crying child with equal ease.

She glanced at her watch on the extended arm. "We don't have much time. We need to get out to the training ground."

"We'll get there. We need to call the sheriff too." He began to move the scanner over her arm. When the scanner reached the top outer area of her arm, he paused. "I've got a reading."

She closed her eyes briefly. She'd so hoped there would be nothing. "What's it say?"

"It's a set of numbers. 07623876. Mean anything to you?"

She shook her head. "The ID numbers I use are longer. We've got to get it out, see what we can find out about it."

"How do you do that?"

She sighed. "It will take surgery. I'll have to get it cut out." She glanced at her watch. "We've got to get going."

"Just a minute." He lifted the desk back onto its legs and began to pick up the papers on the floor.

"I can do that later."

"I'm here now." He continued to work until the papers were stacked on the desk again and the furniture was upright. "One of the chair legs is broken. I'll fix it after work." He went toward the door. "I'll call the sheriff on the way. We'll leave the office unlocked for him. It's not like anyone could do any more damage."

She listened to him call in the problem as they drove off. If only she could talk to Mary Beth without interruption, get her to explain the chip. What would have numbers like that? A password? A bank account? If only she knew what she was dealing with.

When they reached the mustang training camp, Jack parked in the lot and didn't get out. Instead he glanced at her, and his green eyes seemed to really *see* her. A person who was scared and hurting, not someone who was in the way of his plans. Shannon found she liked being the focus of his attention.

"Are you okay?" he asked.

Her initial response was to deny her fear, but that would keep the barrier up between them, and she wanted to start removing the bricks in it. She leaned back against the headrest. "I'm scared. Mostly for Mary Beth. I want this to be over."

The back of his hand grazed her cheek. The deliberate touch made her inhale. Her gaze sought his. All the feelings she'd had for him when she was a teenager bubbled to the surface, but she buried them again. He meant nothing but kindness.

"Two blows, one right after the other," Jack said. "I know Faith's reaction to the news hurt you."

"But not you," she said, drawing away so his hand fell. "You want Faith to love and remember Blair."

"Actually, I felt bad," he said. "We are married, whether we like it or not. I can't imagine anything worse than spending the next fifteen years fighting. I'd like us to at least be friends."

A tight bud of pain relaxed. Could he be sincere? Shannon stared at the strong line of his jaw. "I'd like that too." Before she could chicken out, she leaned across the truck and brushed her lips across his, then leaped from the truck before she could read his expression.

19

JACK TOUCHED HIS LIPS AND STARED AFTER SHANNON'S RETREATING BACK. Knowing what he knew now, he was willing to admit to himself that she was exactly what she said: a mother intent on making sure both daughters were cared for and loved. A vet who loved her patients and cared about her community.

And maybe someone he could love. Was Rick right? Was it possible to decide to love someone? To act on it without the emotion being there?

He leaped out of the truck and ran after her. When he caught up with her, Shannon's color was high. Maybe she feared he was going to be upset about the kiss. All the things he wanted to say dried on his tongue. "Make sure you're not alone today," he said. "With that guy breaking into the office and not finding anything, he might be more active today."

"I'm not afraid. I brought my pistol in my pack."

"You might not have time to get to it. There are plenty of people around. Stay out of the barns when they're empty and avoid the bunkhouses."

Her brilliant eyes flashed. "Look, Jack, I'm not some hothouse flower that shrinks back at the first sign of danger. I've lived in a big city in a not-so-nice part of town. I know how to take care of myself."

"I'd be a poor husband if I didn't try to make sure you're safe. We're pulling together in the harness now, Shannon."

The fire in her eyes died, and she shrugged. "Are you my husband?" She bit her lip as though she was sorry the words had escaped.

A slow burn started in his belly. "Some days you make me feel about as welcome in your life as a skunk at a dinner party." He stepped closer until she backed up against the side of the mess hall. He was tired of denying the emotion simmering between them. He cupped her cheek in his palm, then pulled her into his arms. She didn't resist. His mouth came down on hers, and a current seemed to flow through them both, binding them together. Her lips were soft and pliable and she smelled sweeter than a field of bluebells. Her arms crept around his neck. He couldn't think, couldn't breathe.

Catcalls from behind brought him out of the trance. He tore himself away. Her eyes were dreamy, and she blinked. A bemused smile tugged at her mouth, a smile he answered with one of his own.

"This ain't your bedroom," a cowboy called. "Time to get to work."

Jack didn't turn. He was drowning in those amazing eyes. "If you need to go somewhere, don't go alone. Call me on your cell phone and I'll come with you." Lame comment, but it was easier than talking about what had just happened.

She caught her lower lip in her teeth and cleared her throat. "My cell goes dead for no reason," she said. "I might not be able to get you."

"At least try."

She nodded but with obvious reluctance. "It's not easy for me to depend on anyone but myself."

"You need to learn. We're a partnership. What would happen to the girls if that guy killed you?" He wanted to pull her back into his arms but resisted.

"He won't kill me. He wants his money. I only wish I could give it to him and make him free Mary Beth."

"He might come after you for the fun of it." The thought made him wince.

She smiled. "Listen to yourself, Jack. This isn't some shoot-'em-up movie." She waved a hand. "I'll just get this chip out and be done with it."

"You don't believe that," he said. "It's okay to share your worry with someone. You don't have to carry your problems alone. I want to help."

She glanced back at him then, her eyes darkened to indigo. "I'm more afraid of you than of the guy who's threatening me."

"Is this the same woman who just told me she wanted a husband?"

"I didn't say that. Not exactly." She pulled her hair forward, twisting a lock of it in her fingers. She stared at him. "I have to say you're a good kisser."

"I'm not sure you've had much experience to compare," he said dryly, though his pulse galloped at her words. He'd like to practice that again.

Pink stained her cheeks, and she dropped her gaze.

Why was he trying to convince her to depend on him? He'd gone into the marriage with the idea that they would be two people living in the same house for the sake of the girls. He'd never intended that they'd have any real partnership, but he found it intriguing to imagine getting under that beautiful skin to understand her better.

SHANNON FOUND HERSELF THINKING ABOUT THAT KISS AT ODD TIMES DURING the day. Every now and then, she found herself touching her lips and remembering the minty scent of his breath.

When the sun was high overhead, she trotted across an open field to the mess hall. Now that she had a free minute, she was going to try to get hold of Mary Beth again. Yesterday's call had reassured her that her friend was alive, but there was so much she didn't understand. She propped her boot on the lower rung of a fence and got out her cell phone. Drat, the thing was dead again.

A familiar long-legged lope caught her gaze. She squinted in the bright sunshine at the man coming toward her. "Curt, I thought you'd be long gone by now. What are you doing here?"

Her cousin wore an easy grin under his cowboy hat, a genuine Stetson Beaver. The hat covered his blond hair, but his blue eyes were as vivid as Shannon's own. "I went home and came back this morning."

Shannon fell into step with him and they walked toward the building. "Did you find what you were looking for at the ranch?"

"Nope. Not a sign of it, but I got to thinking about Dad's picture albums. I know everything belongs to you, but I'd like to have them if you don't mind."

"Of course you can have them! I wish you'd take half the property. It rightfully belongs to you."

Curt shrugged. "I don't need the money. My business is almost more than I can handle. I told Dad if he left it to me, I'd just sell it. I think he saw leaving it to you as a possible way of keeping it in the family."

Sometimes she thought his bravado was all show, but as she stared at his expensive clothing and caught a peek at his brand new SUV, today wasn't one of those times. He probably was doing every bit as well as he said. She didn't need to dwell on the guilt that plagued her.

"You know where the albums are? I'll stop by the house and get them."

She tried to remember, then shook her head. "I haven't seen them anywhere, but they might be in the attic. There used to be several chests up there, and Uncle Earl squirreled away stuff up there all the time."

Curt grimaced. "There might be bats up there."

Her cousin hated bats. He'd gotten one in his hair once and had run screaming like a girl. "Probably are," she said. "They get in that hole in the west end of the attic. Want me to get them for you?"

"Shannon, girl adventurer," Curt said, his grin widening. "You sure you don't mind?"

"I'll take a tennis racquet up with me."

He shuddered. "Better you than me. I don't know how you stand the things. When should I stop by to get them?"

"It will be this weekend before I have a chance to go. The trainers give the horses a rest on Saturday and Sunday."

"Want me to go with you? The sheriff talked to me about the break-ins out there. Guess he thought I might have had something to do with them. I told him the ranch was good riddance as far as I was concerned."

"Me too," Shannon said. "I was going to live there because I had no choice, but it's in terrible shape."

Curt studied her face. "You happy, Shannon? The marriage working out?"

She'd bet no one dared ask Jack these questions. "I'm happy," she said. "Jack is a good man."

"How long have you known him?"

Her laugh sounded shrill to her ears. "What is this, twenty questions? Since when did you care about my love life, Curt?"

He shrugged. "Seems odd, that's all. A big shot like Jack MacGowan marrying a . . ."

She knew what her uncle and Curt thought of her. "A what? An unwed mother? A slut who doesn't deserve him? A crazy woman the whole town whispered about?"

The tips of his ears reddened. "That's not what I said."

"But it's what you thought." She squared her shoulders and faced him down. Would she never live down her reputation? One mistake and the town had marked her as poor white trash. She saw the expression in people's eyes at the grocery store, at the hardware store. Until they remembered she was the vet now. Then they pasted on a smile. People in small towns had a long memory and they all knew her entire history.

Curt's lips tightened and he shook his finger in her face. "Don't put words in my mouth. I'm glad you managed to overcome your past. You came out smelling like a rose, that's for sure." He flicked a finger toward Jack, who was working his mustang in the corral. "The wealthiest man in the area."

"I'm most proud of making it on my own," Shannon said quietly. "I put myself through college and vet school and came here to start my own practice. I didn't need a man to validate my accomplishments."

"Then why'd you marry him?"

Shannon glanced over at Jack. He still didn't know about her MS.

Would he have married her if she'd revealed her illness? "It's complicated," she said.

"He has a daughter, right? From a previous marriage? I hope you didn't bite off more than you can chew."

She could have told him Faith was her daughter. She could have told him her fears about the future. She might even have explained that Jack had loomed as an important person to her since she was a teenager, but in the end, she shrugged. "For the same reasons anyone gets married. What about you? Any little woman in your future?"

"Not likely. Women just want a guy's money."

Had Jack thought that about her? Shannon hated the thought he might consider her a gold digger.

JACK'S MOUTH WAS AS DRY AS SAND, AND HIS MUSCLES ACHED. A GOOD kind of ache though, one born of hard work and determination. Friday afternoon he looped his rope over his shoulder and walked toward the mess hall. His stomach rumbled, but he was more interested in swilling a bottle of cold water.

A man fell into step beside him. "Got a minute, Mr. MacGowan?"

Jack recognized him as the reporter for a news channel in San Antonio. "Sure." The more publicity the event drew, the more mustangs would find adoptive homes.

The man motioned a videographer to join them. The huge camera focused on Jack's face, and he tried not to notice. He slowed his steps when what he really wanted to do was to rush to the tub of icy water holding the drinks.

"I'm following an interesting story that's popped up," the reporter said. "Shannon Astor returned to town a few weeks ago, and you married her a week later. I've seen her daughter and yours. They're clearly twins. What's the story behind the amazing resemblance?" He thrust a mic in Jack's face.

Jack batted it away and grabbed the tail of his anger as it threatened to escape. "My personal life has nothing to do with anything. Ask me about the mustang training and I'll tell you whatever you want to know. But you leave my wife and daughters out of this."

The reporter jammed the mic under Jack's chin again. "Daughters, Mr. MacGowan? Are both girls your natural daughters? Did you and Ms. Astor break up and each take a child?"

Jack shoved past the reporter. "No comment." He sped up and walked away from the man and the camera. He should have known people would notice. He and Shannon should have figured out what they would say when asked. He ducked under the low-hung door frame. His boots clattered across the wide wooden boards of the old mess hall until he found a deserted corner where he could look over the crowd.

He spotted Shannon by the heavily laden tables of food. His nose picked up barbeque, his favorite. Grabbing a plate, he joined her at the buffet.

She glanced up. Dressed in slim-fitting jeans and a blue shirt that showed the smooth column of her neck, she was as fresh as when she'd left the house this morning. He'd better not get too close, not covered with dust like he was. She nodded, and he filled his plate with coleslaw, pork barbeque, corn, and pie, then followed her to the table.

"What's up?" she asked.

Her light aroma drifted his way, and he shifted to get a better whiff. "A TV reporter is asking questions about the girls. He's seen them and noticed how much they look alike. He thinks I'm their father and we split years ago, each taking one."

Her fork paused en route to her mouth. "Well that's an interesting theory. If he digs around, he'll find where we filed the adoption papers. But why does he care? It's hardly newsworthy."

"I'm the senator's son. We're likely to get more reporters asking questions. If there weren't so many in town because of the training, this probably would have slipped under everyone's radar."

She shook her head, and her shining curtain of blonde hair dusted her shoulders. "Not everyone. The folks who live here see the girls and wonder. They're just too polite to ask."

"We've never come up with what to say when asked."

Her gaze dropped to her plate, and she laid down her fork. "The truth probably works best."

"I was hoping to avoid causing embarrassment to Aunt Verna." He knew he'd said the wrong thing when her cheeks fired with color and her angry gaze skewered him.

"What about all the pain she's caused me?"

"I think it's balanced by the joy she brought me," he countered. "I wouldn't have had these five years with Faith. I wouldn't have a new daughter in my house."

"You wouldn't be burdened with a wife you don't love either." Her voice sounded choked.

Was that what she thought—that he resented her? He cleared his throat. "You're not a burden, Shannon. I'm getting used to having you around."

She smiled, and the pain in her eyes faded. "You mean it?"

"I think we're rubbing along pretty well. The girls enjoy the playtime at night. And you're a nice sight across the dining room table." More than nice. He'd become uncomfortably aware of her. Like now, with the fragrance lingering around her making his head spin.

Her cheeks pinked up again. "I think we should tell the truth if we're asked. That the girls are twins. That's all we have to say. How we came to be married is no one's business. And it's not like we can keep their relationship quiet anyway. The girls tell anyone who will listen."

She stood with her half-full plate, then stumbled and went down on one knee. The plate of food fell from her fingers and dumped onto the floor. Jack jumped up and went to help her, but she was still clumsy and awkward as she struggled to her feet.

"You're eating wheat again," he said, gesturing to the donut on her plate. "Enrica is going to be all over you."

"Not if you don't tell her," she said as he bent to scoop up her plate and to clean the food from the floor. "Sorry I'm such a klutz."

"No problem." He dumped the Styrofoam plate into the trash can, then watched her walk to the restroom door and disappear inside.

She was limping. Had she been injured in her fall? When he got a chance, he was going to suggest she see the doctor.

20

Shannon intended to go to her uncle's before supper and find the pictures she'd promised Curt a few days ago. With Jack, of course. When she went out to the porch, she saw the TV van parked outside the gate to the ranch. She jogged to the barn behind the house. Jack had said she could ride any of the horses in his stable except Devil, his palomino stallion. She had her eye on a sorrel mare called Filly. After watching the trainers all week, she was ready to get into the saddle herself. With Enrica watching the girls, she had a Friday afternoon to herself, an unheard-of occurrence.

Jack was currying Devil when she stepped into the massive barn. His cowboy hat was pushed to the back of his head, and his face glistened from the heat of the day. "You ready to go to your uncle's?"

She nodded. "That nosy reporter is parked outside the gate so I thought I'd ride one of the horses across to the ranch."

"Not without me," he said. "That guy might come back. Besides, maybe I just want to spend some time with you," he said.

Shannon turned away rather than answer him. She saddled the mare and led the animal out of the barn. Before she could mount, Jack led Devil outside too. He wasn't going to let her make any excuses, and the thought of spending the rest of the afternoon in his company brought heat to her cheeks.

She swung up into the saddle and turned Filly's head to the west. Rocky outcroppings rose in the horizon beyond the scrubby shrubs and cactus. She dug her heels into the mare's flank, and Filly broke into a trot across the yard. Shannon had hoped to find Jewel today, but the stallion would be sure to hide with Jack along.

Jack caught up with her when she reached the trail up the desert mountain. "I had a cougar try to get one of the colts last month. Keep an eye peeled on the rocks over your head."

"I'm not a greenhorn, Jack." She tried to soften the words with a smile, but she knew he caught her irritation because he shrugged and didn't return her smile.

She wished she could swallow that sense of independence that held her at arm's length from others. It had seen her through some bad times, but it tended to alienate people who didn't understand how important it was for her to be strong. Then she looked at people like Allie who weren't afraid to be vulnerable. Maybe they were the strong ones.

Shannon's gaze kept wandering to Jack's broad back on the way down to the desert. She wanted to ignore him and the way her nerves came to full alert in his presence. She wished she could be indifferent to him.

A flicker of movement on the rock above Jack's head caught her eye. The yellow eyes of a mountain lion scrutinized them. The lion's tail lashed as he crouched. "Jack, stop!" Shannon lifted her rifle from the pommel of her saddle.

The big cat's muscles flexed. She saw the nose below the whiskers sniffing the air, the little jiggle in its behind that signaled an imminent leap. She wasn't going to be in time. She managed to wrench the rifle loose and brought up the barrel. Jack reined in his horse, then went for his own rifle when he saw the puma, but the cat would be on him before he managed to get it out.

Shannon sighted down the barrel. She didn't want to hurt the mountain lion—just scare it away. Her finger pressed down on the trigger, and the rifle recoiled against her shoulder. The bullet dug into the hillside to the right of the mountain lion, and shards of rock scattered. The big cat snarled and leaped back. The black tip of its tail was her last glimpse of the animal.

"Thanks," Jack said.

Shannon lashed her gun back to the saddle. "It was a big one. Probably eight feet from nose to tip of the tail. You would have done the same for me. I was in a good place to spot it."

He stared at her steadily. "Is there anything you can't do, Shannon? The more you let me in, the better I like you."

And the more she loved him. The realization nearly rocked her from her horse. She'd tried to guard against it, but he'd scaled the walls with ease. Yanking her gaze from his, she dug her heels into the mare's sides and ran from the temptation to tell him how she felt.

THE RANCH HELD NO APPEARANCE OF LIFE. TUMBLEWEEDS PILED AGAINST the barn and the fences. The house was shuttered, and the contrast against the bright sunshine made it seem more forlorn. Jack's gaze swept door and windows, but they were shut tight. At least no one had broken in.

Shannon stretched in the saddle. The sun glimmered off her pale blonde hair. Jack averted his gaze. He had to get a grip. He'd been without a woman so long that any female would be attractive if he was around her long enough. At least that's what he tried to tell himself.

Shannon swung to the ground and rocked on her boots as she stared at the house. Her brow furrowed as she glanced around the property. The sound of an engine and tires on gravel made him turn. A dusty blue pickup rolled over the ruts and holes in the narrow drive.

Shannon shaded her eyes with her hand, and when the man inside the vehicle stepped out, she gasped. She took a step back and grabbed the horse's reins as though she wanted to mount the animal and run.

"What's he doing here?" Jack asked.

Larue hadn't seen them standing by the barn yet. He stood staring at the house. He wore faded jeans and a Harley-Davidson T-shirt. A finger tipped his dusty cowboy hat to the back of his head. The expression on his face was guarded and speculative.

"I . . . it's Tucker. Let's get out of here. I don't want to talk to him." Her voice was barely a whisper, and her white-knuckled grip on the reins tightened even more. She stumbled and Jack caught her fall. "Maybe he'll leave without seeing us."

"Since when are you afraid of Larue?" Jack studied her face. She'd called him Tucker. In a familiar way. He'd seen them talking a time or two out at the camp. He'd wondered then if they had a history.

Jack's movement attracted Larue's attention. His head came up and his smile sprang into view. He came toward them with his hand outstretched. His blue eyes twinkled under his hat, but it was like someone had turned on a light switch. All fake, as far as Jack was concerned.

"I thought I'd find you here," Larue said. When neither Shannon nor Jack made a move to take his hand, he dropped it back to his side, but his smile only widened. "The old place looks the same, still just as run-down as ever."

"What are you doing here, Tucker?" Shannon asked, her voice vibrating with anger.

He shrugged. "Some reporter tracked me down at the camp. She said I had twins. Twins! I had no idea. I only knew about the one kid."

The truth hit Jack like the kick of a bull. His constant rival had fathered the twins. Acid boiled in his gut. Shannon could have told him when he asked instead of deflecting his questions. She let him be sucker-punched. Right now, he couldn't stand even to look at her.

Larue glanced at Jack. "I hear you got one of my daughters. Kind of ironic, ain't it?" A sardonic grin twisted his mouth.

Only Shannon's hand on Jack's arm restrained him from jumping the trainer to wipe that smirk from his face.

Shannon straightened and shot a glare at Larue. "What do you care? You said you wanted nothing to do with a baby."

Jack managed somehow to control his temper. Larue's sudden interest could ruin all their plans. The adoptions weren't final yet. He wanted to speak his piece, but anything he might say would only inflame the situation. There was no love lost between him and Larue.

"You ready to pay about twenty-five thousand dollars in back support?" Shannon asked, her voice hard and inflexible. "It might be more. There's two, after all."

For the first time, Larue's smile wavered. "Back support?" he echoed.

The color was coming back to Shannon's cheeks. "That's what fathers do. They support their kids. You haven't paid one dime for the girls."

"You're sitting pretty anyway." Larue jerked a thumb at Jack. "Mr. Big Shot married you and plans to buy the girls."

Shannon gasped, and for once, her fast reply deserted her. Jack's grip on his emotions evaporated. He took a step forward and grabbed Larue's shirt collar. He lifted the man up until Larue stood on the toes of his boots. "You aren't fit to even be in the same room as my girls," Jack said through gritted teeth. He let go of Larue and gave him a shove backward.

Larue stumbled back before he recovered his balance and jerked his shirt down into place. "Just because you have money doesn't mean you can strip a man of his children," he said.

"They're not your children," Shannon said. "You're not even on the birth certificate."

Larue fingered the bullwhip at his waist. "A paternity test will prove I am. I have rights, you know." He walked stiff-legged back to his truck like a banty rooster. "You'll be hearing from me." He slammed the door behind him and the engine roared as he turned in the drive. Dust billowed from his tires and hid the vehicle from view.

Shannon sagged against the fence. Her lips trembled in her pale face. "This is my worst nightmare come to life," she said. "I can't let him have contact with the girls."

Her voice seemed to be coming from a long distance away. The magnitude of the problem nearly overwhelmed him. He'd thought marrying Shannon would solve all problems with his claim to Faith. *Think, think.* Larue wasn't the father type. He'd had no concern for Shannon or the girls in five years. That told him all he needed to know.

He could yell at Shannon, but it wouldn't accomplish anything. He focused his gaze on her and saw trembling lips and tear-filled eyes. Her tears washed away the last of his anger.

"He doesn't want contact," Jack said in a firm voice, though his knees wobbled.

"What do you mean?" Shannon choked out. "You heard what he said."

Jack took out his handkerchief and handed it to Shannon. "It's all bluff. He wants money."

"Money?" she echoed. She dabbed the tears pooling in her eyes with his hankie.

"Sure. He knows we'll do anything to keep the girls safe and happy. He's a shark moving in for the kill."

She managed a watery smile. "You really think so?" A faint hope gleamed in her eyes.

"He figures we'll pay him off and he'll be home free." Jack intended to pay up without a murmur. "How much do you think I should offer him?" It galled him to think of caving, but he didn't want the girls ever to know this slimeball was their father.

Her eyes widened. "You're going to pay him?"

"You got a better idea? The adoptions aren't final yet."

Her hands were shaking when she gave him back his handkerchief. "Maybe five thousand dollars?"

Jack snorted. "He'll want more than that. A lot more."

She stepped closer and took his hand. Her fingers curled tightly around his. "What if I give him this ranch? I don't want you paying. I hate this place anyway."

Jack returned the pressure of her hand. "It would mean he'd be in the area trying to sell it. I wouldn't want us to run into him when we had the girls."

"I wouldn't either." She bit her lip. "You didn't sign up for this, Jack."

He caught her gaze and saw the anguish there, but it had to be said. "It would have been a lot easier to handle if I'd been prepared. You should have told me the truth when I asked, Shannon."

She dropped her gaze to the ground. "I thought I had time. I was afraid it would just inflame the rivalry between the two of you. Besides, I didn't want you to know what a fool I was. He showered me with attention back then. He seemed dashing, exciting. A rodeo rider has a certain mystique. I was such a fool."

"You were young. I would have understood that, but what I don't understand is your secrets. Every time I turn around, I run into another one."

Her gaze sought his. "I'm just now learning to trust you," she said in a barely audible voice. "You forget how you've broken my trust in the past, Jack. It's been hard to get past that. You've got to give me some time." Her gaze drifted past his shoulder, and her eyes widened. "Jewel," she breathed.

He turned to see the old stallion come loping over the desert. Shannon called to him, and his ears flickered as he broke into a gallop.

Shannon ran to meet the horse, and Jack watched Jewel approach with a trust that spoke volumes to him about this woman he'd married. She was crazy about her daughters. She'd go to any lengths for an animal without regard for herself. She'd worked tirelessly to provide a better life for Kylie.

But Shannon gave nothing of herself to him.

21

SHANNON FLUNG HER ARMS AROUND JEWEL'S NECK AND BREATHED IN THE scent of horse and sage. She ran her hand down his twitching flank. "Jewel, I've missed you. Where have you been hiding out?"

The horse snorted and nibbled on her hair. Shannon vaulted onto his back, and he turned and cantered across the desert. Crouching low over his neck, she clung to his mane as the wind whipped through her hair. Surefooted as ever, the stallion's hooves flew over the rough ground as woman and horse became one beast.

On the back of her old friend and feeling the wind in her hair, Shannon felt her shame melt away. He'd been her only friend in the dark days, and even now as her tears soaked into his coat, his great heart poured out healing. She'd messed up with Jack time and again. If only she knew how to lower her guard and trust him not to hurt her.

"Jewel, you're too old for this kind of exercise," she said, running her hand over Jewel's damp neck. In the distance she could see Jack walking out to meet them as they returned to the old ranch. Sunlight glinted on the rocks and graphite along the ground, sparkling like tiny diamonds.

Jewel's head came up at Jack's approach. "It's okay. He's a friend." Shannon patted the mustang's neck again, and his rapid breathing slowed.

"He's quite a horse," Jack said, nearing them.

Shannon pressed her knees into Jewel's belly, and he stopped. His eyes rolled at Jack's nearness.

"I've never seen a melding of woman and horse like that," Jack said. "You should be the one training the mustangs instead of watching the rest of us do it."

Shannon slid from her mount's back. "Isn't he something?" She rubbed Jewel's nose.

"So was his rider." Jack's gaze lingered on her. "You were like some mythical creature racing across the desert. I could have watched you for hours."

Heat radiated from Shannon's cheeks. "It's all Jewel." She dropped her hand from the horse's neck, and he snorted, then withdrew. He turned for one last glance at her, then his hooves kicked up sand and he raced away to the hills.

"He'll be back," Jack said near her ear.

"I know." But she strained to catch one last glimpse of the stallion.

Jack tucked a strand of hair out of her eyes. Shannon suddenly realized how closely he stood. Close enough for her to catch the scent of his cologne, to smell the hint of mint on his breath, to catch a whiff of the fabric softener on his shirt.

Her mouth went dry at his nearness. Her gaze locked with his, and she saw a new awareness of her in his eyes. The realization that he was beginning to find her attractive made her pulse race faster than the canter with Jewel.

"Shannon, I need to know everything hiding under that beautiful face. Are there any other secrets you want to spill now?"

Shannon fell into his green eyes and nearly opened her mouth to tell him about her illness, but her throat convulsed. She should have told him before he married her—given him an opportunity to back out before being saddled with a sick wife. He'd have to know sooner or later, but she couldn't tell him when he was staring at her with that intense expression.

He made a slight movement as though to lower his head, and she waited for it. Her disappointment was keen when he stepped back. Maybe it was just as well. A kiss would mean nothing to a man like him, but everything to a woman like her.

"There is one thing I can tell you," she said, offering him the only thing she could right now. "I know where the Spanish artifacts are located."

"Just like you know the cause of the Marfa lights, right?" He grinned and tweaked her nose.

"No, really, Jack. I'm serious. My father found them. They're in the cave, sealed up with the bodies of my parents." She knew he understood the magnitude of what she'd said when his smile slackened then warmed again.

"You're serious?" he asked.

"No one knows but me. And now you."

"You said you didn't want their bodies disturbed. How do you know I won't go looking for that treasure? Every guy has a little bit of Indiana Jones in him."

"I . . . I trust you, Jack." *But not enough to tell you I have MS.* That revelation had to wait until they weren't standing in the blazing sun in front of a dilapidated old house. Maybe one night this week after dinner when the kids were in bed. She turned toward the house. "I guess we'd better get inside and find those papers Curt needs."

He led the way. "You could have let him look for them."

"Curt's afraid of bats. We've had several in the attic, and I think that's where Uncle Earl put the box he's looking for." She dug the extra key out of her pocket when they stepped onto the porch.

"Here, let me," Jack said when she had trouble fitting the key into the lock. He took the key from her fingers and fiddled with it until it clicked, and the door swung open. With obvious reluctance, he dropped his hand and let her move forward. He stepped around her. "Let me look inside first."

Before she could protest, he leaped up the steps and disappeared through the doorway. She hurried after him.

"I can handle this," he said. "Tell me what to look for. You can wait out on the porch."

"We'll go up together." She shut the door behind them and locked it. She put her hand on the banister and began to climb the steps.

Jack followed her to the hallway on the second floor. "Where's the attic access?"

"There." She pointed to a door at the end of the hallway.

He got to it first and tugged it open. Stale, dank air made her cough. Dust motes swirled in the entry to the steps. Darkness shrouded the steep stairs. He groped for a light switch and found it halfway up the steps. Weak yellow light showed spiderwebs barring the way. "Got a broom?"

"There's one in the closet. Hang on." She went down the hall to a door at the other end, then returned with a broom in hand. She'd grabbed the tennis racquet they kept in the hall closet as well. "Here you go," she said handing him the broom. The bats she could handle with the racquet.

He took the broom and knocked the spiderwebs down. The tough webs resisted the broom at first, and he stepped back as a fat spider ran toward his boot.

Shannon watched him squash it and shuddered. She grimaced. "I hate black widows."

"They love anyplace where people don't go." He brandished the broom like a weapon and started up the stairs.

There were no more spiderwebs until they stepped onto the wide floorboards. Glancing around, she saw more webs with the characteristic erratic appearance, as though the spider were drunk, but they were high overhead and unlikely to be a bother.

"There are probably brown recluse up here, too, so watch where you put your hands," Jack said.

Shannon skirted the webs on her way to the chests in the center of the room. She reached the first one and leaned down to open it.

"Let me check it first." Jack unlatched the chest and lifted the lid. Papers and books were stacked inside, and the dry odor of decaying paper rose to greet them. "Looks clear," he said.

"The lids are tight fitting," Shannon said. She knelt and began to lift the items out one by one.

"Do we know what we're looking for?"

"Some kind of photo album, Curt said."

"What's so important about it?"

Shannon shrugged. "I guess he has some fond memories of his dad, even though they didn't get along. Maybe he has regrets." She stood and dusted her hands. "It's not in here."

"Maybe the other one." He pointed at another chest under the eaves. "Let me pull it out. It's certain to have spiders on the back of it."

Shannon stepped back and let him swipe behind the chest. He hauled it away from the eaves. He squashed more spiders.

"The sooner we get down from here the better. This place is badly infested," he said with his mouth twisted.

Shannon shuddered. "I'm ready to go as soon as I look in there."

He threw open the chest. "It's empty." He glanced around at the mismatched furniture—mostly chairs and a broken table or two. "Should we start on the boxes?"

Shannon clasped herself. "No, I'm getting out of here. If he wants the pictures that badly, he can come look for them himself." She bolted toward the steps. Her skin crawled from being up here.

Jack followed behind her and she heard him stop. She turned at the top of the stairs to see him staring at a small chest at the far end of the attic. He strode to the wooden box, brushed it with the broom, and opened it.

"What's inside?" She forced herself to walk the few steps to join him. Several photo albums and account books were inside.

"This what you're looking for?" he asked, lifting the photo albums.

She nodded. "I think so. Can you bring it down?" She led the way down the steps and didn't do a very good job of disguising her limp.

Jack followed her to the first floor with his burden. He dropped it onto the sofa and dusted his hands. "You're limping again. We need to have you looked at."

"When did you become a doctor?" She smiled to mask her fear. How would she tell him about her MS? She walked outside and moved toward her horse, and the wind shifted. The sharp tang of smoke came to her nose, and she squinted into the darkness and saw a glow in the west. "Fire!" She pointed out the blaze against the night sky.

"I'll call Rick and have him get some help." He grabbed his cell phone, punched in the numbers and explained the situation in terse words, then shut it. "Any shovels in the barn?"

She nodded. "I'll show you." They both ran toward the outbuildings, and she led him to the rack of tools on the wall just inside the door. They grabbed as many shovels and hoes as they could, then mounted their horses and headed across the desert in the direction of the blaze.

"It's where Jewel usually roams," Shannon said, her voice tight and strained. "He has to be all right."

She was right. Jack urged his horse to a gallop. They were the first to arrive at the blaze. A line of fire raced across the tinder-dry vegetation. The blaze advanced toward a small valley hemmed in at the back by steep desert mountains. He caught a glimmer of movement and stared through the gloom.

"He's there!" Shannon said, pointing in the direction he'd seen movement.

Then Jack saw Jewel. Mustangs as well. They tossed their heads, and he heard one scream with terror as the fire advanced into the valley. A few more minutes and they'd be trapped. "This way!" he shouted, pointing to an opening in the wall of flames.

Devil reared and snorted, and Jack knew he'd never get him through that opening with the cinders whirling all around them. He dismounted. "Come on!" he told Shannon. "Follow me."

She dismounted and dropped all her tools but a shovel, then raced after him through the opening. A piercing whistle came from her lips. Jack saw Jewel's head come up, and the horse screamed, almost as if he were asking for help. He didn't run from Shannon as she jogged toward him. He stepped out to meet her, and she grabbed his mane.

"Come on, boy, we can get you out of here." She led him toward the narrowing window through the flames, and he snorted and backed up before she managed to coax him to move.

Jack watched with his mouth open for a moment, then bent to shovel dirt on the fire as fast as he could. He was fighting a losing battle here, and the heat and smoke seared his lungs. "Hurry!" he shouted above the crackling.

Shannon nodded and led the big stallion closer to the escape. The wild mustangs and burros followed Jewel toward the opening. Shannon stepped past the blaze, then slapped Jewel on the rump, and he took off. The rest of the horses followed.

Jack tore at the ground even harder. They'd saved the horses, but if they didn't get help soon, they'd lose her ranch. Then he heard the rumble of trucks and saw the glow of headlamps. The cavalry had arrived with smokejumper Buck Carter leading the charge.

It was two hours later before the fire was contained, and he and Shannon mounted their horses to ride home. His wife drooped in the saddle, and her face was smudged with soot, but he'd never seen a more beautiful sight. What other woman would have fought for the lives of the horses so hard?

Their gazes met across the manes of their horses. "Thank you, Jack," Shannon said. "You saved Jewel. And the other horses. I'll never forget tonight."

"Neither will I," he said softly. "You're amazing, Shannon."

Her lips trembled, but she didn't look away. "I'm sorry I didn't tell you about Larue when you asked."

"We'll fix it," he said. "We're a family now." And he realized he was beginning to love being able to say that.

22

MONDAY MORNING SHANNON AND JACK SAT OUTSIDE A STUCCO BUILDING nestled in the rocky hillside. Her throat hurt from the smoke inhalation of the night before, and every muscle ached. She knew Jack had to feel the same, because he was moving slowly.

They exchanged a warm glance, then Jack swung open his door. "We'd better get in there or we'll be late."

The structure appeared more like a house than a doctor's office. She dreaded having the doctor poke around in her arm. It might leave her too sore to do her job.

"Ready?" Jack asked. He got out of the truck.

"If I have to be." She climbed out the other side and fell into step with him. "This is a good doctor, right?"

"The best. He retired from the Mayo Clinic and came here for a slower-paced practice. He'll be gentle." He grinned down at her. "I never took you for a coward, Blondie."

She stuck her tongue out at him. "I laugh at pain."

"I can believe that." He opened the door.

Shannon glanced around the room she'd entered. Charles Russell reprints of western scenes hung on the walls. She couldn't help but straighten one that hung crazily. Old issues of *National Geographic* and several hunting magazines were stacked on the oak table in front of the sofa and chairs. She sat on the sofa and riffled through the pile.

Before she could decide on one, a woman in jeans and boots stuck her head in the doorway. Her brown hair curled in tight ringlets around her head, and she wore a smile bright enough to light the room. "Jack, the doctor's ready for your wife."

Shannon shot to her feet and followed Jack's long legs down the hall. The nurse ushered them into a tiny examination room. There were only two chairs, one for the doctor and one for Jack, so Shannon scooted onto the examination table. The paper crinkled under her. Her hands were shaking.

The door opened and a man who could have modeled for Gumby stepped into the room. His legs and arms were long and lanky.

Dr. Hastings glanced from her to Jack from under beetled brows. "You pregnant already?"

Shannon didn't dare look at Jack's face. She was sure her own was beet red. "Um, no, I've got something in my arm that needs to be removed."

"Your arm? What do you mean?" The doctor took hold of the arm Shannon had extended. He ran his long fingers over it.

"We need your discretion on this, Doc. Against her knowledge, someone injected a microchip into her arm. The person it belongs to has been threatening Shannon. We need to get it out and see what's going on."

"A microchip? Do you have any idea where it's located?" He adjusted his glasses and peered at her arm.

"I ran a scanner over my arm. I think it's right here." Shannon pressed on the flesh, high on her upper arm.

"Want to do it now? I'll have to numb it."

"I want it out."

"I've got a larger room with more equipment down the hall." Dr. Hastings turned around and held the door open. "I'll probably need a microscope."

Shannon slipped from the table and moved toward the door. Her feet seemed like logs today, and she stumbled slightly before she reached the door.

The doctor frowned. "How long have you had MS?"

Shannon froze. She wanted to deny his observation, to pretend she didn't hear, but he was staring at her with an intent expression. Behind her, she heard Jack's sharp intake of breath. This wasn't the way she'd wanted to reveal her condition to him. She'd meant to do it this week, but the time had never seemed right.

"MS?" Jack said. "You mean multiple sclerosis?"

The doctor seemed to realize he'd stepped into unknown waters. "This way," he said briskly. His white coattails flapped as he escaped the explosion he'd just launched.

Shannon started after him, but Jack caught her arm. "You have MS?" he asked.

Shannon drew herself up and squared her shoulders. "Yes. I was diagnosed six months ago."

His nostrils flared, and his mouth was a thin line. He was breathing hard. "Why didn't you tell me?"

She rubbed her head. "Does it matter why?"

"Yes, it matters," he said. "Blair went a little crazy when she was diagnosed with breast cancer. She couldn't bear the fight ahead, and she fought it by doing all kinds of wild stuff. I can't go through that again."

"I'm not Blair." Her heart beating hard in her chest, she brushed past him to follow the doctor. One last secret had detonated in her face.

NOT AGAIN. JACK BARELY NOTICED THE DOCTOR PREPPING SHANNON FOR the procedure to remove the chip. She'd betrayed him, sucked him into a relationship without telling him of her major health issues. The words *multiple sclerosis* had sucked him back to the vortex of pain following Blair's death.

The day Shannon had suggested they marry, she'd said she wanted Kylie to be taken care of, but he'd never dreamed she had an urgent reason for that desire. That had to be the real reason she'd proposed marriage. Or maybe to get health insurance for her condition. She needed some patsy on the hook to care for her when she couldn't care for herself.

And he was that patsy. He'd been so desperate to keep Faith, he hadn't investigated Shannon's motives. He stared hard at her, but she didn't look his way. Too ashamed, probably.

"Got it," the doctor said, removing the magnifying glasses he'd worn. "Tiny thing. Not much bigger than a pinhead. Got any idea what's on it?"

Jack struggled to put aside his anger and concentrate on the current problem. "Nope, but Rick's got a friend who can tell us."

The doctor put the tissue containing the chip in a petri dish. He put a lid on it and handed it to Jack. "Let me know what you find out. This is a new one for the books." He glanced back to Shannon. "You doing okay, ma'am? You look a little pale."

"I'm fine. There was no pain," Shannon said. "Can I go now?"

"You bet. Take it easy the rest of the day. I put a couple of butterfly bandages on there to hold the cut closed. Call me if you have any problems." She nodded and the doctor helped her sit. "You need a wheelchair? You seem a little shaky," he said.

"No, I can walk." Perspiration dotted her upper lip, but she slid off the table and started for the door.

Stiff-legged, Jack grabbed the petri dish and followed her down the hall. She paused to grab the wall just before they reached the waiting room. He slipped his arm around her waist and supported her to the door and out to the truck. She sat heavily on the seat and began to fumble with the seat belt. She still hadn't looked at him or said a word.

Typical woman. Not even an apology. His fists clenched, he strode to his side of the truck. He wasn't leaving here without an explanation. Slamming the door shut behind him, he turned to pin her with his gaze. "When were you going to tell me?" he demanded.

Their gazes locked. "I meant to tell you this week," she said. "I didn't want to keep any more secrets from you. I was waiting for the right time."

Her blonde hair and clear blue eyes made her appear so innocent. Like his dad always said, *Just because a chicken has wings doesn't mean it can fly.* He fumbled for his keys. "Why weren't you honest right up front?"

"I was afraid you'd use it against me, take me to court and tell the judge I wasn't fit to raise Faith. Remember, Jack, it was early in our relationship—if you want to call it that—and all I had to go on was the way you'd betrayed me in the past. Did you really expect me to trust you with something like that?"

He'd escaped the money-hungry Texas mamas with their simpering daughters in tow only to be caught by a golden-haired angel whose beauty hid her true motives. "Were you just interested in my money all along?"

That brought her head up, and her eyes flashed fire. "I don't care about your money! How could you think this is about money? You're my daughters' daddy. That's all I wanted. Someone to care about Kylie and Faith. You could have been as poor as me and it wouldn't have mattered." Her voice trailed away, and she twisted her hands in her lap.

"I don't think I believe you," he said shortly. "All my life I've had to contend with people out for what they could get from me. For once I thought a relationship was starting because of something someone else could give." He jammed the key into the ignition and started the truck.

"Believe what you want." She turned her head and stared out the window as the town buildings moved past her head. "Our marriage is based on what's best for the girls. That's all that matters to me."

"And to me," he said through gritted teeth. And to think he'd been starting to find her attractive, to watch her with the girls and wonder what a real marriage with her might be like. He'd been a pure fool. Theirs had been a business transaction, and that was all it would ever be.

He felt her glance as he gunned the engine and raced the truck up the hill toward the house. She'd better not be feeling sorry for him. He couldn't remember when he'd been so mad. He'd begun to dream again, to believe he might even love again. The facade of a sweet little family had dissolved in his hand even as he grabbed for it.

The touch of skin against skin came when she leaned over and laid her hand on his bare forearm. Her fingers pressed into his flesh, and he shot a glance at her. Tears swam in her eyes, a sight that began to melt the ice forming around his heart. *Probably an act*, he reminded himself.

"I'm sorry, Jack. Really, I meant to tell you this week. I'm not like Blair. I'll fight this."

"Don't speak her name," he said, jerking his arm away. "Not once in all the years I knew her did she ever keep something from me, especially not something like this. You're full of secrets, Shannon. We can't have any kind of marriage when you hide things away."

"Okay, so I'm not perfect like Blair," she said, her voice choked. "I was trying to declare a truce for the sake of the girls. You can be mad at me all you want, but don't let the girls see."

"Agreed," he snapped. He would have to be wary of her from now on. Even in his own home. It didn't seem fair that he'd been so completely snowed by her. He'd always prided himself on his good judgment, but when it came to her, his instincts had been off in the worst way.

They reached the long lane back to his ranch. He glanced at the petri dish. "We need to talk to Rick about this chip."

"I'll take it over after supper. He'll send it to his friend."

"Seems like we ought to clean it up or something."

"I can do that."

She wasn't looking at him and her tone was one she might use with a stranger. Their relationship would never be the same.

23

AFTER SUPPER, SHANNON TOOK ALCOHOL, A TOWEL, AND TWEEZERS AND set to work cleaning up the microchip. It was hard to see past the blur of tears. She'd messed up everything by not trusting Jack.

The thing was tiny, and she couldn't imagine what it might contain that was so important. She wiped the petri dish, dropped the minute chip back into it, and capped it.

In the living room, she found Jack playing Candy Land with the girls. Seated on the floor and flanked by the twins, he was smiling and relaxed. Shannon wished she could slough off their argument so easily. She still burned at the memory of the contempt in his eyes.

And she'd deserved it. At the time it seemed best to hold this secret close, but she'd been wrong. "I'm going over to Bluebird Ranch," she said.

Jack glanced up and his smile died. "You want me to come with you?"

"No, Daddy, you have to finish the game!" Faith narrowed her gaze at Shannon.

"No, I'll be fine." Still, it stung that Jack didn't insist. Her gaze caressed Faith. Shannon had made no inroads in getting close to her other daughter. Faith held her at arm's length. Shannon suspected Jack would encourage things to stay that way now. He'd loved his first wife in a way that made Shannon wish she could someday inspire even half that depth of emotion.

But not from Jack. That dream was stillborn. She let her gaze linger on her little family one last time, then went out to her Jeep. The night air was still, and in the distance, a coyote yipped. The scent of the Chihuahuan Desert greeted her: creosote, sage, and the sweet fragrance of blooming roses. She batted away a moth as big as a hummingbird that dived for her head, then ambled to her vehicle.

It was too nice of a night to worry, but she found herself chewing on her lip as she drove to the neighboring ranch. Marriage to Jack had seemed the answer to her problems, but instead, it had only compounded them.

Lights shone from the windows of the Bluebird Youth Ranch. The aroma of chili wafted through the open kitchen window. Jem and Moses came to meet her, their tails wagging. She stopped to rub their shaggy coats and to accept their kisses on her chin. "Good boys," she crooned. One thing she loved about dogs was their total acceptance and love. Unlike humans.

The family hadn't realized she was out here yet. Jem hadn't barked. Shannon stood on the porch and listened to the sound of laughter as Rick teased Allie about looking sexy pregnant. The love in his voice made hot tears well in Shannon's eyes. She had never experienced that kind of love and support.

And after today, she never would.

Dashing the tears from her cheeks with the back of her hand, she rapped on the screen door. The laughter and voices stilled, then Allie appeared on the other side.

Allie opened the door with a smile. "Shannon, I wasn't expecting you until tomorrow."

Shannon stepped into the entry. "I got the chip out of my arm. Rick said he could give it to a friend to decode."

Allie nodded. "Want some chili? It's still hot."

"No thanks, we ate already. Besides, it's only good with crackers, and Enrica has everyone in the house on a strict no-wheat diet. I think it might even help my MS." She followed her friend to the kitchen. "But I'd take some coffee." Rick and Betsy greeted her.

"There's a fresh pot—help yourself," Allie said.

Shannon knew her way around the Bailey kitchen, even better than her own since Enrica hardly let her near the room. She got down a cup and poured the strong coffee into it. She found cream in the refrigerator and sugar in the canister. Being here always infused her with a sense of belonging and love.

If only her own home held this much contentment.

Most days she was on the sidelines looking in at life, just as if she were back in her uncle's house. She took a swig of coffee and sat beside Betsy at the kitchen table. "Hey, Bets, are you going to come play with the girls one of these days?"

Betsy nodded. "Can I come tomorrow?" She looked up at her mother as she spoke.

"If it's okay with Shannon."

"That would be great. Kylie and Faith have been asking about you." She didn't want the twins to get so close they excluded other friends.

"You have the chip out?" Rick asked. His hair hung over his tanned forehead, and he leaned forward in his chair.

Shannon slid the petri dish across the table to him. "There it is."

Allie's glance moved to her arm. "Did it hurt?"

Shannon shook her head. "The doctor numbed it. It aches a little now but nothing major. Take a look—the chip is tiny."

Rick held the dish up to the light. "I can hardly see it. I'll overnight it to Brendan Waddell, my friend in Washington. He'll figure out what it is. You sure you want to do this? That guy might be back for it if he finds out this is what he's been looking for."

"I don't know where Mary Beth is, and I don't want to turn it over to them if she's in danger. It's my only bargaining hope. How long do you think it will be before Waddell gets back to you?"

"I'd give it a week. He might be involved in some big issue at work." Rick rose. "I'll go give him a call, then head out to the barn to check on the horses."

"You might stop by the bunkhouse and make sure no kids have snuck out," Allie said.

He nodded. "We've got a pretty good batch this time. I don't anticipate any problems with them." He glanced at Betsy. "Want to go with me, squirt?"

"Sure, Daddy." Betsy slid from her chair and put her hand in Rick's.

"Thanks," Shannon whispered as they passed. Smart man to know she needed to talk to Allie.

"What's wrong?" Allie demanded as soon as Rick and Betsy were out of earshot. "You're too pale and shaky for it to be caused by digging that little chip out of your arm."

It would be easy to blame Jack for her upset, but the time for truth was here. Shannon didn't want to lose Allie's friendship, but she might react as badly as Jack had to Shannon's secretiveness.

"Jack found out today that I have MS."

Allie's mouth gaped. "You've never told him? Oh, Shannon." Her voice was reproachful.

"I know, I know. I meant to tell him this week. I've been so stupid, Allie. I . . . I wanted him to start to feel something for me, and I thought if he knew everything about my past, about my illness, he'd never love me." She rubbed her hands together. "There's more though. You've never asked about the girls' father."

"I thought when you wanted to talk about it, you would."

That would be never. Shannon sighed and took a sip of coffee. "Tucker Larue showed up at my uncle's ranch when we were there Friday. He told Jack he was their father."

"Tucker?" Allie grimaced.

"I know, it seems strange. He wasn't always so out for himself." Shannon lifted her shoulders. "Anyway, Jack was furious and told me he wanted all the secrets out. I should have told him about my MS then, but the time didn't seem right. I was so *stupid*!"

Allie took Shannon's hand. "I'm so sorry. How are you feeling?"

"Okay, but the stress has kicked up my symptoms a little."

"There's a really good naturopath in Alpine. I think you should go up there and see her. I know an MS patient she treated, and you can't even tell my friend has it now."

"Really? I'm willing to try anything. Make me an appointment and I'll go."

Allie nodded and continued to stare at Shannon. "I assume Jack was mad when he found out?"

Shannon winced at the memory of his white face. "Furious. And I can't blame him. I forced him into marriage and didn't tell him the whole story. I was stupid and selfish. I've faced worse than a disease. It's not going to lick me, and we would have been okay without him."

"You married to make sure Kylie was taken care of, right? Surely he can understand that." Allie stood and began to carry the dishes to the sink. Her huge bulk swayed.

Shannon gathered the rest of the dishes and began to put them in the dishwasher. "I was beginning to hope there was a future for me and Jack that was more than . . . than I'd first thought."

Allie leaned her weight against the counter and stared up at Shannon. "You're in love with him," she said.

"He's about as easy to love as a horse fly." Shannon wanted to turn away from the probing blue eyes of her friend. "We're still strangers. I did hope that we could be friends."

A smile played about Allie's lips. "I know the signs, my friend. I tried to ignore my feelings for Rick for way too long. You can deny it all you want, but the evidence is clear."

"Clear as black water." Shannon tried to laugh off Allie's words, but they sank deep, down to her soul.

She had tried to talk herself out of her initial realization that she loved Jack. She could admire his tenderness with the girls and his commitment to his first wife without being in love with him. It was fine to watch his broad shoulders across the paddock and see his gentleness with the mustangs without allowing it to go any further. Noticing his strength and unswerving integrity didn't mean she had given her heart with no hope of retrieval.

Did it?

Her throat closed. Was there anything more pathetic than being in love with a man who despised her?

"Your emotions are right on your face," Allie said. "It's okay to love him. He's your husband, after all. When I married Rick, I thought it was for Betsy's sake and would be temporary, but Rick realized our vows were sacred. He decided to love me in action and hoped the feelings would come later. They did."

Shannon had never witnessed a happier union than Rick and Allie's. Maybe there was hope for her and Jack after all. "Jack doesn't love me. He's still in love with Blair."

"Fight for him, Shannon." Allie's gaze locked with Shannon's. "He might not love you right now, but show him love and respect anyway. Once he gets to know you better, he can't help but love you. Anyone would."

"You're prejudiced." Shannon smiled weakly. "I don't know if I can do this. Or even if I *want* to do it. I've had a lot of rejection in my life. I'm not sure I can face a rejection that would hurt so much."

"No pain, no gain," Allie said. "I know that sounds flippant, but it's life, girl. Would you trade the joy you've had with Kylie to avoid the pain that's gone along with it?"

"No," Shannon said. "Not in a million years."

"Then try. Shower Jack with love and respect and see what happens."

Shannon's pulse gave a jump at the thought of going out on a limb that way. "I'll think about it," was all she could manage to say.

DRIVING HOME UNDER THE STARS, THE ROMANTIC IDEALS ALLIE HAD talked about seemed easy to put into action. Jack was an easy man to respect—and love. Facing the reality of his aloof expression was something else. The girls were in bed when she got home, and he sat watching the sports replays on the news.

When she passed the door to the den, he called to her. "Shannon, you won't believe what the sheriff said. Come here a minute." He leaped from his leather chair when she came into the room. "You'll need to sit down."

He was scaring her. "What's wrong?" She shook him off when he tried to push her into a chair.

"I think it might all be over. It was your cousin Curt all along."

"What are you talking about?"

"Sheriff Borland was driving past your uncle's place and saw a light inside the house. He shut off his cruiser by the road and walked onto the property, found Curt on the porch with a box of papers. Curt tried to talk his way out and said you'd given him permission to be there, but he dropped the box and Borland found old stocks inside. When he started to call you, Curt objected. The sheriff didn't like his manner but let him go. Borland kept the stocks though. He checked them out and they're worth a tidy sum. He wants to know if you authorized Curt to take stocks from the house. I told him no, so he's going to pick Curt up for questioning."

"So that's what Curt's been after. But why? He has plenty of money."

Jack shook his head. "Not so much. He's on the verge of bankruptcy. He lost an important case about six months ago, and his practice has tanked. It's over, Shannon. He's been behind all this."

"But what about Mary Beth?"

"Borland is sure he can get Curt to sing."

A thought began to hover. "Maybe if I take the stocks to the guy who's been assaulting me, he'll let Mary Beth go. This might be what he's been looking for."

"You're not in danger anymore. Or the girls."

Shannon stepped closer. Her arms came up around his waist, and she clung to him. Did his lips just brush her hair? She hugged him tighter, words of love hovering on her lips.

But no. He would never believe it. She had to show it, like Allie said. Dropping her arms, she stepped away and directed a full-wattage smile his way. He nearly reeled when she did. "I'm glad I heard it from you," she whispered. She turned toward the door. "I want to talk to Curt and get those stocks."

"I'll come with you." He got up from the sofa and followed her. He called his intentions to Enrica.

Shannon tried her phone after piling into Jack's truck. Jack pulled out onto the main road. "Stupid thing is dead again," she muttered.

Jack fished his cell phone out of his pocket. "Here, use mine. Who are you calling?"

"Mary Beth's phone." She was going to take charge of this situation and put an end to it. She plugged her phone in to charge, then punched in the number and listened to it ring. When she got Mary Beth's voice mail, she left a message for the captor saying she had what he wanted.

Jack parked his truck in front of the sheriff's office, a single-story stucco building that was showing signs of weathering on the corners. Shannon let Jack explain what they wanted while she thought about how to handle Curt. What did she even feel about what he'd done?

Acceptance. That's what this sense of peace was all about. All the property should have belonged to Curt anyway. She'd tell him he could have it all, but she had to take the stocks to his partners so Mary Beth could go free. She followed Jack and the deputy back to the cells and faced Curt through the bars.

He sat on a bunk with his head in his hands. He leaped to his feet when he saw her. "Shannon, you've got to tell them I wasn't doing anything wrong."

"I'm going to," she said. "I'm not pressing charges. But why didn't you just tell me what you wanted, Curt? I would have let you have anything you wanted. Or wouldn't your partners let you?"

"What partners?" He shook his head. "If you're talking about that crazy idea of Borland's that I had something to do with a kidnapping and some attacks on you, it's not true."

She didn't want to believe him. "I'm going to take the stocks to your partners, and you can go free. I'm also going to sign over the ranch to you."

He gave a harsh laugh. "That place isn't worth the kerosene to burn it down. I don't want it. But I need the stocks."

She shook her head and walked away, ignoring his shouts. Jack pointed out the sheriff's office, and she stopped long enough to take possession of the box of stocks and tell him she wasn't pressing charges.

When she stepped outside, she stopped in her tracks at the sight of Verna talking with reporters. She and Jack exchanged glances, then approached the tangle of media. "What's going on?" she asked.

Verna's gaze was direct. "I'm telling the truth, Shannon. All of it. I can't sleep, can't eat, can't even take pleasure in my garden. People ha-have been saying wrong things about you and Jack. I'm not standing for it anymore."

Shannon's eyes welled, and she blinked back the tears. "Thank you, Verna." Jack murmured his thanks, too, and ignoring the shouted questions from the media, they pressed past the crush of people to his truck.

By the time they reached the vehicle, her cell phone was ringing. She and Jack locked gazes. "It's Mary Beth's cell phone," she said.

"He's returning my call." Her pulse was thumping loudly in her ears, and she unplugged the phone, then flipped it open. Jack bent his head to listen in.

The man's voice came through the phone. "You ready to play ball? Where do you want to meet?"

"I want to know that Mary Beth is okay first."

"You're in no position to call the shots, lady. No money and the woman goes bye-bye."

"Look, I have the stocks right here in my hand. I'll turn them over to you, but not without Mary Beth."

"Stocks? What stocks? Is this some kind of scam?"

"You . . . you aren't after my uncle's stocks?" Confusion swept over her.

"We want our eight million," he snapped. "Not some stupid stocks. Don't get cute with me. It's not good for your health. Or the broad's."

The phone went dead. Shannon closed it and stared at Jack. "Eight million dollars," she said, her voice awed. "I don't understand."

"Maybe it's something to do with that number on the chip. We'll have to wait and see what Rick's friend finds out."

Shannon's earlier elation drained away. She had no idea what to do next. About anything.

24

SUNDAY AFTERNOON AFTER CHURCH, AS HE DROVE THE TRUCK ALONG THE deserted road, Jack passed a piñon that was as twisted by the wind as he was by his emotions. He glanced at Shannon from the corner of his eye on the way. She wore a cute little pink dress that showed off her tanned arms. Very froufrou and unlike her normal attire of jeans and T-shirt.

He was too aware of her: the long curtain of silken hair, the way she chewed on her lower lip when she was thinking, the strength of the love she showed the girls—even Faith, who didn't respond. After her secrets, he wanted to pretend she was nothing more than a guest in the house, but all week, it seemed as though she was going out of her way to be appealing.

"Let's play Candy Land after lunch," Shannon said.

"Daddy said he'd take us horseback riding," Faith said. "Just me and Kylie. Not *you*."

Shannon's smile faded, and she turned her head, but not so fast that Jack missed the liquid sheen of her eyes. "We'd like you to come with us," he said, then wished he hadn't.

"You can take the girls and have fun," she said. "I've got a book I've been wanting to read."

"Mommy *has* to go," Kylie said. "You're being mean, Faith."

Faith had been taking a big sister's leadership role. Jack watched in the rearview mirror to see how she would take her younger sister's assertive tone.

"My mommy is in heaven." Faith frowned, then turned to look out the window without saying anything.

Jack studied her in the mirror. Having her mother back had been her dream since Blair died, but Faith was unable to accept the love Shannon extended. He wasn't sure how to get to the root of the problem. Maybe have a talk with Faith. Or maybe Blair's parents, though he suspected it would take more than that. They hadn't seen her since Faith found out the truth.

Was Faith jealous of his relationship—such as it was—with Shannon? Jealous of Kylie? Maybe Faith wanted her own mother, not someone else's. Still, the two girls had become inseparable, so that didn't seem likely.

Jack parked the truck. "Everyone get changed. I'll have Enrica pack us a lunch. Take your swimsuits too." The girls unsnapped their seat belts and slid out of their booster seats in the back. He got out to open the door for them. They jumped from the backseat and raced to the house.

Shannon stopped, her hand poised on the door handle. "Swimsuits?"

"There's a great pool this time of year in the back canyon. It will be cold though." He grinned when she shivered.

"I know the place," she said. "You three go on."

"The girls would be disappointed to leave you behind." She was still shaking her head, and the words "I want you to come too" slipped out of his mouth.

The sway of her head stopped. Her gaze examined his. "You do?"

"Yes. Very much." He let her see into his soul a bit before he broke the connection and looked away. He hadn't wanted to trust her again, but his wall had developed a hairline crack. Much of her distrust was his fault, so he didn't have much of a right to beef. The more he'd thought about it, the more he'd realized he wouldn't have told her he was sick either.

"I'll get changed." Her voice was resigned as she got out of the truck and jogged up the walk to the house.

Was she afraid to be with him, or did she hate the canyon? It could be a spooky place, and legends abounded of lost gold, evil spirits, and flash floods.

While the family changed, he got the horses and ponies saddled. Faith's pony, Topsy, billowed out her stomach when he laid the saddle on her back. "Oh no, you don't," he murmured. He kneed her hard and she let the air escape. Faith hated to see him do that, but if he let the pony get by with it, the saddle would slide down the minute Topsy exhaled. Faith would be on the ground and maybe dragged.

His three girls came out of the house. The realization he thought of them like that made his smile freeze in place. The children were so like Shannon too. Maybe that was where these stray emotions came from. He couldn't help but be somewhat attached to her when his daughters were so similar.

Psychobabble, that's all it was. He was trying to rationalize something that couldn't be explained. He managed a smile. "Ready?"

The girls squealed and ran to the ponies. Shannon brushed past him closely enough for him to catch the scent of her hair. He watched her hips sway as she walked to her horse. Every woman should look as good in jeans as she did. Spending the day with her was trouble.

He mounted Rascal and led his family over hardpan past sagebrush, yucca, and prickly pear. A gentle wind blew back his hair and filled his nose with the scent of the desert—sage, creosote, and clean air. He couldn't remember when he'd been so contented.

He slanted a glance at Shannon. She rode in the saddle like she'd been born there, her knees guiding the mare, her head up and surveying all they passed. Her tan cowboy hat framed her beautiful face.

He'd fallen in love with her.

THE CLEAR MOUNTAIN POOL WAS AS CLOSE TO PARADISE AS SHE WAS LIKELY to get this side of heaven. Shannon dangled her feet in the cold water and shivered when the breeze touched her bare skin. Almost before the shiver began, Jack dropped a towel around her bare shoulders.

She glanced up. He was smiling, and the expression in his eyes drew her. She shook off the notion that he was expressing anything other than kindness. "Thanks."

"If you want to get out of that wet suit and get dressed, there's a cave back there. I checked it for critters, and it's clear."

The girls still swam and shrieked in the cold water. The pool was only three feet deep, perfect for the children. "I'll wait until the girls are ready to change." She felt great and had for the last two days. Enrica had begun pushing some homeopathic concoctions down her as well as doing acupressure treatments. Shannon hoped it was working.

He sat beside her and dropped his bare feet back into the water. Her pulse was too erratic to dare a glance his way. "Have you talked to Tucker about our offer?"

"Not yet. I'm letting him sweat a little." The warmth in his voice had turned as cold as the water.

Shannon paddled her feet in the cold water. "My parents used to bring me here. Up that path and around on the other side of the mountain is the cave I told you about," she said in a low voice.

"The treasure?"

She nodded. "If you tunneled through the rock right behind us, the Spanish artifacts and gold would be right there, heaped on rock shelves like the day it was hidden. I've never seen anything like it."

Jack turned a speculative glance behind him. "You trying to see if I'll break? I won't. Your secrets are safe with me. I wouldn't go looking for that treasure unless you wanted me to. And I don't think that's ever going to happen."

He put his arm around her and she leaned into his embrace. Maybe fell would be a more appropriate way to put it, since the shock of his gesture stole her strength. His cold skin was starting to warm in the heat of the sun. If she dared, she'd tip up her head and invite a kiss, but she didn't want to press her luck.

Jack gave her a squeeze, then removed his arm. "I think I'll get dressed." He rose and moved away from the spring.

The girls came sputtering up out of the water. Kylie climbed into Shannon's lap. Her cold little body made Shannon gasp, but she wrapped a towel around her daughter and drew her closer. She held out her other arm for Faith. "Cold, sweetie?" To Shannon's surprise, Faith glanced at her father's retreating back, then crawled into Shannon's lap. She wrapped the other side of the towel around the shivering child.

It probably wouldn't work, but a thought struck her. She leaned over the still water with the girls. Their reflections shimmered back up at them. "Look at us, girls."

"We look just like you, Mommy," Kylie said. "Me and Faith. Are we going to be as pretty as you?"

"Prettier," Shannon said, sitting back with her arms tight around the girls.

Faith touched her face and stared at her. "Are you really my mom?" she whispered.

Why the sudden interest? Shannon hugged the little girl tightly. "*You* tell *me*, Faith. Look at my eyes and hair. My mouth. Then look at your own in the water."

The child studied her, then leaned over the water again and stared at her reflection. When she sat back against Shannon, the stiffness had gone out of her small body. "Maybe you are," she whispered.

"It's okay to love me and love your other mommy," Shannon said, pressing a kiss against her daughter's hair. "We're a family now—you, me, Kylie, and Daddy. I won't take the place of your other mommy."

"I can't hardly remember how she looked," Faith said in a small voice.

Shannon's heart broke for her daughter. "It's okay," she whispered. "You'll see her again someday in heaven. And she's watching out for you now, praying for you, loving you."

Faith stiffened. "She'll be sad if I love you," she wailed, tears beginning to flow.

So that was it. "No, she'll be glad you have a new mommy to take care of you. She was sad to leave you and was worried about you being alone."

"No, no, she wasn't," Faith said. "She left because she wanted to go. She didn't love me enough."

Shannon rocked her children, one sobbing and the other trying to console. "I'm sure she wishes she'd been wiser," she whispered. "I know you don't understand, but even mommies make mistakes. But I know she loved you very much, sweetheart. And I love you. I'll never leave you willingly."

"Me too, Mommy?" Kylie asked.

Shannon's arm tightened around Kylie. "I love you both just as much." Had Kylie felt neglected during Shannon's attempt to show Faith her love? "More than anything."

"More than Daddy?" Kylie asked.

Shannon heard the rumble of a laugh over her head and glanced up to see Jack looming over them. Amusement gleamed in his eyes.

"Let's go get dressed and we'll look for butterflies," she said. Her distraction worked, and the girls slid off her lap and ran to get their clothes. Hugging the towel around her, she scrambled to her feet.

"Faith seems to be warming up to you," Jack said.

He was standing too close for Shannon's peace of mind. The clean scent of the spring still clung to his skin.

He reached out and caught a lock of wet hair. "You hair smells like sunshine all the time. How do you do that?"

"I . . . it's my shampoo," she stammered. She should go help the girls get dressed, but she couldn't move.

His thumb stroked her cheek. "You're driving me crazy, Shannon," he muttered.

She stared into his eyes and couldn't say a word. His lips brushed hers and she was still frozen in place.

A small hand tugged at her fingers. "Mommy, you said we were going to look for butterflies."

Shannon's laugh betrayed her nervousness, and she stepped away from Jack even though there was nowhere she'd rather be. "I've got to get dressed," she said.

"Too bad," he whispered.

She ran for the cave and her sanity.

SHANNON SAT ON A BAR STOOL AT THE COUNTER. SHE PROPPED HER ELBOWS on the granite top and leaned her chin into her palm. The children were in bed, and Jack was checking on the horses before turning in himself. It was only her and Enrica, and Shannon had questions she'd longed to ask when no one was around.

She watched the plump housekeeper wipe down the counters one last time. "Enrica, what was Mr. Jack's first wife like?"

Enrica put down the dishrag. Her dark eyes appraised Shannon. "Miss Blair was flesh-and-blood woman with faults like you and me. She love Mr. Jack and Faith. But she is gone now. You good for Mr. Jack. He need strong woman to work beside him. Mr. Jack, he love you now."

Shannon shook her head. "I'm not so sure, Enrica. I'm a nuisance to him." But in spite of her denial, she couldn't help remembering the expression in his eyes out at the mountain pool.

Enrica's smile flashed, then disappeared, and she shook her head. "Mr. Jack stubborn. He don't want to love you, but I see it in his eyes when he watch you. He need help to admit it. You tell him you love him."

Shannon opened her mouth to deny loving him, but she closed it again. This was one secret impossible to keep. "You're right," she whispered. "But I don't want him to know. Don't tell him, Enrica."

"You tell him," Enrica said again. She walked around the counter and cupped Shannon's cheek in her rough brown hand. Her dark eyes bored into Shannon's. "Mr. Jack, he need you. You tell." She dropped her hand and left Shannon in the kitchen.

Could it be true? Shannon wished she could believe it. There were times she thought she caught a glimpse of love in his eyes before he quickly cloaked it. Like today up at the swimming hole. That kiss had left her breathless with hope, but she'd been afraid to believe, afraid to let down her guard.

Sometimes she daydreamed about what life would be like if Jack loved her. What if she were brave and managed to speak? But what if she told Jack how she felt and saw only pity in his eyes in return? It would be more than she could bear.

Shannon hadn't yet seen any real sign of love from him. He mostly kept his distance, though today things had seemed to shift. Maybe Enrica was right. Shannon had faced other challenges in her life. She'd never run from anything. Losing her parents had been hard, but at least she'd seen the way her dad watched her mom with love in his eyes. Dad might have always been after a quick buck, but everything he did was for her and her mother. And her girls needed the security of knowing their parents would never split. They would thrive in a loving home where they saw parents who modeled a good marriage. She couldn't let her fear rob her girls.

She rose and went up the stairs to her room. Glancing around at the pale pink carpet, the beautiful four-poster bed, the feminine wallpaper, she knew she couldn't spend her life alone in this room. If it took laying bare her heart, she had to do it. When the years passed and nothing changed, she would regret not trying.

She shut the door and opened her dresser. The scent of cedar from the new dresser rushed to her nose. She moved her cotton pajamas out of the way and smiled as she always did at the Scottish terriers in the pattern. They'd been a gift from Mary Beth. Her smile faded at the thought of her friend.

There'd still been no word on her whereabouts since she'd told the man about the stocks. Curt still claimed to know nothing. Shannon was beginning to fear Mary Beth was dead. She dug down to the bottom of the drawer, under two more sets of pajamas, to reveal the beige lace gown Allie had bought for her during the outing in San Antonio. She lifted it out and held it up. Did she dare? Her lungs squeezed. There was only one way to find out Jack's reaction.

She shucked her jeans and T-shirt, then raced to the bathroom, where she took a quick shower. Glancing at the shampoo, she decided she would take time to wash and dry her hair since Jack seemed to like the smell of her hair products.

Half an hour later, she tugged a comb through her freshly dried hair. She stared at her reflection again, then tucked her hair behind her ears. No, that showed too much of her face, so she combed it again. Makeup might help. She dusted on a trace of powder and blush, then stroked some subtle color on her lids.

Padding across the carpet to the bed, she told herself to have courage. Nothing ventured, nothing gained. She dropped the gossamer nightgown over her head and tugged it into place. Surveying herself in the full-length mirror, she eyed her pale face and tremulous mouth. She tried a smile on for size. Better, but the fear in her eyes was still there. If he noticed that fear, maybe it would inspire him to be gentle with her heart. She grabbed a tube of lip gloss that had a hint of color.

If she didn't know better, she'd think the gown was a corset, she was having such trouble catching her breath. Glancing at her watch, she knew it was now or never. She took a deep breath and turned to the door. She eased open the door and listened. The news was playing on the TV downstairs, Jack's final ritual of the day. He'd be up to bed after the newscast showed the football scores, another fifteen minutes. There was still time to chicken out.

Shannon bit her lip. Maybe Enrica was wrong. Shannon rejected the thought. The way he'd kissed her today spoke more of attraction than irritation. He might not be willing to admit he had feelings for her, but a woman always knew. She had to cling to that hope.

On her way down the hall, she peeked in on the girls. They slept entwined in Kylie's bed. Shannon tugged the blankets around them, then dropped a kiss on each soft cheek. She was doing this for them too. For all of them.

She stepped back into the hall and tiptoed to the door at the end. Jack's room. She stepped into the room and flipped on the bedside lamp before glancing around. Her gaze fastened on the bed. She didn't have the courage to wait there. It was too bold a move, even for her.

She tore her eyes from the king-size bed and moved to the easy chair by the window. He might not see her the second he came into the bedroom, and she'd have time to gather her courage after the reality of his presence unnerved her. The chair welcomed her, and she hid herself in its embrace. Panic seized her and she nearly fought her way out of the grip of the chair. She should leave now, before she faced utter humiliation. She hadn't even practiced what to say. Or even how to go about seducing her own husband.

She wet her lips. This was all wrong. Better to hurry back to her room, tear this nightgown off, and forget this whole plan. She had half risen when she heard Jack's tread on the steps. Even if she left now, he'd see her exiting his room and interrogate her. Sitting back down and placing her palm on the pit of her stomach, she drew in a deep breath. Adrenaline surged through her. After tonight, no one would ever say Shannon MacGowan feared anything.

Jack entered the room and shut the door. She observed him again, his shock of dark hair—a black MacGowan as he'd be known in Scotland. Muscular shoulders and arms. Legs as strong as tree trunks. A man who turned heads, both male and female. A fierce love and possessiveness swept over her. He was hers. Neither of them believed in divorce, so what she planned was right and good. She clung to the belief when he turned toward the bathroom.

His eyes lit on her, and his mouth dropped as she rose. "Shannon?"

Was that hope in his face? She saw his eyes darken. She rose and faced him. "The horses okay?" she said in a voice that was barely a throaty whisper.

He took a couple of steps closer. Shannon knew he was no fool. He would have known why she was here the second he noticed the gown with no robe. She took hope in his response and matched his steps.

His gaze never left her face. "Wha-what are you doing here?"

Shannon took several more steps until she was in his personal space, close enough to inhale the scent of hay clinging to his shirt. She reached out and touched his chest, and he flinched.

His hands gripped her arms and he stared into her face.

"Don't send me back to my room," Shannon whispered. "We're married, and the girls need to see a normal marriage modeled."

His throat worked. "Is that the only reason you're here?"

It would be so easy to nod, to keep her pride intact, but she wasn't a coward. It was all or nothing. She shook her head. "I love you, Jack." The blood roared in her ears as she waited to see if he would hold her or thrust her away.

A groan escaped his lips. His fingers bit into her arms, then he crushed her to his chest and his lips found hers.

25

THE DIM LIGHT OF APPROACHING SUNRISE WOKE JACK. HE ROLLED OVER and found himself nose to nose with a woman. Shannon. He studied the delicacy of her closed lids, the long lashes fanning her cheeks, the blush of color on her face from sleep. It had taken a lot of courage for her to come to his room and force them to face their feelings.

Had he even told her last night that he loved her? Maybe not. Today he'd make sure she knew how much he loved her and how happy he was they were a real family. Maybe they'd even have another child. His smile faded. It still seemed disloyal to Blair to be contemplating a new life with Shannon.

Still, it was up to him to make sure their family stayed intact. He'd visit Wally and see if he could hurry the adoptions along. Find out what their options were about Larue and how much they should offer the guy. The Mustang Makeover was coming up at the end of the week, and he had a lot of work still to do with his horses. So much to do this week.

Shannon sighed and rolled over, and he realized she was going to sleep for a while. She'd gotten a call about a foaling mare in trouble and had gone out around one, then come back at two thirty and crawled back into his arms. He had a feeling this was going to be their lives, and the middle-of-the-night stuff was going to take some adjustment.

He slipped out of bed, pulled on his jeans, grabbed his boots, and tiptoed out of the room. The rest of the house slumbered on too. Jack glanced at his watch and realized it was only six. He could go to work with the mustangs early, then take a break and run to town to see Wally. Passing the kitchen, he grabbed a couple of boiled eggs out of the fridge, then went out to his truck.

When he reached the camp and got to his corral, the mustangs nickered at his appearance and Dancer trotted to thrust her nose in Jack's hand. They were tamed well enough that they'd do him proud on Saturday.

Buzz put a boot on the fence rail beside him. "You're here early, partner."

"I have an errand later today. Thought I'd get an early start."

Buzz chewed on his unlit cigar. "They look good. You're ready."

"How are the rest looking?" His main goal was to find homes for the mustangs. The prize money meant nothing to him.

"Good. We'll be the media stars for our thirty seconds of fame."

"Hopefully it's enough to place a lot of horses."

Buzz nodded to the two horses. "You takin' these two?"

Jack grinned. "How'd you know?"

"Never seen you pass up a horse that grew on you." Buzz spit out the tip of his cigar. "You and the little lady gettin' along okay?"

Jack couldn't help the huge grin that split his face. "Hunky-dory."

"What about Larue?"

Larue was the main worry on his mind. He eyed Buzz's furrowed brow and the concern in his eyes. "What about him?"

"Say you beat him. He might get vindictive."

"No might about it." Which was why Jack had to nail down the adoption before the competition this Saturday.

"Got an idea, Jacky." Buzz took another bite of his cigar and spit it out. "What if you let him win?"

The idea was so ludicrous Jack laughed. At first. Until the wisdom of Buzz's words soaked in. The money—and beating Jack—might be enough to salve Larue's wounded ego.

"How do you know about the situation with him?"

"He's a blowhard. He's told half the camp he's got twins. It didn't take much to put two and two together. He's been talking to the media too. I reckon there will be an article in the paper."

No wonder the reporter had left off harassing him and Shannon. He had a pipeline to the other side of the problem. A newspaper article should answer the questions flying around town about whether Jack had an affair with Shannon. It went against the grain to let Larue win. Jack wanted his mustangs to do well to prove gentle training methods were best. If he let Larue win, ranchers might hire him to work with their horses. Did Jack go with his gut or with Buzz's wisdom?

"I'll think about it," was what he finally could promise.

SHANNON STRETCHED AND RUBBED HER EYES. BRILLIANT LIGHT SHONE IN her windows. She must have overslept. When she looked around, she realized she wasn't in her own bed, and the memory of the night before flooded back. Heat rushed to her cheeks as joy did the same to her soul. Jack loved her. He hadn't said the words, but she knew it.

She rolled over to kiss him good morning and found him—gone. An indentation of his head in the pillow told her it was no dream. But he'd left without a word, left her sleeping. Surely he'd left a note. She sat up and felt the covers, searched the bed table. Nothing.

Her euphoria dissipated, but she refused to give in to the hovering depression. He'd probably wanted to let her sleep. She awakened deciding to appeal to Larue's better nature. Jack would scoff at her, but she had to try.

Scrambling out of bed, she got ready for work and hurried down the steps. When she asked Enrica where the girls were, the housekeeper told her they were at the barn with two of Jack's most trusted hands. She forced down a bit of Enrica's omelet, stopped to kiss the girls goodbye, then bolted for her car. Usually she and Jack rode to work together, so his leaving her behind without a word was even more inexplicable. Didn't he realize a woman needed some reassurance?

She made a detour to Wally's office to ask him for a release-of-rights form. His secretary said he wasn't in yet, but the woman had a standard one available. Shannon stuffed it in her purse and ran for the door. She was already way late.

The camp already bustled with activity when she wove her way through the cowboys and horses. Today was supposed to be one of three "dress rehearsals," as Buzz called them. The trainers would put the horses through their hoops as if the country were watching. Shannon climbed a fence to watch.

Jack's horses were third in line. He caught her eye and smiled, and Shannon's fears melted way. The horses performed well, the black stallion especially. With Jack on his back, the big mustang galloped around the cones in record time. He'd be a great rodeo mount.

Several other horses performed well—especially Tucker's bay mare. Shannon couldn't help admiring the mustang's clean lines and tight circles around the cones. It would be a close race between her and Jack's stallion.

Tucker was smiling as he rode out of the corral. His gaze locked with hers and he cantered over to where she stood. Would he listen to a plea from her? She hadn't tried a direct assault on the man he used to be.

"Nice job," she said, returning his smile with as much warmth as she could muster. It must have been enough, because his eyes widened and his eyes brightened. "Care if I walk back to your corral with you?" she asked.

"Want to ride?" His grin held a smirk.

"Only if it's by myself. I'm a married woman." She spoke lightly so he didn't take offense.

"I'll walk with you then." He swung down and looped the reins around his palm.

Jack's gaze landed on Shannon. He frowned and beckoned to her with his finger. She shook her head and tore her gaze from his. Something had to be done about the situation with Tucker, so she had to try. Hopefully she'd have good news to share with him after her talk with Tucker.

"I assume you've come to make me an offer," Tucker said when they reached his corral behind the barn.

She stopped and put her hand on his arm. "Not really. I just wanted to talk a minute. I don't want us to be enemies. We were friends once."

"More than friends," he said, leering.

Her cheeks burned, but she held his glance. "It was never about sex, Tucker. You were a good friend when I needed one. You cared about me, about when I was hurt and crying. You helped me study for my final that one Easter, remember?"

He dropped his gaze, and his smile fell with it. "Don't be gettin' all touchy-feely with me, Shannon. It's bad for the image."

"Tucker, I know you've got good in you. Don't try to hurt me or the girls in your vendetta with Jack. Be a man and walk away and let us have our lives."

His boots shuffled in the dirt, and he still couldn't seem to meet her gaze. "Aw, Shannon, do you have to put it like that?"

"Yes, I think I do," she said softly. "Be the person I know you can be, Tucker. For my sake and the sake of the girls."

He looked up then. "I hate Jack, you know. I've got the perfect weapon and you're asking me not to use it."

Shannon stared into his eyes and saw a glimpse of the man she'd once cared about. "I'm asking that of you."

"I'll have to think about it," he said, his voice hard. "They're going to want to know who their daddy is someday."

"Jack is their daddy. But you're their father."

He narrowed his eyes. "Someday the girls will want to meet me."

"I know. Make sure I always have your current address, and when that time comes, I'll give it to them."

The fire banked in his eyes and he sighed. "You got a release form handy?"

She did. She whipped it from the back pocket of her jeans and unfolded it. Yanking a pen from the other pocket, she handed it to him.

The pen paused over the paper. "Pretty confident, weren't you?" He shook his head. "I can't believe I'm doing this."

She watched him shrug, scrawl his name on the paper and pass it back to her. "God will bless you for this, Tucker." She tucked the precious paper back into her pocket.

"Yeah, well I hope he blesses me with a win on Saturday," he grumbled.

"Shannon? What's going on here?" Jack's voice spoke from behind them.

Shannon whirled to see her husband standing with his feet apart and his hands on his hips. "Jack, Tucker just signed the papers releasing all rights to the girls."

"You ready to go see Wally?" he asked in an even tone.

"The least you could do is say thanks," Tucker grumbled. "I wish I'd never signed that paper." He brushed past Jack.

THE RIDE TO TOWN HAD BEEN SILENT. SHANNON COULD SENSE JACK'S anger brewing. The visit to the lawyer's hadn't calmed him either. She handed the paper to Wally, and he'd promised to get the adoptions finalized.

When they got back to the truck, she snapped her seat belt in place, then turned to glare at him. "Just yell at me and be done with it. I can't take this brooding silence anymore."

He didn't look at her. "I don't know what to say, Shannon. You promised no more secrets. Don't you trust me enough to tell me what you're up to?"

"I didn't plan it beforehand! You weren't there when I woke up this morning thinking about it. I just decided to flat out ask Tucker to be a man and step aside. I had no real idea it would work, but I had to try. You should be glad he said yes."

He rubbed his forehead. "I reckon it's going to take me some time to get rid of suspicion," he said. He reached over and took her hand. "No more secrets, Shannon?"

She turned and faced him. "You know everything now, Jack. Everything. I hadn't planned this until I got up this morning and decided to try, so I took the paper with me. That was it. If you'd been here, I would have told you."

"And I would have asked you not to. I . . . I don't like the way he looks at you."

He's jealous! She managed to hide her smile, but her spirits lifted. "Why did you leave without even a good-morning kiss?"

"You were sleeping so peacefully, I wanted to let you rest." His eyes were tender.

She leaned over and brushed her lips across his. "I forgive you," she whispered.

Once inside the house, Shannon checked on the girls, who were napping, then went to her room. Her room. She'd thought Jack would ask her to move into his, but he hadn't said anything. Was he still fighting guilt about Blair?

The leather book she'd found at the old apartment caught her eye, and she picked it up. Shannon turned the ledger over in her hands. There had to be a clue here, but she didn't know where else to look. She'd even tried slitting the back cover in a discreet place to see if Mary Beth had hidden another paper there. Nothing. Just an account book of some kind, with numbers and initials. And the letter written to some lover. She'd tried to find clues in it, but Mary Beth could have written it to anyone. It spoke of a dinner at the hotel and how much she loved him. That was it.

Shannon flipped to the first page. Jack had wireless in the house, so she flipped open her MacBook and called up Safari. It was probably useless, but she put in several of the unfamiliar letter combinations. What popped up in Google made her jaw drop.

Horses! Why hadn't she thought of that? She studied the row of initials. KD could be the Kentucky Derby. TP might be the Preakness. Was BS the Belmont Stakes? And the row of numbers was how much had been won. A huge grin split her face. She'd figured out something about it. The smile faded. So what? It still told her nothing.

She was sure this wasn't Mary Beth's book. She never would have had the money to bet this high. Was this what the man who'd broken into her house had wanted? She flipped to the back of the book and the total there. Nearly eight million. The number jived with what the guy had asked for.

Jack's figure loomed in the doorway. His gaze went to the book in her hands. "What are you doing with my father's ledger?"

Shannon glanced down at the leather-bound book and frowned. "It's not your father's."

He advanced across the pale pink carpet. "Sure it is. Look here." He traced the embossed design on the cover. "This is the MacGowan arms. I've seen him put entries into it for years."

"He bet at horse races?"

"Yeah. When our horses race." He opened the book and began to flip through the pages. A frown crouched between his eyes. "Wow, he's made nearly eight million dollars."

"Is that even possible in horse racing?"

Jack stared at the book. He didn't seem to hear her question. "I had no idea he had that much money," he muttered.

"Just from betting on horses?" Shannon asked again. At least he was talking to her.

"He's done it a lot of years," Jack said. "But you're right—that's a lot of money."

Could Jack Senior have made this money in other ways—maybe by running a bookmaking business? But the even bigger question was how had Mary Beth gotten this book? And why did she hide it? Shannon dreaded the answers to the questions. And why the same sum the big guy had demanded from her?

Jack focused in on her face. "You never said where you got this."

Shannon didn't want to tell him. It was going to hurt. She didn't want to see the light in his eyes go out, the questions that were sure to come when he found out. She kept her gaze locked on his, willing him to realize she wasn't involved in any of this. "Remember when I had to go back to my apartment for something?" she asked. "The day we went shopping for the wedding?" She waited until he nodded. "I wanted to see if I could find any clues to what Mary Beth had been up to. I had no idea why I was being harassed. When I got to the apartment, Mary Beth's room had been tossed. But I knew about the hiding place where we'd often put valuables, so I decided to check there and hope the intruders hadn't found it. I found this book there."

Jack ran his hand over the embossed leather. "Mary Beth had my father's ledger? I don't understand."

"I don't either." Shannon rubbed her temple. "She volunteered at the Republican headquarters last year. Maybe she met your father there and stole this journal. I'd forgotten about it because it doesn't seem to tell us anything. Or so I thought. I had no idea it was your dad's."

The color drained from Jack's face. "That would mean my father could be involved with her disappearance." He stared at the ledger. "And the eight million dollars—that's the same sum the guy wanted."

The pain lines around his mouth broke her heart. "This book might have nothing to do with Mary Beth's kidnapping."

His mouth twisted. "Nice try, Shannon, but I'm smart enough to realize the implications of this. I'm going to take it to my office and look it over." He tucked it under his arm and went down the stairs.

Shannon winced when the office door closed downstairs. If something bad came out of this, would he blame her? Her fluffy pink room was a prison right this minute, and she paced the plush carpet as she waited to hear his office door open again. When she couldn't take another minute of being alone, she slipped out and went downstairs.

She found Enrica in the kitchen browning hamburger. With the beans on the counter, she guessed the housekeeper was making chili.

Enrica wiped her hands on her apron. "Miss Shannon, you not sleep in your bed last night. You take my advice, *sí*?"

"Yes," Shannon said, smiling. She slid onto a bar stool at the island and leaned on the granite counter. Remembering his manner in the truck on the drive home, she knew he loved her, even if he hadn't said the words yet. He would.

Enrica wagged an onion-scented finger under Shannon's nose. "You not give up, Miss Shannon."

"Don't worry, I'm not giving up." Her cell phone played, and she pulled it out from the holster at her waist. The number was local but not familiar. Probably someone with a sick animal. "This is Dr. MacGowan."

"Shannon, how are you?" her father-in-law asked.

Walking out of the kitchen, she tried to think why he'd call her. To invite them to a political event maybe. "Fine, sir. How about you?" She stepped out onto the porch and settled onto a chair.

"Not so good, missy, not so good. Are you alone?"

"Yes, I'm on the porch. Are you ill?" His voice was tremulous. But why call her if he was sick?

"No, but I will be. I'd like to talk to you about something very important."

"Okay."

"Do you know the old copper mine at the end of Larson Road?" he asked. "There's a mining shack at the end of it. I'll meet you there in two hours. And Shannon, one more thing. Bring my ledger."

"Sir?" Surely she'd misheard him. He had no idea she had it.

"Bring my ledger with you. And don't tell Jack."

"You've got Mary Beth?" Everything she thought she knew about what was going on took a 180-degree shift.

"It's not what you think," he said.

"I don't want to know any more than that Mary Beth is safe. I'll bring the ledger if you bring Mary Beth."

The senator didn't answer, and she heard a faint click. He'd hung up on her. Did that mean he wasn't bringing Mary Beth? Shannon wasn't going to be a fool about it. If the senator thought he could send his goons to get the ledger without giving up Mary Beth, they'd find out they were wrong.

She went inside and up the stairs to check on the girls. They were playing with their dolls in the little tent they'd made of blankets in Faith's room. She stood watching them a moment. They were more important than anything in her life. The easiest thing to do would be to hand over the ledger and try to forget their grandfather was some kind of crook.

She went down the steps again to the closed office door and tapped on it. "Jack?"

"Come on in, hon."

The doorknob turned under her hand, so he hadn't locked the door. She stepped into the office and found Jack seated at the desk with the leather ledger open.

"You decipher it yet?" she asked.

He looked up from his perusal of the ledger and shook his head. "I tried to call Dad to ask him about this, but I had to leave a message on his voice mail. I told him you'd found a ledger I think might belong to him."

"But if he's involved—"

Jack held up his hand. "What if it was stolen from him? He can help us shed some light on this mess. I've figured out a few things. Rick called. He heard from his friend Brendan. The number that was on the chip in your arm is a Swiss bank account. I think that's where this money is stored. I don't know what your friend Mary Beth was up to. Maybe she was trying to extort the money from my dad." His eyes bored into hers. "Were you in on this scheme, Shannon?"

"Of course not! I can't believe you would even suspect me." Did last night mean nothing to him? "Jack, I'm your wife. I wouldn't hurt you." She'd come in here with every intention of telling him his father had called, but his reaction proved he'd defend the senator and suspect her. She tried to blame the air conditioner on the sudden shiver that trembled down her back.

No more secrets. But what if telling him this one destroyed everything they'd built so far? She couldn't believe he even suspected her. She'd given him no reason to think she might be a criminal.

The accusing light in his eyes faded, and he nodded. "I had to ask. I don't believe my father would do anything to hurt your friend. But he's got powerful enemies. Maybe they were using her. I'm going to have to talk to Dad." He stood and came around the desk. His hands came up as though to embrace her, then they dropped back to his sides when she stepped back. "Wally called, and there was one place on the adoption papers I missed signing. I have to run to town and do that. I'll be back in a couple of hours and then I'll try to find out what this is all about."

He pressed a kiss on Shannon's forehead before he brushed past her to the door. Shannon hugged herself and felt the prick of tears at the back of her eyes. She blinked furiously. He suspected her of being an extortioner.

It just went to show that it was never good to have any positive expectations of anyone.

26

SHANNON GLANCED AT THE LEATHER JOURNAL LYING ON THE SEAT OF HER Jeep as she drove to the mine. She had to get this done and return home before Jack suspected she'd taken it. She'd promised him no more secrets, but he'd given her no choice. Tears still burned her eyes.

There's always a choice. The choice to do right.

The voice that whispered in her head reproached her. She rubbed her forehead. This whole marriage thing was more than she'd bargained for. It wasn't about just living in the same house or even sharing the same bedroom. It wasn't only about feeling loved or wanted. It was about being *one*. She'd heard that in church, but it had never soaked in until now.

Her years of independence had to come to an end if she wanted her marriage to Jack to be more than a business arrangement. The excuse she'd used to act alone right now didn't hold water. She'd rationalized during the drive that she wanted the girls to have at least one parent if this plan backfired, but Jack Senior wouldn't harm his own son. She was nearly to the rendezvous spot. She pulled into a narrow opening in the mesquite and dug out her cell phone.

She called Jack and got his voice mail. "Jack, I'm sorry but I took the journal. Your father called and wants it back in exchange for Mary Beth's freedom. I'm meeting your dad at the old miner's shack at the end of Larson Road. Please come. I . . . I need you."

The plea for help didn't come easily, but as the words escaped her mouth, she realized how true they were. She hung up and buried her face in her hands. She could finally admit the truth. She couldn't exist without Jack, couldn't function without his love and approval. What she felt was more than love—it was need too. She, who had prided herself on being self-sufficient, needed him with every fiber of her being.

Instead of horrifying her, the realization was almost . . . freeing. She closed her phone and it chirped almost immediately. She flipped it open again. "Jack?"

"Shannon, it's me," Mary Beth's voice whispered. "I need you to come get me before he finds me again."

"Mary Beth, where are you?" More questions could wait until she had her friend out of danger.

"I'm at Mitchell Pass." She ended on a sob.

Shannon sagged in the seat. "What are you doing there? Never mind, I'll come. Where will I find you?"

"I'll be hiding behind the big rock that looks like a buffalo."

Shannon knew the spot. And Mitchell Pass. Her parents were buried in the cave there. Coincidence? Or a plot by the senator to make her reveal where the gold was buried? His curiosity about the Spanish treasure couldn't be coincidence.

It didn't matter. She couldn't ignore her friend's plea. She promised to come right away, then tried Jack again. When she didn't get him, she left another message with the news of where she was heading next. Just as she was about to hang up, the low-battery beep sounded in her ear. Stupid phone was acting up again. Just her luck. She tried to call the sheriff, but the phone was dead before he picked up on the other end.

Jack would come though. And he'd get help. Shannon clung to the thought as she put her SUV into drive and headed to find Mary Beth.

JACK KNEW HIS ANGER WAS OUT OF PROPORTION TO THE CIRCUMSTANCES. The reason for the anger went far deeper than seeing Shannon with Larue. She had kept so many secrets from him that he doubted her every word, and that wasn't a good approach. He'd actually suspected her of scheming to blackmail his dad. Had he been nuts? She wasn't that kind of woman.

The dreams he'd awakened with this morning seemed to belong to another man.

But a lot of that was his fault. He pushed his hat off his forehead. He'd kept secrets of his own. They'd both danced a jig around the truth. He'd never even admitted he loved her. When he got home tonight, he'd lay it all out and demand she do the same.

After he signed the line he'd missed, he went back out to his truck. His phone signaled a voice mail, and he grabbed it from where he'd left it on the seat. When he heard Shannon's voice and what she had to say, he tried to call her back, but the canned message said the phone was unavailable.

He gunned the truck back out of town. On the way, he tried to call the sheriff, but the dispatcher told him Sheriff Borland was down with the flu. He considered trying one of the Texas Rangers in the area, but they were likely hours away, up in Alpine. Maybe Rick. He called his friend, then stopped to pick him up at the end of the Bluebird Ranch lane.

"So your dad is involved in this somehow?" Rick asked after Jack explained what he knew.

"Looks like it." Jack had tried not to focus on that fact.

"I always thought the senator was a straight shooter," Rick said. "If he made the money from legal gambling, why hide it away in a Swiss bank account?"

"I don't know." Jack tried to piece it together. "He sent one of his goons after Shannon, so he must have thought she had something. Either this book or . . ." He stopped, remembering the box they'd found belonging to Shannon's dad.

"Or what?" Rick pressed.

"You know that horse Shannon is crazy about? Jewel?"

"Sure. I've kept an eye on him for her for years."

"He's a stolen racehorse. I don't know how he fits into the puzzle, but I've got a feeling there's some link."

"Five Lives?" Rick guessed.

"How'd you know?"

"Your dad mentioned him once. Said he was the greatest horse ever to put his hooves on the track."

"I don't get it. The horse belonged to Shannon's parents. If Dad had the horse, why would he let him run free? Why not utilize him as a stud?"

"No idea," Rick said. "I suspect we'll find out before the day is over." His cell phone sang out a tune and he pulled it from his belt.

"Hi, honey," he said. His brows winged up as he listened. "I'll be right there." He put the phone away. "Sorry, buddy, I need you to run me home. Allie's water just broke."

"Holy cow." Jack swung the truck around and raced back the way they'd come.

Five minutes later he dropped Rick in front of the house, made him promise to call when the new arrival made an appearance, then accelerated back down the drive.

SHANNON KNEW THESE CRAGS AND HILLS LIKE KYLIE'S WORN-OUT CandyLand board. She paused to catch her breath when a stitch cramped her side. Fixing the landmarks in her mind, she decided this was as good a place as any to hide the ledger.

Not at eye level. If she wasn't mistaken, there was a crevice at the base of the striated rock formations that looked like soldiers. She forced the ledger into the nearly invisible opening. Only she would ever know it was there and she wasn't telling.

She had no weapons, only her wits. Before she finished the climb, she glanced back the way she'd come in case she saw Jack's broad shoulders coming to rescue her. But no, there was only the cry of an eagle from his craggy perch high over her head and the sound of the wind in the mesquite.

He would come. She just had to stay alive until he did.

She resumed her climb up the narrow path. Below her, the Rio Grande wound through the mesquite and cedar elm. Above her head, the black igneous rock, left over from the massive volcanoes when this region was formed, showed striation marks from the centuries of wind and rain.

Her legs ached from the climb. She stopped again and wondered if she should have tried the gentler climb on the other side. But no, if this was a trap, the senator would expect her to choose the easiest way up. The old mining shaft where her parents' bones lay interred by tons of rock was just over the crest of the path. Shannon forced herself forward until she stood at the rockfall.

No one would ever know this heap of rocks was anything more than the other piles in the area. But she knew. And Jack knew. She'd told him her most closely guarded secret. Tearing her gaze from it, she pressed on the last few yards. She crouched behind a cat's-claw shrub and let her gaze sweep the area. A flicker of movement caught her eye, and she spied Mary Beth's head. Nearly all her hair was shorn. Shannon saw her mouth move, but she couldn't see anyone else there. Maybe she was wired.

Just what she should do wasn't clear to Shannon. The whole setup smelled like a trap. Before she could decide, she heard pebbles tumble down the path behind her. Ducking behind a rock, she peered down the trail. Her spirit leaped when she recognized her husband coming up the trail. He wore a somber, determined expression.

Keeping a low profile, she moved to meet him. His eyes recorded his joy at finding her, but he didn't smile, and she knew she was in trouble. Again.

When she reached him, he took her shoulders in his hands. "Shannon, you have to stop this. We can't have a marriage without being a team. I love you, and—"

She held up her hand. "Wait, say that again."

"Say what again?"

"That you love me."

His mouth softened. "I love you. I've loved you for a long time. But we've got to start working together."

"I know. That's why I called you. I knew I was wrong. I need you, Jack. Not just for this, but in my life in every way."

He cradled her against his chest. "It's about time we both woke up."

Reluctantly she pulled away and gestured behind her. "Mary Beth is back there, at Mitchell Pass. I saw her mouth moving like she was talking, but I couldn't see anyone."

"She's wired?"

"That's what I wondered. I told her I'd come get her. She may hide if you show up though. I've got to go in there alone." She thought Jack would object, but he nodded.

He slapped his hand onto his holstered gun. "I got this out of the truck just in case. I'll cover you. Dad won't hurt you though, even if he's involved with this."

"You don't believe me?"

"It's not that. I know he called you, asked you to come. But maybe he was forced into it."

He sounded much more confident in his father than Shannon, who was beginning to believe the senator would dispatch her without a qualm. But she didn't tell Jack her misgivings. He loved his father, which was as it should be. "There's a good place to hide up here. I'll show you." She led him to the shrub and waited until he hunkered down and pulled out his revolver. She started for the path, but he grabbed her hand and pulled her down beside him.

"Wait," he said. He kissed her. "A kiss for safety," he said. "Be careful."

She clung to him for a minute, then rose and hurried down the path. The connection she had with Jack was something she'd never experienced. And he *trusted* her. Trusted her enough to let her rescue her friend.

Mary Beth didn't see Shannon until she nearly reached the overlook into the river valley. She rose, her face eager. Shannon examined her friend and noticed the bruises on her left cheek, the way she limped when she hurried to meet Shannon, and the lump on her forehead. Whatever had happened, Mary Beth had been an unwilling participant.

The women embraced. Mary Beth clung to Shannon. "I knew you'd come," she whispered.

Shannon stepped back. "Where is the senator, Mary Beth?"

Mary Beth put her hand over her mouth. "Sh," she whispered.

"I know you're probably wired. I saw you talking earlier." Her gaze scanned the shrubs and trees around the spot where they stood. "Come on out, Senator. I know you're there," she called.

"Don't," Mary Beth begged. Her eyes flickered to the left. "Let's get out of here."

Shannon's gut instinct swung in the direction Mary Beth had looked. "Senator? Be a man and come out and talk to me."

The mesquite bush rustled, and a man stepped into view. It wasn't the senator, but his lackey. The big guy Shannon had encountered several times already.

"You don't think the senator has time to take care of his own messes, do you?" the man asked, his black eyes hard.

Mary Beth pulled on Shannon's arm. "Run!" she screamed.

So Shannon did. She couldn't reason with a tree trunk like this guy. He blocked the path back to Jack, chuckling, so she grabbed Mary Beth's hand and half dragged her in the opposite direction. This guy couldn't possibly know the area like Shannon did. There was a rock ledge just around the bend in the trail that couldn't be seen unless you leaned over the edge. They could hide there until he passed, then climb back up and join Jack.

He was probably in hot pursuit of the guy chasing them, though she wished he'd fire his gun and save them the trouble of running. Shannon spared no more thought for anything other than escape. This man was the type who would enjoy the chase and take his time. Which was to their advantage.

They reached the spot where she knew the ledge to be. "Climb down," she told Mary Beth.

Mary Beth backed away. "I can't," she whispered. "I'm afraid of heights."

Too late Shannon remembered how Mary Beth wouldn't even look out the window of their apartment. "Don't look down," she said. "Look at me and I'll lower you. It's not far to the ledge—maybe four feet."

Mary Beth was shaking her head and backing away. Shannon grabbed her by the hands. "Do you want him to kill us?" she hissed. "This is the only way out. Do what I say. Don't look down, look at me."

To her surprise, Mary Beth nodded. "Don't let me fall," she pleaded.

Mary Beth got on her hands and knees. Shannon grabbed her wrists and began to ease her over the edge. The ledge was closer than Shannon remembered, maybe forty inches down, and Mary Beth's face brightened when her toe reached it. Shannon let her go, and Mary Beth ducked down onto the ledge. Shannon slid over the side and onto the rocky surface just seconds before she heard their pursuer round the rock. She and Mary Beth lay flat on their stomachs on the ledge, and Shannon prayed there were no scorpions or spiders lurking about. She held her breath and heard the man shuffle on the trail.

He gave an exasperated sigh. "You can't hide from me, ladies. Make it easier on yourselves and come out now while I'm in a good mood." But his voice held amusement. Another shuffle came on the rocks, then his steps began to move away.

Shannon let out the breath she'd been holding. They'd have to wait a few more seconds before they climbed up so the sound didn't attract his attention again. She dared to glance around and saw a scorpion headed their way. She took a loose rock and knocked it off the ledge.

Poking her head over the top, she glanced around. The guy was nowhere to be seen. "Let's go," she told Mary Beth. She stood and boosted Mary Beth up, then pulled herself up onto the path as well.

"Jack is following us too," she said. "He's got a gun." But she was surprised as they went back down the trail that they didn't run into her husband.

Until they arrived at the rockfall that hid her parents and found Jack unconscious. His father loomed over him with Jack's gun in his hand.

The senator waved the gun in the air. "Quentin, get over here!" he called. "I've got the girls."

Shannon knelt by Jack and touched his head. A trickle of blood oozed from a goose egg on his forehead. "What did you do to him?"

He shook his head. "How does Jack put up with you? You got enough tongue for ten rows of teeth. 'Course, I didn't hurt him more than a little tap on the head." He gestured with the gun. "Leave him be and get me my property."

She'd expected this. Putting her hands behind her back, she stared him down. "I don't have the ledger."

"I said get my property. I didn't say ledger." He grinned, revealing perfectly capped white teeth. "Missy, you're runnin' with the big dogs now. Don't try my patience."

He stepped to Mary Beth and circled her neck in a choke hold with his free arm. She shrieked and squirmed as he dragged her to the edge of the trail. "Get it now or she goes over the edge." Mary Beth's screams grew pinched and she beat at his arm with her fists, but he held her fast.

"All right, all right," Shannon called. "Don't hurt her." She'd have been able to deal with his gun but not the thought of him tossing Mary Beth down the cliff. What did he want if it wasn't the ledger?

He let go of his captive, then swatted her behind as she left him. That one movement told Shannon everything. "You were having an affair with the senator?" she asked Mary Beth. "He's too old for you."

"Hey there, I'm only sixty," the senator protested. "Missy, you'll be the first to go over the cliff if you keep talking like that."

Mary Beth hung her head. "Power can be compelling."

"I didn't expect my dolly to steal from me," the senator growled. "Eight million dollars just whisked away right under my nose. I want it back. Now."

"I don't have it."

"Do I have to throw her over the edge?" He made a grab for Mary Beth again, and she screamed.

"You do have it, Shannon," Mary Beth said, panting. "It's in your name in a Swiss bank account. I destroyed all copies of the number once I put the chip in your arm. I wanted to make sure only you had access to the money. It seemed only right that you have it. He killed your parents!"

"Shut up, Mary Beth!" The senator made a grab for her and she darted behind Shannon.

"He arranged for that rock avalanche," Mary Beth said. "Ask him. It's true."

Shannon watched the senator's cheeks turn a mottled red. "You killed my parents?" she whispered.

Tears sprang to her eyes. Her mother and father rested right behind her. If he'd realized what they'd found, he wouldn't have been so quick to entomb them. For just a moment, the temptation to tell him trembled on her tongue. No, he'd dig it up. Or at least he'd tell others from prison.

"Why?" she asked, her voice hard and angry.

"Your daddy was always after a quick buck."

"That's no reason to kill him."

"Your daddy double-crossed him," Mary Beth said. "One of the senator's hobbies was stealing racehorses to up the quality of his stock, and he sometimes sold them to unscrupulous buyers.

"His horses won more races, and their values shot up. Stud values too. He salted it all away in a special account, the one he kept track of in that ledger. The gambling money was all legal, but the amounts for the stolen horses went in there, too, and it grew pretty fast."

"Five Lives was the best racehorse to ever set hoof on a track," the senator muttered. "And your daddy sold him, then refused to tell me who the buyer was."

"Five Lives wasn't sold," Shannon blurted out before she could lock the words behind her teeth. "He's been right here all along. He's mine. I loved him and he loved me from the first minute he came." Her father had cared enough about her happiness that he'd lied to this man. And paid for it with his life.

The senator's smile widened. "This ain't my first rodeo, missy. You're lying to delay handing over my money."

Trying not to be obvious, she scanned the area for a weapon. "I don't have the money."

"A chiseler's pup doesn't wander far from the litter, I see. But I know you've got it. I beat the truth out of her. It's in your arm in a chip."

"Not anymore. I found it with my chip scanner and had it removed."

His cocky smile faded. "What'd you do with it?"

"I don't have it anymore." Not a lie. She'd given it to Rick to send to his friend.

His eyes went round. "You threw it away?" He slapped his forehead with his free palm and muttered something derogatory about women in general and Shannon in particular. "You had to have written down the number. Hand it over." He advanced with the gun held steady.

"You're not going to kill me. A body with a bullet would require too much explanation."

"You might have something there, missy." He seized her around the neck and dragged her to the precipice. "If you don't have the number, I don't have anything to lose by getting rid of the evidence."

"Would you want Jack to hate you forever?" she choked out.

The senator snorted a laugh. "Women have been after Jack since he first strapped on a buckle. He'll replace you in no time."

Shannon fought the choking hold on her throat. Spots danced in her vision, and she felt her legs going weak.

"Dad." Jack's voice came from her right. "Let her go, Dad." He wobbled to his feet and stumbled toward them. "Let her go."

"Jack," the senator mumbled.

His hold on her slackened a fraction, and Shannon took the opportunity to jerk from his grasp and run to her husband. His strong right arm circled her. They faced his father as one.

The senator held out his hands but seemed to have forgotten he had Jack's gun. "Look, Son, it's not what you think."

"No, it's worse. I heard it all as I was coming awake. You murdered a man and his wife, Dad. You've stolen and—" His voice broke off as a horse came up the trail.

"Jewel," Shannon breathed.

The senator stood riveted. "Five Lives. What you said was true?" he whispered.

From the other direction, the senator's hired thug came down the trail. His boss motioned to him, and Quentin turned his gun on Shannon and Mary Beth.

The horse trotted to Shannon and she rubbed the blaze on his face. She knew he sensed her agitation, because he snorted and blew into her palm. "It's okay," she soothed.

The senator brought a lump of sugar out of his pocket. "Here you go, Five Lives," he crooned.

The horse's head came up, and he took a step closer to the senator. Shannon looped her arm around Jewel's neck. "Stay," she said in a commanding voice. The stallion stopped.

"Let him go," Quentin said, turning his gun on Mary Beth.

Shannon dropped her arm. The senator would never catch Jewel anyway. The horse was wily and nervous around strangers. Jewel snorted again and advanced toward the senator. The stallion nibbled the sugar from the man's palm. While Jewel's neck was down, the senator grabbed his mane and vaulted onto the horse's back.

No one had ridden Jewel except Shannon in fifteen years. The stallion screamed, a heart-stopping sound that made Shannon want to cover her ears. Jewel reared and screamed again, then all four hooves left the rocky path as he arched his back. With such wild gyrations, the senator couldn't keep his hold on the horse's mane. He somersaulted from Jewel's shiny black back—right over the edge of the precipice.

Both Jack and Shannon rushed to the edge in time to hear his despairing scream. Jack buried his face in Shannon's shoulder before the body hit the boulders below. She held him tight as he trembled.

Shannon would give anything to be able to ease some of his pain. She was dimly aware of Quentin running off down the trail now that his boss wasn't around to protect him. He likely hoped they couldn't identify him.

"I'm so sorry, Jack," she murmured.

"He was an evil man, but he was still my dad," he muttered, wiping his eyes when he pulled away. "Do you hate me?"

She cupped his face in her hands. "Why would I hate you?"

His eyes searched hers for reassurance. "My father killed your parents."

"But you didn't." She kissed him, and he clung to her again.

She never intended to let him go.

27

SPECTATORS FILLED THE COHEN STADIUM IN EL PASO, WHERE THE MUS-tangs and their trainers would strut their stuff for the final time. Jack's gaze sought and found his wife sitting with their two daughters as close as possible to the fence. And the girls were truly his—both of them now. He and Shannon had formally adopted them both just to cross every *t*.

His eyes misted when he thought of his father, who wasn't here to watch the competition. But then, he'd rarely been there for Jack. His political aspirations were always more important. His mother had wanted a huge funeral, and Jack hadn't told her the full story. Right now, his dad lay in state in the Texas capitol, awaiting the funeral on Monday. No one had to know but him, Shannon, and Mary Beth. Mary Beth had been quick to head back to the city and put this disaster behind her. Doing that would take Jack a little longer.

Shannon had insisted they stop on the way here to check on Allie and the baby. Little Justin and his mama were doing just fine. The same couldn't be said for Rick, who wore the harried expression of being called on to do something unfamiliar. Jack thought he might look like that when his son was born too.

Jack watched Larue put his mustangs through their paces. After Shannon's talk with Larue, Jack had noticed the man seemed gentler, more restrained. Maybe she'd touched something in him that no one else could. She'd sure touched something in Jack.

The crowd roared at Larue's great performance. Jack's turn would be next. All the trainers had done a good job with their mounts, and Jack expected many mustangs would find a home. It would be worth all the work of the past weeks.

A man wove his way through the crowd, and Jack recognized him from pictures. In that instant, he knew what he should do with the money in the Swiss account. Give it back to its rightful owners. All of it. He'd search for the owners of the stolen racehorses and return it all. He motioned to Shannon, who grabbed the girls' hands and hurried to meet him as he left the arena.

"Jack, you'll miss your turn." Buzz grabbed his arm and bellowed over the noise and dust.

"It doesn't matter," Jack shouted back. "My contribution won't make it more or less of a success. Hundreds of mustangs will find a home after this. You did it, Buzz! Great job." He clapped Buzz on the back and walked away to meet Shannon.

"What's wrong?" she asked as he hefted Kylie into his arms.

"We've got to get him before he gets away." He took off through the throng.

"Who?" Shannon asked.

"Leo Brister."

She stopped. "He's here?" Catching at his arm, she tugged him to a stop. "We don't want to talk to him. I can't give up Jewel."

"We're going to buy him back with the money."

She didn't ask what he meant, since they'd been discussing what to do with the cash all week. Her brow furrowed. "Do you think he'll go for it?"

"Jewel is eighteen years old. What good is he to Brister?"

"Stud fees? Or maybe he loves him like I do."

He started again toward the man, who was nearing the parking lot. "He's had fifteen years to forget about that horse. I think we've got a shot."

She hurried along beside Jack. He called out, "Mr. Brister," and the man stopped and turned.

"You're one of the contestants," he said. "I saw you practicing." Surely he was in his eighties or nearly there. White hair and eyebrows, blue eyes dimmed by years of sun. An enormous white Stetson perched on his head.

"That's right, but I need to talk to you and it couldn't wait." Jack searched the man's eyes to assess his character and took heart in the smile lines.

Brister's gaze lit on Shannon and the girls, and that smile widened. "Pretty family you got there, cowboy."

"Yes, sir." He tried to decide how to approach the subject, but Shannon took the lead.

"Mr. Brister, I have your horse."

His bushy white brows raised. "My horse, ma'am?"

"Five Lives."

He rocked back on his heels, and Jack grabbed his forearm. "Are you okay?"

"Fine, I'm fine, son. You have Five Lives, you say? I didn't dream it? I talk to myself all the time, and one of these days I'm going to start making up stories."

Jack grinned. He liked the old cowboy. "You heard her right. Five Lives has been boarding at her ranch for the past fifteen years, and the two of them have a love affair you have to see to believe."

"Is that right?" His faded blue eyes squinted at Shannon. "And you're finally ready to give him up? What about all the lost revenue you've stolen from me?"

Shannon's lips quivered, and Faith frowned. "You made my mommy cry."

He put a gnarled hand on the little girl's head. "A Texas gentleman never makes a lady cry. I apologize if I upset you, ma'am." He turned his laser gaze on Jack. "But what about my lost revenue?"

"We'd like to buy Five Lives from you. For a million dollars."

"Whoa, son, that's what he was worth in his prime. He's old now. He'll have a little value left as a stud, but he's not worth that kind of money."

Jack nodded. "Let me tell you a story," he began, launching into the circumstances he knew.

Brister listened intently, his gaze never leaving Jack's. "The old coot," he said when he heard about the senator's theft. "So basically you want me to take some of the tainted money off your hands."

"Pretty much," Shannon said, smiling.

"Then I'll be happy to oblige. But I'd like to see Five Lives one more time, see if he recognizes me."

"Sure thing," Jack said. "When do you want to come?"

Brister glanced up at the cloudless sky. "Good day for flying. How about we go now? When you get to be my age, you make hay while the sun shines."

"We came in a friend's plane, so that will work. Let me tell him we're going with you." Jack took Shannon's hand, and they walked off to find Rick.

"I wish he hadn't wanted to see Jewel," Shannon grumbled. "He might want him back."

"He's an honorable guy, hon. I think it will be all right."

SHANNON WHISTLED FOR JEWEL, BUT SHE WASN'T SURE IF SHE WANTED THE stallion to answer her. She rubbed wet palms down her jeans and tried again.

"There he is," Brister said with awe in his trembling voice. The desert sun gleamed on Jewel's black coat as he came running across the desert.

"Mommy, is that a unicorn?" Kylie whispered, pointing.

Shannon saw it too—the illusion of a horn between Jewel's eyes.

Brister wore a strange expression, almost of wonder. "I always thought . . ." He shook his head. "Fantasy. Let me call to him, see if he recognizes me after all this time."

Without waiting for Shannon's agreement, he stepped out in front of the group and gave a strange whistle, a trembling call that ended on a high note. The horse's ears pricked, and he snorted. His legs stretched out as he picked up his speed.

"He recognizes you after all this time," Shannon said, her heart just a little grieved. She'd thought Jewel loved only her.

The stallion came straight to the old man, who flung trembling arms around the horse's neck. The two formed a snapshot Shannon would never forget. The man clinging to the horse, the stallion snuffling into his neck—all silhouetted against the harsh but beautiful desert.

Then Brister dropped his arms, and the horse turned toward Shannon. He breathed into her hair, and his big, soft lips nuzzled her neck. Jewel pranced back. His great head swung from Shannon to Brister, then he turned and galloped away.

"Thank you for that," Brister said, his eyes wet. "I deserve every dollar of that money to give up a horse like that. He might live forever, you know."

Shannon's gaze swung back to catch a final glimpse of her horse. "I know." She knew it was impossible, but wasn't that what faith was all about? Believing when you couldn't quite see?

She and her family took the old man back to the MacGowan ranch and watched until his plane lifted into the approaching twilight. Jack walked hand in hand with the girls back to the house, where Enrica met them to spirit the girls off to their baths. Jack went up behind them taking two steps at a time.

Shannon was as tired as she'd ever been. She put on a pot of coffee to help her get through the evening, then decided to take a shower herself while it brewed. She dragged herself up the stairs and down the hall to her bedroom.

Where she found Jack with an armload of her clothes. "Wha-what are you doing?" she asked, following him down the hall to his bedroom. Though sweet words of love had been spoken, they hadn't had the heart-to-heart talk that Shannon longed for. Jack still grieved his father, and the final days of practice had taken every moment.

Jack dumped the clothes on the bed and turned to take her in his arms. "I should have done this the first night," he muttered in her hair. "I knew I loved you, but some last remnant of loyalty to Blair kept me from moving you in here. Watching Jewel tonight made me see how foolish I've been."

"I don't understand." She relished the sensation of his strong arms, his skin against her cheek, the brush of his lips.

"Jewel still had feeling for Brister, and it was okay. Love is never wasted. Jewel moved on and kept some warmth, and I can do the same. I'll never forget Blair, but my heart is yours now. I want you here with me all the time where we can share our hearts, our dreams."

"I want that too," she whispered. "You're never getting rid of me."

"Thank the good Lord," he said, smiling. "Now let's get your stuff."

Shannon went to the bed to grab her clothes and hang them in Jack's closet. He hadn't closed the shades on the window yet, and she caught her breath when she glanced outside. A shadow moved through the light shining from the back of the barn. Jewel. He'd followed Shannon home.

The girls came running in, fresh from their baths. They ran to the window. "Mommy, the unicorn came!" Faith said.

Shannon had been waiting so long for this moment, and when she first heard the word *Mommy* on Faith's lips, it was so natural. Her gaze met Jack's. He knew how long she'd been waiting.

She and Jack joined the girls at the window. Jack put his arm around her and they watched the horse come up to drink from the trough. "He's come to watch over you," he whispered. "And I promise to do the same until I'm dead."

"Sh," she said. "If you go, you have to take me with you." She kissed him before he could say anything else.

Love was never wasted.

READING GROUP GUIDE

1. Are there certain types of people you find it hard *not* to judge? Why or why not?

2. Aunt Verna thought she was helping two people with her lie. Or did she just deceive herself?

3. Have you ever lost someone you love? Did you find yourself remembering only the good like Jack? Why do you think we do that?

4. Have you ever know twins or seen the connection they sometimes have? Why do you think that happens?

5. Shannon felt her occasional glimpses of the "unicorn" were a peek between heaven and earth. Do you ever think you catch a glimpse of something supernatural?

6. Shannon went home, the last place she wanted to go. In the end, she found it was the best thing she could have done. Have you ever seen God turn what seemed a bad thing into something for your good?

7. What did you think when Shannon proposed marriage—that it was stupid or a brilliant way out of her mess?

8. What did you think of Jack's statement that it wasn't necessary to seek the limelight to live up to your potential, that to raise your family and be part of the community can be the best thing? Is striving for something more always good or bad?

9. Shannon had trouble trusting and sharing herself. Do you ever do that? If so, why?

10. When should Shannon have told Jack who the girls' father was?

11. Allie told Shannon love was a choice. Do you believe that? Why or why not?

12. When do you think Shannon should have told Jack about her MS?

ACKNOWLEDGMENTS

Dear Reader,

It was so fun for me to go back to Big Bend, Texas! The place has a stark beauty that draws me, and I've enjoyed hearing from you all about the first book in this series, *Lonestar Sanctuary.* I try to remember every day that love is a choice for all of us in every relationship we enjoy.

My unending love and gratitude go out to my Thomas Nelson family: publisher Allen Arnold, who was the midwife—er, midhusband—for this series; senior acquisitions editor Ami McConnell, my friend and cheerleader, who has amazing insight into story; editor extraordinaire Natalie Hanemann, who puts up with my numerous requests for help with a smile and a hug; marketing manager Jennifer Deshler, who brings both friendship and fabulous marketing ideas to the table;

superorganized publicist Katie Schroder, who helps me plan the right strategies and is always willing to listen; fabulous cover guru Mark Ross (you *so* rock!), who works hard to create the perfect cover—and does it; fellow Hoosier Lisa Young, who lends a shoulder to cry on when needed; editor Amanda Bostic, who is still my friend even though she doesn't work on my books anymore; and Becky Monds and Jocelyn Bailey, who fill in with more help than I even know. I love you all more than I can say.

My agent, Karen Solem, is my biggest cheerleader, and that includes kicking an idea to the curb when necessary. I wouldn't be anywhere without her. Thanks, Karen—you're the best!

Erin Healy is the best freelance editor in the business—bar none. Her magic touch on my book has to be seen to be believed. Thanks, Erin! I couldn't do it without you.

Writing can be a lonely business, but God has blessed me with great writing friends and critique partners. Kristin Billerbeck, Diann Hunt, and Denise Hunter make up the Girls Write Out squad (www.GirlsWriteOut.blogspot.com). I couldn't make it through a day without my peeps! And another one of those is Robin Miller, president of ACFW (www.acfw.com), who spots inconsistencies in a suspense plot with an eagle eye. Thanks to all of you for the work you do on my behalf and for your friendship.

I have a supersupportive family that puts up with my crazy work schedule. My husband, Dave, carts me around from city to city, washes towels, and runs after dinner without complaint. Thanks, honey! I couldn't do anything without you. My kids, Dave and Kara (and now Donna) Coble, and my new grandsons, James and Jorden Packer, love and support me in every way possible. Love you guys! And thanks to my parents, George and Peggy Rhoads; my brothers,

Rick and Dave Rhoads; their wives, Mary and Teresa; and my "other parents," Carroll and Lena Coble. One of them is often the first to hear a new idea, and they never laugh at me. Love you all!

Most important, I give my thanks to God, who has opened such amazing doors for me and makes the journey a golden one.

I love to hear from readers! Drop me an e-mail at colleen@colleencoble.com and check out my Web site at www.colleencoble.com. There's a forum to chat about books, and I try to stop in, since books are my favorite things in the world. Thank you all for spending your most precious commodity—*time*—with me and my stories.

Colleen's Gift to You

With your purchase of *Lonestar Secrets*, you are invited to download *Alaska Twilight* as our free gift to you. Visit http://tinyurl.com/alaskatwilightgiveaway and enter the code Twilight467 to start reading tonight!

LIMITED TIME OFFER!

ESCAPE TO BLUEBIRD RANCH

Also available from Colleen Coble

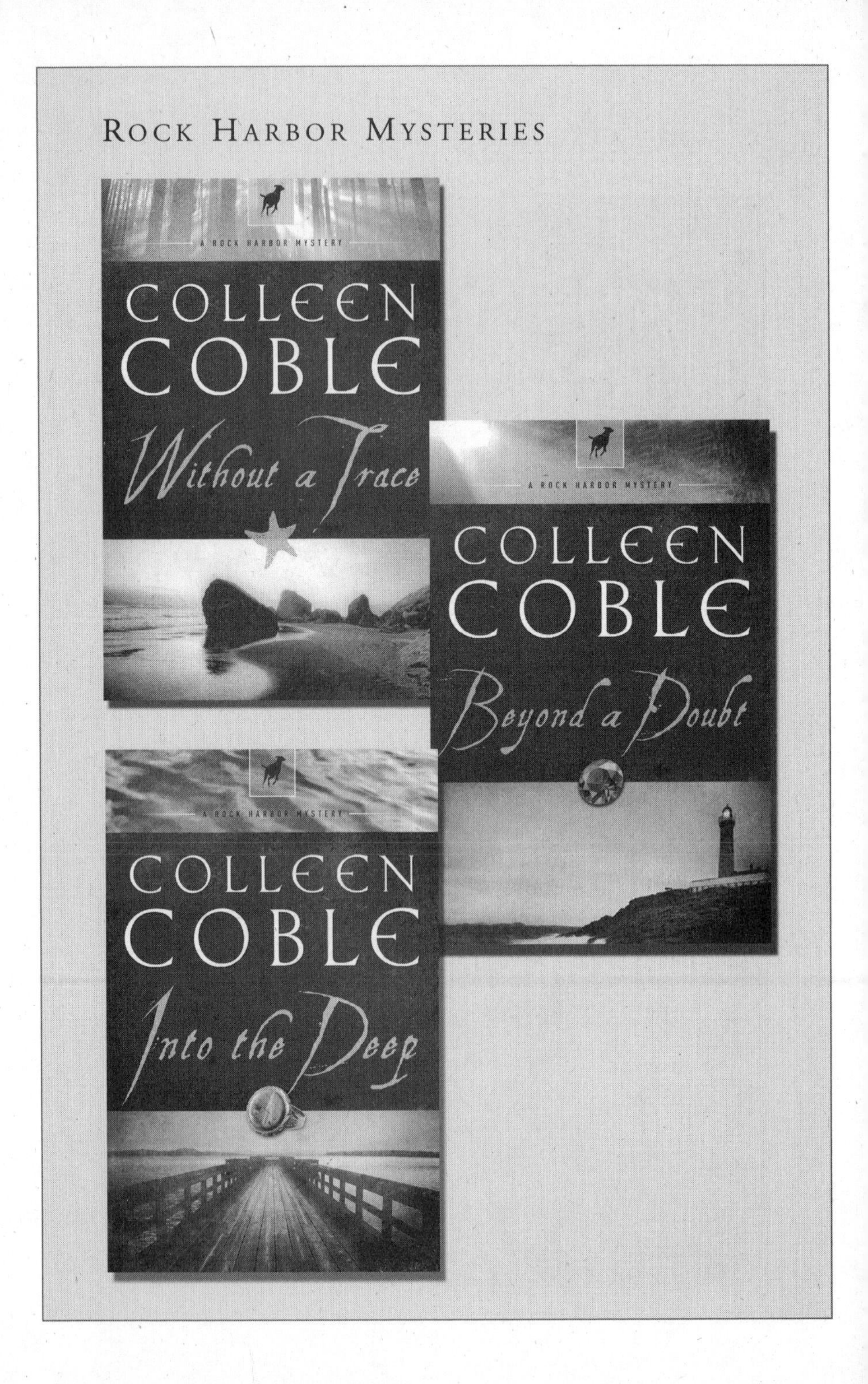

Rock Harbor Mysteries
A Rock Harbor Mystery
Colleen Coble
Without a Trace
A Rock Harbor Mystery
Colleen Coble
Beyond a Doubt
A Rock Harbor Mystery
Colleen Coble
Into the Deep